To Joan
with th
bert w

Jim

Sept 2016

C000227141

THE DEMENTED LADY
DETECTIVES' CLUB

A Novel by

JIM WILLIAMS

Print Edition 2015

Licensed by Marble City Publishing

Copyright © 2015 Jim Williams

ISBN 10 1-908943-73-4

ISBN 13 978-1-908943-73-6

Praise for Jim Williams' books

Farewell to Russia

"There are going to be very few novels of any kind that are as well written. Totally authentic. Totally readable. Far too good to miss." *Ted Allbeury*

The Hitler Diaries

"…steadily builds up an impressive atmosphere of menace." *Times Literary Supplement*

"…well written and full of suspense." *Glasgow Herald*

Last Judgement

"…the author journalists read for their next scoop." *Sunday Telegraph*

Scherzo

"Sparkling and utterly charming. Devilishly clever plot and deceitful finale." *Frances Fyfield – Mail on Sunday*

Recherché

"A skilful exercise, bizarre and dangerous in a lineage that includes Fowles' *The Magus*." *Guardian*

The Strange Death of a Romantic

"This is an extraordinarily witty and assured novel." *T J Binyon – Evening Standard*

"…seriously good…technically brilliant…constantly suggestive… dreamy but sinister glamour." *Times Literary Supplement*

With love to Shirley, a present on our 45th Anniversary,
and
to Adrienne, "Toots", Sue and all my other wonderful
women friends.

1

A man takes his wife to the doctor. The doctor says: "Your wife has Aids or Alzheimer's. I can't say which. The tests will take a fortnight."
The man says, "Well that's no use. Isn't there a quicker way of telling?"
"Well," says the doctor, "you could try taking her for a walk, and, when she isn't looking, clear off and leave her."
"And?"
"If she finds her way home ... don't have sex!"

I don't have Aids.

This morning I woke up confused, with a vague sense of panic. It'd be wrong to say I didn't know where I was: where else could I be but my own bedroom? But it had lost its sense of familiarity. It wasn't strange or unknown in the ordinary meaning. It wasn't anywhere at all. It had lost its sense of 'thereness'.

I got out of bed (the Boss was out buying the paper, thank God), and began my routine of showering and getting ready. This was something I hadn't forgotten: something ingrained in my body, as automatic as breathing. The movements came in the usual way, but I'd no real idea why I was doing them. I recall looking at a tray of pots and creams on my dressing table. My fingers hovered. I knew I was supposed to do something, but for the life of me couldn't remember what or why. All I could do was stand over the tray, dithering and on the point of crying. I'm not a crying woman.

I went back to the bedroom to get dressed. I found myself staring into the wardrobe, unable to choose what to wear. What day was it? What was I dressing for? To have

1

friends round? To see clients? To go shopping? To work in the garden? I picked things at random. A brown blouse and a grey skirt.

I never wear brown with grey. They don't suit me.

It only lasted a few minutes. I'd recovered by the time the Boss came home with a copy of *The Telegraph*. Slobber was on his heels, tail wagging cheerily. I grabbed a kitchen towel and wiped the strings of spittle from Slobber's chops. No one mentions, when you buy a pedigree dog, that the damn thing will spend its days frothing at the mouth and sliming everything. In other respects he's a decent pooch, good-natured and a sight better company than our foul cat, That Thing, who'll sink her claws into you as soon as look at you. We used to have a cat years ago, a sweet-tempered rescue-kitten. This one simply moved in and wouldn't be budged. Slobber objected, of course, but once she'd given him a good hiding, he bowed to the inevitable. As did we. Both of us hate the cat, but it seems there's nothing to be done about her. You'd think the answer would be easy, wouldn't you? Drown her or something? Apparently we're neither of us cat slayers, whatever other kind of murderer some of us may be.

Note: Google "senile dementia" and see where it leads. Pray to God it doesn't describe me and what happened this morning.

Second note: Keep that last note to myself. My first instinct was to write it down and stick it to the fridge with a magnet next to the number for the Indian take-away. Probably not a good idea.

These days we've all become familiar with computers. Even those of 'mature years' as the media call us, making us sound like a ripe cheese. We treat them as extensions of ourselves: repositories of our memories. I may forget stuff but my electronic pal doesn't. I treat it as a friend – no, as a therapist, who listens quietly, takes notes and doesn't judge. On my bad days, I think my scribbles (except one doesn't scribble on a laptop) may turn into a Virginia-bloody-Woolf stream of consciousness novel: *Mrs Dalloway*, which I've had for thirty years in one of those faux leather covered reprints that I've never read and never shall.

If I go barmy, this will be the record of my barmyness. If I commit a crime – not that I have anything in mind – this will be the record of my crime. Some record! It'll be scattered with shopping lists, recipes and telephone numbers.

Maybe I'm depressed rather than senile? I wonder which is preferable? Has anyone ever asked? Taken a poll?

I should send *Mrs Dalloway* to the charity shop for some poor sod to pick up. Sometimes I'm not a nice person.

I've seen a client. Boring. The Boss is dozing on the couch, roaring away in his sleep. That Thing is sitting on his chest looking at him evilly as if she knows her fur makes him sneeze. Slobber is drooling in his basket and occasionally amusing himself by gnawing the edge; I'm for ever sweeping up bits of wicker work.

When the Boss sleeps, his face relaxes. These days it's full of wrinkles and slack flesh. The pores in his nose are like strawberry pips. His eyebrows are an untrimmed thicket. The changes creep up so slowly one gets used to them and never makes a judgment. I don't see him with the same starkness as when I examine the old codgers queuing at the post office. Something comes between my eyes and him: the ghost of the man I fell in love with; a gossamer face that overlays the one I'm looking at. God but he used to be handsome! Some women say he still is, but we lie about these things to be sociable.

A man takes his wife to the doctor is the beginning of a

joke. A woman goes to the doctor is the beginning of a tragedy. We know these things instinctively.

I should probably go to the doctor. Perhaps it's just a vitamin deficiency? Or my shoes are too tight?

Actually this pair is too tight: Gabor aren't always what they're cracked up to be.

I need to find out if anything's wrong with me, because I have an idea in my head and I want to know if it's true.

I have this notion that the Boss has killed someone.

2

Janet stood on the platform of Dartcross station waiting for the Manchester train to draw in. There was also a heritage steam engine that carried tourists to Buckminster through meadows by the river. It left from a separate station that smelled of coke and was decorated with enamelled signs selling boot polish. Television crews sometimes used it for period background and Janet thought of it now because even the regular station, quiet and provincial as it was, suggested another time and an England that had probably never existed but in which she felt she'd once lived.

She told herself: When I was younger I took part in a costume drama and never knew it. Do any girls now wear gymslips? Do Ladybird still sell clothes – or even exist? When did I last see a navy blue gabardine raincoat? She would be sixty-five this year. She thought that by now she ought to have a stable impression of the past and yet she didn't. Sometimes it was vivid and immediate, a recollection as fresh as yesterday. At other times it was a faint record of another world when life had been lived in black and white: a jerky motion picture on a fogged film. The strange thing was that she could hold these two feelings together as if both were equally and simultaneously true.

Thank God for friends who would understand what she meant.

The train came in. Most passengers were going on to Plymouth but a few businessmen and tourists got off. April was too early for the main holiday trade, and Dartcross attracted a particular traffic: middle-aged, middle class people who wanted undemanding relaxation, and New Age types who needed their bumps felt by some charlatan or other.

Enough. Here was Belle, squeezing her bulk out of a carriage door and dragging her bags like recalcitrant children. She'd taken advantage of the sunny spring weather to wear one of her voluminous cotton dresses that was gaudy enough to make an African market woman look shy. Janet remembered how, on first meeting her, she'd marvelled at her friend's size. Now she thought only how pretty her face was and how gracefully she moved.

Belle let go of her bags and sighed. 'Hecky thump, that's the last time I book a seat with a table in front of me! God knows how many sizes I'd have to drop to fit in comfortable! Still, never mind, here I am. Give us a kiss, chuck.'

Janet grinned. Belle always made her grin. Or laugh. They hugged and exchanged kisses.

'Mind my buzooms while you're at it; you're not humping the furniture about. How are you? You look well. Do you live far? Not a ruddy trek, I hope; I had enough of that when we were living in France and that poor cow, Joy, kept dragging us up mountains. Hey, but it's good to see you! Are we taking a taxi? Is Dartcross far from the sea? I should have checked. I've brought my cozzy in case we go swimming. I know that seeing me in a cozzy will ruin some folks' day, but I don't care because I'm on holiday and going to enjoy myself. Oh, it is good to see you – no, I've said that! Hasn't the weather been terrible? And don't get me going about the cost of things since I came back to England! I've brought my raincoat. It's a new one I got in M & S's sale.'

Janet took one of the bags and they made their way to her VW Golf. Belle continued to prattle. It wasn't nerves. Excitement rather. Belle had a knack of seeing freshness in everything: an occasion for marvel or gossip. At odd moments she made Janet feel like a girl again; and that Belle would drag her from the dance floor to the toilets to talk about some boy who'd spoken to them. It was no wonder she loved her friend.

A short detour by the Buckminster road to avoid the town centre and they were home. It was one of a terrace of smallish cottages with painted stucco fronts and the crazy lines of old buildings that have settled into the ground. 'I bet you don't half get draughts from them windows,' said Belle. 'Still, I suppose the Council wouldn't let them put PVC in – I'm surmising it's a conservation area. Maybe even a listed building?'

'I'll make a cup of tea before you unpack,' Janet suggested. Belle was looking around the contents of the small lounge and dining room. It largely comprised Edwardian furniture in beech and elm that could be picked up in sale rooms for a song. A gate-legged table with barley sugar legs. A sideboard with linen fold doors and tear drop handles. A mismatched set of dining chairs with rush seats.

'I don't recognise anything – I mean apart from the photos of David and your Helen. I thought it would be like your place in Puybrun.'

'If you remember, I rented that one furnished.'

'So you did.'

Janet had taken this one furnished too. The plan after David's death had been to settle in France if she found it congenial, which she did. She'd made such wonderful friends among the Englishwomen of Puybrun until … well. Circumstances had intervened and she'd been forced to return to England.

'Do you intend to stay here?' Belle cast an eye around. 'Is this house on the market? What are property values like? More expensive than Clitheroe, I bet, though you'd be surprised what a semi goes for round our way. We're becoming quite posh. Some people's curtains – you'd think they'd joined the aristocracy.'

'I haven't asked.' Janet was getting used to living among other people's furniture and even enjoyed it after a fashion. There was an attractive danger in the notion that she wasn't rooted in any one location, though at times an image would come of one of those genteel ladies in distressed circumstances who live at the seaside in rented rooms. Did they really exist? Probably not outside Victorian novels. Janet liked to try out storylines, even weaving them into her own existence, just to see how things would look.

'Those are Baxter prints,' Belle said. She pointed at a small picture framing half a dozen labels from boxes of sewing thread or something similar. They showed the Crystal Palace, women in crinolines and men in stovepipe hats. 'Alice collected them for a while – along with the tatting, and the pots with flowers on them, and the thimbles: ruddy thousands of them – thimbles I mean – though they didn't take up space, thank God.' Belle sounded disgusted.

'Is she still alive, your mother?'

'Isn't she! I've only had to move her! The last home insisted, you know – *after the fire*. They couldn't prove nowt, but they said their insurance company was kicking up a fuss. I haven't mentioned it to the new one. What they don't know won't hurt them. If there's another fire, I'll say it's just a coincidence.'

Belle had an inexhaustible fund of stories about Alice, all of them funny, the way she told them. And all of them deeply sad, too. You knew because they kept popping up in conversation. Janet wondered if Belle had gone over the same fraught ground with her husband, Charlie, trying to explain the alchemy of her relationship with Alice. Probably, but to no effect because men relate to their mothers in a different way. For all the affection of their marriage, whenever Belle raised the subject of Alice, Charlie would have had one ear to the football results or tried to concentrate on his correspondence as secretary of the local Rotarians, all the while wondering what the bloody woman was wittering on about now. Although they'd never openly quarrelled, decades later Belle was looking for some sort of reconciliation with her mother.

But these days Alice was beyond her.

Belle rummaged in a bag and brought out a small package in greaseproof paper.

'Ta ra!'

'What is it?'

'What is it? Only best genuine Bury black pudding! I bought it at Booths's. I thought we could have it for breakfast with mushrooms and fried tomatoes.'

Janet didn't answer. The two women looked at each other. It was funny, Janet thought, how infrequently people do actually look at each other. Rarely in her experience and not at the same time, not intensely and with sincerity. The mutual emotional nakedness was too intense.

She shrugged inwardly. Sometimes it was necessary; one simply had to do it. She looked at her friend, holding her gaze.

'I'll put this in the fridge,' said Belle, folding the paper with more care than a few bits of blood sausage required. 'We don't want it going off.'

Janet nodded. She wondered how to begin the conversation they each knew they must have.

It was time to talk about death, as well as tell Belle tactfully that she didn't care for black pudding.

3

'What do you mean: you don't like black pudding? You'll be telling me you don't like tripe and chitterlings next.'

'What are "chitterlings"?'

'God knows. Nice word though, eh? Like … "Chlamydia".' Belle rolled her tongue round the syllables. 'Chlamydia Chitterling – isn't it the name of a Roald Dahl character? It should be.'

'You've spent too many years teaching children,' Janet said.

'Yes,' Belle agreed and fell silent. She fingered the mantelpiece ornaments, though they'd tell her little. Porcelain thimbles decorated with the coat of arms of seaside resorts, they came with the house and were none of them personal. The gesture made Janet think: We're picking up and putting down subjects; not really talking about them at all.

'You went home to Clitheroe to sort out Charlie's affairs?'

'His solicitor is there. He had the Will and I was daft enough to think he knew more about Charlie's business than he did. Everything's a mess. I don't know if I'm as rich as God or don't have two pennies to rub together. If Charlie hadn't died I'd have ruddy-well killed him – except that I can't even be certain he was insured.'

'I don't understand.' In fact Janet did, but sometimes one said things because the other person needed to talk.

'You know how it is. Charlie always managed everything and he wouldn't admit he was losing it. The house is full of old bank books and share certificates and insurance policies and Christ knows what. The trouble is that everything these days is done electronically and only Charlie knew the passwords and the PIN numbers – except that at the end, of course, he didn't. I've only got by because, unbeknown to me, he got paranoid about the financial system and drew out a pile of cash; I keep finding bits of it in drawers and shoe boxes. Once that's gone…'

'I'm sure your solicitor will sort it out.'

'I hope so; otherwise I'll be living on soup in your spare room and making do with one change of knickers. Did you have this mess when David died?'

Janet nodded, though in David's case the mess was for different reasons. His company had got into difficulties and David had been out of his depth at the time of his death. Also he had died suddenly and rather ridiculously of a stroke while in a lay-by on the A34. There was no getting away from it: one did so resent the dead, even those one loved. They seemed to pop off leaving their affairs to be sorted out like a teenager's untidy bedroom.

She said, 'My son-in-law Henry helped me.'

'Is he still in prison? Forgive my big mouth.'

'He's on parole. Apparently they don't like cluttering up the jails with fraudsters, and it was a first offence.'

It was Henry's imprisonment after the collapse of David's company that had caused Janet to give up her cottage in France and return to England to help her daughter and grandchild.

'I suppose Helen's forgiven him and taken him back?" Belle said sceptically. 'You don't need to answer. Of course she has. That's why you're here, isn't it? You've been turfed out to fend for yourself now you're no longer needed. Kids! They're an ungrateful lot. And I imagine she thinks she can change him. Fat chance in my experience.'

'It isn't like that…' Janet said. But, as she well knew, it was, and in any case she didn't mind. Even before Henry's early release, she'd outlived her welcome with Helen. It was the mother-daughter thing. They got on tolerably well once they were apart, though it was demeaning to find her company less attractive than that of Horrible Henry – who was another Roald Dahl figure, come to think of it.

'A fine pair we are,' Belle said. 'Two old birds of no damn use to anyone and wondering what we're here for. I was fed up with Charlie towards the end: all that spoon feeding and bottom wiping. But at least he was a reason to get up in the morning, and someone to talk to even if he couldn't follow a word I said. And once in a while I'd see him as he was.... Did you ever do that with your husband? Just look at him and somehow see through the surface to the good looking fellow you married? And did you never wonder if he did the same: looked at you and saw you the way you were?'

Janet remembered that she and Belle had exchanged 'the look' the previous day, assessing the changes since they had each left France.

'Sometimes.' But to truly look at someone was a terrifying act. Always one was seeing the corpse of what had gone before: youth, charm, looks, hope and ambition. With luck one could convert that shared past into reasons for loving – she and David had done so – but the risks of seeing into the heart of a person were enormous because there was so little one could do about the things one saw. Not as one grew older. 'Actually it was just as often the other way round. I had to remind myself that I was looking at an elderly man. I still found him handsome, but he was bald and lined and sixty-four years old when he died, and I don't suppose other women gave him a second glance. The sort of chap you see at a bus stop.' Janet thought it over. 'Yes, it seems I married the sort of person you run into at a bus stop but I didn't think I had, not for a moment. How odd.'

And, of course, she thought, David used to look at me too. And he saw … actually he always told me I was beautiful. You could forgive a man a lot who would say that when you were over sixty.

'Isn't death bloody depressing!' said Belle. 'And at breakfast too. What are we going to do today? Oh, 'scuse me, here I am, acting as if the pair of us are on holiday, and you're probably planning on washing your smalls or waiting for a man to clean your gutters – hey, doesn't that sound dirty? – but you know what I mean.'

'I don't have any plans. I can show you round the town and we can do a little shopping.'

'If you put your mind to it I'm sure you could still get your gutters cleaned. You're a good looking woman when you're scrubbed up. Shopping? Do you have any good shoe shops, here in Dartcross? You know, when I was a kiddy, I could spend all day traipsing round town with my mother, queuing at the cashier's desk at the gas showroom and the TV rental place and the council offices, taking half an hour to pay each bill out of the cash in her purse; no cheque books or credit cards for her. Nowadays I go into town and after ten minutes I wonder why I'm there. Which doesn't mean we shouldn't go.'

So they went into town, on foot, it not being very far. They began at the top end where The Pinches ran into the High Street before its descent through Foregate to the river. Half way down was the old town gate, its arch and clock spanning the road and white in the sunshine.

Belle asked, 'Who was it said that History doesn't repeat itself, but sometimes it rhymes? I keep finding myself living in places with castles: first Clitheroe, then Puybrun and now here – not that I'm living here, strictly speaking, just paying a visit.' She glanced at Janet. Was she just paying a visit? 'Give me a week and I'll probably drive you up the wall. You'll be writing letters to Henry saying how much you miss him.'

The older part of the High Street was lined with medieval buildings jutting over the pavement and sheltering shops, cafés and a toy museum. Although there was a supermarket on Jubilee Road alongside the river, it hadn't driven out the small tradesmen. Always assuming you counted occult bookshops and practitioners of alternative medicine as small tradesmen.

They settled in an old-fashioned tea shop called the Anne Boleyn, though Janet didn't know if there was any connection between Dartcross and the murdered queen. She'd chosen it the first time because the window was full of delicious pastries, and then it became a habit as things do though other places were probably just as good. Today they had morning coffee and fruit scones with too much shortening if truth be told, so they crumbled in one's fingers.

' "Glassy cherries", Alice used to call them,' said Belle, taking hers from the top of her scone and popping it in her mouth. 'Did you see I didn't ask for whipped cream? Got to watch my figure!' She burst out laughing. 'How long have you been living here?'

'A month.'

'Time enough to make some friends.'

'I've spoken to one or two women. Friends? They seem nice enough, but I'm not sure I'd call them friends – not yet, at least.'

They were sitting at a small table by the window and Janet could see across the road Christine from the Heart of Osiris bookshop, who was talking to Sandra. There was some connection between the two women but so far Janet hadn't given much thought to what it might be. She'd met them only because in a moment of distraction she'd wandered into the shop, thinking it was a conventional bookstore and wanting something about cooking for one. Cooking for one – that was what it had come to. But there were no cookbooks unless one counted *Low GI Cooking for your Star Sign* and *Energy Healing Using the Mayan Diet*, both by someone called Sarinda Heavenshine. Christine and Sandra had been chatting – Sandra evidently a customer – and they'd welcomed Janet to talk about the weather and why she was in Dartcross. Nothing was said about the occult. They might have been in the baker's.

Belle followed Janet's eyes. 'I'm not so sure about those two. I always distrust women in skirts made out of recycled tea towels. The one with all the bangles looks as if she smokes and has chipped varnish on her fingernails. And I believe in that red hair like I believe in fairies. It's a Bad Sign.'

It was Sandra with the red hair, and the skirt reminded Janet more of the plush tablecloths with fringes that her grandmother used to have. It was a deep wine colour and complimented by a velvet bolero jacket in the same tone. Christine's skirt was a pale oatmeal and vaguely resembled jute sacking. Between the two of them, Christine was probably better looking, but Sandra had a strange glamour that stopped one from laughing at her. Of course 'better looking' and 'glamour' were relative terms, and both women looked as if their age hovered around the sixty mark and they hadn't resisted the changes or had fought and lost.

4

Across the road from the Anne Boleyn café, Sandra stifled a yawn. She always did when Christine was blathering about some food supplement or other she'd found on the Internet. Apparently this one renewed, balanced and unblocked 'energy'. Not the boring energy you get from coal and oil, of course, but the special New Age sort you pluck from your arse or wherever. Sandra knew all about 'energy'. She had a nice line in amulets bought by the gross from Nepal that were charged to the hilt with the stuff; and on request and for a few quid, she'd wave her hands over anything you cared to name, chant a mantra and bingo! Flogging 'energy' was a nice little sideline to her main career as a psychic.

'I don't know how they manage to sell it so cheaply,' said Christine, meaning the wonderful magic supplement.

I do, thought Sandra. Compressed milk powder, and some herb that's been labelled 'a miracle' by the *Daily Mail*, God bless it. Even if the science isn't dodgy, the method of delivering the goodies will be bollocks, as if you can repair the Forth Bridge by bombing it with sacks of rivets.

'You only have to think of all those research costs,' said Christine. 'Not to mention the packaging and advertising and having it delivered from the United States.'

'Yes, it's incredible, isn't it?' Sandra said while scratching an armpit. 'The company who make it must be idealists.'

'Exactly!'

'Real humanitarians.'

'Yes, they must be, mustn't they?'

Some people have no feeling for irony.

17

Sandra's armpit was still itching – sod it. As the weather warmed up, velvet brought her out in a rash. If it went on, she'd have to switch to linen, which meant months of going about looking as if she were wearing a paper bag. Cotton was too hit and miss – leastways when it was new. She was allergic to something in the finishing process. Silicones maybe? After her breast implants, her neck and face had swelled up till she could have passed for a red-haired hamster. That was when, for business reasons not to mention the enjoyment of her then boyfriend, she'd wanted to make a striking impression. In the end she'd had to settle for tattoos instead of tits. Not a bad idea but she wished she hadn't been drunk when she chose the design. Fairies in general might be considered New Age, but not Tinkerbell. And why on her bum for God's sake? What had she been thinking of? Still, at least it meant she didn't forever have to explain it away. These days there wasn't much chance to take off her knickers in company. More's the pity.

Christine was still droning on. She had one of those soft, inexpressive children's voices that made you want to smack her until an adult popped out – though, naturally, Sandra couldn't smack her, not with her being her best friend apparently. Sandra herself had a pleasingly husky thirty fags a day growl. The punters loved it; thought it deeply mysterious, especially with the measured delivery she was forced to use in order to get rid of her Brummie accent.

Back in the early days Sandra had discovered that you couldn't succeed in the psychic game with a Brummie accent. In fact you couldn't succeed at anything much. It was a bit like racial prejudice with the added disadvantage that people laughed at you. There Birmingham was: all two million plus people – three if you chucked in the outskirts – and once you got beyond Wolverhampton you'd never know the place existed; not to judge by the voices people admitted to. Now she thought of it, the

Spirits never spoke in Brummie accents. Either people from Birmingham didn't die or they practised discrimination in the Afterlife. Always assuming there was an Afterlife, which Sandra rather doubted. Joanie Threadgold (alias Madame Goldheart) hailed from Edgbaston, but you'd never guess it when she was more or less sober and wearing her respectable head. All her contacts on the Other Side sounded like that woman in the old TV cookery programmes, Fanny Whatsherface, with too much sherry inside her. That or Chinese or Paleface-Speak-With-Forked-Tongue Indian (sorry – Native American as you have to call them nowadays). Sandra stuck to the growl. You could come a cropper putting on funny accents and making up odd ways of speaking that owed more to Hollywood than to any race of people known to Anthropology. It had happened to Joanie.

Poor Joanie in her ladylike clothes, if you could imagine the late Queen Mum in C&A pearls (when there was a C&A). As old-fashioned as they come. Still had an oriental Spirit Guide, Master Foo Ling, who used to hobnob with Confucius, apparently, and could always be relied on for some high flown gibberish that meant whatever the punters wanted it to mean. Three sheets to the wind, Joanie once let slip how a client had caught her; not saying in terms that she'd been rumbled – because she'd never admit to not having a genuine Gift – but it amounted to the same thing.

'And you'd never have thought it,' she said in her faux-posh alto, a bit Maggie Thatcher plus amateur dramatics. 'There she was, all nice pin curls and smelling of Yardley. Husband six months dead and the usual unfeeling kids. Wanting a bit of comfort like they all do. And there's Yours Truly and Master Foo Ling willing to give it. Couldn't be easier, you'd have said. Anyway, I got into my stride – well, the Master did, strictly speaking – telling her what the Sage of Lu – that's what they called Confucius – telling her what the Sage of Lu had to say on

19

the subject…'

'Open the curtains and get out more often?' Sandra suggested.

'As you say. And what does she do, eh? What does she do instead of sitting there all meek and dabbing her eyes with a hankie? Only starts asking Master Foo Ling questions *in Chinese*, that's what! I didn't know where to put myself – I mean, how was I supposed to know she'd been a missionary? What are the odds, eh? What do you think Joe Coral would give you? I'm not psychic … well, I am, but you know what I mean.'

'What did you do?' Sandra asked.

'A missionary! I thought they only sent them to Africa. Or to that other place – the one where you get eaten – Borneo? Brixton? – somewhere beginning with a 'B' anyway.'

'And?'

'Oh, Master Foo Ling told her sharpish that she should stick to English. It stands to reason that they've had to compromise on the Other Side and all speak a single lingo if they're to rub along for the rest of Eternity. And English it is.'

'Yes, I can see that,' Sandra agreed but couldn't help saying, 'Still, you'd think, in that case, the Spirit language would be Chinese, wouldn't you? Given that there are more Chinese than any other people?'

'Not in Edgbaston,' said Joanie. 'I can't speak for anywhere else.' Seeming to think this answer might be inadequate, she added, 'I expect TV and films have had an effect.'

I should probably do my roots, Sandra thought. That morning in the mirror she'd spotted some grey. She wondered if other people had difficulty paying attention to their friends, and, for that matter, how it was that one acquired them. Some of hers were like stray cats who just seemed to have followed her home. She smiled at Christine who was making one of the weird remarks people made when you weren't listening, though you couldn't be sure they'd make sense even if you had been.

'...and it's very important to drink hot water. I mean when you have a high fibre diet. Well, of course, you'd know that.'

'Absolutely.'

The sun was reflecting on the window of the café across the road (the Anne Boleyn – silly name in Sandra's opinion), but she could see the new woman, Janet Something-or-other, who seemed to be talking to a head perched on top of a chintz-covered settee. Sandra remembered her coming into Christine's shop looking for – a cookery book, was it? She seemed an intelligent person. Very pretty and well turned out, too, even if she had said goodbye to sixty. Sandra was tired of her own 'look' – all the bangles, velvet, tassels and henna – but she'd got stuck with it for professional reasons. Her own choice. Joanie didn't follow it. A different generation and clientele.

'I need to buy some scones,' she said to Christine and was half way across the road almost before there was a reply. Janet was engaged in conversation and, on inspection, the settee was a fat woman who had a sparkling jolly face.

'I spotted you and wondered how you were getting on. Whether you'd settled in?' The words sounded feeble but Janet didn't seem to notice. She made introductions. The fat woman gave her name and added that she came from Clitheroe, though Sandra hadn't asked.

'I thought we would wander down to the river,' Janet said. 'Belle hasn't seen it.'

'I'll come with you,' Sandra said. She smiled. She had a nice smile: regular teeth, if a little stained by the fags and red wine, which was one of Life's Dirty Tricks as you got older. 'Sorry – you don't mind, do you? If you're going to stay here, you'll find yourself running into the same people again and again, and some of us small-town types are definitely a bit weird.' She put her hand to her mouth. 'Oh, God! Am I talking about myself? Freudian slip or what, ha ha!'

Belle laughed with her, a nice open laugh, and Janet gave a warm smile, but all Sandra could think was: They must think I'm an idiot.

But apparently not. Which went to prove you could never tell with people. Instead Janet said, 'That'd be really kind. Belle doesn't know anyone except me and I've met only a handful of people: you and Christine and one or two others.'

They set off down Foregate towards the bridge and turned onto the towpath. Unasked, Belle explained about the death of her husband Charlie and her old mother banged up in a home and a lot more that Sandra was glad to listen to but couldn't remember. Belle was one of those people who seemed to open themselves freely, though with the odd result that one was left wondering that there was something they were not saying. Sandra stored what she could and would write some notes once she got home. They might come in useful if the other woman ever turned up at one of her séances; quite possible, given the dead husband.

Sandra didn't disclose that she was a psychic and a medium. Outside of touting for business, she rarely did, at least not on first acquaintance. Most folk were sceptical and she didn't like to tell lies to people who might become friends, though that left the problem of explaining her clothes. Not exactly from ... well, not exactly from anywhere you'd care to put a name to. More charity shop than Chanel, though the occasional second hand Hermès scarf had been known to find a place in the ensemble.

She thought: I probably look like someone who lives on benefits and gets a regular bashing from her husband. Which at one time had been more or less the truth. In the end, twenty years of misery, a set of dodgy plastic tits and a miscarriage, all courtesy of Mr Raymond Stanley 'Wide as They Come' Wallace, had been enough for Sandra. Last heard of, until the property crash, he'd thrown in his lot with some bimbo and was doing nicely owning a bar, a golf club and a bunch of villas and she could have wished it had stayed that way. She hated to think back at the pastings she'd taken for a wardrobe of posh frocks, a few holidays and a nice house in Solihull. All behind her and good riddance; but where had the Spirits been when a friendly warning might have been in order? Bloody nowhere, that's where.

And so here they were on the towpath, and there was some yellow plastic tape strung across it.

'I'm afraid you can't come past,' said a lady copper, a young woman, a bit dykey to look at though that was probably just the clothes. 'A body has been found in the water.'

5

They've found one of the Boss's victims in the river. Well, probably it isn't. More likely it's one of those notions that keep popping into my head and that I pay more attention to than I really should. I've always enjoyed thought experiments: imagining the lives I might have had but didn't. Women in my online writers' group are always saying how imaginative I am, though I suspect they say the same to every aspiring writer so they don't die or go mad out of sadness and disappointment. A bit of kindness costs nothing, and people on the Internet never meet each other so they can say what they like with no consequences. They call the nasty ones 'Trolls'. I don't know what they call the nice ones. In fact they don't seem to talk about them at all, though in my experience there are plenty of them about: folk who'll chip in with a kind word or a piece of comforting advice. 'Pixies'? It pairs nicely with Trolls – Trolls and Pixies.

I haven't told anyone yet that I'm frightened of becoming senile. I doubt the Pixies could help me, and the Trolls would probably say I was showing off or it served me right.

According to the *Dartcross Advertiser*, the body was found washed up against the river bank at that dead spot by the path and the builder's yard where bottles and pizza cartons collect, if I understand them rightly. I don't know why people throw bottles and pizza cartons in the river; you'd think that if they bother to walk there, they must like the place and would take care of it, but they don't. Old tyres, too. And once, a mattress, which I've always found puzzling because of all the effort it would take to drag a mattress down to the river. You'd think somewhere else would be more convenient. A roundabout, maybe?

Not that the river in general is a dirty place, quite the contrary. Just that gloomy spot where a willow hangs over and a corpse could lie around for days. At the moment the celandines are out and the primroses, and I've great hopes for the ramsons. I love that faint smell of wild garlic when I'm walking in shade by water.

Per the *Advertiser*, the corpse is an elderly man. No name. I quote: 'UNIDENTIFIED BODY FOUND IN RIVER'. Actually it wasn't even the main story. That was something about an extension to the supermarket in Jubilee Road. 'TESCO PLANS SPELL DEATH TO HIGH STREET!' – apparently. The clue is in that word 'elderly', meaning somebody that no one much cares about. They think the body had been in the river about forty-eight hours, yet it's still unidentified, which rather proves my point. He hasn't been missed.

Actually the paper doesn't say he's been murdered, but I'm surmising he has been, or the story would have been on an inside page. A copper will have dropped a hint to the *Advertiser*'s man and he's waiting for confirmation. Which means the old chap was killed in the evening 3 days ago, after making allowances for the *Advertiser* to be printed. Evening because there are too many people strolling by the river in daytime.

Evening is time for walking dogs.

That Thing has brought home a bird. I found her dismembering it on the kitchen floor, the poor creature still alive and looking pitiful, much good it did where That Thing is concerned. A crow, which I've always thought of as a thuggish bird from the way they lord it over the garden. But, like the rest of us, this one was no match for the cat. I shoved both bird and cat outside with the help of a brush, but beyond that I don't have the courage to take That Thing on. As it was, she gave me a look that would shiver concrete into dust. I'll clear up the remains when she's finished.

*

The Boss walks the dog in the evenings, so regular it's not something I think about. He did so three nights ago. Being civic minded he carries a plastic bag and a sort of grabber-on-a-stick like park attendants used to have, and he picks up litter from the path and the river. For example that still pool by the overhanging willow, where bottles, pizza cartons, tyres, mattresses and the occasional corpse turn up. Except I don't recall his mentioning the corpse, and even with my memory I think I'd remember.

The dog is the problem in this scenario. What is Slobber up to while the Boss is murdering UNIDENTIFIED BODY FOUND IN RIVER? It's a version of the question of the dog that barked in the night – or didn't, if Sherlock Holmes is to be believed. Slobber is a good-natured hound, and in the ordinary way he'd be footling in the bushes, sniffing at those little black bags of dog mess people so obligingly leave around once they've gone to the trouble of picking it up in the first place. On the other hand, if there was any mayhem on the riverside path – namely the Boss doing in UBFIR with rope, lead pipe, revolver, dagger, spanner or any candlestick he happened to be carrying – Slobber would have wanted to join in the fun. It would help if I knew how the murder was committed.

I suppose the Boss could have fastened Slobber to a tree, though I struggle to imagine what UBFIR was doing or thinking while his prospective killer was tying up a drooling dog.

One problem with murder mysteries – as I'm always trying to point out to the others in my writers' group – is that they don't account for small practical details like these.

Later – The Boss says he didn't walk Slobber by the river

three nights ago. Once in a while he takes a path that runs by the Castle and out into the country. I have to concede he sometimes does this. I'd forgotten. It doesn't mean he's telling the truth on this occasion.

'Why do you ask?' he says.

I see no harm in telling him – not my suspicions that he's a murderer, obviously. 'According to the paper, a body has been found in the river. It went in three nights ago and drifted into that pool by the builders' yard, the one you're always complaining about, where the rubbish gathers. You might have seen it.'

'It would depend on whether the poor fellow drowned before or after I went past. Except not in this case because I didn't take the river walk that night.'

Being a man, he has an answer for everything. But I think he's lying. He came home one night fuming because Slobber had been in the river, then rolled over in something completely disgusting and smeared it over the Boss's clothes.

Into the bath with Slobber.

Into the bin with the Boss's clothes.

They were taken away in this morning's collection along with any blood or DNA belonging to UBFIR. Old clothes and no great loss, as the Boss pointed out at the time, which is why there was no point in washing them.

The question is: Can I be sure this incident occurred on the night of the murder? Was it the night before? The night afterwards? Once upon a time I would have been certain, but since I began going bonkers (or whatever it is that's happening), I can't be certain.

I wonder if the Boss is giving me drugs?

Later – I don't think the Boss is giving me drugs. He was considerate about clearing up the dead crow and risking the wrath of That Thing, though it wasn't much of a risk since she'd lost interest, the way cats do. Then he took Slobber out for another walk. I searched the house while he was gone.

Nothing – well, nothing obvious anyway. It's astonishing how much stuff there is in a house and you can't test everything otherwise they'd find me slumped by the toilet bowl, frothing at the mouth, with a bottle of bleach in my hand. Within reason, though, I'm fairly sure the Boss isn't drugging me.

Now I think about it, I'm not sure that's a comfort. Not if the alternative is senility.

If I'm going to lay this thing to rest, I've got to get more information. The paper won't tell me much. I have to get alongside someone with more experience of ferreting information out of the police.

What am I saying? The whole problem may go away if they discover the death is an accident or UBFIR topped himself. I suppose that's what I should hope for. The last thing I need is material to feed my suspicions.

Yet where did they come from? Not from the article in the *Advertiser*, that's for sure. In fact not from any specific incident or discovery. I think that with age I'm losing my inhibitions – I've heard that can happen – and knowledge that I've suppressed for years, decades even, has come bubbling to the surface.

I hope that losing my inhibitions doesn't mean I'll start swearing in the street or showing my bottom to strangers.

You see, I think I've always known my husband is a criminal.

Notes for shopping:
– Sun-dried tomatoes
– Parmesan
– Green pesto
– Linguine
– Bottled water (precaution against drugs)

6

Janet found herself having one of those small-world moments that happen on a handful of occasions in a lifetime. She remembered when she and David had done a safari in South Africa only for David to find that he and the group leader ('ranger' or whatever it was they called him) had been in the same class at primary school until his parents had emigrated.

'What are the odds, eh?' David asked.

'Stupendous if you'd predicted it and your prediction had come true,' said Janet, 'but you didn't predict it, did you?'

'Nothing much impresses you, does it?' The smile on his face told her the comment was meant affectionately. 'I'm always surprised that I did – that I impressed you enough that you married me.'

'I like a challenge. And you made me laugh.'

Janet laughed now, but what she said was true, and that was what she missed most since David's death: his cheerful silliness. As for bizarre coincidences, no matter how striking, they were almost invariably meaningless. David and Gordon (was it Gordon?) had nothing in common and the friendship of a pair of seven-year-olds was never going to revive from a stray meeting on the veldt decades later. So what was the meaning of this extraordinary encounter that Fate or God or whatever had brought about?

Absolutely nothing, it seems.

This time it was Stephen Gregg (Detective Inspector?), met on one previous occasion at her rented cottage in France, though spoken to on the phone several times. He was standing outside the Toy Museum in the High Street, evidently waiting for someone. What are the odds, eh? His

31

stamping ground was Manchester and hers until lately was Puybrun. They had no business running into each other.

'Good God!' he said and grinned. 'As I live and breathe, it's Janet Bretherton, suspected murderess and embezzler. And happily innocent of both crimes.'

One of his qualities was his easy familiarity; you would think they were friends. In another man it would have been intrusive, unwarranted, but in his case Janet had warmed to him from the beginning. The vagaries of personal chemistry, she supposed. She was surprised that she'd recognised him or he her.

Even more surprised when he kissed her on the cheek, though these days, since England discovered it was a Mediterranean country, everyone did.

'That was a peace offering,' he said. 'I'm not here to feel your collar.'

Janet wondered where he got his assurance from. Truthfully he was nothing much to look at: her own height and of stocky build. His nose was broad, his eyes deep set and mischievous, and his tousled hair brown, flecked with grey.

'Are you laughing?' he asked.

Janet was stifling a giggle. The thought had sprung into her head that he looked for all the world like someone who might do a Tom Jones tribute act in a working men's club somewhere in darkest Wales. And here he was, in his Debenhams leisure wear, like a million other men.

'I was trying not to sneeze,' she lied. 'The sun has that effect. You in Dartcross on holiday?'

'Yes and no. You?'

'No, I've rented a place.' Janet explained something of the affairs of Helen and Horrible Henry, whom Stephen Gregg knew of from their previous dealings. And, interestingly, he seemed to intuit – as most men probably wouldn't have – that the complexities of mother-daughter relationships lay behind her move.

'Dad! Dad!'

A boy was coming up the High Street with an ice cream in one hand and change in the other. Janet guessed his age at eleven or so, though small for his years.

'He looks like you,' she said to Gregg.

'Poor bugger.'

'Yuk!' said the boy

'Yes. Yuk!' said his father and pinched his ear. Janet reflected on Stephen Gregg's age. Somewhere in his late forties? And I'm sixty-five. Not that it mattered. She didn't think she had romance in mind. It was just an effect of growing older that she revisited the memories and feelings of youth to see if there was any life still in them. She might not be looking for romance, but the remembered experience was vivid and delicious.

'You must take my mobile number,' he said. He waited while she fumbled in her bag for her iPhone and dutifully entered each recited digit. 'And now yours.'

'What? Oh, yes, of course.' How could she refuse? She gave him the details.

Is he going to phone me? she wondered. But why should he? He was here with his son (she caught the name 'Larry' – extraordinary that there were any 'Larrys' in this day and age) and presumably his wife as well, whose name Janet didn't know; it had probably never cropped up in their conversations. And if he did phone, it was difficult to imagine what they would talk about. Murder and embezzlement weren't promising themes. Certainly she wasn't going to call him. What would be the point? In any case it would be liable to misconstruction. She might come over as a predatory widow.

I don't know why I think so, but he is an attractive man, she told herself.

It had to be because of his rich brown voice. She was convinced that actors on the radio were wonderfully good-looking except for those that had ugly voices. Then there was a football player who modelled and was astonishingly handsome, but when he opened his mouth a flaccid, piping sound came out and his eyes looked empty. His glamorous wife was welcome to him, in Janet's opinion. In any case, he had tattoos.

Needing to say something, Janet remarked, 'They've found a body by the river.' It seemed like something a policeman might be interested in. Death as small talk.

'Yes – a murder.'

'Really? I don't recall that being mentioned in the paper.'

'It wasn't, but the post mortem has confirmed it. I'm not telling you anything confidential.'

'No. I'd guessed in any case. How…?'

'I see I've whet your appetite.'

'I'm a writer,' said Janet.

'As I well know.'

They both smiled at a shared memory of an occasion when she found him in her cottage in France, reading her manuscript – though, now she thought about it, it was shocking, the way he'd entered the place in her absence and started ferreting among her things. She had no business forgiving him, but apparently she had.

And then she suddenly realised she wanted to bring this conversation to an end. She didn't want her feelings and memories stirred to no purpose, when all she had in mind was a bit of shopping for green grocery.

Stephen Gregg took the initiative. 'I've interrupted you when you have things to do.'

'I imagine young Larry could think of better things than listening to us two talking.'

'Yuk!' said Larry, who beamed with a little of his father's cheekiness.

They made their friendly farewells, and Janet watched father and son set off down the High Street, apparently with the river and boating in mind. She found herself feeling strangely upset; yet the encounter hadn't been unpleasant; quite the opposite if anything. Part of the aftermath of grief, she supposed. David was dead these five years and in a general way she was over it. Then something would happen, or it might be she would see or hear something, and her mind would be reaching out to David to talk it over with him. But, of course, he wasn't there, and the effect was that all these undiscussed experiences seemed somehow less substantial. Her life was thinner and at times she was conscious of herself as an elderly lady walking down the street and wondered if she was as transparent as other elderly ladies seemed to be.

Except that Stephen Gregg seemed to find her attractive.

She met Belle for tea and asked about her day.

'I've been pottering. I dropped in that Christine's bookshop. You wouldn't credit the stuff that some people believe in! That said, I can't see that shop making a living in Clitheroe. It's not that we're less gullible, but I think we're stingier. I ran into that daft hap'orth, Sandra. These psychics don't keep regular hours. Before I knew where I was she'd whisked me off to a pub. A pub, at this time of day! Mind you, it was one of those gastropubs, you know? One of those where they do funny things with scallops and bits of greenery that look like weeds. She drinks stout – Sandra, I mean. My grandma was partial to stout, but you don't find many women drinking it nowadays. On account of the iron, she says, though I put her looks down to smoking too much not lack of iron. Between you and me, I think she's a bit of a boozer or I don't know a red wine stain when I see one.'

'Would you believe Stephen Gregg is here in Dartcross?' Janet said. 'You remember, the policeman who came once to Puybrun? He's on holiday with his family,' she added, then recalled that Stephen had said nothing about his wife or if he had children other than Larry.

'I only met him once,' Belle said without much interest. 'He reminded me of my Uncle Arthur, who used to do a ventriloquist act in the evenings. He was an undertaker during the day.'

Janet felt again that sensation of thinning. Belle didn't want to talk about Stephen Gregg, and so she would have to keep her thoughts and feelings to herself.

'Sandra was banging on about her friends,' Belle said. 'Trying to be kind – which I'm not against. She has a notion that, with you being a writer, you might be a bit famous – chance would be a fine thing, eh? Any road, reading between the lines, I fancy she'd like to show you off to her pals. What do you think?'

'I don't know. What do they do?'

'Apparently, they're heavily into murder,' said Belle.

7

The implications of Belle's conversation came to Janet and she challenged her over breakfast next day.

She said, 'You told Sandra I was a writer?'

'I might have let it slip,' said Belle cautiously. 'It's nowt to be ashamed of, is it?'

Janet supposed not. Indeed, at one level she was proud of her skill. Then again, at another level she wasn't. Once she'd got over her initial enthusiasm at the acceptance of her first novel, she thought there was something morally dubious about delving into the human psyche, in particular when she used friends or people she'd met to construct characters. She always ended up distorting them for the sake of effect. The number of times she had made her husband David into a murderer – well, it was shameful, really, because in a general way he was the most amiable of men. At all events she suspected there was something callous in the way that she and other writers used other people: something cold-hearted.

She asked, 'Why did you tell her? And what does it have to do with murder?'

'She's in a readers' group. I didn't give her your pen name or say what kinds of books you wrote.'

Belle sounded ashamed as if she'd gone too far. Janet was sorry if she'd snapped at her. That was how one lost friends: in ill-judged exchanges that would have been different if only one could have seen them from the outside.

She said, 'I'm sorry. I don't mean to be…'

'I learned something in return,' Belle went on, 'though it was Christine not Sandra who told me. She's a psychic. Does it for a living. That's why she dresses like Snow White's wicked stepmother. You don't have to tell the truth if you don't want to get dragged into something. Say you write books about How to Do Tatting. That'll shut 'em up.'

Janet smiled. During their time at Puybrun, Belle had taught their women's group how to do tatting, which was a talent she'd learned from Alice.

'Any road,' said Belle, 'what it amounts to is that Sandra, Christine and a few others are in this group. I expect you know all about readers' groups?'

Janet nodded. She'd never been a member of one, but she'd addressed a few in order to oblige her publisher and promote her books. She supposed some writers must enjoy them but she had felt like a bit of a fraud. There was always someone who didn't really get into the book, never finished it and was faking her interest. Someone else hated the book but would never say so because she was a nice person. And finally there was the one who could actually see into the heart of the text, more so even than Janet, which was to be expected because Janet only wrote the damn things and couldn't be expected to know what they were about. People were always surprised when Janet told them she was only guessing at what her books meant; always assuming they meant anything at all. But the uncertainty, the feeling that she was exploring and perhaps discovering something previously unknown to her – aspects of her own character and relationships as much as anything – was one of the reasons she wrote.

'They stick to murder mysteries, by and large,' said Belle. 'They don't claim to be intellectuals.' She caught herself and laughed. 'Sorry, that didn't come out right, did it? It makes you sound like a moron fit for writing nowt bar rubbish. Shall I dig a bigger pit for falling into? You know what I'm driving at.'

'It's all right. I'm just surprised that you've got to know people so well and so quickly.'

'That's me and my big gob and being nosey. Give me the time of day and before I know where I am I'm asking the names of your grandchildren and telling you about my hysterectomy. What do you say? They're having a meeting tonight.'

'What book…?'

'Frances Fyfield's latest.'

'She gave me a nice review once.'

'Name dropper.'

Janet shook her head wistfully. In a writing career of more than thirty years she'd met only a handful of other authors at festivals and the like, and at a pinch they might remember her face but not her name. What she knew of them – those things that weren't common knowledge – were stories and stray facts mentioned by her agent and publisher: bits of gossip and quite likely untrue. Unless one got on the media circuit, writing was a solitary business and networking online wasn't a substitute for human contact. By and large Janet avoided writers' groups. She had a suspicion – no doubt unjustified – that the members were self-obsessed and a little mad. There were no other writers among her friends. Her day job with the local authority had brought her into contact with social workers and people in education – women like Belle for example, who'd been a teacher – and she found them congenial.

'You're too modest, you are,' said Belle. 'If it were me, I'd be collaring folk, treating them to my charm, and getting them to buy my books.'

'They'd be too frightened not to.'

'Are you having a crack at my size?' Belle shuffled her bosom as if moving furniture, but she didn't wait for an answer. 'Anyway I can see you're up for it. I'll tell Sandra. I don't know what the etiquette is, but it's usually a safe bet to take a bottle of plonk on these occasions so we can all get plastered. I don't see Sandra serving up any dainties. If I know anything, her oven won't stand close inspection. Maybe I should pick up something from Tesco's you can shove in a microwave? Sausage rolls or falafel, depending on how posh we're feeling.'

They ran into Stephen Gregg outside the gents' outfitter in The Pinches and without his lad.

He said, 'I'm told that one of the signs of middle age is that you think you look good in a panama.' He pointed to the one in the window. 'What do you think?'

Made in Ecuador and forty pounds. Not a bad price in Janet's view.

'My husband David used to wear one.'

'And did you like it?'

Janet smiled guiltily. She did think it was a sign of middle age, even if she was too polite to say so, but David had set his heart on it. As it happened, it became part of David's vaguely raffish style. Had he stopped wearing the panama, she would have noticed and he would have seemed diminished. So perhaps his instinct had been right all along.

She said, 'The question is: do you see yourself as a panama hat person?'

Mentally she tried to fit that image to Stephen Gregg. Panama hats seemed to go with both ends of the dress spectrum: respectable old fellows in flannels and blazers with regimental badges, and louche types in rumpled linen suits and espadrilles. What am I doing? Janet realised she was creating a mental sketch so that she could slot this curious policeman into a book. How disgraceful!

'Perhaps I'll pass for the time being,' he said.

Janet glanced round and saw that Belle had sloped off to rummage in the vintage clothes shop. It was her notion of tact. Belle was playing with the girlish idea that Stephen Gregg 'fancied' Janet. She'd hinted as much both when they lived in Puybrun and first ran into him, and again after they met him in the High Street. 'Hinted' insofar as anything Belle said was indirect enough to qualify as a hint. 'Shouted' might be nearer the truth.

For a moment they studied each other in silence,

neither of them particularly uncomfortable with the other.

'Your boy…' Janet began.

'I've packed him off this morning on the train back to school.' He named the school, which Janet recognised. She was surprised the boy was a boarder. Not what she imagined of an ordinary copper's child.

'I thought you were in Dartcross on holiday; isn't that what you said?'

'I think I said "yes and no" when you asked. I'm here on business, but it's a nice place and it was handy for Larry to have a break for a couple of days.'

Something in what he was saying didn't compute for Janet and she reminded herself to give it more thought later. For now she asked, 'So you've been seconded here from Manchester?' She remembered Stephen Gregg had claimed a background in accountancy before his transmutation into a policeman. 'I shouldn't have thought Dartcross was the hub of financial crime.'

'Manchester? I'm based in London.'

Janet was flustered, thinking for a moment that she was being stupid.

He understood. 'Oh yes, of course. I was working out of Manchester during that business with your husband's company. Well, as it happens I was on secondment that time as well.'

'I wouldn't have thought my husband's company merited that kind of attention – I mean enough to bring in an expert from London.' She was floundering. It wasn't as though she knew all that much about police procedure. She faked what there was of it in her books. She thought the local fraud squad should have been well capable of unravelling the after effects of David's incompetence without the need to bring in a heavyweight from London.

Then again, perhaps he wasn't a heavyweight? Perhaps quite the opposite? One of those people one can afford to lend out as a stand-in when somebody is having a knee replacement because, frankly, they aren't exactly indispensable. She considered this possibility as an alternative image for her catalogue of not-wholly-fictional characters.

Being on secondment would explain why there was no sight of Stephen Gregg's wife. Obviously she would be at home in London. Quite likely she had a job of her own; a nurse or a teacher: jobs suited to the wife of an intelligent unpretentious man in his forties.

'Is it the murder that brings you here, then?' she asked and caught herself laughing. 'I'm sorry. Can you imagine someone overhearing us?'

'You mean the small talk of other people.'

'Yes, those stray remarks you catch when you're sitting on the train that make sense in context but sound bizarre to strangers. Murder – it's not exactly talking about the weather, is it?'

He grinned. 'No, not the weather. But it wasn't the murder that brought me here. I arrived the day before.' His friendly brown eyes held hers but he showed no inclination to elaborate. Reticence or deceit?

'I'll say goodbye,' she said at last. Not to be abrupt, she added, 'No doubt I'll see you about – I mean, if you're seconded here for a while. Dartcross isn't much more than a village and one is bumping into people all the time.'

And here was Belle to save the day, carrying something from the vintage shop in a recycled plastic bag.

'Summat that caught my eye,' she said. She treated Stephen Gregg to a smile, which he returned before walking off. Turning to Janet she went on, 'What do you make of this fascinator? I thought it might do for one of those weddings where you don't want to splash out too much because you don't know why you've been invited. Frieda in the shop says she'll take it back if I decide I don't like it'. She put it on. 'Does it suit or does it look like the holly on a Christmas pudding?'

'Frieda in the shop?'

'Is that your answer? So it's holly on a Christmas

pudding. Pity.'

'And Frieda?' Janet was sure Belle hadn't been in the shop before; yet here she was brandishing a name. 'I suppose you know the names of her grandchildren and have swapped details of your operations.'

'Since you ask, she has a granddaughter called Maisie, and what those doctors did to *her* was absolutely shocking. You'll get to meet her – Frieda I mean. She sells that clobber that Sandra wears. That's all you need to know. And how did you get on with Sexy Stevie? Does he still fancy you?'

Janet looked away and glimpsed him in the distance walking into the High Street. In the way of things if you gave them enough time, she now understood the business about his boy being at boarding school.

Stephen Gregg was a widower.

8

They've identified UNIDENTIFIED BODY FOUND IN RIVER. The *Advertiser* was just looking for a touch of mystery or maybe too lazy to do its homework when it said that no one knew his identity. The local TV news says his name is Stanislaw Walacaszewski – which I can spell but can't pronounce. It also said he was 'elderly', but fifty-seven isn't 'elderly' in my book. Then again these days everyone over thirty is 'elderly'. Or it may be that lying in the river for days on end among all the rubbish in that pool by the willow has done nothing for his complexion. If he'd stayed there any longer his face would probably have floated off, and then where would we be?

Apart from his name, we've been told nothing about him. Most people probably think he's a Polish plumber rather than a Russian gangster. 'Stanislaw Walacaszewski', how do we know it's his real moniker (if that's the right slang word)? Spies and crooks use false names and I have my doubts about a lot of the people that the Boss used to introduce me to. First and foremost Gerald Wyngard Wyngard Wyngard de Saint-Foix (which I swear to except for the exact number of 'Wyngards'), and his wife Hermione W W W de S F. Those two came across so posh they'd almost lost the power of speaking English.

Gerald – 'Call Me Gerry' – and his wife, paramour or whatever she was were always taking us to restaurants. And the holidays, well! This when we were living in Hampstead back in the day when one could still meet a nice class of homosexual and before the place filled up with Russian spivs. Said he was a banker, and I admit he looked the part, given the creepy reputation the species has these days. Hermione claimed to be a model, and she had that strange vacuity of models, as if they are only templates of real women, waiting for Life to fill in some interesting details.

It was Call Me Gerry and his pals that brought about the disaster that has been my life.

This morning the Boss made a bonfire in the garden. A pile of stuff in one of those galvanised contraptions like an old-fashioned dustbin with a chimney on it, so I couldn't see what he was burning. Slobber went bonkers, running around in circles with lashings of spit hanging from his chops and barking his head off. That Thing paraded up and down the garage roof with half a mouse in her mouth. Which reminds me: I should ask the Boss to get on the ladders and clear the roof with a long brush. Last time we did it, it was like an abattoir up there. More crows, pigeons, blackbirds and blue tits than you'd find in an aviary. Also the hind leg off a badger – God knows how.

Reminder – Get him to cut back the ivy while he's at it. It blocks the gutter.

So the Boss is burning stuff in the garden? So what? The so whattery is that it's spring not autumn. The place isn't exactly full of leaves and windfall branches.

'Hi, darling!' I coo. 'What are you burning?'

He turns round cheerily and says, 'Oh, just prunings and such.'

'You seem to have put a lot of paper in the … thingy.'

'Oh, you know how it is. Green stuff doesn't burn easily; so you need to get it going.'

He's right of course. Green stuff doesn't burn easily. But it burns with a sight more smoke than is coming out of the whatsitsname. Paper on the other hand….

These days I realise too well that Call Me Gerry was more important than I first gave him credit for. If you laugh at people, it's difficult to take them seriously. The first time I saw him he was wearing a chalk stripe suit, a pale blue shirt with a white collar, red braces and a bowtie, and he was showing that little triangle of bare belly that men never notice but women do. As for Hermione, she didn't buy her clothes at any charity shop I ever went in.

Now I think about it, back in the eighties I didn't buy clothes at charity shops either. Quite the contrary: Hermione ('I just know we're going to be great friends') and I went to a lot of shows over the years; every fashionable designer in the book. It seemed to be all she was interested in; the curse of being a model, I suppose. Once, years after our first meeting, when in retrospect I think she was already going over the hill, we went to an Alexander McQueen show. Not especially my taste, but in the dim and distant I had enough money to buy anything I pleased, even if it amounted to something better suited to an adventurous production of *The Merry Widow*. I always wondered what happened to that Alexander McQueen dress. I once saw a very pretty Goth wearing something like it, and it looked rather fetching with black knee-high torture boots. Who would have thought?

Here in Dartcross there's a decent Oxfam shop where I picked up a nice Givenchy cocktail dress, which made me think back to the days of Dior, Chanel and Alexander McQueen. I haven't worn the cocktail dress. You know how it is that you buy something thinking it's absolutely right for that special occasion, but it turns out the occasions aren't all that special. Not in Dartcross. I take it out every now and again and pose in front of the mirror with the dress still on its hanger and a glass of wine in my spare hand. Nowadays, in the beau monde of our little town, I get by with an old scrap of Laura Ashley and a few accessories or the occasional haute couture souvenir of another life. I think that's a bit sad. In fact I think a lot of my life is sad, but it's a case of chin up and carrying on, isn't it? If you want a solution to depression I recommend yoga and cheap Tesco's plonk in equal proportions. Pilates is probably as good as yoga.

Anyway and back to my story – not that anyone is reading it – here comes the Boss with Call Me Gerry and Hermione, who at this date I don't know from Adam but we're all laughing and air kissing like characters in an American afternoon soap. Call Me Gerry has a Bentley out front ('Just until I get a Roller, eh?') and we go off to one of those places you read about in the Sunday supplements, though it falls a bit flat because Gerry hasn't booked five years in advance and Max Clifford is eating there and the maître d' doesn't accept coin of the realm even on a cash-no-questions basis. How embarrassing, always assuming C-M-G can be embarrassed by anything. Which he can't.

In the end we go to a gentlemen's club in St. James', not gambling and lap dancers but one of those with libraries full of bound copies of *Landed Families of East Sussex* in ten volumes. And it turns out that Gerry actually is a member! 'A good cheap room when I'm in Town,' he says. I was surprised then, but I'm not so surprised now. But I mustn't get ahead of myself.

As for dinner, no problemo. Unlike *L'Escargot sans Toit* (by appointment to Max Clifford), the Empire & Dominions Club has got a vast empty dining room, all oak panels, dusty chandeliers and bad portraits, and on the off-chance of filling it seems to have boiled the entire cabbage crop of Lincolnshire and made a mountain of steamed pudding with custard.

'The main thing,' says Gerry, 'is the absolutely first rate cellar.'

So we settle to a bottle apiece (not Tesco's finest). Which is probably wise in the circumstances.

What is it all about? I wondered then and wonder now. Friendship? Hardly, even if at times we seem to be living out of each other's pockets. My new best friend Hermione slithers alongside (I think it's one of those years when snakeskin and leopard spots are in fashion and in my experience they do make women rather slithery) and tries to engage me in conversation, but at this date I think we have nothing in common. Her interests are in horses, which she's been brought up with in Cambridgeshire or Byelorussia or wherever it is that Daddy has a racing stable – or so she says. And I try to explain my involvement in writing, and tell her about writers' groups and so forth. I don't think there's anything pathetic about being a member of writers' and readers' groups with a lot of other nice women, but Hermione looks at me as if it's the saddest thing she's ever heard. The sort of group you would join when you'd lost a child.

I've got my dates wrong. Back in the eighties ordinary people weren't involved in writers' and readers' groups. The truth is I can't remember what we talked about.

When I first met Call Me Gerry and Hermione, Angela hadn't been born and hadn't died. And I was still capable of being happy.

Anyway the Boss has been burning stuff that may be garden waste or may be papers containing all the dope on his Guilty Secret. Once the ashes have cooled I shall root around with a stick and find out which. If it turns out to be papers, I don't know what I'll do with them. My problem is to understand if I'm right in my suspicions – I mean about the spying and crookery and murdering. Is that really what was going on?

Back to the Empire & Dominions Club. On reflection I'm confusing this first meeting with years later and Gerry and Hermione as they were when we last saw them, just before the Boss made his decision to retire. That was fifteen or more years after our first meeting and by then Gerry was fleshy and had high blood pressure and his lips were pursed and thick as if he could kiss the opposite wall, and Hermione was a raddled old baggage who didn't know it. Cleavage like a washboard and breasts like a pair of old socks.

49

But not that first time. I'm forgetting how glamorous we once were. How rich – or faking it, which is much the same thing. Now that I recall, in those early days Gerry was very handsome with that long hair and floppy quiff which public school men can carry off into middle age and he was charming, not the lascivious old groper of his mature years. And as for Hermione, she was a model for god's sake! Of course she was beautiful! Better than beautiful. Ethereal, like a fairy or spirit in one of those soft porn Victorian paintings, all gauzy flesh and air-brushed you-know-what, not a hair in sight so to speak. How could I have forgotten?

How could I have forgotten? I don't put this down to senility but only to the ordinary tricks of memory and understanding. Some impressions come to the fore and some don't, and that last meeting between the four of us was one that none of us is likely to forget in a hurry, which is why I'm getting confused with how things used to be.

I have to keep reminding myself that the Boss was also handsome in those days and, despite the wrinkles and the sagging flesh which I see as his wife but others apparently don't, I suppose he's still good-looking for his age; but he no longer has the ruthless energy that at one time showed him to be a man on the make and made him so immensely sexy. Only the years would reveal him as a crook and murderer – or accomplice to murder at least.

In retrospect he hasn't been a very good husband. It became obvious after Angela died. Coldness or indifference; I'm not sure which.

On this first night the Boss has prepped me to be on my best. 'Potentially a top drawer client,' he says. To date his career has been more show than substance, though I'm guessing. I've no idea where the money comes from or how we happen to be living in Hampstead. Only now do I realise that he used to treat me like an idiot, doling out an allowance for pin money while he managed the rest. Much as his father used to do with his mother, I fancy, because I never saw a more downtrodden woman, though hiding it behind the cut glass manners. You'd have thought I'd have picked up some women's lib notions by the time I was in my twenties, but the fact is a lot of us didn't. We tend to characterise an age by its exceptions rather than its rules, and the truth is that for many the subject of 'liberation' never got much beyond sex. And I wonder who decided that?

But I digress. This evening at the E & D I am minding my Ps & Qs in front of a valuable client and trying to understand what's going on and who these people are. The Boss and Gerry are a pair of dogs, sniffing each other's bottoms. Hermione and I are more like each other than I care to admit: two lovely budgies looking at our reflections in the mirror. What I recall is that Gerry comes out with some tale about having been to Fettes, which is where Tony Blair went to school so I'll say no more. The Boss counters with a slightly glossier version of the strict truth, which was that he'd been to a perfectly good public school no one has heard of ('All the buggery and none of the kudos,' as he likes to say) and then to Oxford. These days, says Gerry, he runs the London branch of the Leeward Islands and Southern Antilles Commerce Bank. And the Boss says he's principal partner in a firm of investment brokers

I never heard of any junior partners.

I have no idea what an 'investment broker' is, except that at the time it was apparently supporting us at our place in Hampstead and keeping me away from the joys of buying my clothes at the Dartcross Oxfam shop.

So much for my first meeting with Gerald Wyngard Wyngard Wyngard de Saint-Foix.

Shopping List
– Fruit (cheapest in season)
– Onions, carrots, bunch thyme
– 8 oz brisket

*– Replacement rubber mouse for the one That Thing
ripped to pieces*
*– White wine for readers' group (do they still do Blue Nun
or am I showing my age?)*
– Teach Yourself Russian (second hand if possible).
*– Suitable poking stick for rummaging in the thingummy if
I can't find one around the house.*

9

Sandra Wallace's house turned out to be a pebble-dashed semi along Station Road. So much for the lair of a practising psychic, thought Janet, suddenly realising she'd expected something a bit more gothic – older at all events. But there was no accounting for taste, or pockets for that matter. She knew next to nothing of the occult business but suspected the majority of practitioners found the pickings thin; certainly not enough for a large gloomy mansion with turrets at the corners and a drive lined with yew trees. As she was aware from experience, most writers, artists and entertainers had to take a day job, and putting on séances and telling the future didn't seem so far removed from playing gigs in pubs or doing readings at literary festivals. In fact Janet recalled pubs with signs advertising forthcoming psychic attractions.

'Well, this is a bit of a bit of a let-down,' said Belle. 'What's that Sandra doing, living all respectable?'

'You were looking for Dracula's castle?'

'Don't be daft. Still, a few bin bags full of incense sticks and empty gin bottles wouldn't come amiss. And look at those curtains! There's no way those are off Preston market. I know Sanderson when I see it.'

A short flight of steps led to a newly-painted door with a glass roundel patterned with a sunburst, very Art Deco. Sandra answered the bell and smiled with what looked like genuine pleasure.

'You're the last to arrive. That should make the intros easier. And what's this?' Grinning at Belle. 'A bottle of red wine! Maybe it's you that's the mind reader not me. And what's in the bag?'

'Falafel and a few other bits and pieces. I don't know what you usually do.'

'Oh, you are good!'

This evening Sandra was wearing a celadon green silk blouse and brown boot-cut slacks. Her red hair was pinned up and she wore some simple jewellery, discs of … abalone, Janet thought.

While Sandra put away coats, Belle whispered, 'What happened to Gypsy Rose Lee?'

Janet shrugged. She'd no more expected this transformation than her friend. But wasn't that the lovely thing about people: their capacity to surprise? Though the truth was that they were always consistent with their nature; it was just that one was ignorant as to what that might be. Some people, for example, were consistent in their inconsistency. It was a damned nuisance for writers.

'Let me make the introductions,' said Sandra.

She led them into a neat sitting room, giving names as she did so. 'I don't suppose you'll remember them straight away but you'll get used.'

Joanie – smiling and white haired, a neat little body like everyone's favourite aunt (or Miss Marple, thought Janet) – not clear what she did: retired presumably.

Jean – short black hair – Scottish (that harsh Glaswegian accent was off-putting, but as often as not hid a perfectly good nature) – taxi driver – lesbian?

Diana – homeopath or similar nonsense – a bit 'county', what with the Alice band and the pearls – high cheek bones and good looks.

Frieda – ran the vintage clothes shop – dressed there as well, to judge from appearances – rabbit teeth and a smoker's cough – dog hairs on her skirt – clunky beads made out of seeds and nuts.

Christine – already met at the Heart of Osiris bookshop – linen and homespun and a bit New Age – 'and short of some marzipan on top of her carrot cake' in Belle's opinion, but pretty and amiable.

And not a surname between the lot of them, though no doubt that would come. In the meantime Janet took in the room looking for signs of Sandra's profession and finding nothing except a few books in the IKEA bookcase, though, even here, most of them were murder mysteries and a bit of Mary Wesley not stuff about fairies and angel magic in pink and lilac covers. For the rest Sandra had gone in for magnolia emulsion, a fireplace with a teak surround, scented candles, a bit of Clarice Cliff, and one of those paintings – Montmartre by Moonlight – bought on holiday and regretted afterwards because it had probably been painted in China. Janet found herself warming to Sandra as she did to people who seemed decent and without pretensions – other than claiming to be a psychic.

'Belle has brought us some falafel and...'

'Pakoras.'

'Pakoras,' repeated Sandra, and as an aside, 'We normally go in for corn snacks and cashew nuts, but these are much appreciated. Joanie love, don't eat the pakoras because there's onion in them and you know it repeats on you. I can't swear to the falafel. Belle – Janet – have some wine.'

So they dived in among strangers. Belle enjoyed herself. 'I could have been in Clitheroe,' she said afterwards, and Janet knew what she meant. As with other readers' groups she'd attended, this one was preoccupied with family news and the latest rumours, and only when these had been gone through, which took about an hour, did they turn to the ostensible matter in hand: Frances Fyfield's latest. Naturally they had opinions.

Of one of the male characters: 'What a pillock!'

Of a female: 'A right cow.'

Actually, in Janet's opinion, the characters in question were a pillock and a right cow, and as literary criticism goes, the comments were on the mark. And at least everyone had read the book. What's more, with the author not actually present! Impressive or what? She could remember a couple of dismal occasions in her own history when that hadn't been the case. At the time, of course, she could do nothing but smile and pretend she hadn't noticed.

She gave Belle her head and kept her own opinions to herself, preferring to watch the other women, 'my new friends' as she thought of them, the way that she had once thought of the women of Puybrun when she lived in France. New friends and old friends. Meetings and partings. It was an aspect of being a widow that she hadn't foreseen: the need to go out and actively seek friends if she weren't to die of loneliness. I shouldn't have had that glass of wine; it's making me maudlin. Old Joanie is drunk but putting on a good show. I don't think Jean is really a lesbian; it just seems like that if you're Glaswegian, cut your hair short and drive a taxi. Diana – it's very difficult to penetrate her sort of good manners and find out what lies underneath. Frieda dresses too young, and of course it has the opposite effect, drawing attention to her age. Christine has that gushing desire to see the other person's point of view that makes her come across as an idiot, though I don't suppose for a moment that she is.

I wish I could stop coldly studying other people. It's not a very attractive character trait. Apart from Joanie, I'm the oldest here, though none of us are young. We're the sort of women who make up theatre audiences, not the ones who tear at each other's hair outside night clubs or push their children around in buggies. There are no such things as groups of random people: there's always a factor that makes us comprehensible to each other. Which makes me wonder if it's truly possible to solve a crime simply because people always remind one of others one has known? Or is that a bit too 'Miss Marple'?

As a writer Janet felt torn in that regard: relying on stereotypes so the reader didn't have to vex her head over subtleties of characterisation; yet fighting against this inclination in order to make her women interesting. As for Miss M, in Janet's opinion her insights into village life didn't reflect acute intelligence but only the prejudices of her creator's class and time and a mild suspicion of Jews.

The truth was Janet couldn't resist picking up clues, even if her inferences were sometimes mistaken. All the women in this group were married – even old Joanie – excepting Janet herself and Belle who were widows, and Sandra who was divorced 'always assuming a Spanish divorce means anything'. There was no mention of children; then again they were of an age when the kids had grown up and left. Not, of course, that that meant one was free of them (shades of Helen), but they didn't intrude into conversation in quite the same insistent way as the little ones who were always having to be picked up from school or taken to ballet class or whatever. No doubt there would be an adolescent somewhere, living in squalor in his bedroom, or a daughter who'd married the wrong man called Dave, and Janet would find out in due course. Meanwhile she felt a little ashamed at looking forward to learning about her new friends. No, I'm not a nice person, she thought, and smiled.

And then the elephant in the room.

The subject of Frances Fyfield was finished with and Sandra put her glass down on an occasional table next to the latest *Advertiser* with its story about the dead body, and announced, 'Well, if our guest, Janet, is too modest to tell you, I will. We've got a celebrity among us! Janet here is no less than *the* Janet Bretherton, the famous writer!'

Ooh! Aah!

Yes, well…. People in readers' groups were always too polite to ask who 'Janet Bretherton' was when she was at home. Some would attempt an excuse that her books were not in a genre that they read. It was worse if they pretended they'd heard of her in order that she wouldn't feel offended, which meant that Janet would have to cleverly feed them snippets of information so it would seem they knew things about her all along, even though they obviously didn't. Janet was too experienced a mid-list author to expect recognition and had long given up caring, but this little ritual of mutual face-saving was such an embarrassment, and it was so difficult to pitch her response exactly. If she acknowledged her fictitious celebrity, the others would think she was 'too full of herself', and if she didn't they would reproach her with false modesty; in fact hadn't Sandra implied as much in her introduction?

Janet thought sometimes that it would be nice to be guilty of the sin of false modesty. Instead, her lowly position in the world of literature meant she'd had to put up with the virtue of genuine article, which was tedious and only slightly preferable to being 'full of herself'.

Deftly Sandra steered the conversation away from the particulars of her guest's unread books to the more general subject of writing murder mysteries. Janet didn't mind expressing some opinions on this, though she knew they were unoriginal. She made a few comments about plot development and suspense and controlling the release of information to the reader; but all along she was thinking: If I really knew anything about this, I'd be reviewing Frances Fyfield's books for the Sunday papers and not the other way round. The bit she found difficult to explain was that at the outset of her novels she was never a hundred percent certain who actually did 'do it' and that the writing didn't so much expound a preconceived solution as unravel a puzzle that was as mystifying to her as it was to anyone else. For instance, she was always finding bits and pieces littered about her text that turned out to be clues, though she'd never deliberately planted them. What sort of a writing technique was that? Janet was slightly ashamed of it and never explained her methods if she could get away without an answer. There were times when she felt she wrote books like a cowboy builder fixing a leaky roof.

'Is your preference for the amateur detective or the professional?' asked she of the buck teeth and vintage clothes (Frieda, wasn't it? The surname would come to her.)

That was actually a good question.

'There are problems with both,' Janet said. 'We're not coppers and so it's difficult to get the police procedures right, but if your detective is an amateur, you don't have to involve yourself in the detail of all that. On the other hand, it means you don't have the resources of the police to do things like check fingerprints and DNA and motor vehicle registrations and all those things you need in order to get the plot to work.'

'So what do you do?' Christine asked.

Janet grinned. 'I'm afraid we cheat. We usually provide our hero or heroine with some sort of tame policeman as a friend or contact in order to deal with the technical stuff that in reality we don't understand. The difficulty is to provide a credible basis for that relationship. In the real world the police would run a mile from the likes of Sherlock Holmes and Hercule Poirot and do them for obstruction of justice if they tried to interfere. The British bobby only gives information for ready cash, and usually only to journalists. Amateur detectives can go whistle.'

'That's a bit depressing for the amateur,' old Joanie said, then changed the subject slightly. She asked, 'Doesn't solving fictional murder mysteries make one wonder that one might have a flair for the real thing? And then again, some of us have a certain...' she gave a delicate cough '...talent. A certain *special ability* that one doesn't always want to mention.'

Oh God! thought Janet. She's a psychic like Sandra.

'Have you never considered that? I mean as a writer? Having a detective with that *special ability*? I don't say you should, but on the other hand you might. And if you needed some ideas ... some consultancy services...' Her voice trailed off as if she had lost the train of her own thoughts, and Sandra intervened.

'Here, Joanie, get another glass of wine down your gullet.'

'What? Oh yes,' muttered Joanie.

'Doo lally,' mouthed Belle in Janet's direction.

Someone else said, 'I can't really believe in a psychic detective, and it would make things too easy, wouldn't it? I mean always having the spirits to lend a helping hand. But what about the alternative of a women's group? Like us for example? Could you imagine us doing it in real life? I mean with a real case like the man whose body was found by the river?' It wasn't clear if this was meant seriously, and, whatever the case, no one took up the suggestion. It was only social conversation and Janet was tired and not paying attention and afterwards couldn't remember exactly who said what. It was enough that tonight she'd met some women she liked, and they fell to discussing other things they might do together: watching the latest play produced by the local amateur theatre (*Witness for the Prosecution*, wouldn't you know it? Agatha Christie getting everywhere), or the ceilidh at the town hall organised by the Mayor's Fund, or perhaps all of them attending a séance as Joanie suggested.

It was drizzling as the women left in a flurry of air kisses and various reminders and promises that they would all go to the ceilidh and might even give the theatre a try since Christine was the prompter and Frieda providing help with costumes. In the vestibule they sorted out coats and scarves and Sandra reminded Joanie, 'Take your stick; you left it when you dropped in last week,' and Joanie looked confused as though she couldn't remember having a stick or suspected Sandra of stealing it. Janet and Belle were both slightly elevated by a couple of glasses of wine, and, as they walked home, Belle gave thumbnail sketches of the other women that were good-natured if not altogether charitable.

'I'm not convinced that Joanie is completely with it, and not just because of all the pop she put away. Poor old thing doesn't know if she's coming or going – with or without her stick! As for Sandra, I thought it was a bit of cheek when she hinted that the Departed Spirits had blown the whistle to her on you being a writer. I'd told her you were and a quick search on Google would have filled in the details. And then somebody or other came up with the daft idea that we all investigate the murder of whatshisface – Stanislaw Welfare State or however you pronounce it – that they pulled out of the river. A bunch of silly beggars like us. I can just see that – *The Demented Lady Detectives' Club*! Did you see their reaction when I came out with the name? I mean: most of us wouldn't know a clue if it bit us on the bum.'

'No … you're right,' Janet said, although something was niggling at her that might or might not be significant.

Belle stared at her. 'Oh, bloody hell, I can hear the cogs churning. Do cogs churn? Churning or spinning or whatever it is cogs do. Go on, spit it out.'

'Well, it probably isn't important.'

'I've heard that before.'

'It's just that, if I'm not mistaken, somebody there tonight knows the dead man. You see: someone drew a circle round the newspaper article – it was on the occasional table. I noticed.'

'You noticed?'

'It was a Parker Knoll table,' said Janet; then, 'I'm sorry. I can't help it.'

10

The Boss has gone for his morning constitutional with
Slobber. That Thing trotted on their heels. She's that sort
of cat, which is how we acquired her in the first place
when she followed the dog home. I just hope she doesn't
slope off to pick a fight with a Yorkshire terrier as has
been known. It occurs to me now that no one ever came
looking for her even though her owner must live fairly
close by. We thought nothing of it at the time, nor why the
'found' notices pinned on lampposts didn't produce a
response.

Nowadays it's obvious.

I've had no repetition of the episode of confusion. I
wonder if it wasn't a 'transient ischemic attack' or 'TIA'
(which I used to think was an American airline). I had
hoped the fact that I'm able to contemplate calmly the
prospect of losing my marbles might be a sign that that I'm
not losing my marbles. But apparently it isn't. Meanwhile
I try to hang on to things by exporting my memories into
this whatever-you-call-it on the computer or into notes
stuck on the fridge. I've protected my stuff with a
password in case the Boss decides to pry.

Last night we had a meeting of our Readers' Group.
Sandra dragged along a pair of newcomers. Janet B-
something and Belle something-else, a name I didn't
catch. Janet is somewhere in her mid-sixties and, on close
inspection, looks her age but she has something about her,
a spark, a sort of liveliness. She smiles a lot and is
enthusiastic (or is the word 'gay' in the old-fashioned
sense?). She carries herself well and has a good sense of
style, though her clothes are Zara or similar. Belle is a
touch younger, though I can't be sure because her

plumpness hides the wrinkles. Well, actually, she's very fat. I couldn't say where she gets her clothes from. Nigeria, possibly. And not in the smartest shops.

Belle has a thing about Clitheroe. I had to look the place up on an AA road map. Apparently it is, for practical purposes, the Centre of the Universe, the touchstone by which to judge everywhere else; and, if it hasn't happened in Clitheroe, it hasn't happened anywhere. So one lives and learns. She tells me that Booths is a very good supermarket. I've never shopped there, but now I think I'd like to. She has that effect.

We talked about Frances Fyfield's latest – my suggestion at the last meeting. And then God help us if Sandra didn't come out with the fact that Janet was a 'famous author' – though I don't think any of us had ever heard of her, and she was obviously embarrassed. We had to hide our ignorance. I pretended I knew the name and said that, although I hadn't actually read one of her books, they were on my list. Janet smiled and said her books were on a lot of people's lists and she had the sales figures to prove it. I think she was being sarcastic. But in a nice way.

Then Sandra asked how she would characterise her books.

She said they were 'Aga Slaughters', which apparently is a bit like 'Aga Sagas' but with bodies face down in the virgin olive oil and more balsamic vinegar than blood. It struck me that it was a remark she'd made before and she was repeating it because it sounded good, which it did. Having put so much effort into forming well-turned phrases, writers probably end up by quoting themselves rather than lose them.

There was some discussion about writing. Most of us joined in though not good old Diana for obvious reasons. She just keeps her mouth shut and listens. I found it interesting even if I'm too old to have aspirations any longer in that direction other than this whatever-it-is that I'm writing now. And the notes on the fridge, which sometimes read like Japanese poetry.

Green pesto – red pesto – which?
Parmesan – whole and grated.

It feels as if there's a Buddhist message in there, just waiting to be got out.

I did a creative writing course when I was in my forties. It was a local authority thing, not one of those that seem to launch young women on a writing career. From what I hear it doesn't do them any favours in the long run. In my case I like to think it makes this whatchamacallum witty and stylish, but what do I know? I have no intention of running this stuff across my online writers' group.

Should fictional detectives be amateurs or professionals? That question came up. Either or both or who cares? Someone asked if we – meaning us – could be amateur detectives, and I thought: well, one of us is already. Me.

For example, said … was it Sandra? No. For example – said somebody who wasn't Sandra – there's that dead body found by the river. Isn't that the sort of crime we could solve, since it's local and this is a small town where everyone knows each other? We already have the man's name because it was given out on TV.

So the mystery is: Who killed the late Stanislaw Walacaszewski?

I kept quiet because I know the answer even if I can't prove it. The Boss killed him.

The Boss hasn't come back from his walk yet. I'm not expecting any clients. Someone came to the door. Not the usual Mormon missionaries or Jehovah's Witnesses or one of those bedraggled hoodies selling car cleaning materials as part of a 'job creation programme'. I couldn't see clearly through the gap in the roller blinds, but it was a dark-haired man, tolerably smart and carrying a black bag. If I were any sort of real detective, I'd be able to describe him in detail, but I can't. For some reason I was in a panic as if he was someone I ought to be afraid of and that put any other thoughts out of mind. He rang the doorbell and I stood in the vestibule twisting my hands as if I was squeezing water out of a window leather and muttering to myself. I had an idea that the bag was the sort a hired hitman would use to carry a weapon, even though he was more likely a double-glazing salesman carrying a laptop.

Now I recall, the previous owners installed UPVC windows, so I don't think he was a double glazing salesman.

Having written that I've had no repeat of the confusion episode, I just found myself in the kitchen in some sort of fugue, staring at a shelf full of cookery books. Then I realised that an old copy of Elizabeth David's *French Country Cooking* had caught my eye. The pages were full of those stains you get in a well-thumbed cookery book, though I don't use any of her recipes today. I'm a rotten cook, but in my time I've bought a lot of cookery books and, except for Delia, I don't think I've got more than one or two recipes out of any of them, and even then I forget them after a while. But that isn't why we buy cookery books, is it? We do it to exercise our imagination and go on exotic journeys; and after we're finished we keep them like old family photographs because they remind us of the woman we once were. My shelf of cookery books is a trip down memory lane. On reflection I don't think I was having another funny turn. I was just musing over the past the way that perfectly sensible people do.

I didn't cook much in the early days when the Boss was putting himself about London, drumming up business by eating in restaurants we couldn't afford with people I didn't like. Call Me Gerry is simply an example. A natural double-glazing salesman. When we first got to know him and the glamorous Hermione, he could have sold sand to Arabs (Is that a cliché? Who cares?). He and the Boss brought out everything that was smooth and flashy in each other. Nowadays people would suspect there was something a bit gay between them, but I don't think it was that: more a case of the vanity of each of them reflecting off the other. Perhaps there was something of the same between me and Hermione and we were more alike than I care to give credit for. Perhaps in the eighties I was a brainless bimbo.

After the dinner at the Empire & Dominions Club I didn't see them for a while, but I gather the Boss did. Now and then I'd ask and he'd say, 'Oh, I'm trying to match Gerry with the right client,' whatever that meant; but the fact that I did ask is rather telling, now I think of it. It shows that they'd made an impression and that I wanted to meet them again, even if I didn't care to admit it.

The second meeting was at *L'Escargot sans Toit*, the alleged haunt of Max Clifford. This time Gerry has made the arrangements and the maitre d' welcomes him like a dear friend instead of chucking him out on his ear as happened on the previous occasion. Tonight there's a third couple. I'll describe them for the sake of dramatic effect (whoever you are that's reading this), but for reasons I'll explain, my memory of the event is a bit hazy. I don't think I'm cheating. A lot of the Boss's clients were of the same type and if you've seen one you've seen them all.

He's one of the 'Steves' – of whom there are many in the Boss's early career, divided according to whether they are 'Stephens', 'Stevies' or 'Stevos'. This one is definitely a 'Stevo'. The 'Stephens' come later, when the Boss is more mature in years and has refined his act.

Stevo is about thirty-five and dresses in what I'd call 'professional footballer chic'. You can fill in the details for yourself. I don't think he actually was a footballer, but he may have been. At this period we hobnob with the garage-ocracy rather than the aristocracy. That comes later.

Mrs Stevo is along for the ride, and strange though it seems, they really are married to judge from the wedding ring, a huge thing in keeping with the rest of the bling, and

I don't think she's English. She's a luscious brunette of a kind that won't last well, and I guess that her first language is Spanish. I've forgotten her name and that probably says it all.

French Country Cooking isn't on the menu. Nouvelle cuisine is in but *L'Escargot sans Toit* is still holding out for the Escoffier tradition with lashings of anything calculated to give you a heart attack. There's method in Gerry's choice because an old style French slap-up makes a big statement to the Stevos of this world, especially when accompanied by champagne, wine by the bucket, brandy and cigars, and Cointreau for the ladies.

It was the Boss who brought this pair along for Gerry's scrutiny, though he's also selling Gerry to Stevo. Why remains a mystery. Afterwards Gerry whispers within my hearing, 'He's a bit "other ranks" but he'll do nicely. And you swear the moolah's for real?'

'On the honour of the Regiment,' says the Boss, who was never in the Army.

This bit I remember well: the two of them red-faced on their way back from the gents and Gerry fiddling with his flies. And the sad part is that I'm not ashamed by any of it. I think I'm actually enjoying myself and, whatever my prejudices, Mrs Stevo for all her lusciousness is a nice woman with two children she loves and she lets slip in an affectionate way that she thinks Stevo is a bit of an idiot though sharp as a tack about the things men are interested in, so she clearly isn't without common sense.

I suppose what Stevo, Gerry and the Boss see is three beautiful women, all glamorously togged out at their expense and not a brain cell between them. It's all a matter of perspective.

The meal done, Gerry pays the bill. 'My treat, Stevo' – though the Boss tells me later that he chipped in our share. It is, after all, a business meeting and not to be confused with genuine friendship.

'What say we push on to a club?' the Boss chips in,

following the script.

'T'riffic idea!' bellows Gerry and Stevo agrees though I can see Mrs Stevo is reluctant. Kids and babysitters; she has my sympathy.

So off we go to some place in Mayfair that has a casino where the Three Musketeers play roulette, while we gorgeous babes haunt their shoulders cooing encouragement. Bored to my boots I drink overpriced fizz, which is why I end the evening in a stupor and begin this story by warning you about the hazy details.

To this day I don't know how Gerry and the Boss fix it for Stevo to come out ahead after two hours of gambling, but I'm sure they do. However the Boss loses a thousand pounds on the evening, which we don't have, and after taking a taxi round the corner for the sake of appearances, we slink off home on an all-night bus, where I put on an impromptu cabaret on the top deck for an appreciative audience of West Indian office cleaners.

Yet the truth is this is not a comical story. In the morning, both of us with crushing hangovers, the Boss and I have a furious row about his reckless spending. Yet how can I argue? I haven't a clue where the money is coming from or where it's going, and when all is said and done I'm living in an expensive flat in Hampstead with a wardrobe full of good clothes and some very tasteful jewellery. The Boss's mantra is 'speculate to accumulate', but what does it all mean? This is the eighties and sharp young men are talking like that everywhere. They've heard it from Mrs Thatcher, but I don't think they know what they are on about.

A month or so later the promised shower of money arrives from wherever our money comes from and all is sweetness and light. In the meantime I don't have a penny and am too embarrassed to show my face after the business on the all-night bus. The Boss dines out with his clients and cronies and I live on Special K. Two weeks of this diet and I'm a stone lighter and Hermione tells me I look 'palely interesting'.

Later – The Man with the Bag has been back. He slipped an envelope under the door, but I ignored him and it. That Thing returned on her own and is in the garden gnawing on a dog collar. I hope there wasn't a dog attached when she found it.

The Boss came back from his constitutional, picked up the note or whatever it was from the Man with the Bag and announced that he was taking off on one of his half day walks, his second this week, so I have the place to myself. Is there a connection between the note and the Boss's decision? I haven't a clue except that in the ordinary way I'd think nothing of it, if it weren't for the fact that like last time he hasn't taken the dog with him. The poor beast can't go in the garden because of the cat and he's presently having a nervous breakdown in his basket. Why didn't the Boss take the dog?

I've just re-read that passage about Gerry and Stevo over a cup of tea. I admit I can't see what it has to do with the Boss's career as a crook and murderer, and it may be there's no connection in a direct way. I keep reminding myself that we were young and the Boss was still setting out on his career with a few false starts. Stevo may have nothing to do with the later business. He may have been part of what they call a 'cover'.

After my cup of tea I did what I'd planned to do and went into the garage and rummaged for a poking stick. I found something for supporting beans, then went to the bin-for-burning-stuff thing (I do wish the word would come to me), meaning to rake around in the ashes from the Boss' recent bonfire and see what turned up. But there was nothing there, and that isn't right. There should be charred twigs and half burnt leaves and also some scraps of paper if I'm correct about what he was really up to. And if, for some reason, he's emptied it, the remains should be in the general rubbish bin or on the compost heap, but when I checked those, they weren't.

When the Boss went out for his walk I noticed he was carrying a black plastic bag. I meant to ask what was in it but he spoke to me about something else and it slipped my mind as so many things do if I get distracted.

Yet nobody is perfect. Nobody is that thorough. I scoured the garden, checking the cracks in the paving and the flower beds for anything that might have been caught by a breeze and blown there and I've found something, a few scraps that have been torn before burning.

My first find is a couple of fragments that are part of a letterhead. One consists of incomplete words that read: 'Grand Cay...' The other is a single fragment with the word "Bank" printed on it. I think that 'Grand Cay..." is part of the name of the bank, or possibly its address. It means nothing to me and I can't say if it's important.

However my second find is more shocking because I was coming round to the idea that this whole story I'm concocting about the Boss is some sort of mad fantasy that I've dreamed up because I'm frightened of becoming old and bored and neglected, and perhaps because I've always wanted to be a writer and tell tales that people will believe.

What frightens me is that I can't say what's written on this last bit of paper because I don't understand it.

It's written in Russian.

11

Janet ran into Detective Inspector Gregg again while shopping at Tesco's in Jubilee Road.

'So we meet again,' he said with his usual attractively off-putting cheeriness, adding, 'Before you say a word: are we on Stephen and Janet terms or is it still Mr Gregg and Mrs Bretherton?'

Janet wasn't sure. However she avoided a direct answer, instead saying, 'Stephen and Janet – it makes us sound like characters in a children's reading primer, doesn't it?'

'*Stephen and Janet Go Detecting*? You know, I think I may have read it as a boy.'

Janet burst out laughing.

'I'll take that as a "yes",' Stephen Gregg said.

Janet was pushing a trolley. He was carrying a basket.

She said, 'Shouldn't you be at work at this time in the morning?'

'Ah, the Lady Detective has caught the villain out! However the truth is that one of the advantages of being on secondment is that you work more flexible hours, and no one is to say what I'm up to if I pop out for a while.'

She looked at his basket of groceries, noting wild rocket, pecorino and penne rigate. No ready-made meals. The Detective Inspector had a taste for Italian food and was cooking for himself.

'Doesn't your hotel feed you? No, you're obviously not in a hotel, and not a bed and breakfast either because you wouldn't be able to cook. Have you rented somewhere?'

'Is it a party trick of yours: pulling deductions out of thin air?'

Janet felt a little ashamed, though Stephen Gregg's comment was perfectly good-natured. She kept forgetting

73

that not everyone saw things in the way she did, always drawing conclusions from everyday observations. It came from writing those damned mystery novels she supposed. Or possibly the other way round. Where the interaction of character and action was concerned, one could never be sure that cause and effect were in the right order. Even so it was indecent to be forever scrutinising her friends the way she did.

And fun.

'As it happens,' Stephen Gregg said, 'I'm sharing a house with one of the local men, whose wife has left him. The police station is stuck for space and it suits them if I work out of the office. In my line, provided I have a decent broadband connection, I can work anywhere.'

'I suppose that's because you spend your time going through accounts and company reports. Do you never need to go into the station?'

'Well, if I need a little privacy to beat up a witness.'

'Does that happen a lot?'

'No, not a lot. Look, have you finished your shopping? Shall we walk on?'

Janet didn't say yes, but all the same they kept pace with each other through the store and to the till, and maintained the same light banter but this time about detergents and two for one offers. And at the end he said, 'Once you've put your shopping in the car, shall we find somewhere to get coffee?'

'Yes,' she said. She didn't see how she could have answered otherwise.

They went to the Anne Boleyn because it was the only café she'd tried. They ordered coffee. Walnut cake for him; a scone for her. Janet wondered what they were going to talk about. The framework of their conversation had changed and they were now friends, or close acquaintances at least, and previous experience was only of limited use. What did conventional wisdom have to say on the subject?

Not a lot apparently.

'You've gone silent,' he said.

'You're a man. I was expecting you to talk about yourself and not notice me.'

'That's a pointed response.'

'Sorry.'

He grinned. 'No, it's me who should apologise. I'm afraid coppers don't like exchanging personal information except with very close friends. But we're not that, are we? At all events not yet. And, if you think that answer is too creepy, let's both acknowledge that we may never get there. It just happens that circumstances have brought us to Dartcross and neither of us has much in the way of roots or connections here, and so we talk to the nearest friendly face. Will that do by way of explanation?'

'Yes – for the present.'

'Indeed. So...' he drawled. 'Let's talk about you. Nothing too personal. Not: why are you here, but: how are you spending your time? That's fair enough, isn't it, because I've told you why I'm here; at least so far as police confidentiality lets me.'

Janet considered for a moment then thought: the hell with it; and began to chat about her rented house and the idiosyncrasies of Belle and the wonders of Clitheroe. In response he chuckled warmly and showed no desire to do anything but let her go on; and in the calculating part of her mind she thought it was the reaction of a man who was skilled in relationships and cared about them, and so he had probably been happily married.

'Have you made any new friends?' Stephen Gregg asked when she came to a natural lull.

Had she? Janet wasn't sure how to characterise her situation and a little embarrassed at her guardedness when he seemed so open.

Taking the plunge, she told him about the Women of Dartcross (the title of a book in there perhaps?), giving short pen-portraits of those she'd met. At the same time she thought: you find Stephen Gregg attractive and you're blabbing like a schoolgirl. It's ridiculous. He's Welsh for God's sake and sounds like it! Who ever had a nice Welsh accent except Richard Burton?

One topic led to another and Janet mentioned the Readers' Group and the way they'd discussed the matter of solving the mystery of the Unidentified Body Found In River. How had Belle described the women? The Demented Lady Detectives' Club! Not that there was any question of their detecting anything. In fact, quite wisely, most of them hadn't been interested.

'And is that what you want to do?' Stephen Gregg asked. 'Become a detective?'

'Me? Oh, good lord no. I'm only interested in the idea as a writer. The problem is that one invents these amateur detectives and then runs into the problem that, considered practically, there's so little detecting they can actually do. In the past they were always friends with Colonel Mainwaring, the Chief Constable of Loamshire, but the truth is a real policeman wouldn't share information with some fluffy old body from St. Mary Mead or even the Sleuth of Baker Street, would he?'

'No.'

'No,' Janet repeated and smiled. 'That's what I told the others. It's a pity.'

'I'll pay the bill,' Stephen Gregg said, shuffling his chair to look for the waitress. 'My treat; I think I can afford it even on a copper's wages.' He returned Janet's smile. 'As it happens, I couldn't help you, even if it was permitted. I'm not working the murder, and I know only the gossip going round the station. So, if you can't run DNA tests and don't have access to the Met's data base, how do you solve your problem? I mean as a writer.'

'With what you have: public information, common sense and a little logic.'

'For example?'

'Well,' Janet thought the point over for a moment.

Certain things seemed fairly obvious but not especially remarkable and she was reluctant to say something he might think of as nonsense or, at best, trivial. 'Just as an example: I don't know it for a fact since it wasn't in the paper; but I suspect your victim – Mr Walacaszewski, was it? – was killed by a blow to the head with a blunt instrument.'

'Good Lord!' said Stephen Gregg.

He didn't say that Janet was right, but she knew at that moment that she was.

They left the café and found their paths both led up the High Street. After a moment, he asked, 'Just as a matter of interest, what makes you sure our man was killed by a blow to the head with a blunt instrument?'

'Sure? Oh, I was far from sure: it simply seemed the most probable explanation.'

'How so?'

'Because the newspaper didn't say at first that he was murdered; only that the body of an unidentified man had been found by the river. And you said yourself that it was the post mortem that determined he was murdered.'

'But I didn't say how.'

'No, you didn't. I had to work that out.'

Christine was standing outside the Heart of Osiris bookshop taking in the fresh spring sunshine. Janet returned her wave. 'One of my new friends,' she said to Stephen. 'And a member of the Readers' Group.'

'Another would-be detective?'

'You're laughing at me. No, I don't think Christine would make a good detective. She's a touchy-feely person.' *And not too bright* – though Janet didn't say so, putting the idea away with the rest of those ruthless thoughts of which she was slightly ashamed.

'So the newspaper didn't say he was murdered. So what?'

'It means that the cause of death was invisible or that,

at first sight, it was capable of an innocent explanation: some sort of accident. That rather rules out bullets and daggers, and you wouldn't need a post mortem to recognise if someone had been strangled. I suppose poison is theoretically possible, but it's such a rare event, and people who are poisoned tend to die slowly and messily and not suddenly while going for a walk. Do you see?'

'He might have been drowned.'

'Yes, he might, and I don't rule out that he drowned after he was hit and fell or was placed in the water. But drowning someone is quite a tricky thing to do. They have a knack of fighting back and have to be overpowered in some way. A blow to the head would do it, but I don't see our murderer wrestling with the victim on equal terms, especially with a grown man.'

'Perhaps there was more than one killer and they overpowered the victim by sheer weight of numbers?'

'Perhaps there was. But multiple killers are unusual, and in most cases the result is *more* violence not less and there would be lots of evidence. In any case why make the task complicated and risky when a preliminary knock on the head would do the trick?'

'To hide the fact that the drowning was a murder?'

'That bespeaks premeditation. Possible, I suppose, but it isn't a method I would choose if I wanted to bump someone off. These days everyone knows about trace evidence. Anybody getting to close quarters with the victim would risk leaving fibres, skin – blood even – somewhere on the body. If that was the plan, it was a rotten one.'

Stephen nodded but seemed mildly annoyed. 'Well then: what about a slip and a fall? Head bangs against a branch. Plop into the water. You haven't excluded accident.'

'You mean apart from the fact that the post mortem says it was murder?'

'Yes, apart from that. And, by the way, there hasn't

been a formal finding yet – no inquest.'

'I imagine the difference between accident and murder is obvious from the nature of the wound. A branch would leave an irregular mark and probably traces of dirt or bark, but a man-made object would probably be smoother, cleaner and more regular. I don't suppose you've found the weapon?'

'No,' said Stephen Gregg; then grinned as he realised he'd let slip a piece of information that had not been made public.

They reached the Market Place at the left of the High Street before it turned and narrowed at The Pinches. The Town Hall, a small building constructed to the cheap standards of the sixties, stood at the further end and, today being Friday, the space in front was full of stalls.

Pausing, Stephen asked, 'Who do you suppose buys this stuff?'

Among the vegetables and vintage clothes, several stalls were selling New Age items: lotions, potions and talismans.

'I'm afraid that's the mystery of other people,' said Janet. 'I've never understood who buys half the clothes I see in shops, or why they display so many cloche hats when I've never seen any women wearing them; or for that matter what do people in Leicester do for a living now that we don't have any industry?'

'Why Leicester?'

'Leicester isn't my point. I might equally have asked what we are all of us doing in Dartcross. Surely we're not all living on pensions, serving cream teas or giving palm readings? Not all ten thousand of us or however many it is? Speaking of which, that's my new friend Sandra over there with Belle.'

Janet indicated two tables among the other stalls. Sandra was sitting at one of them, laying out tarot cards before an elderly shopper, and Belle was lending a hand at the other by minding the sale of incense and magnetic

79

bracelets.

'You disapprove of the New Age?' Stephen asked.

'What? Yes, I suppose I do. But it takes all sorts, as they say. My husband David was rather more forthright about what he considered to be irrational thinking.'

There! She'd given Stephen Gregg another chance to respond by saying something about his wife. But he missed his cue, as men did more often than not.

And then he did something she hadn't expected.

On the Town Hall notice board was a poster advertising the ceilidh. It was fixed for the following evening. The women had agreed in a general way that they would all go along with any husbands who volunteered or could be press-ganged.

'I expect that means I'll end up dancing as a fella,' Belle had said. 'I always used to dance as a fella until I met Charlie. He couldn't tell the difference, though he was surprisingly light on his feet for a big chap.'

Janet knew all about Charlie's sociable golf club manner and that he and Belle, strutting their stuff in their outsize glamour, had been a love match.

Like me and David.

'I was thinking – if you feel like it' – said Stephen Gregg, not shyly but with a detectable hesitation – 'that you might like to come with me to the dance. I remember you mentioned once that you and your husband used to dance a lot. If you have nothing better to do?'

Astonishment. 'You dance?' Which was a stupid thing to say since no man would invite a woman to dance unless he felt he could hold his own.

'I don't make any claims, but I've had a few lessons since my wife...' He looked away then forced a smile. 'When you're a widowed copper the choices seem to be alcoholism, fishing, freemasonry or dancing classes.'

'I'd love to go dancing,' said Janet. And truly she thought she would.

12

Wonders never cease. The Boss has agreed to go to the ceilidh at the Town Hall. Immediately my suspicious mind thinks he's trying to butter me up so I don't examine his recent behaviour too closely. That said, what does it amount to? A handful of oddities, that's all.

Paranoia is a symptom of senility. That's worrying.

This morning he took himself off for another of his half-day slogs in the country, leaving Slobber behind moping expectantly. It's the third time this last week. On the previous occasions he didn't pack any sandwiches and I'm certain he didn't drop into a pub because his breath didn't smell of whisky. And this time? After he left, I checked the fridge and the bread bin and there's no sign of activity. He's too snobbish to pick up a panini in town, so where does he eat? And is there a connection with the Man with the Bag? Whoever he is, he hasn't been back. I searched for the envelope he left, but couldn't find it.

'Did you pick up something in the mail?' I asked the Boss as nonchalantly as I could.

'What?' quoth he. 'Oh, yes, it was the usual begging letter from the World Wildlife Fund.'

That was well judged because I forgot about our unknown visitor and went off on one about charities spending all our donations on promotion and advertising instead of doing good. And don't get me going on the subject of Jehovah's Witnesses. Recently they seem to have hidden the ugly ones away. The couple who hand out free books on the High Street are quite young and good-looking and you might even think they were sane. I think that's a deceitful way for religious people to carry on.

Why am I writing about Jehovah's Witnesses? I don't think the Man with the Bag is one. Sometimes, though, I think my clients are as mad as Jehovah's Witnesses. Does that mean I've been wasting my time all these years?

As for the World Wildlife Fund story, it's a lie, of course. Once the Boss had disappeared I rummaged through the waste paper baskets and the outside bins and there's no sign of any letter. I even remembered the toilet and bathroom. Nothing but cotton buds, make-up removal pads and a worrying amount of hair. From the look of it, I need to change my conditioner.

Until recently I never realised how mysterious my past is even to me. L.P. Hartley said that the past is a different country. I suspect it's the Soviet Union.

After Stevo, Stevie and Stephen, and the money showers they brought with them, things started to look up. The Boss and I were so tight with Call Me Gerry and the delectable Hermione that it seemed the most natural thing in the world that we should go on holiday with them.

'Business trip. Tax deductible,' booms Gerry in his best club voice. And we all agree that paying taxes is for Little People and not for whoever it is we're pretending to be.

In the year or so since our first encounter Gerry has acquired monograms on his custom-made shirts, and a crest has appeared on his letterhead. Given that he didn't have them previously, I suspect his fancy surname may not have figured at his christening, though he passes the matter of the crest off as one of those things he's always meant to get round to: reclaiming his heritage after his pa flogged all the ancestral doings to cover his gambling debts.

Not to be outdone, The Boss shelled out for a genealogist, a spotty postgraduate from Oxford who was making money on the side. 'It doesn't hurt to see if there's anything decent in the old family closet,' he said, meaning more than two generations of small-town solicitors. The genealogist came back with a speculative connection to an Irish baronet and after that the subject was dropped. He never said what he found on my side. Tarts and washerwomen I suspect. I only started swanking up after we met Gerry and Hermione. Before I bumped into the Boss and he took a shine to my assets, I was what these days they'd call a 'slapper'. The last I looked, the house I was born in was occupied by a family of Sikhs.

So off we go on a jet to the Caribbean (first class – the taxman chipping in), and a round of the islands: Bahamas, St. Kitts, Grand Cayman to name only a few because they merge into one when all you see is beaches and your head is inside a glass of rum punch. No, that isn't entirely accurate. Hermione and I go shopping, sunbathing, shopping, snorkelling, shopping, and sailing in a glass-bottomed boat with gaggles of American retirees who invite us to play canasta and visit them in Florida. And also shopping. A girly time without the Boys because, strange to say, in part this actually is a business trip. While Hermione and I flounce around the Armani and Gucci stores, the Boss and Gerry are visiting lawyers and bankers, or so they tell it. As proof, we are invited once or twice to dine at country clubs with gentlemanly types in immaculate suits, who speak with a faint and musical local accent and are accompanied by young women of stunning beauty.

Nowadays I have to decide which of my half-dozen outfits is best suited to a ceilidh. I look at my skin and wonder if all those holidays were worth the price.

I'm tired and think I'll have a lie down.

The Boss has come home from his walk. When I asked where he'd been he said something about ambling in the general direction of Buckminster. Why doesn't he take Slobber on these long walks? Too old, apparently, which is a fair point. Not to mention the various injuries the poor old pooch has sustained at the claws of That Thing when she gets it into her head to put him through his paces.

After my rest, I took a stroll into town and did a little shopping: cheap cuts at the butcher which should make a decent stew with a leek and a couple of carrots. I saw Sandra at her pitch in the market and chatted a while, and Belle who came to the Readers' Group. We talked about the ceilidh and they were enthusiastic as far as I can tell, and so, naturally, I was enthusiastic too.

But I'm not enthusiastic. Not about the ceilidh or anything else. The Jehovah's Witnesses had their own stall on the corner of the street, quietly minding their own business, but all I wanted to do was rant at them. Think about that: what sort of person wants to rant at Jehovah's Witnesses? Depressed people – mad people – old women who are losing it, that's who. And the occasional Evangelical, I suppose.

No one seems to notice that there's anything wrong with me. If they did, I think they'd say something or at least give a hint. Admittedly I haven't cultivated close female friends in years, not since we came to Dartcross. The Boss has repeatedly told me it isn't safe – but I don't think that's the explanation. At the least sign of trouble, women, even strangers, pick up the cues and start asking questions out of empathy or nosiness. They can't help themselves, unless you are one of those people who unload everything on anyone who gives you the time of day, in which case they spot it and shut you out. But I'm not one of those.

Partly it's because I have nothing to trade. Feelings and secrets are there to be shared. You tell me yours and I'll tell you mine. But I can't share my secrets and so I offer nothing. I'm seething inside, but the others probably see me as serene.

I can't tell them anything about myself anyway because I'm a fake from head to toe and have been for the last thirty-odd years, which is what happens when you are a crook or the wife of a crook or whatever it is that I am. I've become an object in my own narrative, like any other character. And the sad thing is that I volunteered for it. I lapped it up!

Meantime I have to make what I can of the Boss's demeanour. Belatedly he seems to have realised I have Suspicions. I could be offended that he hasn't spotted it before but I'm not. Instead I wait to see how he'll handle the problem. Not by telling the truth, obviously. Having lied for so long, I don't think it would occur to him. A matter of habit rather than malice; because, of course, I conspired with him, never quizzing him about his relationship with Gerry and the source of the money showers and all the other things that happened and the people we met.

The fact is we have an agreement that I'm a person to be lied to. Apparently it's what I want, though I never realised. So now it seems he's going to deal with the problem of little wifey and her Suspicions with kindness, not truth. Hence he's accompanying me to the ceilidh, for which I am appropriately grateful though my feelings are so disconnected from my conscious mind I can't honestly say whether I'm grateful or not. At all events I speak the words and he smiles warmly – even fondly. And would you believe that his face is beautiful when he smiles? Despite the passage of years, it becomes the face of the man I fell in love with.

I scarcely remember the man I fell in love with. He remade himself just as I did. But today for a moment I put a question to him in the hope that he won't lie, though, of course, he does.

I ask, 'Darling, why are we so poor?'

So there we are, the four of us, twelve months into our relationship and on a holiday-cum-business trip to some West Indian island or other; and today we are doing the polite with Henry and Lorraine.

Henry is Creole: part of the old planter aristocracy turned to banking, casino management and property development, no doubt courtesy of the Cosa Nostra. He is about forty years old, lightly tanned, very handsome and immaculately groomed. Think Roger Moore playing James Bond, though the look has nowadays gone out of fashion. Being still young and a fool, I don't pay attention to what he's saying; I'm concentrating too much on his elegant manners; his mellifluous voice and his gorgeous and expensively clad escort. As for said escort, Lorraine is darker skinned and twenty years younger than him, but a stunner. And the delicately revealing dress she is wearing is lusciously coloured and sets off her skin perfectly. At a short break for a huddle in the ladies room, Hermione and I agree that, in that dress, a pair of pale blondes like us would look like dead fish on a slab. It's *that* good.

We are in an old-fashioned country club on the slope of an extinct volcano somewhere with a view across plantations to the ocean. The main building is low and stuccoed, with a veranda, fly screens and storm shutters; and it stands in an expanse of lawn bounded by bananas and there are bougainvillea and frangipani everywhere. In this place waiters in white coats glide about discretely, gardeners doff their ragged straw hats and hold them in to their breasts as you pass, and old men in linen suits sprawl in rattan chairs, dozing over their glasses of grog. The films don't lie.

God knows why we are there. In the world of the Boss and Call Me Gerry – at least when the ladies are present – business is discussed in oblique terms especially on first introductions, which is the case here; and, as when we met Gerry and Hermione, it isn't clear among the preening and the pleasantries exactly who is cultivating whom. Perhaps it's the wrong question, but I fancy 'cultivating' is the right word because we are heaping manure on each other, out of which that fragile thing, 'a relationship of mutual trust' will grow. Leastways that's what Henry says he wants, and the Boss and Gerry nod because it is clearly the most original and tremendous idea they ever heard, and we can all drink to that – and do.

And then it's over and we are off down the mountain

and back to town in our limousine, with Hermione and me squiffy in the back and the boys braying and cheering as if the team has just won an away game. If anything has been decided, I haven't a clue what it is, but back at the hotel we gather in the bar and add a couple of bottles of best fizz to the tab in order to celebrate the whatever the thing is that we are celebrating. Then back to our room, which whirls like a carousel, and the Boss and I make sloppy love.

And then silence.

We spend a couple of days drinking morosely by the pool. Bored to our boots (or more accurately our manicured toes) Hermione and I are waxed to within an inch of our lives while the boys fret and play cards. There are no mobiles back in the day, and so we are tied to the hotel, waiting for a telephone call from Henry. Occasionally we make a telephone call to Henry and either swear at him or suck up according to whether we are drunk or sober. As time goes on there is more yelling than sucking, but as far as I can gather Henry takes it all in good part. Leastways, when he drops in at the hotel to calm our nerves, he has the suavity of a tele-evangelist assured of salvation.

And, speaking of salvation, the call finally comes; but, to our surprise, not from Henry in person. It's enough that one of the pool boys brings us his name and tells us that the fellow who gave it to him is waiting in the street.

'In the street?' hollers Gerry, who is still in the booming phase of his day. 'What sort of hosts are we not to welcome our guest? Wheel him in!'

'Sorry, sah, but no can do that,' says the pool boy, who manages to look both amused and ashamed, and remains obdurate even after another round of booming. It's curiosity as much as anything that drags us all from pool to lobby to out into the street, the boys leading the way and Hermione and I tottering after them on high-heeled gold sandals while fastening the clasps of our bikini tops. We are looking out for Henry's limo, but there is no sign of it. Instead we see one of the locals in straw hat, cut-offs and red plastic sandals who waves cheerily and shouts, 'Your taxi, sah! Just as you done ordered.' And to make security doubly sure, as we approach, he winks and whispers, 'Mistah Henry done send me, sah. My name is Clarence.'

With hindsight, I suspect Hermione and I were not expected to join the party. It was frustration, surprise and curiosity that drew us from the poolside, and Clarence's instructions were imprecise as to numbers. As for his car, it was an ancient American sedan with bleached paintwork, rotting sills and the ruins of spectacular chrome work; a tribute to the island's mechanics that it still ran.

So we drive out of town trailing sour blue fumes and head for the mountains, but this time not for the country club. After a few miles we cut off onto a steep road surfaced in loose stones and compacted earth. No plantations here, just shacks with cultivated patches, pigs, chickens and goats; and now and again a roadside bar with loungers sitting on crates necking beer straight out of the bottle. Under the stares of the people we pass, the boys tense up and Hermione and I stop giggling.

I've never known the Boss seem frightened before, but now he is.

'You know why we're poor,' the Boss tells me in answer to my question. And I do know. At least I know the official answer, and I'm not going to get a different one today. Because I am a person that you lie to.

We're poor because the Boss plunged into hedge funds and margin calls and, and, and … during the never-ending boom. And when it did end he got caught short (or possibly long – I've never understood the difference) and we had to sell up in a hurry and move out of London.

I remember him telling me. He could always tell a good tale, and his manner was apologetic; indeed I might have believed him for a while. It comes to me now, the reason for my doubts. It was the expression he was trying to hide. Not that of a sorrowful man who'd lost a fortune, but of a frightened man who was about to lose his skin. The man I saw in the West Indies.

But not this first time. It's a false alarm. After the treat of Clarence's driving on the hairpin bends, we emerge onto a sort of terrace cut out of the mountain side; perhaps the remains of a quarry, but, if so, the forest has covered the old workings and a villa has been constructed at the edge with a garden and a spectacular view. One of Henry's places, he tells us later: 'where one can keep tryst with one's amours,' he says smoothly, using those words. Well, we all have love nests in the country, so we can relate to that. And here he is, waiting for us with his arms open expansively, and Lorraine beside him.

What am I to make of this meeting? The afternoon is wearing on and the sky is purpling over for a late storm; the sea is indigo and spangled with sun glitter. We are behaving as friends gathered for cocktails and dinner, except that the boys are in shorts and flip-flops and Hermione and I in bikinis and sandals, giving the lie to any notion that this is an arranged affair.

Still, we go along with the idea. The house boy comes out and takes our orders for drinks, and these days we enjoy a dry martini or a daquiri, not the Babycham of my teenage years. Henry ushers us to the veranda where we sit nursing our glasses, expectant, vaguely embarrassed and making small talk. I don't doubt that it's the presence of 'the ladies' that inhibits a more frank exchange. The most that Henry can squeeze out between pleasantries is, 'There's someone I should like you to meet. A very well-connected person. Very…' he spins a finger, conjuring a word out of the air '…serious.' A few drops of rain begin to fall. Henry's face clouds over. 'He should be here by now. If he's delayed, the rain may cause him to…' But the sentence isn't finished because that moment a car arrives and Henry springs to his feet beaming. As for us, what can we do? We stand, as if waiting for the Queen.

The car makes a circuit of the terrace before stopping. The windows are bronzed and all I can see is a reflection of a darkening sky. My heart is thumping, though I don't know why except that there is a perceptible pause in which nothing happens. Then the tension suddenly eases. The driver gets out and opens the rear door and in turn another man springs out. He is fair, stocky and smooth-shaven, and his face breaks into a winning smile set off with the sparkle of a single gold tooth. He has a bustling walk and rushes towards our host as if overjoyed. His voice bubbles. 'Henry! Lorraine! So long no see! And,' turning to the rest of us, 'you guys! So much I hear! All good, all good! Hah hah!'

Immediately we relax. We like this man in a tussore suit and snakeskin shoes. We are all going to be friends. We can feel it. All the waiting and worry of the last few days are forgotten. The storm is not coming on: instead the sky is clearing.

Henry pulls away from bathing in the radiance of the newcomer's smile and takes him by the elbow to lead him to us and make the formal introductions.

'Please, gentlemen, allow me to present our very good friend.'

I see now that 'our very good friend' is like us, not more than thirty years old. A man on the make with a great future ahead of him. Yes, our very good friend!

'This,' says Henry, 'is Comrade Sergei Nikitich Blok.'

13

Sandra wondered, when did I last go to a ceilidh? Not since I was in my teens. No, I tell a lie, it was Syd's wedding. His second, I think; the one before he got his five stretch for robbery. The bride was Scottish and Syd was feeling flush after his last caper. It was a black tie bash at a Hilton and her side were all in kilts. What does a Scotsman wear under his kilt? A cosh or a set of brass knuckles if he's one of Fiona's relatives. Not that Sandra had looked under a Scotsman's kilt

Syd was a business pal of Mr 'Wide as They Come' Wallace, which is why they were invited, Mr W wearing trews for the occasion because he claimed the right to some tartan or other despite his Brummie accent and the birthplace of both his parents. Trews not a kilt on account of the varicose veins. All that handsome top half resting on a bottom half as knobbly as a vine at grape harvest. It must have been a hell of a shock for the new girlfriend when she first saw them.

Until his legs gave out, Ray Wallace had been a sprightly dancer. Jive, foxtrot, rumba, he'd give all of them a go. He had confidence, good timing and a strong lead, and he could shove his partner anywhere he wanted so that the pair of them looked good even when they were making it up. He'd had 'It' (whatever 'It' was) even in their early teens: the days of youth clubs and Methodist church socials when girls and boys both hung on his word as he lounged at the improvised bar and drank dandelion and burdock with the swagger of a man putting away a shot of bourbon. Ah, the scent of Old Spice on a face as smooth as a baby's bum!

Of course there were some good memories, especially of the early years, and these days Sandra found herself thinking about them rather than the later stuff, the violence and whatnot. The problem with growing older was that you didn't really get wiser, just slower, but you suffered from the illusion of wisdom, so that, for a moment, after Ray cleared off with Chelsea (Chelsea for god's sake!), Sandra had seen a new life in all its possibilities opening before her; she was only forty-five after all. But it had proved an illusion at least so far as the prospect of recreating herself was concerned. The truth was that there weren't many careers open to an uneducated middle-aged woman, and all she'd done during her married life was help her husband out in his business, no more than a bit of book keeping and managing one of his massage parlours when the regular woman was on holiday.

And then Life dealt a wild card, as it does.

'I can see you have an aura,' said Joanie during tea and biscuits before the first séance Sandra attended. Nowadays she knew that Joanie had been eavesdropping for titbits she could use during her psychic readings, but back then she'd been impressed at the comfort the older woman in her false pearls and Queen Mum get-up brought to the poor sad bitches who made up her clientele. *Brought to the likes of me*, she corrected herself, except that Sandra had never been completely sold on the idea of communicating with the dead. It was difficult enough to communicate with people in the here and now and she doubted they got any better in the Afterlife.

Who had she been with that first time? Margaret Something (it'll come to me). She'd lost her husband to cancer. At that date Sandra had been living in two rooms over a laundromat. As she said to anyone who listened, 'You try collecting maintenance from a property developer and owner of a tourist bar.' And that was where they met, after Margaret had been tipped out of her house because she couldn't pay the upkeep, being as lacking in skills as Sandra and without even the benefit of an 'aura'. Thinking of her now, Sandra realised they'd never been true friends.

They had nothing in common, as was to be expected when one was the widow of a local authority planner and the other the wife of Mr 'Wide as They Come' Wallace, whose massage parlours and lap-dancing clubs were as respectable as he ever got until he went into property development.

What she saw in Margaret was *sorrow*, and it was to a degree she had never experienced. It was a shock because Sandra's life hadn't exactly been without its tragedies. After all, she had miscarried at four months thanks to the attentions of Mr W and you'd think ... you'd think ... well you would, wouldn't you? But what Sandra had felt was numbness not grief as she'd understood it: not the thing she saw in Margaret's sorrow-haunted face. *Am I a shallow person?* she wondered. And, of course, it might be that she was; it was difficult to judge these things for oneself. So she found herself watching Margaret in fascination and using the other woman's sorrow as a measure against which to judge what now appeared as her own small losses: an unseen child without a face or a personality, and a waster of a husband. Women got over these things every day.

And having an 'aura' helped pay the bills. Which was more than Margaret got.

'Me and Charlie used to love a good ceilidh,' said Belle as they chatted at the market stall between customers. 'You should have seen us. Charging round the floor like a pair of elephants in heat! That's how we met: dancing classes. There's a good dance scene in Clitheroe. Not as good as Bury, where they all dress up in forties clothes: fellas in baggy pants and painted ties and sixty-year-old women in hair ribbons and bobby sox. But they're daft in Bury. All the same, it's good in Clitheroe.'

Sandra was taken by that image: Belle and Charlie stomping happily around the dance floor. Except for the occasional Rotarian 'do', her own dancing had stopped once Ray got varicose veins and became involved in what he called 'the gentlemen's entertainment industry', and in any case his friends weren't the sort she cared to associate with. Thinking of the clubs he went to, she said, 'My husband was into "exotic dancers".'

'Then I don't suppose he was doing it himself – the exotic dancing. Did you ever give it a go? Showing your lady bits and giving yourself a good rub-a-dub on a pole? Charlie once took me to a lap-dancing club; it's something you do when you're in business, that and Masonics. Once I'd got over laughing, I thought it was boring; not half as much fun as a ceilidh.'

Sandra noticed Christine drifting past with a bag of green groceries and waved. 'She'll be there tomorrow with her hubby,' she said. 'It'll be just you, me and Janet on our lonesome.'

'No, not Janet,' said Belle and gave Sandra a girlish smile. 'She's only gone and found herself a chap!'

So there they all were at the Town Hall. What had Belle called their Readers' Group? The Demented Lady Detectives' Club! You had to laugh. Sandra had kitted herself out Faery Queen style in fichus of lilac chiffon. She hated the dress but the problem with having an 'aura' and earning your crust from it was that you had to live up to the damn thing. That said, Christine, who was always banging the drum about her own 'spirituality', had made few concessions to the occasion beyond piling on the beads; she still looked like a cross between the Earth Mother and a bag lady. Not that she had to. Sandra knew for a fact that Christine had a wardrobe of very posh frocks – very *haute couture* – paid for out of her online business in New Age gear, but she maintained that you couldn't wear that sort of stuff in Dartcross.

'You look a bugger in that dress,' said Belle amiably.

'It takes one…' said Sandra. 'Where did you buy yours; Brixton market?'

'Miaow. Can I get you a drink or summat?'

'Double vodka and orange, please.'

'And there's me, drinking halves of shandy.'

While Belle sloped off to the bar, Sandra took in the room. The Mayor in a kilt and four musicians with more facial hair than sense sitting on the stage with their instruments, fiddling with them the way musicians did and showing no signs of actually playing anything. A DJ with a taste for Police and Take That doing a warm-up before filling in at the interludes. The Chair of the Licensed Victuallers wearing his chain of office and putting on a show for the pub trade; the same for the motor dealers but without the chain. And no doubt enough Masonic handshakes to break your fingers. In fact a jolly crew.

Belle came back with the drinks. She said, 'Have you noticed the Mayor's wearing a Jimmy Wig?'

Sandra looked again. The man was wearing a Tam o' Shanter with a mass of ragged ginger hair sticking out from below.

'Every tourist shop in Edinburgh sells them. I suppose he thinks he has to look stupid for the sake of the voters. I always wondered when it was that people actually wore them. And there's his wife, doing the lady bountiful for all the world as if she's not standing next to an idiot. I wonder if this is what she expected when she married him? Nice legs though – him not her.'

Christine glided over with her husband Keith; met once or twice before, though Sandra couldn't remember what he did; retired teacher, she fancied. She often saw him walking a dishevelled mutt by the river; a tall man, not bad looking for his age but with the long, loping stride she associated with people who mutter to themselves in the street. From the look of him he wasn't above fifty-five; but that was teachers for you: if you could stand the kids you got to retire early. Christine began to witter about some new book on the subject of 'energy medicine'; she was going to give it a try for her memory problems in conjunction with a gluten-free diet and mineral supplements. Keith smiled benignly, and Sandra knew he wasn't paying his wife any attention; not that Christine noticed. She probably thought that the glazed-over looks were normal because that was how everyone reacted to her. Wasn't Sandra herself grinning like a half-wit?

Belle had an escape plan. 'Look, there's Janet!' pointing to the door where the other woman had come in with a stocky fellow in a tweed jacket and off-the-peg slacks. 'I need to talk to her about duvet covers.'

Duvet covers? Sandra was too surprised to think of a good reason to join her, but then Keith took advantage of the conversational lull to say, 'This reminds me of a concert I went to in Sofia many years ago. The same tacky furnishings and warm white wine.'

'You were on holiday?' Sandra found herself paying more attention to him than before. She noted a sly humour in his voice that was quite attractive, though there was an unkind implication they were having a joke at Christine's expense. A man who tolerated his wife and on most days never asked himself if he loved her or not. Of course most people didn't, having better things to do. It had taken Sandra years before she twigged that she couldn't stand her husband. Marriages were often like a pair of shoes you kept for years, telling yourself they had to fit, given the price you'd paid for them.

'I was there on business,' Keith said.

Not a teacher, then. It was annoying when one's prejudices weren't supported by the facts. On the other hand the information was intriguing and gave Keith a faint air of mystery. The men Sandra knew were more likely to do business in Soho than Sofia.

He added, 'The concert was in aid of Bulgaria – German Democratic Republic Friendship Week.'

Sandra nodded. After all, there wasn't a lot you could say to that.

14

He took Janet to the Royal George for dinner. It was that, the Nabob, or the brasserie at the top of the High Street that was full of young people and had live music at weekends, which wasn't conducive to conversation. Elderly tourists with comfortable incomes stayed at the Royal George and usually dined in the restaurant. The men wore navy blazers and their wives were over-coiffed as if wearing wigs even when they weren't. Janet had spent most of her life in the Manchester area and she found that whole swathes of conservative England still had a vaguely fictional feel, as if contrived for a low budget TV murder mystery set in an imaginary version of the 1950s. For her part she'd have thought twice before setting a scene in a restaurant decorated with hunting prints and brasswork.

'I hope this place is alright by you?' Stephen Gregg said in a departure from his usual wry, confident manner.

She found herself responding with the same uncertainty, squeezing a small bright note into 'Yes, it's fine!' as if she were lying about it and it wasn't fine at all.

The explanation, as she well knew, was that she and Inspector Gregg – *Stephen* as she must get used to calling him – were crossing a threshold in their relationship, each of them wondering where it was going and was this what they really wanted? In Janet's case she was definitely doubtful, but her curiosity and mischievous inclination had got the better of her. And she did like him, which had to count for something.

Belle liked him too. Looking Janet up and down before letting her loose on the world, she said, 'You'll do. I'll see you later at the Town Hall. Go on, love. Enjoy yourself. Just don't get pregnant.'

Over dinner they talked of their respective

backgrounds. It made Janet aware of the age difference between them and again she found herself wondering: what was he seeing? An intelligent, elegant, elderly woman or the faint ghost of a dead wife?

They chatted a while about music. Janet's taste was Swing and Rock, a legacy of her dancing days. Stephen Gregg liked opera – a surprise, that; an opera-loving policeman; she'd always supposed that like burglars they preferred beer and football and at best could dance to Agadoo if pressed. They were both fond of holidays in France and Italy, though different regions. Their tastes in books weren't the same. He didn't care for crime fiction because the anti-authoritarian heroes would never survive in the real Force and the procedural details were always wrong. She liked crime fiction, not least because she wrote it. He liked…. She liked…. Where was this going?

He paid the bill and refused her contribution. He held her coat for her to put it on. As they stepped out of the Royal George, the evening was dark and clear, with a spring chill so that Janet found herself walking close to this man for his warmth, the same way she had with David. The street was full of young people spilling out of pubs and restaurants and fooling around on the pavement, but she and Stephen seemed to glide between them in a cone of comfortable silence. She found herself smiling and at one point gave a short laugh, which caused her companion to look at her quizzically. She didn't tell him that, stupid though it might be, she rather liked the idea that she was still an attractive woman with whom a funny little Welshman was pleased to be seen.

Because of dinner they were among the last to arrive at the ceilidh. The dancing had started and the Mayor had already shed his Jimmy Wig, which lay on a chair like a spiteful ginger cat. He was dancing a furious reel with every woman in sight, while his wife wore a see-what-I-have-to-put-up-with look and was going cross-eyed as she tried to talk to people while keeping watch over her husband.

'There they are,' said Janet. Her friends from the Readers' Group had gravitated to a couple of tables near the bar. Belle in a dress that contrived to be both successful and indescribable. Sandra in a fly-away thing of lilac chiffon that might have worked for Mia Farrow forty years before but looked distinctly odd at this time and place. Christine in a variation of her New Age ensemble. Janet began to introduce Stephen and became quickly conscious that she knew little about most of the women and next to nothing of their husbands.

'This is Jean and…'

'Stuart,' barked Jean over the music, and she dragged her reluctant consort into the circle. To Janet's eyes he looked a good few years older than his wife, thin faced with worn, smoker's skin and a grizzled Pancho Villa moustache like a minor villain in a Spaghetti Western. He said something but Janet struggled to understand what it was or, indeed, if it was in English.

'I suppose you'll be familiar with ceilidhs?' Janet offered hopefully.

'Stuart disna dance these days,' snapped Jean. 'And ceilidhs are for the Highlands and posh nobs in Morningside, not for Glasgow. Mind, you should ha' seen his break dancing before he did his hip in. Magic wasn't it, pet?' She smiled at him affectionately, a petite brunette in an all-black outfit with hints of aging Goth

Stuart smiled and tapped his hip.

Then, from nowhere, a smooth but unfamiliar voice said, 'I dance at ceilidhs. It used to go with the job.' Janet turned. A tall, slender man was extending a hand and smiling.

Diana said, 'Janet, I don't think you've met Pierce. Pierce – Janet – Janet – Pierce. In the old days – before he retired – people used to call him "Rev". That's the job he was referring to.'

'A month scarcely seemed to go by without there was a ceilidh in the church hall, though I'm probably exaggerating,' said Pierce, 'it just seemed like it.'

Janet looked at him more closely now, though she'd noticed him earlier when (she was ashamed to say) she'd been more interested in Diana's frock, which was a bias-cut number in grey silk that hung beautifully on her contours in restrained sexiness. And, of course, Diana, with her fine bones, was still a beautiful woman in Janet's estimation, just as Pierce in his youth had probably been a very handsome man. Now she supposed he must be pushing sixty, but he was one of those men who had kept a head of thick dark hair of which he was evidently proud, and it gave him the air of a suave movie idol of the kind who was paired with much younger women. In the cinema one was less aware of these things, but outside of films it was an unfortunate look more suited to a Tory politician, a vampire or a sexual predator and not something to parade about the streets of a provincial town. *But that's probably just my prejudices*, Janet thought. Everyone else seemed comfortable with Pierce and indeed his manner was perfectly pleasant and his cool upper class voice rather beguiling.

During these introductions the husbands of old Joanie and Frieda were at the bar. Joanie seemed already two drinks ahead and her husband brought her a glass of white wine and a pint for himself.

'We're doing introductions, Kenneth dear,' said Joanie in her best genteel voice. 'I've mentioned Janet to you already, and this is Frederick – I tell a lie, *Stephen* – who is her companion for the evening.'

'Pleased to meet you,' said Kenneth cheerily. Having been treated to Joanie's Queen Mother and Madame Arcate act, Janet had been unsure what to expect of her husband. He turned out to be a plump, sandy-haired old fellow in his seventies, whose notion of style was a blue Adidas track suit, freshly washed and pressed, and a pair of sparkling Nike trainers. 'I gather you're a policeman,' he said waggishly to Stephen Gregg. 'I'll have to watch my step. I don't suppose my past would bear close inspection, eh? Used to be an estate agent. They've not made it criminal yet.'

Joanie rolled her eyes upwards and to no one in particular intoned, 'I sense that Stephen has recently suffered a bereavement.' Then, when the others seemed unimpressed at this revelation from the Spirit World, she turned to her husband and snapped, 'What did I tell you, Ken? I specifically said *no lemonade* in it.' And to the others added with a superior smile, 'It kills the bouquet.'

Stephen rescued them both by remarking that a new dance was about to start, a Virginia Reel.

'Yes, that would be lovely!' said Janet, though she couldn't recall the steps; then again, most people were in the same position and there was a caller who took them through the various figures. So there she was, formed into a set with the other revellers and wondering yet again at the oddity of things.

What a motley lot we are, she thought. All shapes, sizes and ages. Here a father dancing with his daughter, there a biker cavorting with a punk; and even a crumbling old fellow in a kilt, ninety if he was a day, dancing with a jolly young girl who had Down's syndrome. Up and down the hall they went, faster and faster as the musicians upped the tempo, the dance gradually losing its timing and the figures falling into a confusion of stamping and laughter. How joyful! Janet thought. How innocent! She loved the sight of people harmlessly having fun. Round they went, peeling off at the head of the line, forming an arch at the foot, and all the while praying to God they were still with their partner. More hooting. Now and then a cheer. Faces glistening with sweat. Old people red-faced and panting. Young ones glossy with life and giggling that they'd got themselves involved in this absurd business: how on earth to explain it to their friends? The musicians playing frantically. The caller beating the rhythm with his foot and letting the music go on and on out of malice and beyond reason or so it seemed. And then, suddenly, it stopped and the dancers for a moment looked shocked and confused before they recalled who they were and what they'd been doing. What were they supposed to do? Bow to their partners? One or two did. The rest grinned foolishly, and one by one everybody made their way back to their seats.

During all this, Stephen kept good time. His dancing was spritely. 'Light on his feet,' Janet would have said at one time, though she had a notion that these days the expression had been appropriated to describe homosexuals – a loss to the language if she was right. His face still kept its sly, Puckish expression as if he could see a joke that everyone else was missing. *I could get to like this*, she told herself, not because she believed it but to try out how the idea felt.

'Enough!' he said, when the music finished. The next piece was a Gay Gordon, but there was a tacit agreement between them that a second dance at the same pace as the first would quite likely kill them.

They went to the bar to order soft drinks and a pitcher of water. Frieda from the vintage clothes shop was still there, wearing an improbable sixties ensemble including a mini-skirt and a pair of white PVC boots. *Like Twiggy returned as one of the Undead*. Janet told herself it was an uncharitable thought; Frieda was flushed and smiling broadly, and in this outfit – too young for her by decades – she looked weirdly attractive. *Because she's having fun.* Janet looked at the table where the others sat, chatting animatedly. *We're all having fun, and who gives a damn how we look?* An elderly person's perspective. Young people cared.

Frieda interrupted. 'You've not met Harry, have you?'

She pulled Harry forward. He was a tall, lumbering man with hair carefully oiled and combed into the remnant of a Johnny Cash quiff, and in the same vein he wore a pale blue western-cut jacket with fringed sleeves, a bootlace tie and pointed boots stitched with medallions. He said cheerfully, 'Me and Frieda prefer line dancing. Regular devils for it. Ceilidhs aren't bad, though. I saw you two and you looked as if you could trip the light fantastic. Do it a lot, do you?'

'We haven't danced together before,' said Stephen Gregg. 'Can I get the drinks? Guinness and rum and Coke, wasn't it?'

'Next round maybe. Someone said you was in the police. You look too young to have retired. Here on business?'

'I was taking a break with my boy.'

'Dartcross is a nice place for it. Frieda and me used to come here – well, Paignton – a lot before I decided to give up the building business. She still keeps her hand in with the shop, but I'm a gentleman of leisure, as they say. Walking the dog is about my limit.'

Janet was good for a Saint Bernard's Waltz, so they did one. When they returned to their table everyone was there. Belle had danced a couple of times with Sandra but now she was out of breath and a little bored ('I just knew I'd end up being the ruddy fella!' she whispered). Noticing that their company was complete she suddenly announced: 'I now declare this meeting of The Demented Lady Detectives' Club in session!'

The various husbands looked at their wives and each other.

'It's just a joke,' Belle said. 'We've decided to solve the mystery of that bloke who was murdered by the river. Who killed Mister Wonder Boy? Remember? No? Suit yourself. Any road, we can ask Inspector Gregg of Scotland Yard for the latest lowdown.'

Janet glanced at Stephen who chuckled. 'Assuming I was allowed to tell you – which I'm not – I don't have anything to say. I don't work for the Devon police and I've nothing to do with murder investigations. Janet knows I'm not much more than a glorified accountant.'

Belle snorted. 'Oh, you're a spoilsport, you are. Janet's a better detective than you. She's never seen the body and yet she worked out that he must have been bashed over the head with a "blunt instrument" – whatever one of those is when it's at home.'

'Is that right?' Sandra asked, and when Stephen Gregg didn't answer she asked Janet, 'How do you know?'

'I don't *know*,' Janet said. 'All I can do is draw inferences from whatever facts are released to the public. Some things just seem to me to be...' she was struggling for a word and came out with '...*obvious*. I mean that we sometimes make things more mysterious than they need be and that if we think things through with a bit of common sense and experience, there's a good chance of coming up with an explanation and it's likely to be true.'

'Hark at Miss Marple,' said Jean.

Janet grinned. Perhaps she was.

Joanie's Kenneth chipped in. 'It's a good parlour game, this, isn't it? Are you going to explain about the "blunt instrument" thing?'

Janet could think of no reason not to, and the others seemed eager to listen, so she took them through her reasoning as she'd explained it to Stephen Gregg. Going over it again, it occurred to her that the whole argument turned on one simple fact: that the first newspaper account didn't say that the dead man had been murdered, from which she'd concluded that the police hadn't felt able to rule out an accident. But it could be that, for some other reason that she couldn't fathom, they'd merely decided not to reveal their suspicions. Of course there was the matter of Stephen's reaction, which confirmed she was right, but again it might be that she was reading too much into his behaviour.

Except that I'm not.

'Is this a game that anyone can play?' asked handsome former 'Rev', these days simply Pierce.

'No,' said Belle firmly. 'In case you hadn't heard, we're the *Lady Detectives*.'

'Fair enough. Well? Does anyone except Janet have an inkling of a solution? I mean: whodunit?'

The women looked among themselves and shrugged. Pierce smiled at Diana and asked, 'Is that the Valeta they're playing? I feel the need for some terpsichorean exercise coming on. Shall we give this a try, darling?'

'So are you still detecting?' Stephen asked. The ceilidh was finished and he was walking Janet home after Belle had sloped off with Jean and Stuart for a last drink somewhere. Again she was reminded of David. After an evening out they had always preferred to walk rather than take the car. Walking allowed them to discuss the experience they had just shared and by discussing it make it richer and more intense. *I don't like being alone*, Janet thought. Not the most profound insight into her situation, but true for all that.

'I don't think of it as "detecting",' she said. 'I suppose I just can't stop myself from trying to puzzle out mysteries – not that I'm likely to make any progress with this one.' Not when all she had was a couple of newspaper reports on which she'd built a suspicion that at best was only half confirmed. The police *might* have known all along who the dead man was. But she was sure they didn't. There were conventions about these things. If they had known his name but suppressed it, the paper would have said, 'The police have not released the dead man's name at this time' because the reporter would have asked and been turned down. Instead the *Advertiser* in the first report said he was 'unknown' because that's precisely what they'd been told.

How then had the police discovered the murdered man was called Stanislaw Walacaszewski? Why didn't they know straight away?

'Penny for them,' said Stephen.

'What? Sorry. I was just thinking.... I told you I

JIM WILLIAMS

couldn't stop myself.'

'And have you discovered anything else?'

Janet had to smile because her speculations had to be ridiculous. She said, 'I don't think he was a local man. Most likely he'd just come to Dartcross for the day.'

'Oh, I see.'

'Am I right?'

'How should I know? But tell me all the same how you arrive at your conclusions.' He looked at her intently, and she felt flustered and surprised at the outrageous idea that she might actually be right.

She said, 'It's all to do with timing. The newspaper came out on Wednesday but was presumably put to bed the night before. The report said the man had been dead about forty-eight hours and, since it's unlikely he was killed in daylight on a fairly busy path, the murder most likely happened on Sunday night. Not that the exact day matters for the moment. The point is that he disappeared for two and quite possibly three nights and no one had reported his absence to the police or they would have made the connection and known his identity. I don't suppose it counts, but my friends'–

'The Demented Lady Detectives' Club?'

– '*my friends* would have picked up any rumour that he was a local man, especially in a small town like Dartcross. And of course the *Advertiser* would have been onto it like a shot, yet their second report, when they gave the dead man's name, said nothing about his being a local.'

'It might be an oversight?'

'Hardly likely. Two things newspapers never miss is the local angle to a story and the value of property, as if the importance of a murder is that another house is on the market. I imagine the *Advertiser* announced the end of the Second Word War with the headline *"DARTCROSS MAN VISITS FUEHRER'S £10,000,000 BUNKER!!!"* Oh no, there's no possibility they'd have overlooked the local angle.'

They walked on a while and found themselves outside Frieda's shop where a dim light burned and the display of disembodied flapper dresses and old fur coats looked like extravagantly clad ghosts. Stephen Gregg seemed pre-occupied.

'Have I said something tactless?' Janet asked. With strangers it was always possible, and, of course, they were still strangers.

'Not at all,' he said and smiled to reassure her. 'But, just for the sake of completeness, what makes you think that our Mr Walacaszewski was in Dartcross only for the day.'

'You mean you're interested? Well … to be frank, I may be wrong.'

'Ah – modest are we?'

'I hope so,' said Janet, a little annoyed. She sighed. 'Look, I'm guessing that your Mr Walacaszewski didn't have a suitcase with him; it would be a very odd thing to be carrying by the river on a Sunday night. It's possible, of course, that he'd left his luggage in a hotel or a B&B and that they wouldn't think it necessary to call the police if he were missing for a night or two. But once the first story appeared in the *Advertiser*, I think they'd have been concerned about their missing guest. At that point they'd have gone to the police and in that case I'd expect the police to release the details of the hotel or whatever at the same time they gave out his name. It would be an obvious way of finding witnesses. But they didn't because no one had come forward. So I'm supposing he didn't stay in a hotel or B&B and was in town only for the day.'

They had reached Janet's rented cottage. The lights were off. The night was clear, dry and starlit. A flash of memory brought images of the boys who had brought her home in her teenage years and the final tender fumblings before she turned her key in the lock; her father still dozing in his armchair with the test card showing on the television; her mother in curlers, making Horlicks in the kitchen.

'Thank you for taking me to the ceilidh,' she said.

'It was a pleasure,' he said.

'You dance nicely.'

'We must do it again.'

Again?

She nodded and, when he didn't immediately turn and leave, she gave him a quick peck on the cheek before opening the door. She didn't invite him in.

15

'Another small victory over adversity,' says the Boss, using his pompous voice. He means we got through the ceilidh and yet again no one rumbled us as a pair of phoneys. Whatever it is we're doing, we're good at it.

He says with a cheeky grin, 'On these occasions when we're on public view I always feel as if my flies are undone and there's nothing I can do about it.'

I don't know what my equivalent would be. Walking around with the hem of my dress tucked in my knickers, I suppose.

As it happens, and to my surprise, I actually enjoyed myself last night. I danced with all the men, even Dai the Police or whatever Janet's beau is called. I thought that was bold if he's out to pin a murder beef on the Boss. I don't know if he is. He says he's no more than an accountant.

I recognised him from somewhere. I don't know where. A fleeting impression. Perhaps I'm thinking of one of those quiz shows where the contestants are sportsmen or comedians whose names you can't remember? Why do they always dress like they won third prize in a Primark raffle? I'm sure the BBC must pay them well.

Stephen Gregg, he's called – it just came to me. He's actually quite attractive in his own odd way, which may be why he reminds me of a comedian. His manner is easy and cheerful and he's a natural dancer, though I don't think he's been to many classes. I like him. But he frightens me. There's something knowing about him.

Belle went on again about The Demented Lady Detectives' Club, and Janet gave her explanation about how the dead man was killed. I could see that everyone was impressed. When the subject of a murder investigation first came up at the Readers' Group, I thought no one was particularly interested, not beyond laughing at the name. But tonight I could see the others were paying attention; Sandra was hanging on Janet's every word. I was terrified she was about to come out with some dreadful revelation that would lead straight to me and the Boss; and I wouldn't put it past her because she's very sharp. But last night she didn't.

I haven't discussed my fears with the Boss. In fact I haven't mentioned the murder at all. Even if I did, he wouldn't come clean. He'd just treat me to one of his putdowns. He'd tell me I must be going senile.

And I'm still frightened that I am.

SHOPPING LIST
– *Vim or one of those other old-fashioned scouring powders that are difficult to find these days.*
– *Large bag of Tesco's cheapest doggie chunks for Slobber.*
– *Bay leaves.*
– *Tinned diamonds or whatever it is That Thing deigns to eat these days. NOTE: empty the cupboard of all the stuff she's turned her nose up at. Feed it to the dog.*

I need *Vim* because, in my misspent youth, I never learned to cook. My collection of cookery books qualifies more as romantic literature than as practical help. These days, when I'm forced to try my hand, I keep burning the pans. My forgetfulness also has something to do with it.

Now that I think about it, I did take cookery lessons at school. Girls used to. I believe the subject was dropped from the curriculum at some point, but I don't know for sure since I never had daughters who could tell me – only one who couldn't. Whatever the case, the lessons I had in the seventies wouldn't have helped. As I recall they'd have come in handy only if war broke out and rationing came back. They wouldn't have been much use when we were living high on the hog with Call Me Gerry and Hermione. Whenever we had to entertain, we dined out or got caterers in and I would lie about my accomplishments. I'm quite a practised liar.

I don't suppose Hermione was much of a hand around the kitchen either, though for a time she put it around that she'd been to a Swiss finishing school. That is until someone spoke to her in French.

We used to think prawn cocktails and Black Forest gateau were sophisticated until we learned better. Nowadays I can't afford them. Not even at Iceland.

I don't have a daughter to tell me about cookery classes at school because Angela died.

The Boss says he went walking for most of the day without Slobber as per his recent habit. Except that he didn't.

The Boss despises me, though, oddly enough, I don't think he knows. In fact he says he loves me, and maybe he does in his way. The two aren't incompatible. His contempt shows in small ways as well as big. Although he sees me pounding away on this laptop (self taught – I'm rather proud of that), writing this whatever-it-is, he never asks what I'm doing. It's some female thing beneath his notice. He never asks why I take online writing lessons or whether I'm any good at it. I think I am, though I don't expect to be published.

The problem with despising people is that you become sloppy, thinking the other person is too stupid to notice. When he goes walking, the Boss wears a clumpy pair of brown brogues, handmade by Lobbs, a survivor of the wreckage of our lives. In an odd fashion they're a thing of beauty, the way that relics of our past are. Years of TLC have given them a deep shine and patina. Women's shoes don't survive in the same way. I have lots of old pairs and half of them look as if I've got drunk and been in a fight. It's because they're covered in plastic or patent leather, and whatever you do, you can't protect the heels. I don't know why I keep them.

I think it's to preserve my femininity: to make me feel I have choices.

While the Boss was away I got out a pile of shoes and a tube of UHU and tried to glue the little flaps of leather you get when you scuff some types of heel. The result wasn't good no matter how I squinted and tried to persuade myself that you couldn't tell. It wasn't the first time and I could see the old repairs I'd made; the dirt around the edges where I'd left a trace of glue; the sticky prints because I hadn't cleaned the stuff off my fingers. I don't know why they make the heels of black shoes out of grey plastic. It shows when they get scraped.

Today the Boss wore a pair of tan loafers. I remember buying them at Clarks. So he's lying. However he spent his day, it wasn't walking.

Why am I writing about cookery and old shoes and crying?

NOTE:
– Take old shoes to charity shop.
– Buy box of soft tissues.

The explanation of everything – the dead man, the Boss's strange new ways, the crying over cookery and old shoes – is somewhere in my half-remembered past. Half-remembered not because I'm going senile but simply because of the lapse of years and the fact that I wasn't paying attention to my own life.

Who was Stanislaw Walacaszewski that he turns up now only to get himself killed? The name means nothing; but it may be I've simply forgotten. For that matter, who was Sergei Nikitich Blok and what were we doing schmoozing with him on some island in the Caribbean? I can only guess. The Boss never explained beyond saying our Russian pal was connected with business. And as far as I can gather, Gerry never explained to Hermione, or if he did, she didn't let on. More strangely, she and I never spoke to each other about our mutual state of ignorance. Were we too light-headed or too ashamed? A bit of both, I suspect.

If I tried to explain the way we carried on, I think a feminist would tear her hair out. But feminism has only ever been a minority thing – like being Jewish.

I remember the first wave of feminism – Germaine Greer and all that. At least I suppose it was the first wave; I never heard of an earlier one unless Women's Votes counts. Then again it wasn't something that happened in my world. It was mainly a university thing. Those of us who were living in bimbo-land didn't hear much about it.

I think about it now – feminism – when I contemplate the years I spent following the Boss around, not knowing much of what was going on. In that respect I don't think I was so different from my mother who only ever had a vague idea of what my dad did for a living. She'd say knowingly that he worked in 'light engineering' but she had no more idea of what that meant than I have about 'investment banking'. The difference is that she was probably unaware of her own ignorance but I'm painfully aware of mine.

I'd like to know more about feminism, but I fancy I wouldn't understand the books if I bothered to read them. I don't suppose they do remedial classes at night school.

After that first meeting, which seems a bit improvised as if our new friend wants to catch the Boss and Gerry off-guard in order to take their measure, the Boys and Comrade Blok meet every day for the rest of the week, while Hermione and I carry on shopping, playing canasta with the American widows, and getting a tan. And then nothing more for months. I mean nothing involving me. The Boys and Blok are in constant contact to judge from the telephone calls and the stray remarks.

We acquire a new 'friend', Oliver Makepeace Hemsley.

He's a handsome man in his twenties with a twinkle in his eye and a modest smile. When I say 'handsome' I mean male model handsome, and he has the impeccable manners of the maitre d' of a good hotel; the sort that aristocrats are supposed to have but don't. Even so he has more genuine class in his little finger than the Boss and Call Me Gerry can muster between the pair of them. Wearing handmade shirts and silk ties, his hair groomed and his face powdered and shaved, he is frankly gorgeous. You may trust Hermione and me on this point of manners if on nothing else.

'A top drawer corporate lawyer!' booms Gerry at our introductory dinner; the boat being pushed out at the good old Empire & Dominions; all the roast beef, mash and sprouts you can eat, and enough of their tasty plonk to float any number of boats.

'Don't get carried away,' says the Boss afterwards. Perhaps he's noticed that Oliver's cool good looks and diffidence are appealing, especially in comparison with the racket typically coming from Gerry. 'He has a gambling habit and he's queer.'

Is that true or is it one of the Boss's flashes of spite? Still the fact remains that handsome Ollie has turned up sans girlfriend, though in other respects I wouldn't say there was anything conspicuously gay about him, except that general whiff of campness the upper classes always have in the eyes of the lower orders. Clearly there's nothing about him to put me and Hermione off. We talk about him in the toilets, and our language isn't ladylike. I'm not sure we actually mind if he's homosexual or not. Women often find gay men attractive because many of them seem to care more for us than the other lot. I mean that they care about important things and not just sex – at least not with us.

I see Mr Hemsley only occasionally after this dinner and so I struggle to understand how he fits into the

114

schemes of the Boss, Gerry and Sergei Nikitich Blok. He isn't quite in our charmed circle and is kept at arm's length from the client – always supposing Comrade Blok is the client. Gerry, when in his cups, lets slip the occasional clue but I don't really grasp the whole.

'The boy is a mere technician – a legal hood,' he says on one occasion.

And on another, 'The morals of a City of London solicitor would make Al Capone blush.'

When I ask the Boss as tactfully as I can how things stand with Oliver, he gives me the Evil Eye and says, 'We've taken him on board to handle Sergei's legal work.'

On reflection I don't feel any wiser. What is Sergei's 'legal work' and what does it have to do with us? Then again, perhaps Oliver isn't a lawyer? The story may all be part of the cover.

Thinking again of Oliver Makepeace Hemsley, it occurs to me that the late Stanislaw Walacaszewski may fall into the same category. I don't mean that he was a lawyer – for all I know he could be a 'second storey man', whatever that is and assuming such a thing is needed in our business. I mean that he may have been one of the hangers-on I glimpsed from time to time, whose roles were never explained to me.

I hate to think about what happened to Oliver.

I don't see Sergei again until Nice. This is perhaps a year later and even then, he turns up out of the blue. If you believe it.

Ostensibly we are buying or renting a property in Monte Carlo. It's a complicated story to do with tax avoidance and rights of residence. Apparently Oliver has been taken on to deal with some of this because it's what City lawyers do and Oliver speaks French. He's based in Paris for the duration and flying up and down as need arises, though I never see him.

Sergei gives a clue why Oliver isn't 'one of us'. He

says, 'He is no you guys. He likes flowers and art and fancy music of sort I am not liking. I have seen his kind. Clever but not reliable. I work all time with reliable people who sleep with women in regular way. So keep the fuck away from me, eh?'

I think this suits the Boys, especially if Sergei is the source of the money showers, as I suspect he is. Or his bosses in the KGB.

We run into Sergei when we're lunching at a place on the Promenade des Anglais. The sea is white with sunlight and the day so hot the air seems grainy like an old photograph. And here he comes, Sergei Nikitich Blok, in a white suit and two-tone shoes, sliding carelessly into a chair while calling to the waiter to bring another chair for his lady, even though there's a vacant one behind him and he need only deign to reach for it.

'Jeezus H Christopher! Here you! Here me! Who expect?' he says for the benefit of me and Hermione. 'It must be God is making us see our friends – if there is God, which I no believing.'

Is the woman a natural blonde? I wouldn't care to say, but she's a tall and very expensive number – Hermione and I tot up the bill afterwards to within a thousand pounds 1980s money, depending on whether the shoes and bag are real or fake (and our experienced eye says real). She waves the waiter away and places the chair herself as only a woman would do, who is too self-assured to care if she is seen to be waited on. She introduces herself, talking over Sergei – which we never do – and gives her name as Ludmila.

And who is Ludmila? Nobody. Because none of us women are anybody in this story. Or, if you like, we are everybody because the only authentic people we seem to meet are other women and I wonder sometimes if the men are truly real when the action involving them takes place for the most part offstage and we see only the parts they choose to reveal like conjuring tricks. The play – which we women are only attending rather than taking part in – is one long interval in which we, the audience, wait until we lose interest and talk to each other; and in the end the only subject matter becomes ourselves.

I didn't make that last bit up. I was too stupid to recognise it until Ludmila told me because she is unique in my experience of bimbodom. No idiot she. Quite the contrary. She is *Doctor* Ludmila: graduate in archaeology and classical literature from Leningrad University.

'I am Penelope and Sergei is Odysseus,' she says in her lovely liquid Russian drawl. 'I am at home spinning and he is listening to sexy sirens and killing one-eyed monsters – as if I believe a word he says, hah hah! All lies! He is whoring and drinking with his friends, which is all Odysseus ever does, and the rest is just men-stories.'

There's no money in archaeology and classical literature; and Ludmila has a child back home in some place I can't pronounce, 'but no worry because no one can pronounce'. She pretends that Sergei doesn't know. He probably does, she admits, but for as long as the child's existence is unacknowledged he doesn't care. 'She is not Sergei Nikitich's daughter, you understand? Which is problem because in ancient stories unwanted child is left in forest and raised by wolves, or maybe put in basket on river like Moses. Either way very bad news if you not Moses.' In the meantime she sends money home to her mother in order to raise her daughter.

Ludmila is fearsomely intelligent and I think she understands precisely what the Boys and Sergei Nikitich are up to, but she isn't letting on to me and Hermione. If we find out it may be that we shall be left in the forest for the wolves to find or put in a basket on the river. Either way very bad news, because we're not Moses.

Instead we make a girly trip in a hire car to Grasse and do a tour of the perfume factories and ooh! and aah! at the sight of fields of lavender. In the evening we go to the casino in Monte and play roulette. Ludmila has studied this role to perfection. She drapes herself over Sergei's shoulder and her long fingers play with the lobe of his left ear, which he affects to brush off like a fly. And all the while she smiles dreamily at Hermione and me in a way that excites us and we can't explain.

16

It seemed natural that they should exchange telephone numbers; so Janet shouldn't have been surprised when he called on a Friday morning as she and Belle were cleaning the house.

Or was it natural? There was nothing ordinary at Janet's age in giving her telephone number to an attractive man without a clear idea of why she was having anything to do with him at all.

Six days had gone by since the ceilidh, during which they hadn't seen each other not even by chance. Politeness required that she ask how his week had been.

'Oh, a slow business, going over bank accounts and figures,' Stephen Gregg said without mentioning whose bank accounts or what figures. 'And you? How are the Demented Ladies getting on? Have you discovered the killer of the late Mr Walacaszewski?'

'No,' said Janet, mildly annoyed because she suspected him of making fun of her. 'Then again, neither have the police as far as I'm aware. Don't they say that, if a murder isn't solved in the first forty-eight hours the odds of a solution fall dramatically? How long has it been in this case? Twelve days?'

'*Touché*. My only excuse is that it isn't my problem.'

They were silent for a moment. It occurred to Janet that he was about to say his work was finished and he was returning to London.

'I enjoyed myself last Saturday,' he said.

I did too,' said Janet and asked herself why, of all the things he might have said, the matter of his returning to London was the one that had popped into her head, and why it had caused a slight pang.

'It seems I'm going to be stuck here for a while yet.'

'Poor you.'

'What? Oh, yes – poor me. Which makes me wonder if you wouldn't care to come to the rescue; I mean that there's a play on at the local amateur theatre tomorrow night and it looks … well, it looks as though it might be fun. Would you like to go with me?'

'I'm sorry but I've got something on,' said Janet. Then it occurred to her that she was busy because she was going to see the amateur play with The Demented Lady Detectives' Club (as she supposed she should get used to calling her friends after Belle gave them that damned name). She explained her problem. 'But, of course, you could come with us if you wanted – I mean that some of the husbands will be tagging along…' She stopped.

'I'd be delighted,' he said.

'You sound as if I've just told a joke.'

He laughed. 'Yes. Well, there is a funny side in finding myself a copper among a bunch of women bent on solving a murder.'

'Well, as far as tomorrow is concerned, we're just going to the theatre. The murder thing is' – what exactly? – 'a sort of game, that's all. It came from a chance remark my friend Belle made at our Readers' Group. No one takes it seriously.'

Or do they? Did she? At times it seemed the thing had taken on a life of its own.

'I should think not,' said Stephen Gregg; then asked, 'Do your friends' plans include any food?'

'No.'

'In which case that leaves you free to have dinner with me. A pre-theatre snack at the brasserie – shall we say six o'clock?'

'Yes – yes, I suppose so,' said Janet, unsure if she was pleased or not.

'I heard that,' said Belle, coming out of the kitchen holding a tea towel. 'Ooh, you are a rotten flirt, Janet Bretherton, you are.'

'Oh do shut up!' Janet snapped, cross at her friend for once.

'The truth always hurts,' said Belle.

So they met as arranged; Janet wearing a simple blouse, skirt and jacket that had taken an age to negotiate with Belle as if the latter were her mother, though the terms of the discussion had changed over the years. Once it had been about her neckline ('Too much cleavage, my girl. You don't want to be giving ideas.'): now it was about the crepiness of her skin. Stephen Gregg didn't have to worry about that. He could stick to M&S's Best, as infallible as the Pope for a man of his age with no particular pretensions to style.

The brasserie had bare floorboards and a French-style bar with a zinc top and Art Nouveau posters advertising *Bière d'Alsace* – not that they served it: only Stella, Guinness and a selection of craft beers with names like Stinking Toad that Janet imagined brewed in their cellars by fat men with beards and an unhealthy interest in computer games. The food was a range of inexpensive tapas. Half a dozen cheerful young women were chatting gaily while picking at their food and chugging on a huge carafe of sangria.

What were they to talk about after exhausting the easy subjects during that first dinner at the Royal George? Their late spouses and the circumstances of David's death, which had been puzzling at the time? Even though no one had believed Janet was a killer, she had a sense that people looked at her as if she might manage it when cornered.

And, yes, they did find themselves talking about David. Stephen seemed interested in her take on marriage. What had drawn them together? What had driven them apart? She laughed.

'Why are you laughing?' he asked.

'Oh, I don't know. I suppose because – speaking as a woman – it's difficult to talk about quiet, ordinary marriages without making them sound like dog training classes. And knocking David into a reasonable semblance of a good man really wasn't how I wanted to spend my time; it was just something that happened because of who David and I were. I came to realise that every relationship is uneven.'

'You want companionship and your dog wants his belly rubbed.'

'Isn't this a terrible way to talk about my husband?'

And you? she wondered. What were the asymmetries in your marriage? Why are you talking to me and seeking my company? Surprisingly he wasn't banging on about his wife or anything else: more interested in her, it seemed. Which frankly made a change.

She said, 'You haven't told me your wife's name.'

'Anne. She died of breast cancer two years ago. It surprised me because I thought that these days breast cancer was curable, but apparently sometimes it isn't.'

Janet formed a picture of Anne – or it might be herself – standing in front of a bathroom mirror feeling her breasts as part of her daily routine: the clinical touch of her own hands, not the embrace of a husband; the uncertainty that followed the discovery of that first lump – was it real or an illusion born of anxiety? Had Anne been offered a radical mastectomy and declined because her breasts were so bound up with her image of her own femininity that the prospect of their loss filled her with feelings of horror and inadequacy? Or perhaps she and Stephen had discussed an operation and (because he was a man and had researched the matter on Google) he had persuaded her that there were other, better procedures; and, when these had failed, the final days of her life had been tainted with an unexpressed reproach and what would have been loving memories of his wife were destroyed by remorse?

There are some conversations one cannot have.

'I understand what you mean about unevenness,' he said.

122

Janet nodded with what she hoped showed as sympathy, but a cruel part of her didn't want to hear the tale of his regrets. Nobody got an exemption ticket and she had nothing wise or especially comforting to say – and certainly nothing original – but she had to say something.

'What did Anne do – her job?' Of all pointless questions, this was a prize winner. What could she possibly do with the answer?

'She was a nursing assistant.' Unexpectedly he grinned and Janet realised gratefully that the conversation wasn't going to go down that direction. Instead he changed the subject to dancing. 'There's a thrill in it, isn't there?'

'Yes, there's a thrill,' she agreed.

There was a thrill even in dancing the Gay Gordon in a provincial town hall with a man one scarcely knew.

He asked, 'Why are you laughing?'

'I was thinking of the Mayor dancing a jig in a ginger Jimmy Wig.'

The Dartcross Players had converted a former Wesleyan chapel into a theatre. The ground floor had been stripped of pews in favour of stacker chairs and the balcony was a dump for scenery flats and props. A bar occupied the small vestry and dispensed wine, strong tea and cheap instant coffee in disposable plastic cups.

The Demented Lady Detectives' Club turned up in full strength. Those with husbands brought them, except for Jean who explained, 'I canna afford to take a Saturday night off; so Stuart volunteered to drive the taxi. Anyway, theatre's no really his thing. If Clint Eastwood isna killing people, he canna get too excited.'

'Well, there's a murder in this play,' said the elegant Pierce who was there with the equally elegant if understated Diana. 'Though it's a creaky old piece.'

The play was Agatha Christie's *Witness for the Prosecution* and Janet shared Pierce's opinion. The Queen of Crime might have been the mistress of cleverly constructed plots but her instincts for stage craft were shaky. Court room scenes left the actors too fixed to one spot and the device of having a character wear disguise was impossible to pull off in a modern drama. The audience could see right through it; so why not the other people in the play?

'It's stupid, really, isn't it?' said Belle at the interval. 'I remember the film with Marlene Dietrich in the lead.'

'And Charles Laughton!' said Christine's Keith with his slightly skeletal grin. Christine, never especially talkative except about her New Age nonsense, was almost mute when with her spouse. Tonight, perhaps because she was acting as prompter, she'd swapped her usual fey style for what looked like an expensive dress.

'So it was; I'd forgotten. Any road, there was Marlene Dietrich in make-up and a veil, but she's in close-up, so she's not fooling anybody. And where was Agatha Christie coming from when she has this woman speaking with a German accent one minute and the same woman talking broad Cockney the next? – which Marlene Dietrich could no more do than I can speak Chinese. Everybody knows it's the same person, except for the idiots in the play, so where's the surprise?'

'At least it's truthful in one respect,' said Janet.

'How?' asked Diana.

'The murderers and the victims know each other. These days the fashion seems to be for serial killers or terrorists, but in the real world murders by strangers are so rare. We're far more likely to be murdered by someone close to us. Husbands kill wives. Wives kill husbands. And dangerous boyfriends slaughter the children of poor abused young women – always the saddest thing, I think.'

'So who killed our Mr Walacaszewski?' asked Pierce in a tone Janet found slightly supercilious. 'I think the police would know if there was a Mrs Walacaszewski living in Dartcross. What do you say, Stephen?'

'I can't say what the police do or don't know.'

'Very circumspect of you.'

'But, speaking generally, if there were a Mrs Walacaszewski, I'd expect her to be found sooner or later.'

'And I don't suppose our late friend was wearing a disguise?'

'No. That would be a little too theatrical.'

'No surprises there,' said Belle once the play had finished. ''I'd have guessed the ending even if I hadn't seen the film.'

'Well, I thought they did it rather well,' said old Joanie grandly.

'I'm not complaining, though in my opinion the woman playing the lead looked old enough to be the villain's mother rather than his wife. I don't think her teeth fit any too well; it made my gums ache to look at her.'

'That's amateur dramatics for you,' said Sandra. 'They have to work with what they're given, and if the juvenile lead won't see fifty again they're stuck with it.'

Stephen Gregg offered Janet his arm but she didn't take it. Belle's comment had reminded her of the discrepancy of age between the two of them.

'I think a nightcap would be in order,' Joanie announced. 'Kenneth, dear, you'll do the honours, won't you?'

Kenneth looked as if he'd prefer not to and muttered something about how much money he'd brought along with him.

'That's all right,' Belle chipped in. 'We'll pay for ourselves.'

They went to the Ring o' Bells, a small Tudor relic with a Georgian front and a sign in the window advertising karaoke on Thursday and Eric the DJ on Saturdays. Fortunately Eric had been brought low by a hernia and so the bar wasn't too noisy. In the confusion at the counter, Stephen bought the drinks. 'I'll put it down to expenses,' he said as he handed a fruit juice to Janet and a rum and

Coke to Belle. Then, noticing Janet's mood change he said, 'Someone looks distracted.'

'What? Oh, forgive me; I'm tired.' In fact the business about the difference in age of the actors had made her slightly depressed.

'Forget her,' Belle interrupted to spare them from silence. 'I used to have a cat like that, all moody and not fit company. Hey, look at Joanie! She's already got one glass of wine down her neck and she's after a second before we've got started. What I want to know,' she said, turning to Stephen Gregg and without pausing, 'is where did the police get Stanislaw Wal-Mart's name from, eh? One minute he's a fella found dead by the river without a name to bless himself with, and the next he's got one and no explanation where he or it came from. Nobody in Dartcross knows him; so how come the police do?'

Stephen Gregg smiled. 'Good question,' he said. But he didn't give an answer.

By couples they left: Joanie supported by Kenneth; Christine with Keith; Frieda and Harry quietly singing a Country and Western number and trying out some line dancing steps; Diana and Rev Pierce trailing slightly behind as if they were somehow above the others. Sandra and Belle linked arms and Janet walked with Stephen Gregg, still maintaining a slight cool distance and uncomfortable with herself.

When they split up in the High Street to go their various ways, Janet didn't offer her cheek to be kissed and she thought Stephen looked hurt; but all he said was, 'It was an enjoyable evening. We should do something again. Go dancing perhaps?'

Janet nodded and watched him walk away, lending a friendly hand to keep Joanie on her feet. Sandra and Jean had gone and she was alone with Belle at her shoulder.

'Have you two fallen out?' Belle asked.

'No, I was just tired, like I said.'

'Tell me another one.' Belle took her friend by the arm and said, 'Come on, my girl: beddy-byes!'

They reached the door of Janet's cottage and were taking off their coats when Janet said, 'Before I forget: I want you to go to the police station on Monday and ask them about that mobile phone you lost.'

Belle looked puzzled. 'What mobile phone? I haven't lost a mobile phone.'

'Yes you have. You lost it on the path by the river.'

17

I've had another turn and I'm frightened. The first one I was able to put down to an accident – not forget it exactly, but treat it as something that probably wouldn't happen again. A bug I'd caught. Something I ate.

I don't know if I ever believed that.

I forget if I did.

Now I know that something is wrong with me.

Among the general confusion when it happened, I had a sense that Angela was present. The feeling was intense. It had the conviction you get in dreams, the unquestioning acceptance of another reality. Angela had always been with us. We'd never lost her. It was her death that was the illusion and at any moment I'd remember what she and I had done in all the missing years. But for now, I sat on the edge of the bed, trying to recall what I was trying to do when it happened. Get up? Go to bed? I was paralysed: not physically, but incapable of doing anything because I didn't know what I wanted to do. And there was Angela: not visible or audible, but just there. I tried to call out – to Angela? to the Boss? – but my lips just mumbled.

After Angela died, I wanted to kill myself but didn't. I was one of those would-be suicides who succeed or fail according to their competence; and it turned out that I wasn't very good at it, which I suppose is typical. I was locked up for a month and given tablets and therapy for a year, and they worked after a fashion because since then I haven't tried again. Apparently I'm not a chronic depressive, just a mother who's lost her child, and – so they assured me back then – wanting to kill myself falls within the realm of the expected, though for some reason I'm supposed to put on a brave face and carry on.

I've carried on. I'm not sure why. Habit? Lack of imagination? Certainly not fear of retribution in any afterlife – which I don't believe in anyway. A loving God wouldn't have killed Angela. This is a stark truth built into the very notion of love and beyond any excuse or explanation. The churches don't have an answer. Despite the evidence they just mutter nonsense about being tested and faith and mysteries. On that basis you can make a case that the Earth is flat. Atheism is something the Boss and I don't agree about.

Whatever, I got over my turn and remembered Angela was dead, shrugged my shoulders and spent the rest of the day cooking and cleaning. You would have seen me at the stove or with the vacuum cleaner and been unable to detect the state of terror inside. Fortunately I didn't have any clients visiting. The Boss was out with the dog, after my recent comments that he seemed to be walking on his own rather too much. Yesterday he took That Thing to the vet to have her teeth seen to, though they seem serviceable enough to judge from the havoc she causes among the local wildlife. Cats and their teeth! They do it out of spite.

I still haven't told the Boss about my turns, and I don't think I shall.

Last night we went to see The Dartcross Players: all of us in my Readers' Group plus most of the husbands. I like amateur theatre because the actors are so much closer to failing than the professionals. I sense their danger and find myself rooting for them.

Afterwards there was more talk about the murder. I kept my mouth shut, frightened I'd let something out. Earlier we discussed the play and the fact that the female lead disguises herself and has to switch from a German accent to a Cockney one. Agatha Christie has the same problem as God: she contradicts common sense. I mean, if her character could speak English well enough to be a convincing Cockney, why would she have a German accent in the first place? It made me think about the late Stanislaw Walacaszewski. From the name I imagine he was Polish, and in my experience Polish accents are quite strong. Yet one gets no sense that anyone in Dartcross had noticed he was here. How is that possible?

Belle made the same point to Dai the Police. How had Mr Walacaszewski transformed from being Unknown Body Found in River to getting himself a name? D the P wasn't letting on – claims he doesn't know or can't say. Still, it's a good question and the answer might tell us more about the deceased. It seems fairly clear that there was no identification on the corpse. Janet – the clever clogs – worked that out quite convincingly from the silence in the newspaper report, and Inspector Gregg didn't deny it. He makes a point of not committing himself but sometimes silence speaks volumes. I think Janet knows this and tests him. She's very cunning. I'm frightened that she sees through me.

The feeling that I know Inspector Gregg from somewhere persists. I don't think it's just a symptom of my 'funny turns'. I catch him glancing at me every now and again and, as with the eloquent silences, there's a message in his eyes for those who can read it.

I think he pities me. But I don't know why.

Time to get back to the Story of my Life. That or making shopping lists.

Where the Fabulous Four are concerned, there's this to be said in favour of the money showers. They keep us in a high old style throughout the 1980s.

'And there are even better times to come. Trust me on this,' booms Call Me Gerry.

He has taken to tapping the side of his nose to indicate that he knows how many beans make five – which is six in his case. I'm always surprised that anyone ever falls for his act but it may be that that stuff about Fettes and Oxford and the ancestral acres is genuine after all. Privilege makes some posh people vulgar, and they're certainly no more honest than the rest of us, though less self-aware. At least burglars know they're crooks. Gerry thinks of himself as a wealth creator: an entrepreneur. He turns greed into a Higher Calling: Maggie Thatcher's version of New Age thinking.

I have no room to talk. I was spending the loot.

I don't know where the 'better times' are to come from but they've something to do with changes in the Soviet Union. Gorbachev is in power and acting like Mister Popularity. On the odd occasion I see Comrade Blok, I can't tell if Sergei Nikitich loves him or hates him, but in my opinion he's definitely sexy and his wife reminds me of Ludmila – her glamour.

'Who is believing?' says Sergei Nikitich as we pour vodka and sweet Russian champagne down our throats. 'Here is heir of Stalin and he is become film star – not John Wayne but other one. Except'– he taps his scalp where Gorbachev has a birthmark –'my mother says he have mark of Satan; so maybe we give him time and he is killing people in old-fashioned way and we all do normal business.'

'Let's drink to that!' says Gerry who, when push comes to shove between democracy and business, votes for business. And not alone in my experience.

Then, as if in contradiction, Sergei Nikitich becomes gloomily philosophical. He says, 'Still, maybe shake up everything not so bad, huh? Like cards, you are having to shuffle the deck now and sometimes, and who know but we are all lucky?'

'Well, there is that to be said for it,' Gerry agrees.

So we all drink to Gorbachev: his success or his downfall; one or the other but I'm blessed if I know which.

In all our junketing, which covers for whatever it is the Boys are up to, now and again we go to Moscow and stay at the Mezhdunarodnaya, which is an enormous warehouse for visitors where the sullen staff serve bad food. For entertainment we eat in restaurants where the atmosphere is 'folkloric' – the word Sergei Nikitich uses. It means the waiters dress like peasants on a feast day and the food is accompanied by flames and balalaika music. There are also clubs and striptease, where prostitutes hang out, but we don't go there, though I fancy the Boys do when they're free of our company. As for the shopping, it's rubbish.

Why do Hermione and I accompany the Boys to a place we don't even like? Because you take the rough with the smooth and because it feeds our self-image of international glamour girls. And perhaps, now that I look back after so many years, it is because of Ludmila.

Perhaps that most of all.

Ludmila accompanies Sergei Nikitich whenever we see him. She has a way of draping herself over his arm or shoulder, always hanging back slightly so that we can see her facial expression but he can't. Her presence is a sly commentary on everything that is going on. She sees us in our greed and absurd pretensions to style and is hugely amused, but in an affectionate way as one is with children. Or harmless idiots.

I have only one photograph of us both. Hermione took it and I suppose she must have its companion: the one I took of them. This was in the days of shoulder pads and big hair and I look like a character in a low budget American soap, whose name is probably Tiffany. But not Ludmila. Somehow she contrives to be of no particular time like the women in the Florentine quattrocento paintings at the National Gallery where she takes me whenever she comes to London. Ludmila has the high forehead and fair hair; the slightly pointed, slightly retroussé nose; and the air of looking at something the rest of us can't see. And she has green eyes. I don't know anyone else who has green eyes.

In her cups Hermione asks, 'Why don't you marry

Sergei Nikitich?'

Ludmila looks at her: not angrily but with an air of surprise as if Hermione should know the answer but apparently doesn't. She says, 'Sergei Nikitich has a wife. Nice person – not that matters; if he want rid of her, is easy get divorce or she have accident or something, but no point. If I marry him, is not possible for me to travel abroad. Security – you understand?'

'What exactly is your job? You've never said. You do have a job, don't you?'

'Oh yes! Everyone has job in Communist Paradise! I am secretary in Ministry of Something, but I have friend who does whatever I am doing and I give her money. We have joke, you see. Under communism they pretend to pay us and we pretend to work. So I have job in Russia and Sergei Nikitich has wife in Russia and it means we can travel abroad together. Is very romantic, yes?'

Yes, it is romantic because her life seems impossibly dangerous. I am frightened for her. Between the twin terrors of the Soviet system and jolly Sergei Nikitich Blok, she is walking a high wire – and surely it's only a matter of time before she falls? She knows this. I see it in her green eyes and in the moments when her gaze gives way to introspection before returning to face the world with her flashing smile. But, knowing what she knows of her fate, she still walks the high wire one day and one step at a time for the sake of her daughter.

When the Boss came back yesterday with That Thing, she was spitting at being penned up in her carrier for the trip to the vet. She whizzed out through the cat flap and, if she runs true to form, we may not see her for a couple of days. I keep hoping she'll get flattened by a lorry, but so far no luck

Today the Boss asked, 'Why are you crying?' Not about the cat, obviously. For some reason, this last couple of weeks, as his behaviour has become more mysterious, he's also become more solicitous. I don't know what the connection is.

'A bit of hay fever,' I said, though it's early in the season. He accepted the answer.

I couldn't tell him I was crying over my memories. I can't judge whether I have cause to or whether I'm simply becoming maudlin with age. Another sign of senility? Either way, I couldn't carry on writing about Ludmila. I decided I would push off into town about some shopping. Now that I'm back and writing these words, he's 'gone walking' with Slobber – or at least that's what his note says, if you believe it. Because I have a nasty and suspicious mind where the Boss is concerned, once I'd read the note, I checked the shoe cupboard. His pair of Lobbs' brogues is still there. QED. Wherever he's gone with the dog it isn't on one of the innumerable country walks hereabouts.

I went to Tesco's in Jubilee Road.

Note: White wine is on offer. Half a dozen bottles in one of those cardboard thingies with a handle. A second box at half price. I didn't have the car and couldn't carry them.

I don't know what to make of Stanislaw Walacaszewski. Being dead and unknown, he seems a romantic man of mystery, but, when we were chatting after the theatre, Janet said that's simply because we don't have the facts. The facts being that he's somebody's father, husband or boyfriend whose name seems exotic simply because we don't live in Poland or Russia or wherever the hell he came from; and the explanation of his murder will be banal.

The Boss killed him. Is that banal? In the world of Sergei Nikitich Blok, I fancy murderers are as common as plumbers, so I suppose it is.

As I say, while the Boss was out with Slobber, I wandered through the town to Tesco's, which is why my thoughts drifted in the direction of the late Mr Walacaszewski because his mug was on every lamppost on the High Street and by the tills in the supermarket. Apparently they still haven't pinned down his movements from his arrival in Dartcross to his departure on the towpath.

I've seen his photograph for the first time; there wasn't one in the *Advertiser* but now it's on the posters. It was taken from the corpse and it had 'the look'. It doesn't seem to matter how they tart up dead bodies, the owners always look as if they've been drinking cider and sleeping under railway bridges; at least so far as pictures in the newspapers are concerned. I expected to recognise him but I didn't. I scanned the photo for tattoos because Sergei Nikitich and his mates were tattooed like you wouldn't believe; but I couldn't see any. They may have been hidden by the sheet.

I felt disappointed

When you think about it, that's a perverse reaction. I should have been pleased that the picture didn't confirm that the Boss is a killer.

The reason for the posters is that the police are trying to find witnesses who saw our man after 16.13 pm on the Sunday afternoon. Search me why that particular time, but I wish them luck. There aren't many places in Dartcross open late on Sunday afternoon, so witnesses will be few and far between. On the other hand you'd think someone would notice if there were a Polish tramp with a heavy accent wandering round the place.

Perhaps he wasn't Polish? Perhaps he wasn't a tramp? Sometimes Reality is as demented as I am.

I keep thinking of Ludmila. I shouldn't. It makes me sad.

She wears her tragedy like her clothes, tailored to every contour of her figure. Beautiful. Stylish. A tragedy you would like to have instead of the shoddy stuff that passes for misery in your own sad life.

In London we go to the opera – a first for me. Othello.

'I'd rather listen to cats wailing,' confides Hermione, and I nod. But I know I'm missing something because there in the dark Ludmila is smiling and a tear curls down her right cheek. In this moment she is living more intensely than I am and I want to know why.

Oliver is with us.

'Poof by Appointment to Queen Ludmila,' says Gerry. He and the Boss have taken Sergei Nikitich to a casino and Oliver is conscripted to accompany us to the opera as Chief Eunuch to our little harem. On closer acquaintance he is good-looking beyond belief and his manners are unfailingly considerate.

When we are alone, Hermione hazards a piece of artistic criticism. 'That Othello! Bloody men, eh?'

It may not be subtle, but at least it's accurate. We're in the Ladies, powdering our noses while Ludmila and Oliver chat over cocktails. Hermione asks, 'Did you catch Her Ladyship sobbing her heart out? What was that about? Does she see Sergei as Othello?'

'Do you?'

'Not if I know men. I can imagine him knocking her about a bit – though I've not seen any signs of bruising and whatnot. But I don't think he has the passion for killing her, and I should think she's a sight too clever to give him any grounds.'

I think the same. The tears remain a mystery. Perhaps they are simply one of the ways one responds to art.

London – Moscow – Monaco – the Caribbean. Something is in the air in those heady days and I don't think even the Boys know what it is. They've caught Sergei Nikitich by the coat tails and are now being dragged along for the ride – no questions asked as long as the money showers continue. Hermione and I traipse along as their fragrant better halves and lend a bit of class, because by comparison with the other women in the Blok entourage we are true English Ladies, don't you know?

Only Oliver doesn't come to Moscow.

'My friends are simple people and not understanding him,' Sergei Nikitich explains. 'I sure he is very nice fellow. And as lawyer he is real business for definite. Not an honest bone in his body, hah! But...' he waggles his hand. '...we not wanting misunderstanding among friends.'

No we don't want that. And the truth is that none of us understand Oliver – perhaps not even Ludmila.

I am in Moscow when the Soviet Old Guard stage their coup against Gorbachev and Boris Yeltsin comes into power, which is a game changer for everything we and everyone else in Russia are doing.

I am in Moscow, cowering with the Boys in our hotel in case someone out there decides incidentally to kill us.

I am in Moscow when I receive the news that Angela is dead.

My daughter is dead.

18

Monday came and Janet decided to Google her friends'
names to see what turned up. It might be shameful – in fact
she thought it was – but writers and detectives were known
for being ruthless in the way they poked into other
people's lives and there was nothing to be done about it.
Unless she gave up her activities, of course. Which Janet
wasn't about to do.

She arrived at her decision after thinking again about
the meeting of the Readers' Group. She'd noticed that
someone had drawn a circle around the article in the
Advertiser about an unknown corpse found in the river,
and she asked herself the question: why would you bother
for an unnamed stranger, unless you already knew the
person and didn't need the name?

The *Advertiser* came out on Wednesdays. The name
was first announced on TV news on Thursday evening
only an hour before the women met. It was possible the
newspaper had simply lain around unmarked until then,
but hardly likely given the narrow window of time
between the TV report and the meeting. More probable
was that someone saw the article and knew immediately
who it referred to. In any case it was the fact that someone
thought the story was worth noting that was important.
The actual timing affected only the degree of significance.

First things first. Before starting on her friends, Janet
searched against Stanislaw Walacaszewski himself,
surprised she hadn't done it before. She scored plenty of
hits but there wasn't a lot to them. Top of the list were the
items on regional TV news beginning with the one that
first put a name to the dead man. A couple of updates
followed but with no more information the story was
dropped. The national newspapers followed the same

pattern except that the incident was given no particular prominence, and again there was no new information.

Way down the page came the accounts in the *Dartcross Advertiser*. There were two of these: the first almost a fortnight ago reported the discovery of the body, and the second, dating from last Wednesday, named the dead man but seemed to be just a rehash of the TV news from the previous week. Presumably there would be an update in this week's edition, but Janet suspected it would contain nothing more except details taken from the posters put up by the police

Finally there were pages of stuff written in Polish. Janet had no idea what they said: some of them were clearly unremarkable business websites; others contained photographs that didn't resemble the one on the posters. Janet was certain they had nothing to do with the case but she pulled some fairly unintelligible translations off Google Translate and, so far as she could tell, they were of no interest.

I'm not the police, she reminded herself. This is just a game or curiosity on my part. Not an attractive thought.

Annoyed with the dead man, Janet keyed 'Sandra Wallace' and, as expected for a fairly ordinary name, got a number of hits. Less expected was that they didn't mention astrology, 'energy medicine' or anything else of a New Age character; and none of the plausible pages on Facebook seemed to refer to the Sandra she knew, and in fact Sandra had implied she didn't have an entry when Janet had suggested they might become 'friends'. How then did she promote her business? Surely not the old-fashioned way through the trade press and point of sale advertising? Janet thought the matter over before reaching the obvious answer that Sandra must have a professional name that simply hadn't cropped up in her hearing. How annoying. She could always ask the woman, she supposed, but it niggled her not to be able to work it out for herself. Surely she'd seen it written somewhere?

Janet thought back to her visit to the Heart of Osiris, which she'd initially mistaken for a conventional bookshop. Christine would certainly have put up posters and given out fliers for any event involving her fellow aged hippie; in fact Janet had quite probably seen some but had no reason to pay attention.

I can ask Belle to drop in and get me the name, she told herself and reached for her iPhone. The easy solution: no mental effort involved. Not satisfactory though. An admission of defeat.

What she did remember was a cookery book that, until she saw the title – something about the Mayans – was the only thing in the shop for which she might have had any use. It had been on a table, copies piled high like a best-seller, a dozen at least.

A best-seller about New Age Mayan cookery?

In Dartcross?

Janet had a memory of doing book signings, dismal affairs at which she'd been lucky to sell one or two copies of her latest. Not an uncommon experience for mid-list writers. A fellow sufferer, on a promotion tour of Northern Ireland, was so hesitant at revealing himself as an author that he spent an entire hour sitting behind his table in a Belfast bookshop, searching the customers' bags for IRA bombs.

'Make sure you sign every copy in the place,' Janet's publisher had told her. 'That way they can't return them unsold.' Good advice that did wonders for hardback sales.

Applying her experience to the matter in hand, Janet knew that Christine had stocked a dozen unsaleable cookery books only because they'd been written by her friend: Sandra Wallace, *alias* – Janet typed the name – *Sarinda Heavenshine*. And there she was!

And a disappointment. The website was a fancily designed puff for Sandra's career as a psychic: a platform to sell her books and talismans and advertise her forthcoming appearances. All of this with an entourage of pop-ups offering more of the same to the gullible, and various testimonials from Airhead of Swindon and his or her friends praising the insights of Ms Heavenshine. Janet found it depressing. More to the point, there was next to nothing in the way of Sandra's biography beyond a dubious account of years spent at various ashrams in the Himalayas and her induction into a secret cult of Mayans in the Andes (though Janet was fairly sure the Maya had never inhabited the Andes). Nowadays Sarinda Heavenshine lived in Dartcross because her Spirit Guide had directed her to bring enlightenment there.

Lucky old Dartcross.

'Did you go to the police station about the phone?' she asked when Belle returned with a heap of shopping.

'Give me chance to get my breath back.' Belle put her bags down, took off her shoes and collapsed in an armchair.

'Well?'

'No, since you asked. It was a toss-up between solving a murder and buying a large pack of toilet rolls on special offer, and the toilet rolls won. But never fear, I'll see to it once I've had a bite to eat and a rest. It's a long shot anyway. Somebody finds Mr Walacaszewski's mobile and hands it in and the coppers don't make the connection? I mean: is it likely? What I did do was bring one of these back.' She handed over a police flier.

'I've seen it.'

'Right – well that puts me in my place. Tea? Coffee? Not that it tells us anything beyond providing a mugshot of our man, who looks a bit poorly, what with being dead.'

'No, it tells us a little more than that. We know he most likely came here from London.'

Belle stared at Janet and shook her head, 'I'm going to regret asking this because I know for a fact that the poster doesn't say where he came from.'

'It asks for witnesses who saw him after 4.13 in the

afternoon. It's a very precise time. I checked and it's when a London train gets in. Someone must have identified him, which is why the police are only concerned with his later movements.'

'It doesn't have to be London he came from. The train stops in all sorts of places,' Belle said. 'He could be from … I don't know … Didcot?'

'Yes, he could. London is just the most likely place.'

'Meaning people from Didcot don't get murdered? No, I don't suppose they do. All right, he probably came from London, though I don't see that it takes us much further forward. Then again, I'm thick I am. Let's have a cuppa and you can tell me about your morning.'

They took coffee and Belle set about preparing a snack while Janet recited her searches on the Internet.

'Well we're not going to get much out of the Polish websites,' said Belle, 'unless we intend to make a career out of this thing – which God forbid, we're not, are we?

'No.'

'Good. As for Sandra, you've been a clever beggar as per usual, but you'd have made life easier for yourself if you'd just asked me what her professional name was.'

'You knew she was Sarinda Heavenshine?'

'It's not exactly a secret. You forget that I see her more often than you do because I'm a sociable person – or a nosey parker, take your pick. As a matter of fact I ran into her while I was out and we had a drink and a snack at the brasserie. God, she can put it away can that one; but that's bye the bye. She told me about Sarinda Whatsherface. In any case she has a pile of hand-outs with her name and photo on. I was a bit surprised that she doesn't have a Twitter account, but some people don't take to it.'

Janet didn't have one. 'You do, I suppose?'

'It goes with having a big gob and a lot of opinions. Actually I have a guilty secret. I follow Justin Bieber. I want to mother him.'

They agreed that humanity was not ready for this news.

Janet returned to her Internet searches while Belle, once she'd eaten, went out again.

Christine had a Facebook page and readily welcomed Janet. Her website was under 'Heart of Osiris', and ranked some way below a computer game of the same name.

From her Facebook profile and her 'Meditations', Janet gathered that Christine valued 'spirituality' and desired everyone to be happy, which was fair enough if unoriginal. She had something over 5000 online friends, most of them would-be spouses and fraudsters and quite likely both, because it seemed her habit was to accept every friend request. The rest largely comprised members of the New Age community, who enthused over various therapies, diets and gurus.

The Heart of Osiris website was of a piece with this general picture, but it was evident Christine had had professional help. It displayed unsuspected business acumen. As far as Janet could tell, it was the portal for an online trade in New Age and magical merchandise that wasn't sold through the shop, and the pricing structure suggested she was selling wholesale to others in the psychic profession. She wondered if there was money to be made from this and what it would mean if there were.

This fresh insight caused her to speculate about Mr Christine. She'd met Keith on only two occasions: once at the ceilidh and once at the theatre. Her first impression had been that he was a teacher but – she was embarrassed to admit – this was simply a case of stereotyping from tweeds, a check shirt and suede shoes, and he'd dispelled it by telling an amusing anecdote about being in Sofia during Bulgaria – German Democratic Republic Friendship Week. She recalled that he'd specifically said he was there on business, even if he hadn't specified what.

At the theatre Janet had decided she quite liked Keith – in small doses at least. He was better looking than she'd first thought, with clear eyes and regular features; indeed she could imagine him and Christine in their younger days as quite a good-looking couple. He displayed flashes of dry wit and was a bit of a flirt. Did he have an online presence? None that she could find, but that wasn't surprising: men being generally less sociable than women. It was only the Bulgarian connection that drew Janet's attention, and it was a stretch to infer from it that Keith had any involvement in Poland. It was no more than marginally likely, in that people doing business in one country of the former Eastern bloc might well be doing the same in another.

In all, several hours of searching online didn't materially add to what Janet already knew or suspected. She decided to break off and go through the remaining names another day, but while she was still online she thought she would pursue an idea that had been niggling at her: something she'd read about and even used in her own books but never in fact tried.

She found a website that sold chemicals. And she went into town and bought herself a walking stick.

Towards evening Belle came back from her expedition to the police station looking put out.

She huffed, 'You're a bit spooky, you are. If you ask my opinion, it's not just Sandra and Joanie who are a touch psychic.'

Janet was astonished. 'Don't tell me you've found the mobile phone?'

'I don't know why you sound so surprised, Gypsy Rose Lee. You knew it'd be at the cop shop.'

'I knew no such thing. I was simply running out of ideas and this one came to me. Really, I didn't expect that it would amount to anything.'

'Well, it hasn't – not yet. The battery is as dead as the proverbial and I had to buy a charger. Put the kettle on while I plug it in.'

While Janet made tea, Belle told her tale of visiting the

lost property office at the police station. 'Not so much an office as a drawer in a desk, but you'd be surprised how many mobile phones people lose. It was full of them and I was a bit pushed when the bloke on duty asked me to describe mine.'

'What did you say?'

'I told him it was yours and that I'd forgotten to ask you what sort.'

'He was happy to hand it over to a person who didn't own it?'

'He didn't seem fussed – probably needed the drawer space. And who in their right mind would wander into a police station to pinch someone else's mobile? Apart from us, obviously.'

They took their mugs of tea to the lounge. Janet noted that the place had begun to feel quite homely despite being filled with someone else's furniture. Perhaps it was because she was sharing the space: something she hadn't done since leaving her daughter's (not that she'd felt at home with Helen: too much tension).

Belle carried on with her story. 'I told the man that you'd been walking by the river that Sunday evening and thought it must have fallen out of your bag when you stumbled on a tree root or summat. I said you'd gone back but it was too dark.'

'And what did he say?'

'He didn't much care how it had been lost. He fished in his drawer, pulled a phone out, checked the tag and said it had been handed in on the Monday by someone who said he'd found it while walking his dog the night before. Of course it doesn't *have* to be you-know-who's; it could have lain there for days. But it's more likely to belong to him than anyone else, and once we get into it we ought to be able to tell fairly quickly. But that's bye the bye: what I want to know is how you knew it'd be there waiting for me.'

'I told you: I didn't,' said Janet. 'It was no more than a

long shot. Look, I've spent the day trying umpteen websites and turned up precisely nothing, but you go to the police lost property office and turn up … well, something or other. That's how luck works. Buy enough raffle tickets and sooner or later you win a prize.'

'Yes but…'

'This is Dartcross. People are mostly honest. If anyone found Walacaszewski's mobile there was a fair chance they'd hand it in at the police station.'

'But why didn't the police make the connection with the murder?'

'Because on Monday, when the phone was handed in, the body was still lying in the water. There *was* no murder to connect it to. Who was manning the desk when you were there?'

'Some old bobby waiting for his pension.'

'Precisely. You don't think for a moment he's one of the investigating team, do you? He wouldn't give anything as routine as a lost phone a second thought. Until you asked, he'd probably forgotten when this one was handed in. And two weeks afterwards, he probably doesn't remember what day the murder happened. One thing I was certain of was that if the phone had been handed in, no one would have connected it to the crime.'

'You know,' said Belle, 'there are times when I could hit you.'

'Let's have that cup of tea,' said Janet. 'You can hit me later.'

They drank their tea while looking at the phone and its charger.

'What do you think it's going to tell us?' Belle asked.

'Not very much, I suspect.' Janet's initial feeling that the gods were with her and her investigations had passed. As she'd remarked before, her experience of remarkable coincidences was that they almost invariably meant next to nothing – as witness David bumping into his old friend

147

Gordon while on safari. People made too much of these strange occurrences. With so many possible combinations of events it was inevitable that some of them would actually occur.

She asked Belle, 'What would you do if you found a mobile phone?'

'Assuming I didn't keep it for myself? Only if it was a nice one of course.'

'Be serious.'

'Well ... I suppose I'd go into the list of stored numbers and try some of them out. If I phoned one of his friends, it would normally throw up a name at the other end, and I could ask whoever answered whose phone I'd got, then take it from there.'

'Yes,' said Janet, 'that's what I thought. And I imagine there are other ways, and presumably the police use them. So...'

'So why hasn't the owner of this one been found?'

Janet nodded. 'Yes, why?'

'There were a lot of phones in that drawer,' Belle said and then sighed. 'Oh, sod it: they're all broken, aren't they? They've been trod on or left out in the rain or found in a puddle or.... I suppose it means this one's bust.'

'It's a possibility.'

'Well that's just wonderful. I guess we'll find out in the morning when it's charged up. Meanwhile I'm going to watch TV then go to bed.'

19

Angela was eight when she died. And I was in Moscow.

I don't think I was a neglectful mother – no, that's wrong. I *was* a neglectful mother. Just not a cruel one. It would have showed. Angela was happy. Or so I tell myself, and I don't think I'm lying.

We were living in Hampstead and awash with money or the appearance of money, though I can't be sure since Gerry and the Boss used to joke that even their suits were owned by some company in Panama. One sign is that we had a live-in nanny and Angela was at a private day school. The nanny was called Mercedes like the car but pronounced with a lisp and she was nineteen or twenty. We called her 'Nanny' because it sounded posher and suggested someone more caring: like Mary Poppins rather than a Spanish teenager doing a job. Not that any blame attached to Mercedes for what happened.

Angela was run over by a car while coming home from school. It happens to children all the time, though that nugget of fact has no real meaning, does it? They were on the pavement, Angela and her friend Eleanor, fooling about in a bit of horse play while waiting for the taxi to arrive, when Angela was jostled into the road and knocked down by another parent's car. Re-run this scenario with me there instead of Nanny and Angela is still run over by a car. So you see, neither of us was to blame.

I feel it as a tragedy but all it merited was a couple of paragraphs in the *Hampstead Highgate Express*. Not Shakespeare, is it? Not even Charles Dickens and Little Nell. I think it adds to the real tragedies of our lives that for other people they haven't even happened. Angela's death was reported next to a longer item about a change to local parking regulations as illustrated by one of those photos of a glum shopkeeper staring at the double yellow lines outside his shop as if we are too stupid to get the point. No photograph of Angela, though. I refused to give one.

At the time they said, 'You shouldn't feel guilty.'

Shouldn't I? It wouldn't have occurred to them to say it if they didn't feel in their hearts that I *was* guilty. The only question is guilty of what? Of a nameless crime like the man in Kafka's book, which Ludmila explained to me, though I've never read it. I mean the crime we are all guilty of. And of which we are innocent.

Ludmila never said I shouldn't feel guilty. She had a daughter and a boyfriend who would cut her throat and bury her in the woods if the mood took him that way.

Ludmila was trapped and crushed by guilt, which is why I think her smiles were so tender and poignant.

The Boss went off with Slobber this morning as per usual. The pooch is looking quite chipper since That Thing disappeared in a huff after the business with her teeth. The scar on his nose looks as though it might heal and his appetite has come back now that the cat hasn't hawked a fur ball into his breakfast. I'm frightened to say 'good riddance' in case it acts as a spell to bring her back, but I still live in hope that some friendly bread van or brewers' dray will do us all a favour.

I can't live with this not knowing what the Boss is up to and I'm frightened to wait until Janet has finished her investigations, about which I'm careful not to make any enquiry. Another meeting of the Readers' Group is planned and the subject is one of her books. She had the grace to blush when it was suggested, but she didn't refuse. Modesty only goes so far and she's probably glad to sell a few copies, since, frankly, none of us had ever heard of her until she turned up in Dartcross. I'm assuming the occasion will turn into another conclave of The Demented Lady Detectives' Club and we'll get an update about the murder. So far it seems the police are getting nowhere. I don't know if I'm glad or not.

I've racked my brains about the Boss and the only idea I've come up with is to follow him. Easier said than done. When I tried it out today, the first problem was the time it takes to make the transformation from looking as though I was spending the morning at home, to slipping on a decent pair of shoes and a coat and scarf. I dare anyone to do it in less than a minute, by which time both master and dog had vanished and I wasn't sure in which direction.

As it happens, after a moment of panic, I found them. But that gave rise to the second problem. The Boss was striding out with his back to me while I hung about shiftily a hundred yards to the rear. He didn't see me but the dog, of course, picked up my scent and kept looking back and waiting for me to catch up. Every time he parked his backside on the pavement he pulled the Boss up short, causing some bad-tempered reflections on the poor mutt's parentage. Fortunately the Boss was too concerned with the dog and I escaped by dissolving into the scenery, staring at my feet or the sky or any damn thing until they set off again. I became invisible like a child in a game.

Angela for example.

What I'm saying is: following people isn't easy.

So far as the walk was concerned, it began innocently enough. The pair of them took the turn from The Pinches down Castle Street: not the route you'd pick if you were heading for the river to exercise the dog and bump off any stray Polish visitors you might run into, but fair enough if the Boss wanted to let Slobber loose in the Meadow at the bottom or head further afield to the town park. However, when they reached Station Road, instead of crossing it they turned right as if going to the river after all, only to turn left at the big roundabout this side of Caesar Bridge, which leads into a handful of streets, most of which go nowhere. Not obvious dog-walking territory when the river with its footpath is only a few hundred yards away.

And that's where I lost them.

My first thought was they'd taken another left into the road that flanks the park having decided for some reason to enter it from the bottom end rather than the more logical top, which would have spared them the haul down Station Road. But when I went through the gate and looked around, there was no sight of the pair. Unless they were lurking in the undergrowth (to shake me off perhaps?) they'd not come this way. Which means what, precisely? Presumably that they'd gone into one of the nearby houses.

Which is how things stand after this, my first effort at being a sleuth. I don't know which house they went into; indeed I'm not even certain which street. I debated hanging about to keep watch but quickly decided against it. On his recent performance the Boss might have kept me waiting for hours, and I could easily have found myself in the wrong place and missed him when he emerged. Also I needed to get back home because I had a client to see and I can't afford to lose her, finances being what they are.

All the same, I feel encouraged. I'm not entirely mad: the Boss is definitely up to something. And Janet isn't the only detective.

Meanwhile in the Land of Oz, Sergei Nikitich's fortunes have improved and he has laid hands on a dacha a few miles from Moscow. I used to know the name of the village, but in twenty years I've forgotten. Sometimes we assume we know something and it's only when we search our memories that we find we don't. We think we remember it but the truth is we remember only having once remembered it: a memory of a memory if that makes sense. If I hadn't started writing this whatchamacallum and had to call on my recollections I would never have realised.

I could Google the name if I was bothered. Famous artists and writers have cottages there, Ludmila tells me, though 'famous' in Russian terms isn't as Hermione and I understand it: it doesn't actually mean we've ever heard of them; still less that we've seen them in *Hello!* magazine talking about their boyfriends and boob jobs. At all events the village isn't exactly the back of beyond. So shall I look it up? I think not. The knowledge that I can find it if I want to is enough. Without a name the place retains its mystery. There's a seductive beauty in ignorance. It's what keeps the churches in business.

The dacha is just one sign that things are changing. For one thing, since Yeltsin came into power Sergei Nikitich has become a democrat. He tells us, 'That Boris Nikolayevich, what a great guy! Gorbachev I am taking or not taking, but Yeltsin, what is not to like?'

'Definitely!' booms Call Me Gerry, as if affirming his belief in the Holy Trinity and the Resurrection of the Dead to Eternal Life. 'Didn't I always say so?' he adds, though he never did that I can recall. Then again, on professional grounds Gerry agrees with anyone who can serve his purpose. The Boss has never quite mastered this trick, and, as a foil to Gerry's banging on, he comes the wise and silent. A bit like a comedy duo now I think of it, with the Boss playing the straight man. I don't think Sergei Nikitich ever sees through their act, not entirely. I suspect that at heart he's just a poor boy from the sticks. When Gerry flannels him with all that English-gentleman-word-is-my-bond stuff, Comrade Blok believes him.

Where dachas are concerned, I have no idea what to expect. A hut with an outside toilet for all I know, this being Russia. In fact they come in all shapes and sizes, some of them flanking the road and others up lanes that wind between birch trees into the woods. Sergei Nikitich's place is one of the latter and bloody enormous and he has the builders in.

'I am buying only a few months,' he says, opening his arms to show us his new estate, while me, Hermione and the Boys pick our way between heaps of wood and brick and discover that Russian builders have smiles on their bums just like ours. 'Guy who owns, he is *nekulturny*. Also bastard Communists not doing shit for maintain.'

'Bastard Communists,' Gerry agrees, and I understand what he's getting at, because a touch of Laura Ashley wouldn't go amiss. Half the floor in the main room is up and even I can see the joists are rotten. A carpenter is measuring up for a new window.

Why are we here? We arrive in two cars, the second one driven by some character I don't know, who treats Sergei Nikitich with deference. In the boot is all the stuff for a picnic, and the gofer sets it up in the sunshine on a stretch of uncut grass, dotted at the margins with a carpet of celandines stretching into the trees, and a blackbird is hunting for worms.

More tea, vicar? The folding garden furniture is old but the porcelain is Wedgewood; I remember Ludmila buying it at Harrods. The tea is Liptons; the biscuits are damp; and inevitably there's a half litre of vodka on the table. If we don't run to cucumber sandwiches, it's only because Comrade Blok hasn't heard of them.

Why am I writing about this, when nothing much happened on the day? I think it's because this peek behind the curtains of Sergei Nikitich's private life signals that whatever we were doing in the eighties, it isn't what we are doing now. Whoever we were then, it isn't who we are now.

Call Me Gerry captures the new spirit in his own inimitable way, when he proclaims, 'Doing up old country cottages is the devil of a job! I have a place in Devon and there's not much you can tell me about electricians that I haven't heard, and I could tell you stories about plumbers that would chill your blood.'

I have only half an ear for this because Hermione is whispering, 'If I go for a wee will you come with me? I hate to think what we'll find.' I notice that, to my surprise, our host is listening intently to Gerry and nodding to show he understands. When Gerry pauses for breath, Sergei Nikitich interjects a comment about the difficulty of getting good quality fittings to do the old homestead up, 'so is like English castle though not so big.'

'Not a problem, dear boy,' says Gerry. 'Give me a list of what you want and we'll fill up a lorry at Wickes and send it to you. On the house!'

And suddenly I realise that in some strange way we've become style consultants and interior designers.

The Boss has come back. I ask in my nice-as-pie voice what he had got up to, but he still gives me a suspicious look.

'I took the dog to Castle Meadow for a run around and then we walked by the river.'

Gotcha!

'Did he go in the water?' I ask. We can both see that he didn't because the pooch is in his basket in the kitchen, dry as a bone and contentedly licking his testicles.

'I kept him on the lead. I thought you wouldn't appreciate the mud, not when you've mopped the floor.'

'You're being very considerate all of a sudden.'

'That's a little unfair.'

Actually it is. When we were younger the Boss was inconsiderate in the way that all men are. Partly it's because of a blindness as to relationships and how things might seem in the other person's eyes, and partly because men see any form of adjustment to their behaviour as a loss of control. Fortunately some of them change with age. I don't know whether they grow wiser or we simply wear them down. Either way these days the Boss can be relied on for a timely cup of tea and the odd spot of ironing.

While I am nursing my little pang of guilt, he says, 'You do know I would never want to hurt you, don't you?'

I nod without immediately answering because I'm slightly thrown. It's a false note: a remark that doesn't follow from what he's just said: I mean it's almost but not quite appropriate, as if he has something else on his mind and has slotted it into the conversation as best he can.

I suppose I'm to understand that, whatever he's up to, he's saying it's for my own good.

'Aren't I the best judge of whether or not something will hurt me?' I say.

He bites his lip and offers to make coffee.

It's the middle of the night and I'm still writing. It's probably not a good sign, but the fact is I find it increasingly difficult to sleep. I understand it's an age thing and not necessarily because I'm going doolally.

I've been going over our last conversation, trying to make sense of it. Is it possible that the Boss did walk Slobber by the river? The route he took wasn't the most direct, but who is to say you have to take the shortest one when you're exercising the dog? The fact is that I lost sight of him in those streets off Station Road. I didn't actually *see* him go into one of the houses: it was just an inference based on the assumption that he couldn't be heading for the river. But the reality is that, in a roundabout way, he could have been doing exactly that.

One of the symptoms of dementia is paranoia. I think I may have written that already. Repeating yourself is another one.

He said: 'I would never *want* to hurt you.'

Not: 'I would never hurt you.'

There's a difference.

Am I quibbling over words or does he have something in mind: something he knows will be hurtful but which he feels compelled to do? And what can it be?

He may feel compelled to put me in a home. For my own good, naturally. Yet, even if I am showing signs of dementia rather than being simply depressed, surely things haven't got to a stage where there can be any question of going into care? A couple of funny turns and the occasional lapse of memory are still years away from being gaga. No, the idea is ridiculous. Paranoid.

Later.

I've read over everything I've written. I can see that it may be considered a bit colourful and far-fetched, but it's perfectly coherent. Not exactly something you'd expect from an old biddy with drool on her chin who keeps asking if your name is Sheila. In fact I think my writing classes have had an effect on style if not on content. I've tried to keep it light-hearted, which is what sensible people do when misery stares them in the face. Otherwise it's despair not senility that would get us. At all events I think I'm safe from the old people's home for the time-being.

Which means the Boss was driving at something else when he said what he said.

I went for a walk in the wee small hours. The town dark and the sky a slate grey around a full moon. Wandering the streets at night isn't normal, but what else can I do when I can't sleep and my mind is racing? The arcading in front of the shops at the top of the High Street has a rhythm of moonlight and shadow. Ludmila once showed me a book with paintings by an Italian called Georgio di … something. Arcades and empty squares and sometimes a statue. I have to play the part of the statue. The painting has a meaning, but it always hovers on the tip of your tongue and you will never be able to express it.

When I came home I found half a mouse in the middle of the kitchen floor. A peace offering from the cat.

20

'Who's going to do the honours?' Belle asked over breakfast.

They stared at the mobile phone standing among the cereal bowls and the vase of daffodils like an object in a modern still life. Considering the secrets it might hold, its unremarkable appearance made the anticipation rather anticlimactic. But that was the nature of evidence, Janet thought: it mostly comprised the stuff of everyday life and its significance had to be explained. At the end of the day even serial killers bought their axes at B&Q and their daggers at an army surplus store.

'You had all the trouble of finding it,' she said.

'But it was your idea in the first place.'

Janet supposed it was, but she was feeling generous. 'Go on, I'll make some more tea.'

'If you say so.'

Belle examined the phone more carefully. She called out to the kitchen, 'It's just a piece of cheapo rubbish, isn't it? Fit for telephone calls and not much else. You can tell our Mr Wally Cashew Nut (or however you say it) was getting on a bit: no teenager would be seen dead with it. We're not going to find emails or any record of what he's been Googling.'

'We may not find anything at all,' Janet answered. 'The police didn't.'

'Assuming that lazy sod who gave it to me even tried. Which I wouldn't put money on.'

'I suppose it's possible he didn't.'

By the time Janet brought the coffee, Belle had switched the phone on.

'Well, now it's charged, it seems to be working. So that's not why the police didn't find the owner.'

She opened the message archive and sighed. 'Bugger all, and why aren't I surprised?'

'Try the address book.'

'Here goes ... and ... *nowt*. You've got to be kidding! Who doesn't have any numbers in the address book?'

'Incoming calls?'

'Zip – zilch – nada.' Belle laughed. 'Hey, get me! I'm starting to sound like an American private detective.'

'Calls made?'

'Okeydokey. There are ... two. And about ruddy time. Shall I try the numbers?'

'In a moment. What dates were they on?' Janet took a calendar from the wall.

'Let me see. The first one was the 11th.'

'That was a Saturday. He came here the following day.'

'It's an inner London number. And there was me, betting on Didcot.'

'And the other one?'

'Also on the 11th. An 0800 number. I think I recognise it: one of those train information services; I used it myself to get here. We'll get nowt there, but it's easy to guess that he wanted train times from London to Dartcross.'

'Probably.'

'So shall I try the other number?'

Janet nodded. 'Put it on loudspeaker.'

'Righty-ho.' Belle keyed it and punched the call-out button.

'Paradise Traveller Hotel!' chimed a voice with a foreign accent.

Janet pressed the off-button and broke the connection.

They sipped their coffee companionably. Through the cottage window the morning sun slid shadows of trees across the pavement and a breeze sprinkled blossom. For a moment Janet was distracted and thought of other things they might do in this fine weather. Take the train to Buckminster, for example, which Belle had never seen.

Trying to solve a murder seemed a very odd thing to be doing. Then again so did crochet and knitting tea cosies, yet people did both.

'Why did you do that?' Belle asked. 'Put a stop to the call?'

'Because we haven't decided what questions we're going to ask. We may have only one chance and we don't want to ruin it.'

'Fair enough.'

'We should take stock of what we know and see if it suggests any lines of enquiry.'

'Well, that's not going to take long. We know next to nothing unless you're going to do your psychic thing.'

'I'm not psychic.'

'Sez you. Yes, all right: how do you want to do it; write a list?'

'We could do,' said Janet. She hunted in the Edwardian bureau that came with the cottage and came up with a box of notelets made of pastel-coloured paper with flowers printed in the corners, the sort that had a knack of turning up as Christmas presents and whose usefulness Janet had never worked out. Except that they were apparently for writing down clues in murder investigations. Who would have thought it?

'Stop grinning to yourself,' said Belle.

'Sorry.'

1. NAME – Stanislaw Walacaszewski

2. NATIONALITY – Polish

3. AGE – 50 to 60 according to the Advertiser and to judge from the photograph.

4. DIED – Sunday evening, 12 April. Body found on Tuesday 14 April

5. CAUSE OF DEATH – blunt force trauma – weapon not identified.

6. PLACE OF DEATH – footpath by river Dart

'You should mark that last one as a "probable",' said Janet. 'The police have said only where the body was found, not where he was killed.'

'You think he might have been murdered somewhere else?'

'We should at least consider it. The path is well-used yet the body wasn't found for two days.'

'So you *do* think he was killed elsewhere?'

Janet shook her head. 'Not really. I think the delay was most likely just a matter of chance. The body fell from the path or was pushed into the water by the murderer and simply went unnoticed because the location is a backwater overhung by trees, so the current didn't flush it out into the main part of the river. If you were dumping a body, it isn't a place you'd choose: too close to the town; too much risk of being seen; nowhere to park a car without having to carry the corpse a few hundred yards. I'm just trying to distinguish between what we know and what's simply speculation.'

'It's all speculation if you ask me,' said Belle, which Janet knew was largely true. 'And while we're at it, have you considered the possibility he was killed somewhere else and chucked out of a boat?'

'Actually I have, but I don't think it's likely. Almost nothing drifts into that spot under the trees: you'd have to deliberately bring the boat close into the bank and risk getting stuck. Why bother? It's not as though the body was going to stay hidden if you left it there. Sooner or later someone would find it if only by accident, as actually happened. Also we have the phone, which was found on the path not in the water.'

'All right, we'll scratch the boat.'

They returned to the list.

7. THE DEAD MAN HAD NO LUGGAGE?

'It might have been sitting in Lost Property with the phone,' said Belle. 'I never thought to ask. Mind you, I don't know how I'd have explained it as mine once somebody opened it. A razor, a pair of underpants and a dirty magazine. Not exactly me, is it? And then again, it might have been stolen by anybody passing.'

'Not likely since the phone was handed in.'

'Then maybe it fell into the water and police fished it out but aren't letting on.'

'If they did, it mustn't have contained anything to identify the body, because they'd have known who he was by the time the *Advertiser* came out on Wednesday and it's clear they didn't.'

'Then how *did* they find out? There's been no mention of friends or a family who missed him.'

'I haven't worked that out yet.'

'So did he have luggage or not?'

'I don't know,' said Janet. She felt suddenly dispirited. 'The problem is that we're building our case on silence rather than facts. The police don't immediately release his name, so we suppose they don't know. We think he came from London rather than Didcot simply because London is bigger and he seems to have phoned a hotel there, but we don't actually *know*. We think he wasn't identified by friends simply because no one has said he was and because the police put a name to him before the photo was released. And God alone knows where his luggage is.'

'The Paradise Traveller Hotel! Think about it. If he plans to come down only for the day, or he's meeting someone he knows will put him up, he doesn't need luggage. At a pinch he can always pick up a toothbrush and razor at Tesco's, and I've never noticed that blokes are too fussy when it comes to the state of their underpants.'

'It's one possibility. The most likely scenario is that our Mr Walacaszewski arrived in London on the Saturday – maybe from Poland and maybe not; after all, he could have stopped at other places on the way. Whatever the case, he stayed only one night before setting off for Dartcross on the Sunday.' Janet picked the phone up. She said, 'You do know we can't keep this. It's evidence.'

'I know. I'll pop into the police station later and tell them I made a mistake. They'll believe me since I told them it was your phone not mine.'

'You might mention delicately that it was found near the murder spot and might just belong to…'

'I get it,' said Belle. 'I'll do that.'

'The police can probably get more information from it than we can, and…' Janet paused, staring at the phone again. 'Just a moment.' She checked her watch. 'Have you noticed that the clock on this thing is an hour ahead. It could mean nothing, I suppose, but they run on a residual charge, don't they? They don't switch off immediately even when the battery seems to be flat.'

'So? Perhaps it's running on Polish time?'

'Poland is two hours ahead – at least I think it is.'

'So maybe he didn't change the clock when we went over to summer time last month. He wouldn't necessarily do it if he normally relied on a wristwatch. I never do.'

'The clocks go *forward* in spring. If the phone was previously showing the right time and he failed to correct it for the change, it would be an hour behind not an hour ahead.'

'Hmm…. What if he bought it in Poland before the time change? It would be set two hours ahead, right? Then he doesn't bother to alter it and so UK time catches up by an hour. Net result: one hour ahead!'

'I suppose so. But…'

'Oh, no! Please don't give me a "but". I'm fed up with your "buts".'

'The clocks changed nearly three weeks before the murder.'

'Yes…? And…?'

'So, if you're right, he's had the phone at least since some time in the middle of March. Yet he only makes two calls from it. Doesn't that make it far more likely that he bought it more recently, maybe only a few days before he was killed?'

'All right then, I give up. What's your explanation, Wonder Woman?'

'I don't know. But perhaps he came here from a country other than Poland?'

Belle snorted. 'Ooh, Janet Bretherton, you do make things complicated!'

They returned to their list.

8. *THE DEAD MAN DIDN'T WANT TO BE IDENTIFIED.*

'Go on, dazzle me,' said Belle. 'All right, let's say he didn't have any identification on him – and I'll grant you that he probably didn't – lots of people don't. I don't carry a passport or driving licence and I can never find the council tax bill when I want it. There's nothing sinister in it.'

'You're forgetting credit cards. Who doesn't carry credit cards?'

'Then how did he pay for things: hotels – trains? He'd have needed a bundle of cash. There's been no mention of it.'

'The police sometimes withhold key facts in order to deal with hoaxers.'

'Or maybe there *was* no bundle of cash.'

'If he was carrying credit cards the police would have identified him. And if he wasn't, then he didn't want to be traced. And before you object, the phone confirms it. It's just a cheap throw-away bought a day or two before he started travelling, which is why there's no call history to speak of and no address book. Where's his regular phone?'

'OK,' Belle agreed. 'Let's agree that the late Mr Wally Kazoo didn't want anyone to know where he was. Why?'

'I haven't a clue,' said Janet.

'Well, that's a relief! You may be clever, my girl, but it's very wearing on your friends.'

They found the Paradise Travellers Hotel online. It was a budget stopover in Paddington, convenient for the station and trains to the West Country. They called again and this time Janet did the talking.

'Paradise Travellers Hotel – Kinga speaking!' said the same cheerful receptionist with a foreign accent.

'I'm calling on behalf of a friend,' said Janet. 'A guest who stayed with you on the eleventh of April and left some luggage behind. His name is Mr Stanislaw Walacaszewski.'

A giggle at the other end.

'Have I said something funny?'

'No – no. I'm very sorry. You are not Polish, are you?'

'I take it you are.'

'Yes!' said the young woman brightly as if she had just won a prize and Janet found herself warming to her, though Belle rolled her eyes and whispered, 'Don't you hate ruddy kids?'

'It is a Polish name though, isn't it … Kinga?' said Janet, trying to be friendly. But what she got was a wary answer. 'He is your friend, so you are knowing already…' which made her apologise hastily: 'I'm starting to confuse myself.'

It seemed to work. Kinga said, 'Oh, I know! Always I am confusing when speaking other language.' She repeated the name using the Polish pronunciation, which didn't sound like Stanislaw Walacaszewski but no doubt was. 'OK, I check, but I pretty sure he is not staying here. Eleven April? No, I can't find.'

'Perhaps I have the day wrong.'

'No, is not here. Believe me. I am working almost every day and always knowing if Polish person stays. Last time was a month ago and was two girls from my city. We go to club together when I am not working at night.'

Janet tried offering a description, but even she knew it sounded like someone seen at a bus stop and instantly forgotten.

Her new friend said, 'I see hundreds of men like that, but if he is Polish then I remember.' And Janet agreed: she *would* remember. In any case his name or a Polish alias would be in the register if he had been there. Unless –

'I wonder if I could ask you to check another name,' Janet asked. But too late; Kinga was suddenly cautious of passing information to a stranger.

'I'm sorry, but client names is confidential,' she said. 'Thank you for calling.'

'So our Mr Walacaszewski didn't stay at that hotel then,' said Belle once the call was finished. 'Either that or what we have isn't his phone – which is a bit annoying, given all the trouble I went to. There doesn't seem much point in taking it back to the cop shop, does there?'

Janet didn't know how to respond. It was too depressing to think that all her finely judged inferences from the sparse materials had apparently come to nothing. Yet the call to the hotel did fit with the dead man's most probable itinerary, and the phone showed every indication of being what American crime writers called a 'burner'. Surely it had to belong to the dead man? The coincidences were too great; so there must be an explanation of the call to the hotel that accounted for these facts.

She said, 'You should take the phone back to the police station all the same. It may still be his and the police will be able to find out.' Clutching at straws – was that what she was doing? An idea came to her; it didn't convince her but she said it anyway. 'Perhaps he was calling someone else – someone who *was* staying at the hotel.'

'Right. The Mysterious Stranger Who Doesn't Speak Polish? Not to mention that no one has ever said a word about him. Don't you think he's a bit *convenient*? He sounds like a character out of an old-fashioned whodunit: you know: one of those long lost twins who turn up out of the blue after they've been running a plantation in Malaya for the last twenty years, or a suspect who gets up from the dinner table and comes back two minutes later disguised as a waiter and poisons somebody over the coffee, because we're told that no one ever pays attention to waiters, which certainly isn't true in Clitheroe.'

'Are you saying that I write books like that?' Janet

wasn't sure if she was offended. It was one thing to be modest about her work and another to have her nose rubbed in it. She'd always hoped that her modesty was misplaced and that other people thought she had considerable achievements to her credit. Not likely, admittedly, but possible all the same.

'If the cap fits…' Belle laughed and gave Janet an unexpected hug. 'Don't be silly; of course you don't. Tell you what: I'll pop down to Bargain Booze and buy a bottle of cheap plonk. And tonight we'll get sloshed.'

Unmollified, Janet said, 'Then what sort of books do I write?'

'What? Oh, search me, love,' Belle answered. 'I'm your friend. I don't have to read them.'

21

Back in the nineties the change in Comrade Blok's fortunes is mirrored by a change in ours: an increase in pace. I've focussed on Sergei Nikitich, but the truth is he isn't the Boys' only client. There are still plenty of Stephens, Stevies and Stevos around but I see little of them because the Boss and Gerry have taken an office in Mayfair to which they steer their meal tickets. I meet them only when we're putting on a show at the good old Empire & Dominions or feeding them at *L'Escargot sans Toit*. Hermione even suggests we've taken a small stake in the latter; certainly we spend enough to own the place. Not to mention several casinos and a country house hotel in Oxfordshire. I gather we are 'speculating to accumulate.' When the chips are down we'll discover whether we've been doing more speculating than accumulating, but that's a subject for the future.

These days our clients are called 'high net worth individuals'. They're not ashamed of being rich, but they do have a problem with the word. I suppose shame limited to that level might be considered the low calorie version of having a conscience.

This much can be said for our virtues: we aren't racist when it comes to choosing whom we do business with: Africans, Arabs, Italians, Greeks, Russians (naturally). In fact the whole world is welcome with the sole exception of Romanians. 'Because they kill you,' Gerry mutters darkly, but I think he's only mouthing the prejudices of the *Daily Mail*.

We also branch out into real estate, much to Gerry's disgust. 'I'm an investment banker,' he says, 'and they've turned me into a bloody estate agent!' Whatever the case, he swallows his scruples and joshes with the Africans,

Arabs etcetera in his usual hail fellow way.

Sergei Nikitich decides to get in on the property racket, beginning modestly with an apartment in Rotherhithe that has a view across the river to Wapping.

'Is a present for Ludmila Andreyevna,' he explains. 'So she can come to London when she want and do girl things.' He becomes sentimental and hugs both of us tearfully. 'I love you and Hermione. Our English family! If Ludmila Andreyevna live in London maybe you introduce to very snob people, learn ride and things?'

I can't speak for Hermione, whose conversation drops the names of very snob people at every opportunity, but I am light in that department. Then again does it matter? I rub shoulders with plenty of high net worth individuals, and if they are not 'very snob' I doubt that Sergei Nikitich knows the difference.

Ludmila smiles but I can tell she is weary at the thought. What does she really want? To become a nun and worship God? Sometimes the pain in her eyes makes me wonder.

'I want to be with my daughter,' she says, 'I dream we are living in a cottage in your Cotswold province. In nice village with cathedral and an inn and shop where we drink tea. There is a stream in garden and also roses and willow tree. And' – she laughs – 'I learn to ride bicycle!'

As it happens we once went to Burford as a diversion while the Boys and Sergei Nikitich were engaged in the Black Arts in London. Ludmila was with us. Is this where her dream comes from? She says lightly, 'I want to live as a good quiet lady and make jam like a person in novel by Joanna Trollope, which I read on aeroplane.'

I'm not sure she's entirely grasped the nuances of Joanna Trollope, but there's no mistaking her longing. How old is her daughter Katerina – Katya ? She is my Angela's age, of course. She is my Angela taken away from me but always with the hope that I shall see her again: a girl, now in her early teens, walking down the

High Street of Burford or Chipping Camden, staring at her reflection in the traditional shop windows of interior decorators and financial advisors, seeing her image float in splashes of sunlight and shadow, the glimpse of her profile as she turns to glance at a passing Ferrari, the silhouette of her legs visible through the bright, white panels of her summer dress.

During her absence, the cat has been in the wars. Maybe, as the saying goes, you should see the other fellow. Since she's back home, I assume she won whatever altercation she had with whatever species. She's sleeping it off somewhere. She probably suspects that we'd haul her off to the vet again to take care of her injuries and she's having none of it.

The dog is having another nervous breakdown in his basket. The Boss hasn't taken him out except to perform his ablutions. As a break in his recent routine, he's spending the day at home, closeted in the spare room with his papers, going over figures and correspondence. Is this activity connected with his mysterious walks? It's difficult to see how.

It being Wednesday, the *Advertiser* has arrived. The Boss shows no great interest, so I sneak off with it and read it in the loo. The story about the lately murdered Mr Walacaszewski still merits a paragraph on the front page with his photograph but it adds nothing we don't know from the police posters. After satisfying myself on this point, I place the paper in plain view but the Boss still ignores it. I don't know what to make of this. Does it signal guilt or innocence? I could make a case that an innocent man out of the intrinsic interest of the story would want to read about it and so…. But perhaps my paranoia is making me construe everything so as to fit my mad theories?

I can't stay in with him. I can't think of subjects for conversation and the silences are unbearable. Surely it must be the same for him as it is for me, but, if so, I see no sign of it. I could challenge him of course but if I did I know that he'd lie – for my own good, naturally – and I'm frightened that that would be the end of it. I'm used to the petty lies of men, the ones they tell all the time without thinking because they are less trouble than engaging seriously with a woman, but I have a feeling that *this* lie would be one from which there is no going back: the one that changes everything like a confession of adultery.

Is that it? Does he keep a mistress in one of those side streets between the town park and the river? I don't think of Dartcross as a likely place if you're in the market for mistresses but it must happen. Antique dealers with a wandering eye have to get their leg over somewhere.

I mustn't be silly. These days he couldn't afford one.

I went out, telling the Boss I was doing a bit of shopping; and for the sake of appearances I picked up one or two things. The fine spring weather is holding up and now we're past Easter the tourists have begun to arrive. Despite the chill, I see men wearing shorts so they can display their tattooed calves.

I ran into Sandra in the High Street. Her working hours are like mine: dependent on the clients who care to turn up. I had none today and she said she didn't either. How does she make a living? She says she has an online business from people wanting spiritual advice on the Internet. To my mind the fact that you look for spiritual advice on the Internet proves that you need it, but that doesn't mean it's worth anything. What happened to face to face human contact?

'Let's get some coffee at the Anne Boleyn,' she proposed. 'My treat.'

'That would be nice,' I said in my best polite voice and found myself wondering if she noticed that I was talking like someone drunk or agitated, who has to control what she says. But perhaps I wasn't. Perhaps the real me is overlaid with so many layers of pretence that everything I do is controlled and there's nothing to make comparisons with.

We sat at one of the tables where we could stare into the street and the sunshine. When the waitress came over, Sandra ordered fruit scones on a whim and I smiled again. I think I was supposed to say something, introduce a topic, but I've lost the habit of spontaneous conversation. I'm frightened that, if I open my mouth, I'll fire off something inappropriate and yet not know that I'm doing it. A bit like Tourette's, except that I'll reveal a guilty secret instead of shouting 'Fuck!'

'You write, don't you?' Sandra said. 'You've mentioned it. Do you have anything you could bring along to the Readers' Group?'

Where did this flattering suggestion come from I wonder? I hope I haven't suggested that I'm a Writer in the real sense. I suppose I *could* bring this thing-that-doesn't-have-a-name, this mystery-cum-autobiography-cum-shopping-list and watch them pop out of their socks. But I avoided the trap.

'I don't write for publication. I used to have hopes, the way that people do, but these days I just write ... you know: sort of autobiographical bits and pieces.'

'For your children?'

I shake my head. She doesn't know that Angela is dead. It isn't something I tell people because, if I once started, my feelings would cause the tangle of lies that comprises my life to come unravelled.

'Why do you ask?'

'Because we'll be talking about Janet's book, and I wondered. Of course, I write myself, but not fiction.... I try to help people with personal difficulties.'

I suppose she means the Wisdom of the Ancients or Revelations from the Ascended Masters.

She looked at me speculatively but I couldn't tell which way the conversation was supposed to go. Was she going to acknowledge that she's a fraud or not?

She changed the subject. 'What do you think about the murder?'

'I haven't given any thought to it,' I lied. 'Why are you asking?'

'You can be pretty sure that Janet and Belle will have been applying their minds to the subject, and I'm expecting they'll tell us the latest when we meet.'

We looked at each other, but I can no longer fathom what looks mean. It seems more than a coincidence that she raised this subject with me of all people. Does she know something and isn't letting on? I don't see how she could. She's seen only the persona I present here in Dartcross: this respectable fantasy.

She took me by surprise by asking, 'What's your husband like?'

That was near the mark!

'What you see is what you get,' I said, which is anything but the case.

'Mine is…'

I remembered that she'd mentioned him before: Mr Raymond Stanley 'Wide as They Come' Wallace – you don't forget a name like that. Divorced as I recall. Sandra is one of those women who will let you into the minutiae of their lives. Belle is another. It doesn't mean they always tell the truth.

'He used to beat me,' she said. 'Mind you, he could be generous – very generous.'

She gave me instances of his generosity but I've forgotten them. Between the pair of us I was no longer sure whose husband we were talking about. Was she baiting me to open up about mine? I had a sense of a subtext that I was missing. Sandra lives in Station Road. Did the Boss double back to her house yesterday when I lost him? Is she the mistress I don't really believe in?

She said, 'I wonder sometimes how typical my marriage is of other people's.'

'My husband doesn't beat me.'

Fact: he doesn't.

'No, I don't suppose he does. But can you understand what it's like in a marriage where he does?'

That's a good question though not an original one. Do we ever really understand the experience of the lives we aren't living – especially given the difficulty of understanding the one that we *are* living? I suppose it's a question writers like Janet have to wrestle with. I don't know if they succeed or not. To judge I'd have to know more about people than writers do – more than *I* do.

Sandra sipped her coffee and spread butter on her fruit scone. Pastries are an odd accompaniment to a story about wife-beating husbands: part of Life's ragged plotting and lack of any genuine sense of drama. Like Angela being knocked down on the pavement outside school while I am in Moscow doing unmemorable things.

'I couldn't have children,' she said. 'Well, that's not entirely true. I lost one after Ray gave me a good pasting, and after that I never got pregnant again.'

She looked around and called for the bill and when it came, she paid, including my share. Then she placed her hand on mine and grinned.

She said cheerfully, 'Well, this is a fucking depressing conversation, isn't it?'

Back in the day – as the expression has it – our newly acquired interest in the London property market provides legal work for the gorgeous Oliver to do. Property also means furnishings and decoration, as to which Comrade Blok is wholly clueless. Left to himself the place would look like the bar in a Holiday Inn. I know this because I've seen what he's done to the dacha back home.

Now that the Communists are consigned to the dustbin, Ludmila need no longer pretend to work for the Ministry of Whatnot. Sergei Nikitich, basking in prosperity, lets her come to London on her own on the understanding that she is always with one of us. Katya doesn't come with her, of course. She is never spoken of.

As for Oliver, our previous suspicions are confirmed. He is a person of culture and taste and he ushers his three ladies around the galleries and auction houses after several visits first to the V&A, where, in his suave way, he gives us all a course on the development of the applied arts. Armed with this knowledge, Ludmila has the confidence to bid for various pieces and Oliver prevents her from being taken for a ride.

Sergei Nikitich does actually accompany us on one occasion. Since we all embarked on this new phase of life he is trying to acquire a bit of class and is tearing out his first decorative efforts at the dacha even though the paint is barely dry. The refurbishment aims at a style Oliver refers to as Dictators' Rococo: all gilt, plush and curlicues, with a scattering of statuettes of nudes like a gay brothel. We tactfully ignore him and, like many men, he doesn't notice as long as he's allowed to make a noise.

After some thought, Ludmila settles on late Arts & Crafts and the centrepiece is a Swedish watercolour, a quiet study of a woman and a little girl playing in a sunlit nursery, which must have cost a fortune. It isn't the Virgin with Child, but it seems more truthful: the sort of love we can imagine with our own daughters, Angela and Katya, in a house not too remote from our own. Sometimes, when the sunshine brings a dusty light into the house where the Boss and I now live, I feel the room dissolving into the one Ludmila created out of her longing: the room with pale walls, a rug and a scattering of toys on the floor, and a bar of light from the edge of a door that stands ajar, waiting for the girls who will never push it open and come in.

But it doesn't do to think of such things. Everyday life is full of allusions to other things and, if we choose to, we can read it as a code. At times I've found myself in W H Smiths fingering my way through the cards. *Keep Calm and Carry On* pretty much says it all. I've often thought that there is as much wisdom and insight into the human condition in a comic birthday card as there is in the whole of the Bible. Then again, I'm struggling not to go mad, so I'm not sure my opinion is worth much.

Meanwhile Ludmila finds herself free now and again from the sinister jolliness of Sergei Nikitich and off the leash in London. She is a genuinely cultured woman and, although her English isn't always good enough to follow a play, she enjoys ballet and opera. So does Oliver and he accompanies her to the various performances and they sit together and discuss the reviews.

'It's a good job he's a poof,' says Hermione, whose taste in music doesn't run much beyond *Les Misérables*.

I agree. In fact I suspect that it's the presence of Oliver as chaperone and Chief Eunuch that has persuaded Sergei Nikitich to allow Ludmila her freedom. What others make of them, I don't know. In our mid-thirties and loaded with money we all of us shimmer with good looks and opulence as we glide about Town and to select spots in the country. But Oliver and Ludmila have something more: an authentic glamour and mystery, and the sheer sexiness of sadness which all the wealth of the world cannot allay.

22

It was Frieda's turn to hold the next meeting of the Readers' Group. She and Harry lived in a rambling Edwardian house a little way out of the town up a lane lined by hawthorns with a view over the river. A money pit in Sandra's opinion. Far too big for a modern family and with more defects and inconveniences than turned up in a survey. The sort of place that is a trap for people who have fantasies of what they will do if they move to the West Country. Open a commune or an ashram or a Rudolf Steiner school or fill the six bedrooms with an organic vegan B&B. There was no limit to the daft ideas people had. Sandra knew because she made a living out of them.

Frieda had been a teacher, she said – like Belle, come to think of it. Arty stuff with a bit of RI thrown in. Not a skill set easily adapted to the fashion for targets and testing the kids every other week, which was why she'd got out; that and occasional bouts of depression. Harry had been 'a builder', which Sandra suspected meant unemployed and living by his wits half the time. At weekends he'd supplement his earnings playing bass guitar in an Elvis tribute band with occasional solo pub gigs as Johnny Cash. A small inheritance allowed them to move from Doncaster to their white elephant in Dartcross.

'Don't buy a house when you're recovering from depression,' Frieda advised Sandra during one of their heart to hearts over a bottle of Rioja. 'It should have been obvious really; you wouldn't have thought I'd need telling, would you? We had a notion we could make money taking on a fixer-upper. I'd keep us going with craft classes and a bit of B&B as we did up the bedrooms, and Harry would do the actual repairs.'

'And how did that work out?' Sandra asked, though she

had a good idea. The place was old and smelled of damp and dog and things mouldering in odd corners and behind the wallpaper; and Frieda's housekeeping skills struggled to keep pace with her artistic ones. The floors that weren't sticky were crunchy.

'Harry's discovered he isn't up to anything on this scale. It costs thousands just to scaffold out three storeys so you can paint the place or point the brickwork or fix the roof. And as for the drains, they go on for hundreds of feet and are half collapsed and backing up every other week.'

A couple of bedrooms had been recovered for civilisation and housed the occasional tourist, but the craft classes came to nothing. Frieda had opened her shop to sell vintage clothing, for which, Sandra admitted, she had an eye, but it did little more than cover the rent and council tax.

'If we had the capital we could finish the repairs and either make a go of things or sell up for a profit, but the fact is we're skint. We tried the bank but no one is going to lend to folk our age living on a teacher's pension and bits and pieces.'

Sandra tried to imagine this amiable, elderly couple asking for a loan: Frieda with her goofy teeth, smoker's cough and taste for 1960's clothes and Harry with his Elvis quiff and Western threads.

'Banks are bloody unreasonable,' she agreed.

It was Sandra who proposed they bring forward the next meeting of the Group, making it two weeks instead of the usual four since the last one, and that they read one of Janet's books.

I must have been pissed, she thought, trying to work out why she'd done it. Janet was a new face and she'd wanted to be nice; that was half an explanation. Then again there was something a bit glamorous about the other woman, what with her good looks for someone who wouldn't see sixty again, her clothes sense, and her shrewd intelligence. Not to mention that she was a writer, which had to count for something even if no one had ever heard of her.

Belle, whose sociability could wear you out, had given Sandra the lowdown on her friend over another bottle of Rioja. This was on Monday afternoon at the brasserie when things were quiet except for a handful of prosperous retirees settling into alcoholism disguised as lunch. Belle was on her way to the police station to check if someone had handed in her lost mobile phone, which seemed a waste of time to Sandra, given how unlikely it was. It wasn't a planned meeting but in Dartcross women of mature years were always bumping into each other like dodgem cars. Sandra ushered Belle into the brasserie and they were well into their first glass of wine and a plate of falafel before she noticed the lively table of other diners and said to herself, 'This lunchtime boozing is getting a bit too often.'

And then the bombshell, though it came as a throwaway remark among the general chat about people and the next meeting of the Group.

'There were folk as believed she'd murdered her husband,' Belle said, speaking of Janet, and adding quickly, 'Not that there was any truth in it.' Her voice had an excited note as if in her heart she wished it had been true. Sandra understood. She was always half-wishing disasters on people she claimed to like, partly out of *schadenfreude* but mostly for the sake of the gossip. She didn't suppose it was any different for Belle.

'She even solved a murder,' Belle said. 'Mind you, it was someone who was best off dead, so no one was too fussed about handing the murderer in. A bit naughty, I suppose.'

'You mean the murderer went free?'

'She was a nice enough woman and no harm in her. I don't think she'll make a habit of it. It's only serial killers and characters in detective stories who get a taste for slaughter. I fancy that for your average murderer it's a once in a lifetime thing like parachute jumping on your ninetieth birthday.'

Sandra was still taking this in when Belle rambled off into the history of Janet's daughter Helen and her husband, Horrible Henry, and then started on her own family and her marriage to the late Charlie. In return Sandra told her tale of connubial bliss with Mr 'Wide as They Come' Wallace, skating over the more difficult details of his colourful career before they finished the bottle and wound up with some general conclusions about Life, the Universe and Fellas.

Afterwards Sandra mulled over the surprising revelations about the formidable Janet. She thought that Belle had told rather more than she should have: in a small way betraying the confidences of her friend. What would Janet have thought if she'd overheard? It was sad really, but it was what friends did to each other, often out of unrecognised envy or malice; and, of course, it was a blessing for psychics such as herself, because you could always turn this stuff into Revelations from the Beyond. Sandra was more guarded than people thought when it came to throwing light on the shady corners of her own life.

Then Thursday came. Frieda exiled Harry and the dog to the Ring o' Bells and tidied up the large draughty drawing room hung with knitted and appliqué artworks she'd made in her classes: objects conveying the impression that Doncaster must be more 'ethnic' than one first imagined. Her taste in furnishings ran to the clutter of a lifetime, the room dominated by blonde wood chairs, orange upholstery and bookshelves picked up at Habitat when she and Harry were still newly married; and no doubt somewhere there was an unused fondue set or chicken brick gathering a sticky film in the back of a kitchen cupboard. The floor was imperfectly sanded floorboards, scarred from innumerable plumbing and wiring jobs and partly hidden by a scattering of those cheap and never especially interesting *kilims* people had bought as much for the exotic word as for the rugs themselves, and which dogs and the course of years had left looking tatty. The shelves held well-worn Thames & Hudson art books, crime fiction and Booker Prize short lists. Frieda hadn't been immune to *Fifty Shades of Grey* but had given up half way through when she wanted to give the author a good smacking on grounds of residual feminism rather than sexual gratification.

And here we all are, Sandra thought. Belle's little act of treason over lunch on Monday had affected her and depressed her slightly, though a glass of wine would soon fix that. She'd been reminded that we all harbour secrets and have our moments of shame. Not an especially profound thought, but it coloured the way she looked at the others tonight. After a second glass she found herself mentally inventing a new parlour game, *True Confessions*, with prizes or forfeits for the most appalling revelation. Covering up murder must rank pretty high, though Belle didn't seem to think so.

I mustn't drink so much. I'm losing it. Is anyone else keeping pace? Dear old Joanie, obviously, and she suspected that Diana, looking polite and demure, might be on her second glass too, but she was a cool bitch and would never let it show. What must it be like, being married to a vicar? Different from shacking up with the owner of a lap dancing club, that's for sure. Do they shag differently? In a restrained but sexily clerical way: something they learn at vicar school? The handsome Rev Pierce, bollock naked except for a dog collar? Oh Christ, now I'm giggling!

Sandra helped herself to some sort of smoked salmon and cream cheese canapés provided by Belle, slyly checking if anyone had noticed she was … what was the word? Shitfaced? No, she wasn't quite that, though it was a terrific expression; you had to hand it to the Americans: their flair for vivid language. It was a pity there was nothing more substantial to mop up the alcohol, only cheese and something made with prawns, and old faithful tortilla chips.

And then Frieda, as hostess, was doing the polite, welcoming our 'well-known authoress' (*that no one's heard of*) Janet Bretherton and reciting the titles of her novels from a list she'd pulled off Google (*and five will get you ten that we haven't read any of them except the one we had to read for tonight*). It was curious how everyone straightened up almost as if the Queen had come in, and just for a moment Janet was a stranger and they were curious about her.

'Thank you,' Janet said, and a lot more: stuff about writing in general and how she got into it and the whole business of being published and promoted (apparently these days by some idiot in Ireland, sitting in his underpants and working out of his bedroom; but that was the way of the world). She had an attractive voice, educated but with a trace of a Mancunian accent; and natural presence. What had Belle said about her career – something in the Local Authority? – quite a prestigious job, if anything in that field could be considered prestigious. Sandra was having difficulty concentrating: Janet's little speech, snippets dropped by Belle over lunch, her own musings: they were drifting into each other. Joanie was already nodding off over a large glass of Tesco's cabernet sauvignon and Jean, who'd taken a night off taxi-driving, had her nose in a pint of Stella. Sandra began to wonder if they would ever get to the book before she nodded off herself.

As for the book they were supposed to be discussing, Sandra had enjoyed it well enough, even if it was a bit short on sex and violence and the plot didn't make complete sense. Frieda – who seemed to know a bit about writing – said it was 'old-fashioned in structure but witty, clever and filled with post-modernist irony', which was enough to make you want to throw up, assuming you cared much beyond having a good read; but apparently she was making a compliment. Sandra thought Janet made an insightful comment when she said, 'I don't expect all of you to like it; after all you didn't each choose it for yourself and you wouldn't expect to enjoy a book picked at random in a shop, would you?' It was an invitation to be less than complimentary, but probably not one that Janet expected to be taken up. In fact the others said nice things – sincere or not – and made a desperate effort to ask intelligent questions. In Christine's case the effort failed.

She asked, 'Given all the hard work you put into writing your book, why didn't you write a best seller? You know: instead of the book you did write?'

Well, that was Christine for you, and Sandra wondered how it came about that she'd picked a halfwit for a best friend. Or had Christine picked her? Sometimes it was difficult to tell and you thought people were your friends simply because it hadn't occurred to you that they weren't. They were just people who stuck to your life like fluff on a woollen coat.

'I mean,' Christine went on, 'it would make more *sense* to write a best seller, wouldn't it?'

Janet chuckled. Her eyes lit up when she smiled. She nodded and said, straight-faced, 'That's a really good question. I don't know what was going through my head when I chose my subject and decided to write it the way I did. It does seem obvious now that I should have written a best seller instead. Or … what do you think? … perhaps I tried to write a best seller but simply got it wrong?'

Christine nodded in turn and let the subject drop, but Sandra began to wonder if her friend didn't perhaps have a point. After all, if untutored readers in their hundreds of thousands could recognise a best seller, it was a bit dim on the part of authors if they couldn't write one.

*

Janet didn't consider herself a vain or boastful woman but acknowledged she might be wrong on both counts. She hadn't proposed that the others should pick one of her books for their Readers' Group and was embarrassed when they did. On the other hand it did please her if people showed an interest and, she had to admit, she enjoyed being the centre of attention and giving short readings; they appealed to the theatrical in her. Of course there was always the risk that her audience might not in fact like her book, but in her experience people lied about that sort of thing to spare her feelings, which was very good-natured of them. The giveaway was when they tried to say something both literary and thoughtful, and instead let their mouths run away with gibberish. Other people's efforts to be nice were often quite funny but Janet appreciated the sentiment.

'What's with the stick?' said Belle as they left the house to go to the meeting. 'You don't need a stick; I've seen you – the Dancing Queen – tripping the light fantastic at the ceilidh with Sexy Steve.'

'I get the occasional touch of sciatica.'

'Sciatica? Right … why don't I believe you?'

'Because you've got a nasty suspicious mind?'

'Well, that – obviously. But you can't say you haven't given me cause in the past.'

'Then let's say I've had another stupid idea – a bit like the mobile phone – and I'll let you know if anything comes of it.'

'Righty-ho.'

And so they found themselves outside Frieda's pile, looming in the shadows of a fine spring evening.

'I wouldn't fancy cleaning all them windows,' said Belle. 'I'd be spending all my pension on gallon drums of Mr Muscle.'

Once they were inside, Belle rolled her eyes at the

furnishings, but Janet felt a pang of recognition: of the days when she and David, still in their twenties, had been living in a flat in London owned by a kindly white West Indian landlord; days when even an apron or a lemon squeezer bought at Habitat with their own money would have been a token of their aspirations: a break from their parents' lives of mills, coal mines, the Great Depression and wartime rationing. And with that came the thought that none of us can live in a continuous present but must all take a stand on a concrete version of the past: both its objects and its ideas. Which explained why the Readers' Group comprised *these* women of their particular age and backgrounds; and Janet felt an affection for them: fellow travellers all.

Meantime there were the readings and the discussion to be got through. Not too bad, really. Janet didn't consider her books especially complex with deep layers of subtext – they were murder mysteries, after all. On the other hand, some of her own notions and feelings crept in; as much to relieve the boredom of writing as anything else: nothing much more than mental doodlings that she left in if they appealed to her and took out if they didn't. She often wondered if they struck a chord with anyone else and whether it mattered. Did people look to be comforted by the familiar or provoked by the new? Both probably. They were unreasonable like that. Janet didn't think she had some Great Truth to reveal but she hoped she had gleaned something from the common observations of life and that she managed to convey it.

Tonight's group were the usual mixed bunch. Frieda seemed to have enjoyed the book and have a genuine understanding of the technical issues. Sandra had clearly read it thoroughly and made some interesting comments on the rougher edges of the plot. Christine evidently used these gatherings to talk about other matters, from holidays to care of grandchildren. Jean had something to say but it was in unintelligible Glaswegian. Diana kept her demure silence. And poor old Joanie – as Belle said afterwards – was away with the fairies. She seemed uninterested in anything except the previously mentioned forthcoming visit to Southquay by a touring American psychic. There was talk that they would go as a group to see her.

As they were making their way home afterwards, Janet said to her friend, 'I see that you did read my book in the end.'

'Yes, I did,' Belle agreed. 'Just don't expect me to make a habit of it. And, before you ask, yes I did enjoy it. If I didn't say anything, it's only because I didn't want to show off my degree in Eng Lit. Otherwise I'd have pointed out the resemblances between your story and Beowulf.'

'Beowulf?'

'I'm kidding. But what did you make of that Frieda's house, eh? It was like a museum to Terence Conran. Somebody had a bit of money in the seventies but bugger– all since. And what about her clothes! I don't know if it's summat to do with Dartcross – all this mystic New Age stuff – but everybody seems to be getting their clobber out of a dressing-up box.'

The remark brought back a memory just as the house had brought back memories. Janet said, 'I saw a dress in Frieda's shop. It was from Biba. I bought the same one so long ago I scarcely like to think; it was just before David and I got married.'

'Charlie and I hadn't met back then.' Belle looked wistful and Janet remembered that she had married comparatively late: Belle and Charlie, two fat people meeting at a dance class when both had wondered if romance and wedlock were ever to be. Tripping over each other's feet and falling in love over the cha cha cha and rum and Cokes at the interval. 'My time was a bit later than yours. I fancied myself as Annie Hall; bought one of them waistcoats Diane Keaton wore in the film, and thought I looked dead sexy, though, if truth be told, I probably looked as if I was wearing a settee cover.' Belle smiled. 'Still, happy days.'

'Yes, happy days.'

They paused on the slope of the High Street so that Belle could catch her breath. Light was spilling into the night out of the brasserie together with the music that would fill the memories of another generation.

Between breaths Belle said, 'Now I come to think of it – and you probably know this already – there's something I feel I ought to mention.'

'Oh? And what's that?' Janet asked.

'It's just that – well – that stick you're bringing home isn't the one you came out with.'

23

So, fellow demented lady detectives: who killed Mr Walacaszewski?

We had another meeting of the Readers' Group last night. After my encounter with Sandra and our chat at the tea shop I was nervous about turning up. Her conversation was so oblique that I'm still not sure what it was about. Was she hinting that she knows about my connection to the murder? Was she talking about the murder at all? My fear was that I was being prepared for some sort of 'set up', like the big reveal in a classic whodunit, when the detective gets the suspects together in the library and scares the pants off everyone before rounding on the guilty party. I wouldn't put it past Janet.

In the event, I went. Janet said her piece and we all told her how much we enjoyed her book, though Diana, as you would expect knowing her as well as I do, kept her mouth shut in case she let anything slip. And then in the general discussion Janet said a few things about her approach to writing mysteries. She has some sort of theory – I didn't claim to understand it fully – about arriving at the truth by following the trail of 'most probable inferences'. She quoted a proverb I'd never heard of but I grasped it well enough. She said: 'When you hear the sound of hoof beats, think of horses not unicorns.' That seems to make sense. Then again I find so many ideas turn to nonsense once you try to take them apart.

In fiction murders are committed by unicorns. In life they're committed by poor old knackered horses. The Boss for example, who explained that he didn't walk the dog yesterday because he was feeling under the weather; and this morning he stayed in bed – possibly because he was punishing the whisky bottle last night. In novels the murderer doesn't worry about high blood pressure and a swollen prostate. Well, perhaps in Ruth Rendell.

So much for Janet's book. I thought we were going to get away without any discussion of our real life murder mystery, but one thing led to another and the discussion elided from the original subject to the other one. At somebody's suggestion Janet explained her chain of reasoning so far. I can't set it down in all its detail because – to be frank – my powers of concentration aren't what they used to be (drink or dementia – take your pick), but I followed the outline.

Our victim, Stanislaw Walacaszewski, is a Pole. A bit obvious, that one, but I suppose it needs saying.

He arrived in Dartcross on the Sunday, the same day that he died; probably only a few hours before he was killed.

He didn't have any luggage with him and so was either looking for a bed with someone who knew him or he planned to return the same night to wherever he came from. A bit unlikely, given the state of Sunday trains.

As to the last point, Janet thinks he came from London but she had a setback when she tried to prove it because the hotel where she thought he was staying didn't have any Polish guests at the relevant time. 'So he probably came from Didcot!' Belle chipped in, which I think was some sort of private joke. I don't even know where Didcot is.

The revelation – which frankly took us all by surprise – was that Janet had recovered the dead man's mobile phone, which is presently in the hands of the police. 'Strictly speaking, it was me that got it,' said Belle. I don't see that it matters. It had nothing on it beyond a railway enquiry number and a hotel in Paddington, but Janet has a knack of drawing conclusions from silence. Her point is that Walacaszewski was frightened of being traced.

And there we are. We're no further forward as to who the dead man really was, or how the police identified him, or why he was in Dartcross, or who he knew here. I don't want to disparage Janet because she's been very clever, but what she's discovered doesn't amount to much at the end of the day. Then what can you expect of amateurs?

What Janet didn't say is that she suspects one of us, but I know that she does. She came to the meeting using a stick I haven't seen before. 'Sciatica,' she said, but Belle was screwing up her face trying to keep it straight..

Janet was lying about the stick and it means something. She isn't the only one who can see things.

Back in the Land of Oz, one thing I see is that Oliver isn't gay. Hermione thinks he is but I don't agree. He is cultured, not camp; though when you hang around with the likes of Sergei Nikitich, the Boss and Call Me Gerry you're not likely to spot the difference. I'm frightened for him – for *her*, Ludmila – because their safety depends on everyone else misreading whatever it is that is going on between them.

And what is going on, exactly? Are they doing the Dirty Deed at the flat in Rotherhithe, or a hotel in Paddington, or a weekend cottage in the Province of Cotswold? Please God (whom I don't believe in), they aren't doing anything beyond sharing afternoons at a Bond Street gallery and evenings in restaurants or at the ballet or opera or at a play. Romance is in the anticipation, and that is what I see when I look at them. Did I ever exchange such a glance or blush in that way? Did I ever flutter over last minute things while waiting for a man to arrive? The matching of the blouse and skirt that I chose so carefully from my wardrobe but with a judgment I suddenly no longer trust; the non-existent smudging of my lipstick; the colour of my handbag? Did I ever have my Mills & Boon moment, not in a paperback bought on a station platform but in the joy and silliness of actual love?

In public Ludmila has become inconsistent. That's how I know something is going on. One moment her manner towards Oliver is stiff; then the next she is laughing at a joke he tells, or touches the back of his hand when making a point in conversation; and so back to her previous formality. Beneath his light manner, Oliver is a much cooler, controlled customer as you might expect of a public school educated City lawyer. But the clues are there, simply in his presence. Were he really as he appears to be, and knowing what he knows, he would keep a physical distance from Ludmila; remember his previous appointments; stay at home and wash his hair. Instead of which he dances attendance on the three of us and I know it isn't on account of those two cold-eyed, materialistic bitches, Yours Truly and Hermione.

In the press there is talk of 'Russian oligarchs'. I wouldn't know an 'oligarch' if I fell over one; all I know is they are richer than God. I may be mixing my dates. I can't remember if in the mid- and late-nineties they are already buying football teams or not. For that matter I can't imagine why anyone would want one. But the clues are all there that by some species of magic they own all of Russia, and apparently the people are all better off for it. The Boys and Sergei Nikitich have something to do with this, but don't ask me what.

After so many years, the life is starting to tell on us. It goes without saying that Hermione and I are still gorgeous; how could we not be, given the amount of money we spend on our care and maintenance, though Hermione is a little thicker round the midriff on account of two kids, and has a few spider veins on her thighs. I can't say as much for the Boys, especially Gerry. If I have to describe him in these days, I'd say he is red. He is other colours as well: those of his handmade suits and silk shirts, the foulard he affects in all weathers, the flower in his buttonhole and the handkerchief in his breast pocket; but these vary with the seasons and the occasion. The colour I recall is red because he is red all the time from his forehead, via his nose, puffed cheeks and double chin, to the flesh of his hands, which these days sport a pinkie ring of gold and lapis lazuli engraved with his not-so-famous family crest. Not that it doesn't suit him after a fashion. He is imposing. Dignified. His voice has deepened and thickened as if with a mousse of whipped honey and plums. If you want someone to hold your money while you manage a football club, Call Me Gerry is your man.

And the Boss too, though not in the same way. He is still good-looking and, if anything, thinner than he was. But there is something febrile in his manner. He is short-tempered and sleeps badly. He drinks but doesn't get drunk.

These are bad signs.

Come ten o'clock this morning the dog was dying to do his business and fretting for a walk, so I took him for one since the Boss was evidently not going to oblige. The cat did her following thing. She can't stand the dog but has a habit of trailing him when he's taken out. If she was a man you'd say she was a stalker. I don't know how that translates into animal psychology. At some point she vanished; no doubt distracted by a chance for a spot of slaughter.

I discovered why the dog has been dragging his bum on the pavement until the sparks fly. He has worms. *(Note: Buy worming tablets. Tesco's?)*

While I was out I saw Janet chatting in the street with Detective Inspector Gregg. She was wearing a white dress with sprigs of flowers and an artful brooch; rather nineteen fifties in feeling. She prefers dresses with short sleeves and high at the neck to hide any crepiness of her skin. I do the same and I think it's wise if you don't want to look like a collection of bones in a linen bag. Seeing her, I smiled and waved but didn't approach. As things stand, they must be the two most dangerous people in my life. Whatever is going on between them, it's obvious she finds him attractive; her manner is full of small 'tells'. It ought to be ridiculous because she must be the better part of twenty years older than he is, but, seeing them together, it doesn't seem to be. I wonder why that is?

Whatever is going on on that front, I think it's incidental to something else. Sexual attraction so often is. I don't doubt she's filling him in on the details of her amateur murder investigation and he may be feeding her with information and suggestions, enlisting her help – though, now I think of it, at the Readers' Group Janet said that that was something the police and crime writers don't in fact do. In which case there go a hell of a lot of crime novels.

So is it just mutual sexual attraction after all?

I liked that dress.

Because I had the dog with me, I didn't go to Tesco's. I may slip out later for the worming tablets or suggest to the Boss that he get some in a spare moment between murdering people and having an affair. On the way home That Thing picked up our trail and followed. I noticed her licking her chops and there was a fragment of feather she'd missed; so I suppose another sparrow has gone to meet its Maker.

When I got to the house, I found no one there. I shouted upstairs and there was no answer. It was clear the Boss had risen from his sickbed and smartened himself up because there were shaving bristles and soap scum in the bathroom washbasin (yet again). In my absence he'd roused himself and gone out without even the excuse of taking the pooch for walkies. If that isn't suspicious, I don't know what is.

I made myself a cup of tea and decided to look for him. I took Slobber with me as cover, so I'd have an excuse if by chance I ran into him. I went by the same path as when I'd followed him: turning from The Pinches down the hill to Castle Meadow and then by Station Road and into the streets where I'd lost him last time. Nothing.

I was close enough to Tesco's; so to avoid a complete waste of time I tied the dog up, went inside and bought the worming tablets. No three-for-two offer, I notice. I suppose there isn't the demand.

In the end there was nothing for it but to go home, and, of course, when I got there he was sitting in an armchair reading a newspaper as if he hadn't a care in the world.

'Hullo, darling,' he said. 'Where have you been?'

'Dog – worming tablets.'

'You seem out of breath.'

That or fury.

He looked at me with that pitying look he's taken to lately. 'A cup of tea, eh? I think I saw some biscuits in the cupboard.'

'That's the cheap selection for my clients. We don't have any nice ones.'

'Well, I may have one anyway.'

'No! – if you open the packet, they'll go soft before they get eaten.'

'Are you sure you're all right?'

'Yes! Yes!'

But am I?

He went into the kitchen and made the tea and came back with it and a small plate with two pieces of shortbread. I'd treated myself to a packet when I went out this morning for the first time and even eaten one not ten minutes before I decided to go out again. I'd forgotten. I was going to accuse him of having bought them. I was angry because he'd been thoughtful enough to buy some biscuits. Even if I was right, what did it matter? The words were on the tip of my tongue when I remembered and held back, but I couldn't bring myself to apologise for my manner. I was angry that he'd bought the biscuits. I was angry that he hadn't.

'I found these other biscuits in the cupboard,' he said.

'Fuck the biscuits!' I yelled back at him, knocked the plate out of his hand and ran out of the room.

After that outburst, I don't know if I can bring myself to write about Ludmila and Oliver and everything else that led to this present moment when I'm a mad woman living in poverty in Dartcross with a man she doesn't love and who doesn't love her. Or I think we don't love each other. I'm no longer sure. I don't know what love is like. It changes over the years – from day to day – hour to hour – minute to minute.

We forget my harsh words and settle peaceably over our cups of tea – *and biscuits!* – and talk about the weather and the dog and the state of our marriage. The last topic is implicit. The Boss offers to administer the tablets I bought, which I think is a gesture of affection. People show love in small ways. Shovelling worming tablets down the dog's throat is apparently one of them.

Tea drunk, I tell him I want to work on my 'diary' – which is what I've decided to call this thing, and he says, 'Alright,' and slopes off to give Slobber a seeing to. So that's what I'm doing, but concentrating is difficult. Then and now become the same. I hear the Boss coaxing the dog in the next room, a low voice scarcely above a whisper. Yet between the syllables I also hear Ludmila and Oliver exchanging secrets and making plans. When they are in company they say nothing of these matters, but I'm not fooled because I can hear their eyes whisper when they glance at each other; his fingers whisper when his hand is placed on the back of the chair on which Ludmila will sit; her dress whispers as she places the folds carefully before sitting on the proffered chair.

But enough! Let's come down to cases, though don't expect me to be too specific about dates because in those days, unlike now, I don't keep a diary and don't need a shopping list because I have a woman who buys my groceries.

Sergei Nikitich tips up in London after a space of several months, bringing with him a man called Pyotr Afanasich Something-or-Other – it doesn't matter. Age forty or so. Chunky as if a player in a very rough sport. Formerly some sort of KGB officer but not a filing clerk I fancy. During the period I'm speaking about, I've seen his kind by the busload, and this one has only a walk-on part in my story.

To understand, you have to ask yourself: why is Vladimir Putin photographed without his shirt? We joke that the pictures are a little bit gay, but a Russian knows differently and that Vlad is displaying his unadorned chest to prove that he's not a gangster whatever the rumours might say. In contrast these days Pyotr Afanasich is tattooed from his waist to his neckline but this is hidden except where the results peek below the cuffs of his expensive shirt.

Some big business is going on. It involves Russian oil fields and Western oil companies. The Boys don't involve themselves too openly in fronting these deals, which are done by altogether classier crooks, namely the great international banks and City law and accountancy firms. In the edifice of the new capitalism we are just the rats beneath the floorboards, but like the rats we are always there. Gerry has taken to calling himself a 'facilitator'.

As far as I can gather the role of the Boys on this occasion is to do with putting the various parties together and arranging for more confidential conversations to take place, not to mention showing the uninitiated the arcane ways of Switzerland and the Cayman Islands. It involves a lot of travel, a lot of flitting in and out of London and Zurich and whatever the place in the Cayman Islands is called if I could be bothered to look it up. It isn't practical or desirable for the Three Lovelies to be accompanying our menfolk on all these jaunts. Sergei Nikitich never says why on these occasions he doesn't leave Ludmila behind in Moscow or at the dacha, but it seems to be a matter of trust. Even now he is incapable of reading us. Even now we are his 'Beautiful Friends', his 'Western Family'. Back home in Russia he can rely only on venal and brutal men like himself – but we? Hermione and I are English ladies. The Boss and Call Me Gerry are English gentlemen. We earn his highest accolade: we are 'very snob'.

So we splash money on a blow-out at *L'Escargot sans Toit* and then the casino the night before Sergei Nikitich, Pyotr Afanasich and the Boys are to fly off to Zurich on a trip covering the weekend. Oliver isn't involved. Sergei Nikitich, as his confidence grows, has squeezed him out of the inner circle entirely and his legal work is limited to the property empire, and his social engagements to escorting the women as Chief Eunuch. Accordingly tonight he isn't invited. 'I don't want give creeping skin to my friends,' Sergei Nikitich explains.

Ludmila normally drinks moderately or not at all, but tonight she puts away an aperitif and a couple of glasses of wine. Only I notice because the others are honking in self-satisfaction and too noisy to hear her silence. Drink takes Ludmila quietly. Her whispering eyes are looking inward in an internal dialogue and tears creep into their corners.

Noticing that I notice, she smiles at me with affecting radiance and proposes a girls' trip to the loo, bag and makeup in hand. Hermione doesn't see what is going on and stays at the table mouthing ooh! and aah! while the men talk rubbish.

Once we are behind the toilet door – 'What's this about?' I ask sharply and a little cautiously. I know that Ludmila no more needs a pee than I do.

She looks hurt. 'Oh, please, my darling,' she says, 'do not look so hard. I want you to do something for me.'

'Oh yes? What?'

'*Please* – you are normally more kind.'

'What do you want?' I ask, but more softly.

She smiles. 'I want you to book hotel for me – for weekend.'

'For you?'

'For me – and Oliver.'

'You're joking! You're mad! In any case why don't you book it?'

'I can not. You do not know how suspicious Sergei

Nikitich is. I have lot of money but everything I have to explain, every last *kopek*. I can not explain cost of nice hotel in nice place we want to stay.'

'Then get Oliver to book it. He isn't without a few bob.'

'No! You do not understand. This is surprise for him. If I tell him, he will not agree, but if everything is done, he will. *Please*, darling!'

I think: This is absurd. This is horrifying. I can't believe….

'You've known Oliver for what? Ten years?' I say. 'And you've never…?'

'No, never,' she says and there is wonder in her voice.

'But why a hotel? Why not your flat or Oliver's place.'

'Because it is love and I want it to be in some place beautiful.'

Love in some place beautiful. I understand. The risks are fantastic but there is a reason why now of all times. I see it when I catch a glimpse of us both in the mirror. We've become works of artifice and it's starting to fail. For all her beauty, Ludmila is a woman on the cusp of middle age and she has never known love. There is an urgency in her desire.

I look at her and remember that last month I missed my period. And I wasn't pregnant.

24

'I take it you're not going to tell me what it is about that stick?' said Belle. 'Not even whose it is?'

Janet answered reluctantly, aware that she was trying her friend's patience. 'No. It wouldn't be fair; not if my suspicious are unfounded.'

'Right. And when are we going to know that?'

'I'm expecting a parcel.'

'A parcel? It's like waiting for Christmas, living with you. If I didn't have such a saintly nature, I could get cross. Instead, I'm going to do a bit of shopping and drop in the Anne Boleyn in case anyone's about. And if I end up eating a Danish pastry and putting on half a stone, it'll be all your fault.'

'I'm sorry,' Janet said, and meant it. But she was sincere when she said she couldn't disclose her suspicions. Quite apart from possible misconstruction and damage to an innocent person's reputation, she was conscious that she might be accused of tampering with evidence. She was already on thin ice over the business of the mobile phone, and this was definitely worse.

So Belle went out, and Janet decided to resume the task of searching the Internet for whatever she could find concerning the other women and their husbands. In her first effort on Monday, in addition to the dead man, she'd checked out Sandra in her alter ego as 'Sarinda Heavenshine', Christine through her shop the Heart of Osiris, and Christine's husband Keith, who didn't seem to have an online presence. In the end she'd turned up nothing of obvious interest and found the experience time-consuming and disheartening, not least because it exposed her own ignorance so far as the online world was concerned. As she was well aware, there were lots of other sites she might have checked, if only she knew how: Linked In, for example. She excused her omissions by telling herself that someone without a presence on Facebook or Twitter was unlikely to be revealing their secrets anywhere else. But it was just an excuse and there might be something somewhere that she'd overlooked. People were more predictable than they imagined, yet they still had a capacity to surprise. For example, Janet suspected that Sandra was perfectly capable of posting a lap dancing clip on YouTube, as a memento of her disreputable past as Mrs 'Wide as They Come' Wallace. However, Janet would never know for sure.

She made a list:
– *Joanie and Kenneth*
– *Diana and Rev Pierce*
– *Jean and Stuart*
– *Frieda and Harry*

She added: 'Miss Scarlet and Colonel Mustard', then scratched them.

She began with Joanie and found that, lo and behold, exactly as Joanie had said, there she was on both Facebook and Twitter with 'likes' and 'friends' coming out of her ears and a website broadcasting her views to all and sundry. It was quite astonishing, given her age. And the old dear was prolific, too, which was a bonus, Janet supposed, though it increased the mass of material to work through.

Which all amounted to…?

Nothing, as far as Janet could tell. Joanie had a modest clientele for her services as a medium but an army of 'friends' especially in America, who to all appearances spent a lot of time roaming the virtual globe for like-minded souls – 'soul' being a word they used with tedious frequency along with 'spirit'. Joanie seemed to act as an Agony Aunt, dispensing advice on life's problems, some of it good if a bit obvious and some of it nonsense, and in addition expounded generally on the Afterlife. As a natural sceptic, Janet could take little of this seriously but clearly some people did, and that made her cautious. It might be that the motivation behind the murder lay somewhere in this miasma of New Age and Occult vapourings, in which case that would leave Janet where precisely? It was a possibility she didn't care to dwell on.

Fortunately there was nothing on Kenneth, which at least made the task easier after the slog through Joanie's gushing prose. Janet remembered him from the one occasion they'd met, at the ceilidh. An amiable duffer in a freshly washed and ironed track suit. She would have been surprised to find anything, but was thorough enough not to discount the possibility. As it was, he didn't really figure in her line-up of suspects, so it was something of a relief not to have to waste more time on him. She just hoped she'd have no cause to regret it.

Next she tried Diana and found nothing at all. Was that significant or not? It was hard to decide. In some respects Diana was the most sophisticated of the group; her manners the most polished; her dress sense the most tasteful, though Christine appeared to have a secret wardrobe of good clothes. Outside of the Readers' Group, Janet had never spoken to her and so knew next to nothing of her background. It was vaguely 'county' from her voice and general appearance, but that might have been acquired (she thought of Margaret Thatcher). As was often the case, you could put several narratives to a person's life and they all would seem equally plausible. Diana might or might not have a presence in the social media, and absence wasn't necessarily suspicious, but it niggled with Janet.

In contrast she had no problem finding Rev Pierce; not that there was a lot: only two hits. As expected, his name popped up in Crockford's Clerical Directory as one of the runners and riders in the list of Anglican clergy. Unfortunately Crockford's was a subscription service and anything beyond his name was going to cost thirty-five pounds. Was it worth it? It wasn't as if Pierce was in

Janet's first rank of suspects; rather he was of interest only because details of his career might have shed some light on Diana. More to the point, what was likely to turn up in Crockford's that would be worth the cost? Details of some Oxford college and a list of clerical livings. It was unlikely that he'd spent his days addressing the Warsaw branch of the WI or, indeed, that Mr Stanislaw Walacaszewski was a member of the Church of England. Janet reminded herself yet again that her investigations were no more than a piece of silliness and decided it would be doubly ridiculous to spend thirty-five pounds only to discover that Pierce had been a vicar in Scunthorpe.

As it was, she achieved as much as she could reasonably expect from the second hit. Dartcross parish church, a medieval building of Devon sandstone located on the High Street and dedicated to Saint Ivo, had its own website. It was full of goodwill and cheeriness and invitations to join various organisations and events with names that were probably intended to be inspiring but seemed oddly mundane (what was 'Sunshine Club' for God's sake?). However it also contained potted biographies of people involved in its mission, both clergy and laity. And there was Pierce: not the vicar (she was a woman) but a semi-retired supernumerary, who did clerical odd jobs such as holiday cover. The only interesting though not necessarily relevant fact was that he'd come to his calling late in the day, already middle-aged, after a career in unspecified 'business'. As a result he hadn't been a parish priest: rather some sort of industrial chaplain. The details were too brief to draw conclusions but there had to be a small chance that 'business' or 'industry' included an international dimension involving a connection with Poland.

Or possibly not.

Janet felt she could go mad with speculation.

Browsing the Internet with no clear success was

frustrating. Janet decided to take herself off into town on the excuse of buying toiletries at Boots, and perhaps drop in at the tea shop where she might run into Belle or one of the other women. She was walking along the stretch of Tudor arcading by the Toy Museum when Stephen Gregg called out from the other side of the street and came over. He looked his usual cheerful self and was wearing his familiar smart but not very stylish tweed jacket and twill trousers.

He asked, 'What news on the Rialto?'

'Well, yesterday I talked to the Readers' Group about one of my books, and just at this moment I'm looking to buy some foundation cream'– actually it was itchy skin cream but she wasn't going to say that –'so, all in all, the Rialto is fairly quiet. And you, do you have any plans for returning to London?'

'Not immediately. Soon, perhaps.'

They were silent for a moment where ordinary friends would have slid easily into a new subject and mere acquaintances glanced at their watches and said goodbye.

Then he said, 'You don't intend to ask me about the murder investigation?'

Janet was surprised he raised the subject. 'I wasn't going to bother since you told me it wasn't your business and, by implication, not mine either.'

'That's true enough.' He grinned. 'Still, I heard a little story at the station. It isn't confidential; so I think I can share it.'

'Oh?'

'Apparently, on Monday a woman paid a visit to enquire about lost property. It seems a friend had dropped a mobile phone on the path by the river on a Sunday two weeks before. Had it been handed in? Yes, it seems that it had been.'

'That was fortunate.'

'Yes. But then the surprise. It turns out that the phone that had been handed in wasn't the one lost by the lady's friend, which was an altogether different model that remains well and truly lost. We know this because the woman returned, apologised, and gave the phone back – which was public spirited in the circumstances, because the thing was one of those pay-as-you go affairs that you buy for next to nothing with five pounds of credit already on it. Most people wouldn't have bothered. They'd recognise that, after doing nothing for more than a fortnight, the true owner had probably written it off and bought a replacement.'

'Yes, I imagine so.'

'I mean – speaking personally, and I'm a policeman and tolerably honest – I wouldn't have gone to all that trouble, but this lady did. And, what's more, she had an idea that had occurred to her which she wanted to share with the desk sergeant. Her friend – she said – had lost her phone on the very same night and on the very same footpath, where a Polish gentleman had been murdered. What if…? Are you with me?'

'I think so.'

'What if *this* phone – the one that didn't belong to her friend – belonged instead to the dead man? Had that occurred to the police?'

'And had it?' Janet asked.

'No – and I may add that the investigating officers are very grateful for the steer, because it seems the phone *did* belong to the dead man. Not, I fancy, that they would appreciate any more help from that direction.'

'Still,' said Janet, 'it's good to know that an outsider can make a useful contribution Do you know who it was?'

'According to the desk sergeant, it was a fat woman, a *very* fat woman, but unfortunately he didn't take down her particulars correctly; at all events we've been unable to locate her.'

'I'm surprised you've tried. I mean: if she was just a helpful member of the public.'

'Perhaps the investigating team wants to thank her.'

'I see.'

They paused again, but this time each of them was unashamedly taking in the other's expression. Janet broke the silence by saying, 'If your helpful fat member of the public was giving some thought to the murder and the investigating team wanted to show a mark of appreciation, it may be she'd like to know how the police managed to identify the dead man. It might give her more helpful ideas. It would be a way of saying thanks.'

Stephen smiled. 'Yes, if only things worked like that. I can't say. I don't know. But I'm sure the team used one of the standard methods for identifying people at the scene of a crime.' And this time, in the pause, he did check his watch before changing the subject. He said, 'I have to go, but before I do: tomorrow is Saturday and I was wondering…'

Janet had to make a quick mental shift. One moment he was teasing her with matters concerning the investigation (what did he mean by 'standard methods for identifying people'?) and the next he seemed about to propose a date. Surely…?

'There's a dance tomorrow night at the Grand Hotel in Southquay. A big band and a dance competition, but the public are invited and there's general dancing. I thought you might enjoy it – I thought *we* might enjoy it.'

Janet didn't take any time to think. She said calmly, 'Yes, I should like that.'

Janet skipped a visit to the tea shop and went home, where she found Belle had already returned.

'You didn't tell me you'd planned on going out,' Belle said.

'I was bored with searching Facebook and suddenly remembered I needed something from Boots.'

'It means we missed the postman.' Belle waived a red collection slip. 'It must be the parcel you were expecting. It's too late now but I think they're open for a couple of hours on Saturday morning.' She looked at Janet expectantly, but getting no reaction said, 'So how did your researches go? Find a smoking gun?'

'If I did, I didn't recognise it. So far I haven't found anybody with a link to Poland.'

'Maybe you won't. Maybe Walacaszewski's nationality isn't important. Maybe he was just a Polish plumber who did a bad job on somebody's central heating. The world's full of Polish plumbers from what I hear, so the law of averages says that some of them must get themselves murdered. Speaking generally, people hate plumbers more than they hate Poles, so, if you're looking for a motive...'

'You may be right,' Janet acknowledged and offered to make tea for both of them. Busying in the kitchen gave her opportunity to collect her thoughts. Belle's point was a good one of course. In the nature of things, everybody had to come from somewhere, and it didn't follow that that 'somewhere' was important. But if it wasn't, that left Janet where precisely? Walacaszewski's nationality was the only concrete fact as to his identity, and without the victim's identity it was impossible to arrive at a motive and solution to the murder unless it was a random killing.

She returned to the lounge with a tray of tea things and poured for Belle.

She said, 'It matters that he's Polish. You're forgetting the time discrepancy on his phone, which proves he recently came into the country. He was too old to be an immigrant looking for work. Something specific caused him to come to England, and that "something" is the reason he was killed.'

'Always assuming that what we found was his phone.'

'It *was* his phone. Stephen Gregg told me.'

Belle gave a wide-eyed stare. 'Oh, we've been seeing Sexy Stevie, have we? And when were you proposing to tell me about that, my girl?'

'He's asked me to go dancing at the Grand in Southquay tomorrow evening.'

' *"He's asked me to go dancing at the Grand,"* says Her Ladyship, coming the innocent. Is it sex or is there more to your pension than you've told me about?'

Janet couldn't answer. There was nothing to do but join in Belle's laughter at her predicament.

That evening Janet went online again to find what she could about Jean and her husband Stuart. In Jean's case she had volunteered that she subscribed to both Facebook and Twitter and welcomed Janet as a 'friend'. She had even posted a couple of short clips on Instagram. These comprised a video of relatives getting drunk at a family party and a dog making a mess on the carpet probably at the same party. There was no accounting for other people's sense of humour or their attitude to privacy.

Jean was a prolific correspondent with her virtual friends and happy to record the minutiae of her own life and her opinions about media stories involving 'celebrities' Janet had never heard of. Hints in the various postings confirmed the outline Janet had gleaned in conversation at the Readers' Group and the ceilidh. Jean had been raised in Glasgow, given birth to four children and worked as a shop manageress until she and Stuart had moved to Dartcross. Her relationship with her children was chaotic, switching from affection to estrangement seemingly every other week in ways that would provide material for a decent Reality TV show, but no more so than millions of other families. Was this history authentic? Janet had to admit it felt like it, and that if anybody had knocked Stanislaw Walacaszewski on the head because of some faulty plumbing, Jean was a prime candidate; but if he was killed for some other reason it was difficult to see what it was. The only puzzling note in her story was the move from working class Glasgow to genteel Dartcross. It wasn't something one would expect and nothing Janet found explained it.

She switched from Jean to Stuart. Like the other

husbands, he wasn't interested in the social media, but he did get a mention on a website for Wizard Taxis, which turned out to be a two-man firm run by Stuart and a jolly-looking man called Barry. The website was one of the simple kind generated by DIY software: little more than a couple of photographs and some contact details. Unsurprisingly there was no biographical information. Janet probed the theory that the amiable Barry was an old friend living in Dartcross for his own reasons, who'd invited his mate Stuart to join him in their small business. It was plausible as an explanation of the move from Glasgow but there wasn't a shred of evidence to prove it was true. Janet parked the idea as one to follow-up as necessary but didn't think it would be.

And that was surely enough for one day? Belle was calling from the kitchen to say their fish dinner was almost ready; so Janet logged off and shut down her laptop.

'Any joy?' Belle asked over their meal.

Janet looked up bleakly. 'I've no idea. I'm not even sure what I'm looking for. Some sort of connection to Walacaszewski or to Poland, I suppose; but I'm not finding it.'

'I don't really know why you're bothering. I mean: it was fun to start with and I'll agree you've been a bit clever; but hasn't it ever occurred to you that you're barking up the wrong tree? Your suspicions, as I recall, started with that newspaper and somebody drawing a circle around the article about the murder. Hasn't it always been a bit of a stretch to think it means that one of us women is somehow involved?'

'People don't draw circles around articles without a reason,' Janet insisted.

'I agree. But there's reasons and reasons. Maybe the article gave a clue to solving a crossword puzzle? Maybe it was something about the *path*, not the *body* that attracted her interest? I'm only saying that there could be an innocent explanation we just haven't thought of.'

Janet decided she was too tired for this. 'I'm not going to argue with you. You may be right but there's no harm in carrying on.' To close the subject she suggested they wash the dishes. She would wash and Belle would dry. A sort of peace treaty. Afterwards they settled to watch the television; or, rather, Belle watched and Janet brooded over the case, torn between following the slender thread of clues and recognising her own foolishness.

Stephen Gregg had said the police identified the body using what he called 'standard methods for identifying people at the scene of a crime'. What had he meant by that? Not checking lists of missing persons or tips from the public. Something forensic was implied. DNA would qualify. So would fingerprints. But each would require a database. And what in turn did that mean?

She turned to Belle and said, 'You're going to hate me for this.'

Belle gave her a leery look. 'I suppose that means you've been Thinking. OK, go on. Spit it out.'

'Stanislaw Walacaszewski was a criminal.'

25

This morning I woke up suddenly – yanked out of sleep by a crushing headache. It passed but it's left me frightened. I've tried *baryta carbonicum* and *lycopodium* but to no noticeable effect. I keep asking myself if I should go to the regular doctor's. The memory lapses, the odd moments of confusion and now the headache: do these mean something or am I simply plucking symptoms out of the air and the true problem is depression and anxiety? I tell myself there's no risk in going; when all's said and done I've been seeing Doc O'Malley for years with no problems except a cupboard full of medicines I don't take and don't know how to get rid of. Yet this time I have an awful feeling that, if I see him, my world will come apart. I'll tell him everything. I shan't be able to stop myself.

The Boss is out with the dog. The cat is hunting for victims. I wander around the house, glimpsing reflections of an old hag in a worn flannelette dressing gown the sickly colour of raspberry milkshake. I'd get dressed but don't know what to wear. An Evil Fairy has filled my wardrobe with things I don't like.

How do I feel at the thought of dying?

Hmm … so-so. Not too fussed. I can live with it.

The plan for the day? I think I have a client at ten. Janice? Alison? Is there a difference? Half an hour of tea and sympathy – an hour if I can stretch it out, because we need the money.

The client was Edwin. He has an itchy skin rash, but at our age don't we all? He showed me his forearm which looks like it's covered in cheese rind; I declined to look at the rest of him. Afterwards I wandered into town for no particular reason. I saw Belle to wave at but didn't stop to speak. These days when I open my mouth I feel an urge to rant or confess – one or the other. I suspect I've written this before, and that says a lot about me, too.

For want of anything better to do, I made my way to the little complex of streets off the bottom end of Station Road towards the roundabout where I lost the Boss on Tuesday when I followed him. Perhaps I had an idea of spotting him and discovering what he was up to. Instead, in Station Road itself, I bumped into Detective Inspector Gregg and we exchanged a few words.

I'm running late,' he said. 'Not at all like me.' Cheery manner as always. Lovely deep voice.

'You're staying near here?'

'Sharing a house with another copper.'

'And working on Saturday?'

'Nothing better to do, and the sooner I finish here, the sooner I get home to London.'

Well, that all sounds innocent enough, I suppose, though I noticed that he didn't say what his business in Dartcross was. But why should he? As I recall he was here before Mr Walacaszewski got topped; so it seems unlikely that he has anything to do with investigating the murder. Janet says not, and she should know.

Still I have the feeling that I've seen him in some other context.

In the byways of Memory Lane, once I get over the shock of Ludmila's little scheme to spend a weekend away with Oliver, I'm astonished at her naivety. It's one thing to hide the expense of a hotel from Sergei's prying eyes, but how is she to explain what she's been doing with her time? Women like Ludmila don't take themselves off for weekends alone in a foreign country. Men like Sergei Nikitich don't allow it; and clearly she isn't going to tell him Oliver will be with her merely as a chaperone. His status as Chief Eunuch is contingent on good behaviour. Sergei Nikitich is naturally dirty-minded and suspicious, and on this occasion he'd have good reason to be.

When I put this to her, she's crestfallen and we talk the matter over. I suggest, 'Can't you tell Sergei Nikitich that you've spent your time in London visiting places on your own?'

She's angry with me because I bring bad news. She snaps, 'How can I say that? When do I ever go anywhere without my friends? I am prisoner who is never without her guards!'

We are none of us her guards, but this isn't the time to argue the point. It comes to me that the problem isn't the money, which can always be explained if Ludmila is spending it in our company. Neither is it Oliver, her would-be lover, or Yours Truly, her dearest friend, who can obviously be trusted to keep our mouths shut. It's Hermione. We are a foursome and I don't see how she can be excluded from whatever we do.

I can't explain this to Ludmila. 'Oh, is easy!' she cries when I try. 'Hermione is also my dear friend.'

Except that she isn't. I know that in her heart Hermione despises Ludmila because – whether it's her style, her intelligence, her culture or her beauty – there's something about her that's authentic. It's not that Hermione hates her; she doesn't even dislike her very much. But she does find Ludmila incomprehensible and annoying; and I think she would betray her out of casual spite without even recognising what she'd done. I can hear her saying, 'It was just something that slipped out. I can't tell you how sorry I am.' And she would believe this to be true. Insight isn't her most outstanding quality.

I say, 'I think we should try our best to keep Hermione in the dark – for her own protection.'

'OK!' says Ludmila, lightly.

So I make the arrangements because it's better if it appears the whole expedition originates with me and that Ludmila is simply going along with the idea. It's well known that we are in love with the Province of Cotswold and so there's nothing more natural than a visit to Blenheim Palace.

'Boring!' drawls Hermione.

And shopping in Oxford.

'Better.'

I find a country house hotel near Witney – 'four single bedrooms, please, and can you explain the layout?' I've read about Edwardian weekend parties and learned the routine: silent corridor-creeping in the wee small hours so that adulterous lovers may be discreetly paired. As estate agents will tell you, location is everything, and I manage to get adjacent rooms for Ludmila and Oliver. Does Ollie suspect that he's being set up with a romantic assignation? Let's not be silly: of course he knows, but he's a cool customer and doesn't let on.

Janet and Belle aren't the only detectives. For one thing I saw immediately what Belle was up to when I ran into her in the High Street for the second time today and she wanted to chat.

'You don't mind, do you?' she said. 'The thing is that I'm on holiday, and once you've seen the Toy Museum and the Church, there's not much doing in Dartcross – pretty though it is – so I've got a lot of time on my hands for gossiping.'

'You could go for a walk by the river,' I suggested, which only made her smile.

'I don't think so, do you? How shall I put it? I'm not exactly built for exercise. In any case, people get murdered on that riverside path; it's like Chicago, Dartcross is!'

I joined in the laughter, though I would have said Moscow not Chicago.

'Any road,' she went on, 'me and Janet are having fun scratching our noggins over this business of Mr W – not that we expect to solve the mystery: that would be daft, eh?'

'Probably.'

'Yes, probably. So I was thinking: what was I doing on that Sunday evening? You know: so as to rule me out as a suspect – not that I am one, a suspect.'

'I see. And do you have an alibi?'

'That's my point. My alibi is that I was at home in Clitheroe that night and I didn't arrive here until the following day, for which I have a witness because Janet met me off the train.'

'I see – no actually, I don't see.'

'No? Well, the thing is that, when you think about it, Janet doesn't *really* give me an alibi because she can't actually swear to where I was the night before. The fact is I was in the house packing or watching telly when Mr W was getting knocked on the head, but you only have my word for that. I *could* have come down here on the Saturday or early on Sunday and holed up in a B&B for one or two nights and no one would be the wiser. Then, after murdering Walacaszewski on the Sunday evening, it wouldn't have been difficult for me to take a train to somewhere or other nearby on Monday and return the same day in time to be met by Janet.'

I didn't mention that an enormous jolly noisy woman from Clitheroe might be a little noticeable in Dartcross, and it didn't appear to occur to Belle who probably imagines herself differently as we all do. She said, 'I put the same question to Janet: where was she while our friend was being killed? Well, she was at home in that cottage of hers – where else would she be? – and, naturally, she was alone. She no more has an alibi than I do.'

On the other hand Janet doesn't need one. But I do – that's what Belle meant.

'Of course,' she said, 'living on your own doesn't help. Millions of us can't prove where we were that Sunday night, even assuming we remember. Widows – single women – fellas, too, I suppose. A bit sad when you think of it.'

'I'm not a widow, though.'

'No. Still, it's funny, when you think about it, how many of us can't prove we didn't kill Mr Walacaszewski.' She paused. 'Not that we have to, thank God.'

'I was at home, like you and Janet.' Strange how guilty I felt saying that even though it's true. I didn't mention the Boss, who, if I have the timing right, was out walking the dog and killing mysterious Poles for reasons I haven't quite worked out yet. I didn't give him an alibi and didn't claim he supported mine. Not that anybody believes partners alibiing each other. No – correct that: nobody believes wives who alibi their husbands. The reasons are obvious. On the other hand I fancy that husbands who alibi their wives are believed more often than not, since they're not likely to be beaten up by their spouses if they refuse. When you think about it, the difference amounts to sexual discrimination. You could argue it infringes the human rights of female murderers.

Does Belle believe in my innocence as much as I believe in hers? She said, 'I thought that's what you'd say. I mean: where else would you be on a Sunday evening except at home? – especially at our age – not that you're as old as me.'

She's right. It is sad that our lives are so predictable. I imagine that even Sandra was at home when Walacaszewski was done in, for all that she gives the impression of having had a very racy past with Mr 'Wide as They Come' Wallace, when I don't suppose she spent Sunday evenings drinking Ovaltine over a copy of the Radio Times.

But that isn't what this conversation was about. Belle asked about my alibi because, for some reason I can't fathom, she suspects that I killed our Polish friend. I can only imagine I must have let something slip that makes me look like the guilty party and it hasn't occurred to her that I'm covering for the Boss.

Meanwhile, on our weekend trip to the Cotswolds, we

reach a compromise. Ludmila and Oliver will go to Blenheim, while Hermione and I will have a girly time in the shops of Oxford. I compliment myself on being a bit clever about this: priming Hermione with the idea so that in the end it was her who came out with it.

'I mean,' she says, 'just how much Chippendale does one need?' adding quickly, 'I don't mean you, Ludmila. Not a lot of it in Moscow, I know; so you get your fill while you can.'

'And me?' asks Oliver with a raised eyebrow – a bit Cary Grant, now I think of it.

'Oh, Ollie!' she exclaims but doesn't explain. It goes without saying that, if one is inclined 'that way', one is always in the market for a bit of rococo furniture.

So we patrol the streets of Oxford, Hermione and I. These days we are into haute couture, but we don't mind slumming it in Top Shop. There's a secret code in our laughter as we huddle together, inspecting each other in the changing rooms, cooing over the clothes while noting the stretch marks. We are remembering the girls we used to be: the days when we had no money and had to make choices between a lunchtime sandwich and a packet of Silk Cut; the cheap trips to London by coach; the long afternoons browsing the stores in the West End to return with only a pair of tights and a lipstick bought at Selfridges. We may not have known each other in those days and certainly have never admitted to them, but they are why Hermione and I stayed friends and why nowadays I miss her so much.

'Wits and tits got us where we are,' she once said in an unguarded moment. It isn't just philosophers who have insight into the human condition. Not that this was typical of Hermione.

I don't recall if we buy anything on this occasion. Probably we do because, for us, shopping is like breathing: we just can't help it. We return to our hotel to find that Oliver and Ludmila have got back before us and their faces are glowing. And here is the mystery. How long have they known each other? Ten years? Admittedly there have been long gaps in that period, but still it's a long time. Yet now, suddenly, love rears its head – for Ludmila at least; I don't claim to speak for Oliver. Nor do I know what's brought her to this state. I feel so close to her, but I have to remind myself that nine tenths of her life occurs off-stage, so to speak, in Moscow and at the dacha. It occurs to me that so much of my picture of her is made up of guesswork and stereotypes to fill in the blanks she presents to me. Sometimes I wonder if I see her or myself.

'How did you two get on, darlings?' Hermione asks.

'Wonderful!' says Ludmila.

'Buy anything?'

'But of course!'

Again I forget the details, but I know Ludmila picked up the things one buys in tourist shops: books about Victorian servants; biographies of Queen Elizabeth I; lavender soap. I imagine that in the dacha there's a scented candle that has never been lit and, hanging on the wall, a tea towel printed with a picture of Blenheim. These things are a wonder. You can't get them in Moscow.

In England, however, we still have an evening to get through before bed, so we have dinner together. Naturally Oliver knows of a Michelin-starred restaurant in one of the nearby villages, and, although it has a waiting list of months, he has the pull to get us a table. I expect it to be full of soap stars and City wide boys like our favourite haunt, *L'Escargot sans Toit*, but here the clientele are so rich and powerful you don't have a clue who they are. However we've had enough experience to get through the meal with a degree of grace instead of falling face down in the pudding with our spilled glass of *limoncello* – not that we've done that lately: practice has indeed made us perfect.

Afterwards we take the night air. The Cotswold stone is mellow by moonlight and bats are flying. In a show of cunning Ludmila takes my arm and walks with me, leaving Hermione to keep Oliver company. She presses my arm against her side and now and again her head rests on my shoulder. Our heels click on the pavement. A low murmur and occasional squeal of laughter come from Hermione and Oliver who walk ahead of us, but Ludmila and I say nothing. My heart is full of affection and terror for my friend.

So to our car and back to the hotel along dark country lanes: Hermione with Oliver in the front and Ludmila with me in the rear; mist rising from fields either side in billows caught by the headlights; the white ghost of a barn owl; a disc playing sparkling Charles Trenet numbers because Oliver likes French café music. In reception we discuss whether to go straight to our rooms or have a nightcap. Ludmila says she's tired and leaves us. Hermione sits on a bar stool and kicks off her shoes; I plant myself on the next stool; and Oliver leans suavely on the counter and orders whatever the ladies will have and a Laphroaig single malt for himself. We talk lightly of shopping and sight-seeing.

That night I don't sleep. I listen for doors opening and the soft hush of feet sliding along hotel carpet; kisses; voices; sighs. I hear nothing but the hoot of an owl in the silent countryside and the noise of returning revellers making a racket in the car park.

The next morning we return to London. Ludmila says nothing and I can't interpret her looks or body language. She is stiff and undemonstrative. Appalled at her own behaviour, perhaps? Oliver and Hermione keep up a light banter and to all appearances nothing has happened. We drop Ludmila at her apartment where Sergei and the Boys are back from their trip, half drunk and full of themselves and their own glory. Sergei Nikitich displays his bonhomie and in an expansive mood asks Ludmila what she did and how she feels but doesn't listen to the answers. He praises her for the 'very snob' tie clip she bought in the tourist shop and slips it into his pocket from where it never again appears.

We have got away with it, I think. This time. The thought of next time and the time after makes me feel dizzy with fear.

Then, next day, I get a call from Hermione.

'Who'd have thought it?' she says with an indulgent chuckle. 'Our Ollie has been inside Ludmila's knickers, hasn't he? And him a poof, too!'

26

Janet asked Belle, 'Would you do me a favour and collect my parcel from the Post Office?'

'Oh? And what did your last slave die of? Don't answer. Seeing as it's you, I'll do it.'

'I'm sorry if it's an imposition. I just thought you'd be wandering into town anyway.'

'Fair point. And what's your ladyship doing while us serfs are running errands?'

Yes, what? Fooling around with murders was one thing, but Janet had an idea she ought to get down to writing since she claimed to be a professional (if only occasional) writer and had proved it by cleaning her fridge and re-lining the chest of drawers. She said, 'I thought I'd try to finish my Internet searches – not that they seem to be doing any good.'

'Because there's nowt to find.'

Janet feared Belle was right. As likely as not the answers to the mystery of Stanislaw Walacaszewski lay in things not said rather than things said. She made a list of subjects that had sparked her curiosity.

QUESTIONS NEEDING AN ANSWER
Sandra – What was she doing before she came to Dartcross? More of the occult stuff?
Sandra – Why did she and Mr 'Wide as They Come' Wallace split up? She suggested he'd made his livelihood on the fringes and knocked her about. Where does he live these days?
Christine – What business was Keith involved in before he retired? What was his connection with Bulgaria? Does that imply business with Poland?
Diana – What did Rev Pierce do for a living before he saw

the light and became a vicar?
Jean – What caused her to move from Glasgow to
somewhere as unlikely as Dartcross? What was Stuart up
to before he took to driving taxis? Were they forced out of
Glasgow?
Joanie –

Where Joanie was concerned, nothing came to mind. On the surface she was nothing more than a frail old body sliding gracefully into senility with the help of a few bottles of wine. Her husband, Kenneth, seemed cut from the same cloth. There was no reason to suppose she hadn't been a medium for years and Kenneth's business (estate agent, was it?) sounded as tedious as the man himself – unless he was lying, of course, and had been a Man of Mystery: Batman in a track suit and comb-over.

That left only Frieda and Harry. Frieda claimed to have been a handicrafts and RI teacher, which seemed to be true to judge from the contents of her rambling old house. Harry was a barely competent handyman whose career suggested a succession of casual jobs. There were a lot of Poles in the construction industry. Was that the connection? Although their house was dilapidated and needed a fortune spending on it, that didn't disguise the fact that it was large and in a desirable location. Had they really bought it from the proceeds of a small inheritance from a remote relative? As explanations went, it seemed old-fashioned and rather contrived: the sort that Janet, when she was writing rather than fridge-cleaning, would have been inclined to reject for something more plausible.

She booted up her laptop and resumed her searches. She found references to Frieda's B&B business on TripAdvisor: several reviews that described it at best as 'cheap and cheerful' and one that said its no-stars for luxury were fully deserved. There was also a very basic website with amateurish photographs, a map and some contact details. She found nothing in the social media, which was largely par for the group. So far so consistent with Janet's first impressions and still the open question: where had the money to invest in this white elephant come from?

The problem with the list was what to do with it. Quite apart from the relevance of the questions (and they couldn't *all* be relevant unless the solution to the mystery was one of those, like *Murder on the Orient Express*, where all the suspects did it) Janet didn't know how to set about getting answers. She couldn't interrogate her friends: what explanation would she give? She supposed she might try to tease out answers by raising the various matters in ordinary conversation, but she wasn't sure she had that degree of patience or subtlety. Then an idea came to her.

Belle returned from doing bits and pieces of shopping. She dumped the package from the Post Office on the kitchen table.

'Well, aren't you going to open it?'

'I already know what it is, and it can wait. There's something else you can help me with.'

'Oh aye?'

Janet showed Belle her list of questions. 'What do you think?'

'Not bad. I can see the answers might help – as long as you stick with the barmy idea that one of us is involved in the murder.'

'Can you answer any of them?'

'That's not what you really mean, is it? You want me to go wading in and just ask. If the questions come from me, the others won't suspect anything: they'll simply put them down to nosiness.' Belle gave a theatrical sigh. 'What a low opinion you have of my character! Accurate, mind you. All right, love, I'll do it for you.'

Over lunch Belle raised another subject. She asked, 'Have you given any thought to alibis? Where was everybody when Polish Stan was getting done in? You were here alone in this house, assuming you've not been lying. I was at home in Clitheroe, ironing my smalls and doing my packing for coming here.'

Janet shook her head in wonderment: surprised, not for the first time, at her own limitations. 'I'm really not very good at this detecting thing, am I? You know, it hadn't occurred to me to ask.'

'Really? Well, Nosey Parker here *has* been asking, using my famous charm, and I've got the answers for what they're worth. Do you want to make another list?'

So they did.

WHERE WAS EVERYBODY AT THE TIME OF THE MURDER?
Sandra – at home watching telly on her own. No witnesses.
Christine – at home sharing her Wisdom with her online friends. Keith at the pub for part of the evening.
Diana – at home reading. Pierce presumably at church or at home – check.
Jean – taxi driving. Only two fares and the rest of the time sitting in the cab in the station car park. Stuart at home 'doing the accounts' (i.e. probably too drunk to drive).
Joanie – giving readings at a 'Mind and Spirit' event in a pub at Buckminster – should be a lot of witnesses but not checked. Kenneth at home.
Frieda – at home doing something incomprehensible with cloth and glue – Harry walking the dog or at pub.

'It doesn't say a lot to me,' Belle said once they were finished. 'Except for Jean and Joanie, everyone was at home as you'd expect on a Sunday evening. Joanie almost certainly has an alibi if you take the trouble to find the witnesses. Sandra, Christine, Jean and Frieda definitely don't have one, not for the whole evening. Diana may have one, but it's guesswork at the moment as to whether Rev Pierce was with her or not. Then again, is it the women who need an alibi? Just because one of us recognised that story in the paper and drew a ring round it, it doesn't follow that she killed Walacaszewski. She could be covering for her husband. In fact, isn't it more likely that a man committed the murder, fellas being what they are? Where does that leave you?'

Indeed, where did it leave her? Janet thought it over. 'The problem is that we don't have a reliable time of death: only circumstantial evidence suggesting the later part of the evening rather than the earlier because the footpath would be less busy; but even that isn't a very strong inference. Keith may have an alibi, but it depends on when he left Christine and how long he spent in the pub. We have no evidence of where Pierce was, though the church seems likely for at least part of the time, though probably only in the early evening. Stuart and Kenneth were supposedly at home on their own, and so definitely don't have an alibi. Harry may have an alibi for the time he spent in the pub, but not for the time he spent walking the dog unless someone saw him – and I don't know how we can check that. Do you have any thoughts?'

'I don't think it was Harry. Look at it practically. What do you do with a dog while you're beating the victim round the head with a stick or whatever? You can hardly ask Whatshisname to hang on while you tie the ruddy thing up. And you know what dogs are like. If it wasn't tied up it would be going bonkers while you were doing the dastardly deed. I suppose it's possible but I just don't see it. And you're the one who's always going on about what's "probable".'

'Yes, you're right.' Janet had to admit it wasn't probable. It occurred to her: 'Does anyone else have a dog?'

'You mean they'd be excluded if they were taking it for a walk? God help us but you *are* clutching at straws. Let me think. Sandra doesn't: we've been to her house and there was no sign. Christine said summat about having one – something "organic" or "spiritual" knowing her – but

229

I've never seen it. And I think Diana mentioned one as well but I'm not sure though I could probably find out. I've no idea about Jean. Does she strike you as the doggy type? I can imagine Stuart with a pit bull, but that's just my prejudices about Glaswegians. As for Joanie, I haven't a clue.'

'Is it possible to have an "organic" dog?'

'Probably, but only if you want fleas and worms. Look, let's agree that anyone who was walking a dog didn't kill Walacaszewski. Where does it get us? Barring Harry, we don't know who was walking a dog, if anyone, and even in Harry's case we don't know he was walking it at the time of the murder because we don't know the exact time of the murder.'

'He was walking the dog or had it with him in the pub all evening, as I understand it. That puts him pretty much in the clear whenever Walacaszewski was killed.'

'All right. So Harry's probably innocent. One down and a dozen to go. I'm not sure this alibi business is going to get us anywhere. We can probably exclude Joanie because of all the witnesses at that "Mind and Spirit" do in Buckminster, and, at a pinch, we may be able to exclude Keith if he was also in the pub all night and Diana and Pierce *if* they alibi each other and if we can believe them and if the alibis cover the whole evening, of which I'm doubtful. In fact I don't care for any of the alibis except Joanie's.'

'In books the murderer always has what looks like an unshakeable alibi.'

'What's that got to do with the price of sprouts? Are you going to tell this lot that they're cheating and they should go and get themselves an alibi like any self-respecting suspect?'

'Don't get cross with me,' Janet said softly.

Belle sighed and sat down. 'I've had enough of staring over your shoulder at that screen. My ruddy legs are killing me. Who was it wrote *Fifty Shades of Grey*? S &

M's got nothing on my veins when my support stockings are in the wash. Speaking of which, you've been trying to do some writing, haven't you?'

'How do you know?' asked Janet.

'You've cleaned the fridge.'

Belle went to lie down, doze and rest her legs. Janet decided she should get down to a bit of writing and so did some baking instead: lemon drizzle cake. Her head was spinning with trying to work out the permutations of evidence and probabilities in this stupid, *stupid* murder investigation that was never going to come to anything.

What was her latest gem of intuition? Oh yes! Stanislaw Walacaszewski was a crook. And the evidence (when she bothered with things like that)? A remark by Stephen Gregg that Janet chose to interpret in a certain way. He'd said that the police had used 'one of the standard methods for identifying people *at the scene of a crime*'. She'd understood that to mean forensic evidence of some kind, and the only examples she could think of that would lead to the victim's identity were fingerprints or DNA, and that meant they were on a database, which in turn meant they'd been recorded and stored in connection with a crime. Ergo Stanislaw Walacaszewski was a criminal, or at the very least had been a suspect.

Or a victim.

Or had been identified by his teeth, in which case he might be entirely innocent of any offence.

Or Janet had over-interpreted a throwaway remark that Stephen hadn't intended to mean anything in particular.

No! No! She was sure she was right. The only victims whose DNA was likely to be taken and retained were women who'd been raped. And as for dental records, there was no national database: the police would have had to have a good idea of Walacaszewski's identity *before* they could narrow down the search. Stephen had been trying to help her, she was certain of it. A small reward for drawing the attention of the police to the mobile phone.

Forget about murder. Think about lemon drizzle cake – Nigella Lawson's best – a favourite of David when he was alive and Helen before she married Horrible Henry. That was the trouble with favourite recipes: they captured your memories in flour and sugar. Janet couldn't remember when she last baked this one or why she picked it now. But, thinking about it, the memory was a tender one. After all, the three of them had been happy, and David's death and Helen's miserable marriage didn't take that fact away. She thought that, provided one didn't go to extremes, there was nothing wrong with these prompts to recollection. How else could she savour her life and enjoy it in its entirety if she never thought about the past? How could she justify her marriage as having been something worthwhile which she was glad she did?

The cake put in the oven, she recalled there was something else she was supposed to be doing. Working on her new book, obviously – well, hard cheese to that – but something else as well. The package of chemicals she'd ordered on Tuesday, which Belle had collected from the Post Office.

Also at some point she had to get changed in order to go dancing at the Grand in Southquay with Stephen Gregg. Another of her stupid ideas – well, his idea but she never should have agreed to it because…. Because.

She checked her watch. She still had plenty of time before Stephen came to pick her up. Belle was asleep; her breath purring through the bedroom door. Janet opened the small parcel on the kitchen table and checked the swabs and vials inside it. She went into the lounge and from the corner where she'd left it took the walking stick she'd brought home from Frieda's after the last meeting of the Readers' Group. Back in the kitchen she dampened a swab with cold water and ran it over the carved horn handle and the area of wood just below it. Then she applied the chemicals.

'And what are you up to, my girl?' said Belle, standing in the doorway, her hair dishevelled from sleep.

Well, there was no point in hiding the fact. Janet said, 'I'm carrying out the Kastle-Meyer test.'

'I see – no, I don't see. Who's Castle-Thingy when he's at home?'

'It's a test for the presence of blood.'

'Right. Know about that sort of thing, do we?'

'If you mean "have I done it before?" the answer's "no". I've written about it often enough, but only out of books. It's been around since 1903 and seems simple enough: a swab and two chemicals: phenolphthalein and hydrogen peroxide. Sherlock Holmes could have used it.'

'So, my dear Watson, you're surmising that this stick may have been the murder weapon in the Case of the Polish Plumber?'

'It's a possibility.'

'Why is it that nothing surprises me about you? But don't you think the murderer will have wiped any blood off? Call it a wild guess on my part.'

'I'm sure the murderer did, but it's easier said than done. If they used hot water as most people would, it would tend to fix the blood instead of completely washing it away, and the handle and wood are rough surfaces where traces can be caught. The Kastle-Meyer test is really very sensitive.'

'But? There's a "but" there; I heard it.'

Janet glanced at her friend, not sure if she was being reproached for not discussing this earlier. 'Yes, okay. The test isn't specific, and if I haven't done it properly it may be reacting with the copper and nickel in the brass nails holding the handle. In any case the blood isn't *necessarily* human. There's something called the Ouchterlony test for determining that, but it's beyond me.'

Belle nodded. 'I follow. It *may* be blood or it may not. If it is blood, it *may* be human or it may not. If it is human blood it *may* be Thingummy's or it may not. Is that about the size of it? Don't stare at me like that. You're not upset, are you? What's brought this on?'

Janet shook her head. Belle handed her a tissue and she wiped her eyes. Janet remembered that she didn't bake lemon drizzle cake because it made her cry despite the fond memories. And on top of that there was this ... this ... farce! She said, 'Don't criticise me, Belle, *please*. Help me.' She held up the swab to show the pink stain. 'I've been careful. This isn't from the brass nails. It's blood. One of our friends owns a stick and it has blood on the handle.'

'I believe you. Blow your nose. I do believe you. This is the stick that was used to club Stanislaw Walacaszewski to death. So, whose is it?'

'Joanie's.'

27

'Joanie? Joanie! You have got to be kidding. I take back what I just said about believing you. She's the only one among us with a half decent alibi, not to mention that she's too gaga or plastered most of the time to go murdering anybody.'

'We haven't checked her alibi.'

'Don't get all clever with me, Janet Bretherton. You know it'll stand up. If I make a couple of telephone calls, there'll be witnesses coming out of the woodwork to say old Joanie was talking to Big Chief Bollocks, the Spirit Guide, in front of an audience of two hundred at some pub in Buckminster while Stanislaw Walacaszewski was getting his head re-modelled.'

'And the stick?'

'It mustn't be blood that's on it. You made a mistake, that's all. You got a chemical reaction from some brass nails, like you said, or it's red wine or summat else. Get real, love! It's a daft enough idea thinking that one of us silly beggars is involved in the murder without picking on the least likely one out of the lot of us. What other explanation can there be?'

There was another explanation of how the stains got on old Joanie's stick but Janet decided this wasn't the time to give it. As Belle said: she might be wrong.

'Any road, what are you going to do with it?' Belle asked. 'I'm not traipsing down to the cop shop to tell them they should run some tests on the thing. I did my bit with the mobile phone. What sort of story are you going to come up with to explain why they should be investigating some poor old body who hardly has her wits about her?'

'I'll keep it for the time being.'

'You mean you're going to hang on to possible

evidence in a murder case? They lock people up for that.'

Janet nodded. She knew of the risk before she retrieved the stick, but, if she couldn't convince Belle, there was no way she could persuade the police to investigate an old lady's walking stick, which meant that she had to do it herself. The problem was that her tests might have compromised the evidence: opened it to challenge as being contaminated.

Belle looked at her watch. 'Hadn't you better top up your spray tan, wax your lady bits and put on your best thong? What time is Stevie Wonder coming round to pick you up for your date? And, by the way, that's another case of you going off the rails and carrying on like a fifteen year old girl with a hormone rush. If I was your mother.... Go on, get yourself ready.' She gave Janet a hug.

Stephen Gregg arrived at seven. He was dressed in his usual smart chain store look: beige slacks with loafers, a check shirt and a blue lightweight jacket. His expression was the vaguely puckish one that seemed to be normal for him

'Half an hour in the car and a meal before we go dancing. Doors open at seven thirty but I fancy not much happens before nine. You look very nice by the way.' He grinned at Belle. 'I'll have her back by midnight.'

'You make sure you do or I'll have the police on you.'

So they drove to Southquay in quiet traffic with the sky clear and Venus low above the horizon. It was that brief transition to spring when the emerging leaves gave a pale dappling to the trees before the heavy greens of summer. Either side of the road was the early flush of spring flowers: celandines on shaded banks, garlic mustard against the hedges, bluebells at the margins of woods. In the silence Janet had time to notice these things. In the silence … Janet wondered if she should speak but couldn't think what to say.

The Grand stood on Southbay Road fronting a strip of

sand and beach huts: a white pile in Belle Époque style with steeply pitched roofs, balconies, a clutter of extensions added over the years, and a few palm trees to convince holiday makers that this was the Riviera. Janet had been there as a child, never inside the hotel of course but having a jolly raucous time with her parents and siblings at a caravan site near the town. In those days she'd vaguely supposed that the Grand was some sort of palace where princesses lived, somewhere she couldn't enter even in her imagination. Yet now she was here; Stephen was parking the car and soon she would go inside for the first time. But first they ate dinner.

He'd booked a table at an Italian restaurant. 'TripAdvisor's best' he said to avoid any implication that he was a foodie. He had David's taste for *fegato alla Veneziana*. Janet mentioned it and he explained how he'd come across the dish on a holiday in Venice with his wife Anne and their boy Larry. This was six years ago, when David and Anne were still alive, though neither of them referred to that fact. Janet responded with an account of the two occasions she and David had been to Venice, and, because they were talking of holidays, she told him of her feelings about the Grand Hotel.

'There are barriers between different worlds: not just physical barriers but limits to what's conceivable. I didn't *want* to go into the Grand Hotel. I didn't even think of it as something I *could* want.'

Over dinner at the Royal George and then at the brasserie, they'd talked of their respective backgrounds and tastes in music, books and holidays. What were they going to talk about now? Please God not religion, politics and the state of the economy! And not health – Janet had reached the age where, if she asked her friends how they were getting on, they took her at her word and actually told her down to the last symptom and doctor's appointment. What they didn't talk about tonight, except incidentally, was their dead partners. 'When David and I did…' whatever. 'Anne and I once went…' somewhere or other.

In fact she found talking with Stephen Gregg easy.

'You're smiling secretly,' he said.

'Yes, I am, aren't I?' It suited her not to explain.

He was smart enough not to press her. 'I'll get the bill,' he said.

'You paid last time. Let me.'

'I will, if you insist, but I'd prefer to consider it my treat. I'm sure you have other things to do, but I'm just bored in the evenings: watching TV and eating takeaways. So, will you let me?'

Janet let him. It felt like a negotiation between equals and that was enough for her not to feel too obliged to him. Badly judged conversations about bills could be humiliating for one side or the other.

When he invited her, Stephen said the occasion was a dance competition. It had taken over the ballroom and a pair of adjacent lounges and filled them with teachers, pupils and competitors, glittering and overdressed for any event except this one. Elsewhere the ordinary life of the hotel went on and the regular guests, mostly elderly visitors in conservative clothes, haunted the doorways and peered in with an air of puzzlement or embarrassment as if they suspected something mildly indecent was going on among the chandeliers and gilded gesso and plasterwork.

Between the stages of competition there was social dancing to a decent-sized band led by a wrinkled trumpeter who wore a fez and a toupee. A blowzily attractive woman whose hair hinted at a complex history before it finally settled on blonde treated the room to numbers from the Great American Song Book. Janet and Stephen danced a foxtrot.

'What do you think?' he asked

'I like Cole Porter but I've never been a fan of strict tempo; it seems to strip the emotion out of the songs and somehow flatten them.'

'I know what you mean. It's the boiled sprouts of music.'

She laughed at that.

The band next murdered a Count Basie tune and the bandleader, in his introduction to the following number, informed the dancers with pride that he had once played in a Victor Sylvester tribute band.

'Is there such a thing?' Stephen asked. Then, 'Look, I'm sorry if this affair doesn't live up to its billing.'

'No, it's all right,' Janet said. 'There's something zany about it that makes me want to smile.' She gave a slight nod in the direction of two gay men in white tie and tails who were dancing very elegantly. 'I'm having a marvellous time, so don't be disappointed.'

In one of the side rooms, a woman dance teacher in a spangled black dress that, in Janet's opinion, did nothing to flatter her belly or upper arms was running a short class teaching a couple of waltz steps to a recording of *Moon River*.

'Shall we join in?' Janet proposed.

'If you like.' Stephen led her out onto the floor among the other dancers and they giggled at their stumblings as they tried the new figures. In general though, Janet was very comfortable with her partner. He was an accomplished though not a flashy dancer; quite different from David who'd been flashy without being especially accomplished. Quite different, too, from Léon, a young man thirty years her junior, who had once taken her up for innocent though confusing reasons of his own and who was thrilling to dance with. Three men and three styles and she'd enjoyed all of them and been fond of her partners – and loved one in David's case as much for his dancing as his other often infuriating characteristics.

They returned to the main room for the next round of competition. The two gay men did a European ballroom tango to the tune of *Hernando's Hideaway (Olé!)*, which to Janet's mind was one of the silliest dances ever invented, and gave the dancers the air of palsied chickens. Yet it was impossible not to enjoy the spectacle and the good humour and commitment of those taking part. She was clapping with everyone else when her iPhone pinged with an incoming message.

'Are you going to look at that?'

'Do you mind?' Janet turned away and took the phone out of her evening bag. It was a text from Belle: *Joanie's alibi is confirmed.*

'Important?'

Janet shook her head. 'No, it's what I was expecting.'

'From Belle?'

'Are you having a psychic moment?'

'Who else is likely to text you? She worries about you.'

They stayed until eleven and finished the evening with a rumba to *Besame Mucho*. The musicians were wearing white tuxedos and the leader put aside his trumpet to croon the words of the song: there in his fez with coloured lights playing on a backdrop of paper flowers. Unexpectedly, Janet found the banality of the evening transformed by the image of a night in Havana taken from one of the films of the late forties. In it she and David were dancing on the terrace of a hotel filled with mobsters and corrupt politicians with their molls; the Cuban orchestra had dark skins and pencil-thin moustaches; their wavy hair was black and oiled; their smiles said they had seen everything there was to be seen and been impressed by none of it; and waves crashed on the beach below. David and she had often created such word pictures to capture a shared experience and laughed at them as often as not. Janet felt a tear in her eye and hoped Stephen hadn't noticed.

And then they were on their way back to Dartcross. Night had fallen and the hedgerow flowers were pale flecks at the edges of vision and in the headlights they glimpsed a stoat dashing across the road; the scut of a rabbit; a road-kill badger.

Stephen Gregg said, 'Is this the time to talk about your investigation?'

'Are we making small talk?' Janet was surprised by his interest.

'If you like.'

'Why are you asking? You can't tell me anything, and it's unlikely I'll come up with something the police don't already know.'

'Like the phone?'

'Yes, all right, I happened to make a lucky guess in that case.'

'Suit yourself.'

They were silent for a minute. Then Janet said, 'Stanislaw Walacaszewski was a crook. You – I don't mean you personally – identified him from his fingerprints or something else on the CID database.'

'Very good. I'm impressed. Truly.'

'What did he do?'

'Not a great deal after a conviction in his twenties – no, let me rephrase that: nothing he was caught for. But he was suspected of bankrolling and laundering the proceeds of the UXE Bank Vault Raid in two thousand.'

'Remind me.' With few exceptions, 'famous' bank robberies were quickly forgotten and Janet couldn't remember this one.

'One of those bank holiday weekend break-ins into the deposit boxes of the rich and dodgy. Ten million in jewels, cash, and bearer bonds; but it's pure guesswork since the owners either lied to bilk the insurance companies or lied to avoid the Fraud Squad and the Inland Revenue.'

'Why are you telling me this?'

'It'll be in the papers on Wednesday.'

Yes, of course, Janet thought. He wouldn't tell her anything confidential. She didn't know whether to respect him or be annoyed. Both, probably. She said, 'You've known his identity for at least two weeks. Why haven't you revealed all this before?'

'I wish you wouldn't keep saying "you" as if you thought I was responsible.'

'I'm sorry.' Janet wasn't angry with Stephen. What irked her was that she'd beaten her brains out only to arrive at conclusions the police were prepared to give away for free to any moron who could read a paper.

'As a matter of curiosity,' Stephen said, 'why are you pursuing this investigation? Do you expect to solve it when the police can't?'

'No, of course not.' Janet wondered if she meant that. It was a novelist's conceit that the amateur detective was more acute than the slow-witted police. In her case, curiosity and sheer bloody-mindedness were more likely explanations, and it was obvious to her that, if she got anywhere at all, the police would most likely have got there first. Janet was an intelligent, self-confident woman and didn't suppose she could beat the professionals – and for that matter didn't care because she was doing this for herself. She said, 'I'm not really investigating. It's just that things come to me now and again – ideas – theories – whatever.'

She expected Stephen to say something and had primed herself to expect a comment that would be 'understanding' but in some way patronising. She forestalled him. 'Let me guess. The police didn't say anything because they didn't think this bit of history was relevant so long after the event. He was a petty criminal in his twenties and then a suspect in a crime decades later. What happened to the robbers?'

'Three of the stupid ones were caught and sent down for fifteen.'

Janet did the arithmetic. 'Assuming remission, they would have been released years ago. But Walacaszewski wasn't one of them. Did he give evidence against the others? No, he didn't, did he? That and the lapse of time is why the police think his criminal past has nothing to do with his death. The other robbers had no motive to kill him – unless, of course, he ran off with the money; and even in that case they've had at least five years to do something about him. So why now?'

'Congratulations. I'm impressed.'

Janet didn't answer. In fact she was mildly annoyed by the compliment with its implication of a superiority that came only from the fact that he had access to information denied to her. Instead she tried to imagine Stanislaw Walacaszewski from such facts as she had been able to gather. A man aged sixty or so; recently arrived in London before his mysterious journey to Dartcross; disguising his Polish nationality by hiding out under a false name in a budget hotel; using a throwaway phone to avoid being traced. Janet was fairly sure this account was correct though she hadn't confirmed her theory about the hotel, which had no record of a Polish guest on the relevant date; yet she had to be right unless the phone and its recorded numbers were a complete red herring.

Such as it was, the story spoke of some change in Walacaszewski's circumstances that had suddenly set him in motion after so many years. What was it? And why *now*?

'Were you crying during *Besame Mucho*?' Stephen asked, breaking Janet's train of thought.

'I'd hoped you hadn't noticed,' she said. But in a way she was glad he had. It meant he was someone who paid attention, and yet he'd been careful not to intrude in the moment. 'It's a song David and I liked to dance to.'

She thought he would offer something similar: he and Anne dancing to … whatever people twenty years younger than herself danced to. People usually did, thinking they were sharing a human experience without realising that sometimes we need the undiluted illusion of our uniqueness. She was glad he didn't unintentionally diminish her.

In fact he was silent for the rest of the journey, and at

the end smiled at her wistfully and kissed her on the cheek.

28

Because it's Sunday, I went to morning service at St. Ivo's. Although I'm an atheist, I try to fly the flag a couple of times a year. Dartcross is so damned respectable that I have to keep up appearances and, after decades of practice, if there's one thing I'm good at it's keeping up appearances. In fact I'm so good that I'm no longer sure of the boundary between reality and this illusion that I – *we* – have created. Standing there, sniffing in the dust and beeswax and belting out *Ye Holy Angels Bright*, I find myself wondering if at some vague date in the past I didn't go through a conversion experience, and that perhaps I'm really a Christian and have simply forgotten how and when I became one. It's plausible enough, the way I feel at the moment, and God knows I'm easy in the role of occasional worshipper, and comfort myself that Anglicans aren't too fussy about atheism, which they seem to think falls within the area of reasonable doubt. Whatever the case, the least-concerning of my sins is hypocrisy, which in my experience is often a virtue and makes for a more polite world. The main reason I don't go to church more often is simply that it's boring and there's a limit to the number of nice people I can allow into my life without wanting to throw up.

I give Rev Bev as an instance of the latter. After the service she stood in the porch glad-handing everybody as usual. She's one of those pleasant women full of genuine goodwill that I could cheerfully punch. She pressed my hand between both of hers, which is a mark of special affection and sincerity. She does it to everyone. In my case she also commented in a concerned way that she doesn't see me as often as she'd like, using her sympathetic voice as if I was on my death bed and she appreciated that I'd made a painful effort today. I forget what particular lie I told her to excuse my habitual absence, and I doubt she was listening since I've presumably said it before. I left her having a chat with the Boss.

I came home and busied myself with Sunday lunch, though there was no rush since we eat around five. The Boss followed half an hour later. The weather today is beautifully sunny and I suggested we might go for a walk or even take the train to Buckminster and have a wander round the Abbey. The railway follows the Dart valley which is lovely at any time of year, and I have nothing against Catholic monks especially when they make a fortified wine that's calculated to lift the spirits more than somewhat and reputedly does a roaring trade in Glasgow.

'I'm sorry, darling,' he said, 'but I've promised to see someone. Business – I don't want to trouble you with it.'

I hadn't meant to put him on the spot but it's obvious I had. I mean unexplained 'business' – what sort of excuse is that? A leftover from the years spent in the company of Sergei Nikitich and his ilk.

Then he surprised me. He said in a serious voice and as if he cared for me, 'I know we do need to talk about things – about you – about me. This just isn't a good time; I'm under a lot of stress.'

It was the first chink in the armour of lies and silences we've created between us, and I felt a flush of warmth towards him. But why hadn't he recognised the offer contained in my invitation? An afternoon trip to beautiful places. Trees, wild flowers, sunshine and water. Two of us sharing our company.

I was stretching out a hand to him, hoping he would pull me back from the dark forgetful place that frightens me. But he didn't see. Or didn't dare to see.

Ludmila is gone. Back to Moscow. Back to the dacha. Or maybe back to an unmarked grave in the forest. I don't know which because we don't communicate except face to face. She doesn't have a mobile phone. It's not permitted. This is a sinister change. A new edict from Sergei Nikitich. Has Hermione let slip something?

After her first stray remark she and I talk only once about what has happened. She says in her snotty drawl, 'Obviously I misjudged Oliver. He's not the fairy on top of the Christmas tree that I first thought; in fact, given how clever and secretive he's been, I shouldn't be surprised if there isn't a Mrs Ollie and a bunch of little Ollies somewhere in leafy Surrey.'

I can't say, but I'm reminded how, behind his suave affability, Oliver has told us virtually nothing of his personal life in all the years we've known him.

Hermione says, 'It's Ludmila I don't get. What's she playing at? You don't cuddle up to a swine like Sergei and then play a round of one-hole golf with one of his employees. You'd think she'd have more common sense.'

You would – and then again you wouldn't. As a species we're more used to talking about common sense than practising it. In any case it isn't that Ludmila doesn't see the pit that's opening at her feet: on the contrary she's staring into it in all its horrors.

I don't think Ludmila is frightened of death. Rather I think she's decided that she's dead already and wants to come alive again. The joke is that she's chosen to do it with Oliver, who, if I'm right, is nothing more than a handsome piece of emptiness. Ludmila is a heroine, but she's a woman like me, and in women's lives there are no heroes.

After this conversation Hermione drops the subject. There's no new information and so nothing to gossip about.

And then suddenly Ludmila is back, full of kisses, hugs and tears. The business of buying and selling oil assets – and incidentally robbing the Russian people blind – raises its head again. The pace is quickening towards some sort of closure. I imagine it as musical chairs with everyone whirling round until there is only one seat and one winner and everyone else is somewhere I don't like to think about.

Whatever the fate of the losers, the moment is full of excitement. Sergei and Ludmila tip up in London, but this time Sergei Nikitich has two 'associates' with him who call themselves 'Boris' and 'Vanya'. Both speak good English and both are sharply dressed.

'Ex KGB types,' Call Me Jerry lets slip, 'and higher up the food chain than Sergei ever was.' The comparison of a banker and a barrow-boy spring to mind and I'm getting a feel for ex-Comrade Blok's position in the scheme of things. On this trip he's toadying up to his new pals, and one reason they are in London is so that he can introduce them to his 'very snob' friends and win some kudos. Roast beef, cabbage, mash and the best jam roly-poly at the good old Empire & Dominions and they are convinced. Boris and Vanya are models of affability, but the Boys sit silent and rigid through the proceedings. Back at the Hampstead flat, it takes a litre of vodka before the three of them recover.

The next day they fly off to Switzerland leaving Ludmila behind.

Having had what passes for a heart to heart conversation in our marriage, the Boss made small talk about the doings at church. Rev Bev is trying to drum up support for a new campaign of evangelism. In my mind's eye it isn't difficult to envisage Diana listening to this and nodding, for all the world as if she is paying attention behind that impenetrable exterior. No doubt the affair will be given one of those depressingly inspiring names and various discussion groups and events will be arranged at which no one turns up except the organisers and a handful of mad people who use the word 'spiritual' as often as normal people say 'fuck'. You'd think she'd have learned from the complete lack of interest in the Alpha Course. Long after its failure the banner hung outside the church until rain rotted the strings and the wind blew it off. It was much the same with the Toronto Blessing which Rev Bev caught on some foreign trip like a dose of the trots. Dartcross is far too staid for that charismatic stuff, if you ignore the Pentecostals, all six of them, who hold services in a corrugated iron shed. People laughed when she started speaking in tongues. Talk about embarrassed!

Still, not my problem. The Church won't see my face again until Christmas.

Once he'd enquired as to the state of Sunday lunch (a stew in the oven and the remaining veg cut up and ready), the Boss forgot about his alleged business and announced he was taking Slobber for a walk. The fact that he forgot convinces me that 'business' and walking the dog are the same thing. And speaking of 'things', I haven't seen That Thing for a couple of days. As the weather warms up, she's taken to spending more time outside. The local wild life must be talking in whispers. I can't remember when I last heard a bird in our garden.

As for our conversation, such as it was, I waited for the Boss to say something about the state of our marriage, of our life, of my sanity, or whatever else was behind his remarks. Or at least give me a hint. But he didn't. Having told me that there are things we need to talk about, it seems he thinks that's enough for the time being. I've been informed, and apparently that's as much as is necessary until a more convenient time. How I might react to being informed hasn't occurred to him. He doesn't understand that conversations are more than exchanges of information. He probably wonders how many times I need to be told he loves me. Correction – he probably doesn't wonder at all. When all is said and done, we still share a bed, which is proof of his affection, isn't it? I can hear him say that in his 'reasonable' voice.

I'm having a quarrel in my head. I must stop

Instead I'll write a bit more of this whatchamacallum to make sense of this morning. Sometimes I think I have insights, but I have to set them down so that I can remember. I must choose between that and cleaning the windows.

In the end I can't face the writing or the windows, and so I go out. Because the Boss is a creature of habit, I have a fair idea where he's going and don't need to keep him in view. This time I take a book with me. My intention is to find a spot where I can keep an eye on the street I think he's visiting and wait for him to emerge from one of the houses. If he has another woman, I'll find out who she is. And if nothing happens, I'll be able to talk a bit more knowledgeably about Janet's detective stories.

To limit the risk of being seen, I decide to avoid Station Road and approach via the High Street, Foregate and Jubilee Road, which is how I come to be passing the Heart of Osiris. Sandra is coming out of the shop. I'm not especially surprised because she seems to spend as much time in there as she does in Tesco's, though what she buys is a mystery. She has just touched her hair up: it's bright copper and shiny with conditioner. (By way of an aside, in my lifetime hair products have improved enormously and I've noticed how many raggedy old things are walking about with the hair of a twenty-year-old.) Beneath her flaming locks, Sandra's face is worn out and liver-spotted. From all that smoking, I suppose. She also looks worried today, though she puts on a smile when she sees me.

I have no problem sparing five minutes for a conversation. Last time we ran into each other – was it Wednesday? – we talked about the Readers' Group and children and husbands. She told me that Mr 'Wide as they Come' Wallace used to beat her up and caused her to lose a child, and I told her about how Angela died. It's strange how bland these topics sound after a lapse of time. The years go by and we survive our tragedies by stripping away the feelings so that we can talk about them in the street to people we don't know very well. They remind me of titles for school essays. 'Children, I want you to write about Life and Death on two sides of paper. Please pay attention to your spelling.'

She says, 'Where do you think Janet's getting with her investigations?'

I'm not sure what to make of this. I don't know what she suspects, so I try not to sound guarded. Paranoia is a symptom of dementia. But also of a guilty conscience.

I say, 'I asked myself the same question yesterday. I happened to run into Belle and she quizzed me about alibis.'

'Alibis?'

'Yes. I told her I was at home. Where else would I be on a Sunday evening?'

Sandra thinks that over. She says, 'Belle asked me the same question, and I gave her the same answer. I imagine most people would.'

We're both silent for a moment but I can't read anything into Sandra's expression, though she asks the obvious question: 'Does Janet think that one of us is involved?'

'I don't know. How would any of us be involved? Belle seemed to be making a general point: that half the population don't have very good alibis for Mr Walacaszewski's murder. She doesn't claim to have one herself. She was alone at home in Clitheroe. No witnesses to confirm it.'

With that, we drop the subject. I don't think I revealed any more than I told Belle, but I'm curious why Sandra is interested. Of course, it may mean nothing if she's telling the truth and Belle is asking everyone about alibis. It suggests the investigation is getting nowhere.

'I've got to go,' Sandra says. 'I have a client comes for a psychic reading every Sunday at three. Speaking of which, do you remember Joanie banging on about Elspeth van Doorman? American? Psychic? Visiting Southquay? We discussed her at the Readers' Group, and Joanie's only gone and made arrangements for us all to see her. Are you still up for it?'

'Yes, I'd like that,' I say, just to be agreeable, and we part: Sandra to wherever and me to go hunting for the Boss.

As planned I go down Foregate, turn left at the bottom and walk past Tesco's as far as the roundabout by Caesar Bridge, all without seeing hide or hair of my quarry. My problem begins at the handful of streets below the park where I lost the Boss during my first effort as a sleuth. I don't know which one he went into, and, for my purpose, it isn't enough to hang about in Park Crescent. Granted, if I'm right, I'm bound to see him there sooner or later because it funnels all the streets into Station Road. But the point isn't to confirm what I already know: that he visits someone in the area; I need to see *who* he's visiting, or at the very least get the exact address. From my first attempt I've formed an idea of the most likely street. Now I see nothing for it but to back my judgment and keep watch there.

Keeping watch on a suburban byway isn't easy if you want to be inconspicuous. Certainly not on a Sunday afternoon in a street that's empty except for a man washing his car on the drive. After all, why would anyone hang around for an hour, doing nothing in particular? And why on earth have I brought a book? I try to imagine explaining to Mr Car-washer, that a perfect stranger has simply decided to wander into his unfamiliar cul-de-sac and while away her time reading a murder mystery.

I give Mr Car-washer as an example because, between plying the hose and the suds, he's fixing me with the evil eye. But he isn't the only one. My first impression of emptiness is mistaken. Two children are playing ball in a garden, a toddler is pedalling a tricycle up and down a stretch of pavement, and a woman in a glaring green blouse and purple Lycra tights is keeping watch on both them and me. Another man comes out and starts pruning some laurels. A third bloke appears, opens a garage door and does whatever mysterious thing it is that men do in garages. Surely sooner or later one of them is going to ask me what I'm up to?

Or call the police.

It's difficult to say where inspiration comes from. I'm told that dementia loosens one's inhibitions. Whatever the case, an idea comes to me. I take my book, carefully covering the title, and, holding it in front of me, I march up the pathway of the nearest house. I ring the doorbell and wait. An elderly man in a beige cardigan answers in a quivering voice.

'Yes?'

'I have a question I'd like to ask you!' I say as brightly as I can.

'Oh? You're not one of them poll people, are you? What do you want to ask?'

I breathe deeply and launch in. 'How do you intend to spend Eternity?'

'What?'

'Our Lord – do you intend to welcome Our Lord into your heart on the day of His return?'

He scrutinises my face, mulls the point over, and after an age asks, 'He's coming back, is he?'

'Most certainly. It is foretold in this book.' I hold out the book, which happens to be called *Death Cancels All Payments*.

'Is it?' He looks at the book though with more puzzlement than attention. 'Oh, when? Do I need to get changed?'

'What?'

'Who is it you say is coming?'

'Jesus.'

'You'll have to speak up.'

'Jesus!'

'Don't swear – a young woman like you. I'm sorry. Was I doing something? I think I was eating my tea. Look,

253

if it helps, I'm Conservative. Always have been.'

He closes the door.

Perversely, I feel rather disappointed that my first effort at doorstep evangelism has failed and decide to try harder at the next house. A woman answers and I start with an opening I vaguely recall from being on the receiving end.

'I belong to a non-denominational religious organisation,' I say.

'You're a Jehovah's witness,' she says.

And that's that.

At the third house, an unshaven man in his twenties slouches in the doorway. To my question, 'Do you accept the Lord Jesus in your heart?' he says that he's a Plymouth Argyle supporter.

'Are you joking?' I ask.

'Possibly,' he says, and gives me a charmingly sexy smile.

I try half a dozen houses like this and with no luck so far as converts are concerned. It's strange, though, how I want to succeed. I suppose I'm beginning to 'inhabit the role' as actors say. From the corner of my eye I notice that the various spectators in the street have returned to concentrating on their own affairs, so I've accomplished my purpose of explaining my presence in the area. Even so, it seems unwise to stop; so I go to the next house.

To all appearances it's as non-descript as the others; one of a pair of pebble-dashed semis overdue a coat of paint. The curtains on the upstairs windows are closed, which is odd at this time of day, but the door is ajar, possibly to allow a flow of air on a warm afternoon but it may equally be an oversight.

I ring the bell and after a brief wait catch some movement in the corridor and a glimpse of a face, and hear a voice. I pull back in shock and walk away as quickly as I can. I struggle to think how I look: an elderly woman muttering to herself, every bit as mad as I sometimes feel. But the fact is that I recognise both the voice and the face.

The voice is that of the Boss calling from a room where I can't see him, but the face isn't his though I know it only too well. Thinking of it now, I'm struck at how our ability to recognise things is conditioned by context. I've seen this face before in different situations, yet never made the connection that they are sightings of the same person. Only now, glimpsing him at a door, more or less as I'd seen him that first time, do I remember the Man with the Bag who called at our house to speak to the Boss. Only now do I know who he is.

He is Stephen Gregg.

29

'Monday evening seems an odd time for a psychic event. I'd have expected a weekend.' Janet had forgotten about the subject after Joanie mentioned it at the Readers' Group. According to Belle, in order to humour the old girl, they'd all agreed to attend, not expecting that anything would come of it. 'And why Monday?'

'It's because it's part of a tour: Monday it's Southquay; Tuesday it's Plymouth – you know how it goes. They have to make best use of their time, especially if they've come all the way from the States.'

'And you say Joanie has organised this?'

'She's even got Jean's taxi firm to lay on a minibus and take us all. There was me, thinking she was just a silly old beggar who scarcely knows the time of day; then, before you know where you are, she's bludgeoning Poles to death with her walking stick – if you're to be believed – and organising trips for the ladies. What next, we ask? Naked rambling?'

'I never said Joanie killed Stanislaw Walacaszewski, only that there was blood on the handle of her stick.'

'Don't split hairs with me.'

'I'm not splitting hairs.'

'Really? You're talking as if you know who it was that did it. Well? Well? Cat got your tongue?'

Janet wasn't sure how to answer. She knew that at some point she had to produce a solution to the mystery or give up and admit that her investigations had all along been nothing but a piece of fun ... or something else for which she couldn't find the word.

She said, 'I do know who did it.'

'What? This is the first I've heard of it. When did you find out?'

'I've always known,' Janet said, but immediately thought that wasn't right. 'No, let me put it another way: I've *suspected* someone from the very start and I've had no reason to change my mind. Proving it, on the other hand, is a different matter.'

'Right – I see. What is it about you? There are times when you could try the patience of a saint. If you say you know who killed Whatshisface, I suppose you know what you're talking about. Are you going to let me in on the secret?'

Janet shook her head. 'I'm sorry. It wouldn't be fair.'

'You mean because I'm a big mouth and would tell everybody? Well, you're probably right. But it doesn't alter the fact that there are times when you're ruddy annoying. So what are you going to do? Lay it all in front of the police?'

Janet had thought of that but what did she have? No material evidence, just a slender chain of inferences based on observation and a few lucky guesses such as the phone and the stick. No one would treat her seriously except for Stephen, and he wasn't involved in the murder investigation, or so he said. She found herself once again struggling to form a plausible image of herself: frightened that she might be no more than an elderly lady (was sixty-five elderly?) making a last effort to affirm her own significance before descending into senility. Yet she was sure the evidence was there. But only the police had the ability and authority to look for it.

'The police won't pay any attention to what I have to say.'

'No, I don't suppose they will,' Belle agreed. 'So what are you going to do?'

'I'm not sure.' Janet was reluctant to say more; it might sound arrogant. Then on reflection, she thought Belle would correct her if it did; so she said, 'I have an idea, and, if it works, she may confess to me.'

'She? We're talking about the killer?'

258

'I don't think she wanted to kill anybody.'

'No, I don't suppose she did. I doubt that many murderers do. Well, tell me anything you want me to do to help.' Belle smiled. 'Meantime do you fancy a ginger biscuit?'

Sandra decided to wear her hair up with an ivory silk blouse and trim black trousers. She wondered yet again whether it was time for a change of image. All the airy-fairy New Age stuff was a bit old-fashioned and when she stared into the cruel mirror she suspected that these days she looked like a frowsy old boozer rather than the Fount of Wisdom. Not that Christine fared much better: all dressed up like a Faery Queen even though she had a wardrobe of perfectly good clothes. But there was no accounting for Christine. She even managed to square her mystical beliefs with going to church, though she claimed it was for Keith's sake.

The Americans – notably Elspeth van Doorman – were the leaders in psychic fashion as in so many other things and they seemed to have abandoned Sandra's 'look'. Then again they had all sorts of advantages, not least the publicity and TV shows. That was what you got when the stations were owned by Nazi oilmen from Texas. These days van Doorman dressed like the anchor woman on a breakfast programme: beautifully tailored clothes but softened so as not to be intimidating. The Botox and the jewellery weren't to English taste, but a bit of makeup would tone down the Chinese mummy look and if she eased up on the bling she might succeed with the pensioners of Southquay.

OK, so I'm jealous, Sandra admitted to herself.

She kept an eye on others in her profession and wasn't one of the American's admirers. The TV editors did a good job on van Doorman's programmes before they were aired, cutting out the 'misses' and general time-wasting so that she seemed to score a high number of 'hits' in her

259

readings. But Sandra could spot sloppy technique when she saw it and was fairly certain that an army of paid researchers explained some of her competitor's more uncanny predictions.

Being narcissistic, van Doorman had once gone head to head on a chat show against James Randi, and the magician had exposed her for the vain charlatan that she was. However, because she was married to one of the Nazi oilmen, she'd managed to pull the programme though it circulated on YouTube. Not that it did her any harm. The Internet trolls picked on Randi not van Doorman. They poured bile on him for damaging the reputation of 'someone who brings comfort to millions'.

It's a living, Sandra told herself about her own work

So it was Monday evening and there they were in the minibus provided courtesy of Jean with Keith doing the driving. And, surprisingly, they were all as good as their word and showed up: even Diana who was married to a vicar and might be expected to disapprove, and the ever-rational Janet who'd made it quietly clear that she regarded the whole business of psychics and mediums as a fraud. Out of consideration for Joanie, not to mention respect for her own livelihood, Sandra kept her opinions about Elspeth van Doorman to herself. When all was said and done, it was just a couple of hours of harmless entertainment. Instead she gave Joanie her head, and the old dear – half cut already – expounded on the successes of the main attraction.

'She's made *thousands* of correct predictions!' she enthused. 'Many of them about the future. And her powers of remote healing are ... well, she once cured a woman of cancer *over the telephone*. The telephone! The only word for that is *incredible!*'

Tonight the Grand was decked in banners for its half-way famous visitor. Coloured lights dribbled into the quiet sea under a fading evening light. The car park was packed,

260

and Jean and Keith exchanged words in Glaswegian before he drove off with the empty minibus.

'I've told him to find a space somewhere and then take himself to the pub for a few,' Jean said cheerfully. 'I'll drive us home.'

'I was here on Saturday,' Janet said as they went inside. The lobby area was heaving. 'There are a lot more people here tonight. The Afterlife seems to be more popular than dancing to a Victor Sylvester tribute band.'

Belle had told Sandra about Janet's date with Stephen Gregg. Sandra wondered what her own life would have been like if she'd hung about with coppers instead of Ray Wallace. A few timely psychic predictions in that direction might have come in handy, but now it was too late. She couldn't decide if she admired or disliked Janet for her competence. Probably both, and it wasn't something she felt guilty about. Friendship was rarely separable from jealousy.

Van Doorman had come with her entourage. An American with a clean-cut Mormon look was supervising the cloakroom, taking bags and coats from the old ladies and beaming at them as he did so. Sandra looked around and noticed two more Americans mingling with the crowd; it was impossible to mistake the clothes, the earpieces and clip-on mikes. She had to grant that it was a slick operation, exactly what she would have done herself if her business could have stood the cost. No one else seemed to pay attention to these hangers-on or wonder why they were there.

By way of warm up and to draw in the crowd, the event organisers had brought in some home-grown talent. Sandra had been approached but had turned the gig down because van Doorman had a reputation for being patronising which was something she could do without. These lesser stars had set out their stalls in the smaller lounges where dance classes had been held on the previous Saturday. Sandra knew most of them from previous events and they bought

261

some of their stock through the mail order side of Christine's business. Speaking of which, there was the woman herself, saying hello to her customers and gushing about the psychic abilities of their American visitor. Tonight, as predicted, she was wearing all sorts of loose skirts and fly-away shawls in flimsy grey open weave fabric. Presumably some sort of gossamer effect was intended, like Titania in *A Midsummer Night's Dream*, but Sandra thought she looked more like a large pressed cheese.

'They're an ordinary looking lot, aren't they?'

Sandra found Frieda standing by her side. She was wearing a dress that was too much like hard work to think about and a white PVC cap that Audrey Hepburn might have sported in a sixties film. Sometimes, Sandra thought, that vintage shop had a lot to answer for.

'Do you mean the professionals or the public?'

'The public. The professionals, as you call them, look like used car salesmen or paedophiles – I mean the men. The women are all right, though with more chiffon and hair spray than I care for.'

'I take it you're not a believer. What were you expecting?' Sandra glanced at the other women. That goofy-toothed look was a distraction that made it difficult to take Frieda's intelligence seriously. But she had been a teacher, after all.

'I'd always thought that folk who came to this sort of thing were needy.'

'We're all needy. And a lot of them are just here for the entertainment – like us.' In fact Sandra had always thought of her clients as the sort one might meet in a doctor's waiting room: a cross section of society, weighted towards the older end as patients tend to be, but otherwise just normal people coping with the everyday stress of life. She might consider them silly for believing in the stuff she peddled, but she thought none the worse of them for that. It was just a fact that people were stupid – including herself. After all, she'd ended up married to the owner of a lap-dancing club and, among his many other sins, a man who used to beat her; how bright was that?

Sandra was bored. She'd been to too many events like this. Why couldn't she be like Christine, who was ever hopeful that some herb or therapy would work its magic for her, and indeed believed that many of them did? Take that back; it wasn't what she wanted at all. What she wanted was to be truthful in the hope that the truth would set her free, but she didn't really believe that could happen. For one thing she probably wouldn't recognise the truth if she saw it; and for another it would probably make her want to top herself.

Still, at least this event was good for people-watching. Consider Diana, whom she could never figure out. Still beautiful at her age, chic in her dated but classy clothes, and married to Reverend 'melt in your pants' Pierce. Not a good subject for a psychic reading because she never revealed anything of herself beyond her taste in books. Here she was tonight, and looking for what? A revelation from Elspeth van Doorman? Depending how good her researchers had been, it was just possible the latter might oblige. One thing Sandra knew was that even the sceptics, in a corner of their hearts, were hoping that the performance was genuine and they'd be granted something: an insight, a crumb of comfort, a guide to action. Well, good luck with that.

As Sandra was about to join the queue into the main room and find a seat before they were all taken, Janet came alongside, also scanning the crowd rather than looking at Sandra.

'Any progress with solving the murder?' Sandra asked. 'What did Belle call us: "The Demented Lady Detectives' Club"? That never really got off the ground, did it? You and her seem to have been the only ones doing any actual detecting.'

Janet smiled. She had a nice smile as if she and Sandra

actually were friends, which Sandra didn't believe for a minute: not real friends, who share secrets, swap clothes, talk behind each other's backs, and forgive each other.

'I'm always happy to get some help.'

'You think I can help?'

'Not you in particular. Lots of questions just require common sense answers or a fresh point of view.'

'Oh? I'm intrigued. What's your question?'

'The dead man, Walacaszewski – or however we're supposed to pronounce it. I'm certain he stayed at a hotel in Paddington the night before he came to Dartcross.'

'Yes, I think you said that when you updated us at the Readers' Group.'

'The hotel employs Polish staff and I spoke to the girl on the desk. She has no memory of anyone Polish staying that night.'

'He may have registered before or after her shift.'

'She checked the register and there were no Polish names in it, not for that night, and I've yet to meet a Polish person who doesn't have a noticeable accent. So how did our Mr Walacaszewski manage to pass himself off under an English name?'

'Ah.' Sandra hesitated before an answer, finding herself coolly curious at the workings of another person's mind. She said, 'The only explanation I can think of is that the dead man wasn't Polish, despite his name.'

'That's what I think, too. I just wanted to check if there was another explanation. I was misled because these days one thinks of all the Poles coming over here to work as tradesmen or in hotels and restaurants.'

'Or in "Polski skleps", whatever they are.'

'Yes. Yet it's easy to forget that there was an earlier immigration; I mean the soldiers and refugees left behind by the War. They had children, raised here and brought up to speak English like you and me, and many of them will these days be in their sixties: the same age as Stanislaw Walacaszewski. So that's my theory. His parents were

Polish, but he wasn't. What do you think?'

'It's possible.' Sandra admitted. 'But where does it get you? It doesn't solve the mystery of who murdered him.' She glanced at her watch. If they didn't move quickly, all the seats would be gone. 'Sorry to interrupt, but don't you think we should take our places in the main hall? The show's about to begin.'

And indeed the last of the audience were filing through the double doors into the large function room that had previously served for dancing.

Janet hadn't been to a demonstration of psychic powers before. Looking over the audience – older and more female than the general population – she was reminded of people who went to the theatre or ballet; they weren't so very different, and their manner had the same air of expectancy. As for the room, it was set for perhaps three hundred with a dais decorated with lights and scenery flats that van Doorman probably brought with her on all her tours. In the competition for chairs, Janet's party couldn't all sit together. She pointed out Belle, who had reserved a couple of extra seats by putting her bag and coat on them and daring anyone to say differently. Sandra looked around and then joined her.

After a recorded fanfare, a man bounded onto the dais. Janet had a notion he was a 'celebrity' on regional TV; certainly the audience seemed to recognize him and clapped as he extolled the virtues of their visitor in an effervescent voice that reminded Janet of a holiday camp host.

'I'm not surprised his wife divorced him,' was Belle's whispered comment.

Introduction over, the star came onto the stage. Elspeth van Doorman was smaller than Janet had anticipated, but compensated with heels and blonde hair teased to add a couple of inches to her height. Her age was fifty or so, but not the fifty years that ordinary women experience;

instead, the slightly inhuman fifty of media celebrities, not unattractive but disconcerting. To Janet's eye, her clothes, a jacket, blouse and skirt combination, were too studied in their effect, but she suspected that was just prejudice on her part.

The psychic and the male host did the handover, namely praise at her achievements from him and gushing modesty from her in a voice with a Southern accent, as far as Janet understood American accents. And then she began.

'I have a sense of a male presence. I'm getting an M – maybe a Mike? A Malcolm?'

Janet was surprised how quickly this raised a response. A woman in the audience raised a hand and shouted out an excited 'Malcolm!'

'He's concerned that you have a health problem – joints? bones?' said Elspeth van Doorman

'I should ruddy-well think so,' said Belle. 'She's got to be seventy if she's a day.'

'You're visiting – a chiropractor, is it? – an osteopath? Yes. Well keep on doing it, honey. Mal says it's doing you good.'

Malcolm was followed by Sydney and Tom. Sydney's wife was advised to keep taking the tablets for her abdominal problem and Tom said he approved the new curtains, which he mysteriously knew were of a pink flowered pattern. There were more hits and no misses.

Sandra leaned over to Janet and murmured, 'This is a warm up. She's brought her Internet fan club. She's been giving them online advice and is reworking stuff she already knows.'

At the interval the women met at the coffee table and exchanged opinions.

'Isn't she wonderful!' enthused Christine.

'A load of cobblers,' said Frieda.

'Very professional,' said Sandra; and in an aside to Janet, 'Now the audience is primed, she'll take more chances in the second half. She'll make a few more guesses before she gets a response and she may have to hide a few "misses". Look out for them.'

And, of course, Sandra was right, as Janet noticed. At her first effort after the break, Van Doorman pulled a D out of the ether and had to rattle off a half dozen names with no luck until a woman called out 'Desmond!' and the psychic confirmed it. Desmond was discreet and limited his communication to the news that he was doing OK in the Hereafter. He was followed by an Edith, an Alice and a Dereck and then an Alan who wanted to talk about a family secret.

'No takers for that one,' Sandra chuckled when no one rose to the bait.

'It's OK, honey,' said van Doorman as if it was what she expected all along. 'You know who you are. Some stuff you don't like to talk about in public, but if you come backstage after the show, I'll tell you what Al had to say.'

The audience applauded, but Janet thought their enthusiasm was sad and rather dreary. There was nothing entertaining in seeing people parade their grief, their fears and need for comfort. Surely there was a more honest way of addressing these things? She thought of David and of Stephen Gregg and his Anne and felt compassion for those who could still not reconcile themselves to their loss. She wished that she was elsewhere, except that she had come for a purpose and was still waiting to see if she would succeed. The evening was coming to a close and so far she hadn't.

On stage Elspeth van Doorman had changed pace again, aiming to end on a high note with some sharp accurate messages. She disposed of a couple of these and then paused and assumed a serious expression and slowed and lowered the tone of her voice.

'I've been getting a persistent contact all evening,' she said solemnly. 'It's for someone here in this hall but there's a lot of pain. The person on the other side, I'm not sure he's British. I'm getting an S – a Stan? – a Stanley? – a Stanislaw?'

'Oh, fuck!' said Belle.

'Yes, a Stanislaw!' She paused and seemed to listen attentively to an otherworldly sound. She nodded and resumed, 'He died violently. I'm getting a mental picture of a club of some sort – a stick maybe? And water – a river I think. Whatever. He wants you to know he isn't bitter. He doesn't blame you. He knows you have your reasons – that he wasn't the easiest person to live with. I'm speaking to someone here – I mean *right here!* That person is also an S. It's OK to speak up because no one will blame you, honey. But it's OK too if you want to talk afterwards. I'm getting strong vibes when it comes to this name. Oh, yes, I mean *really* strong vibes. I'm getting an S – a Sss … Sa … a Sah…. Have we got a Sarah here?'

'Who the bloody hell is Sarah?' said Sandra.

30

Sarah killed Stanislaw Walacaszewski. Not the Boss. Who is Sarah? Do I know her? Is she someone who fits into my story, whose name and existence I've forgotten because I'm growing old and mad?

My story isn't a fabrication. *It isn't.* I tracked the Boss to a house near Park Crescent and saw Stephen Gregg, the policeman, there. That really happened only two days ago. I can see the house. The curtains of the front bedroom are drawn, and a voice is telling me that it's because there's a third person hiding there. Perhaps it's Mr Walacaszewski. Perhaps he isn't dead. Perhaps it's Sarah.

After my discovery I came home. I expected him to follow and that he would challenge me and that everything would come out, whatever it is. But when he did come home we passed one of our long evening silences together, and yesterday was the same: he vanished most of the day; no doubt to the same house, but I couldn't be bothered to follow. He thinks I didn't recognise him or perhaps that I'm hoping he and Stephen Gregg didn't recognise me. In either case what happened is deniable. And in the interval I've learned that Sarah killed Stanislaw Walacaszewski and I am possibly mad.

Today the Boss has gone out again and I'm waiting for him to return. Each passing minute fills me with horror because I know he'll come like Jesus to judge the quick and the dead and make all things known.

I don't know if I can face true knowledge.

I must write about Ludmila and everything that happened to us, and then perhaps I'll know.

The Boys have gone to Switzerland with Sergei, Vanya

and Boris. Ludmila and Oliver have disappeared. I discover this when I call her flat and then his.

'Well, I'm not going to cover for them,' says Hermione. 'They've made their bed and now they must lie in it – which seems to be exactly what they have been doing.'

'You mustn't tell Sergei!' I urge her, which she finds annoying because she snaps back at me.

'Obviously I'm not going to get on the phone to him. But if he asks me outright, then tough titty is what I say. They're grown up and must take their chances.'

I try my best to dissuade her but she acts as if Sergei is a deceived husband and she is the standard bearer for common decency. She doesn't acknowledge her own jealousy and resentment. For different reasons Ludmila is as important to her as she is to me, but neither of us can see into our own motives.

And then she calls me. Ludmila calls me from the unnamed unimaginable place where she lives. Her voice has laughter and tears in it and the pitch is higher. I can't unscramble the emotions.

'Where are you?' I ask.

'Why do you want to know? Are you worried for me, darling?'

'Of course I'm worried! Is Oliver with you?'

She doesn't answer this question. Instead she says, so excitedly that even over the telephone I feel her joy, 'Katya is free. Katya! My Katya! I have managed to get her out of Russia and she is hidden where Sergei is never finding her. Never! Never!'

All I can say is, 'How?' I'm not prepared for this. She said Katya, not Angela?

'Friends! Yes, I have friends: people who are not liking bastard Sergei Nikitich Blok. Also English friends. Beautiful, beautiful, very snob English friends I am remembering until I die! So I am calling you to say I am free and happy.'

She means she is calling me because we shall never meet again. And I find that thought unbearable.

She puts the phone down without telling me where she is or if she is with Oliver. She does not give me her number. She does not promise to call again. I feel bereft as if someone has died.

The Boss has returned with the dog. From the look he gives me, I see immediately that there are to be no more pretences between us. And now I don't care if he is looking over my shoulder as I write this because he has read everything I've written in this thing I have no word for. I made him do so in order that he understands his wife.

'It's time we have a talk,' he says when he has finished. 'I was waiting for the right moment, and it seems that this is it.'

'Did you kill Stanislaw Walacaszewski?' I ask him, and he looks shocked. He can't even pronounce the name.

'Who is he? I've never heard of him except through your diary.'

'What do you mean? His name was in the paper! He was murdered by the river!'

I don't know why I'm shouting at him. He isn't lying. He doesn't read the *Advertiser*. He's heard mention of the murder but has paid it no attention because it's just a piece of lurid provincial news.

I feel Reality slipping away. I ask, 'Who is Sarah?

'Which Sarah? I know several Sarahs. Rev Bev's second name is Sarah.'

I don't know which Sarah. The question doesn't make sense even to me. I try something different.

I ask, 'Why are we so poor? Why don't we see Gerry or Hermione anymore?'

He's disconcerted but he answers, 'You know why.'

'You lost all our money in futures and derivatives and banks in the Cayman Islands and … and … and…' I scream, *'None of it means anything!'*

271

He's silent. I think he'd forgotten that he lied to me, and now suddenly he remembers. 'I'm sorry,' he says and strokes my hair, and I move my head to nestle in the comforting hollow of his hand and let the tips of his fingers graze my cheek.

'I'll make a pot of tea.' His hand leaves me and he goes to make the tea and returns with two cups. He places one in front of me.

'I'd forgotten what I told you. It was…'

'A lie? Why did we have to abandon our friends and change our names?'

'It wasn't a lie, but only a partial truth. We were betrayed by Sergei.'

'Now there's a surprise!'

We both laugh. But laughter doesn't explain my tears.

'Sergei stole money from Boris and Vanya and the people they all work for, and lost it in speculations.'

'You and Gerry helped him.'

'Yes.'

'You were thieves.'

'We were always thieves. Always from the very beginning.'

And I knew. I always did.

Slobber comes in the room and parks his backside on the worn rug. The Boss gives him a bourbon biscuit – his favourite.

'Sergei saved his own life by blaming us. It suited Boris and Vanya to believe him because, among those people, when violence starts it's impossible to control. But someone had to pay.'

I cast my mind back to that night, when the Boss came home drunk and in a panic and announced that it was all over and we must run. I see him standing by the window, peering through a crack in the curtains into the darkling street while I throw clothes into suitcases: the haute couture that will have to last me a lifetime and the copy of *Mrs Dalloway* in its faux leather binding that I mean to

272

read some day but won't. While I am doing this he tries to reassure me. He says he has money tucked away and a bolthole in the West Country. He has talents he can use. This will all blow over.

But it never does.

'What happened to Gerry and Hermione?'

'We made our separate plans and never told each other what they were. But we had a method to make contact in emergency.'

'And?'

'Hermione died a dozen years ago. Nothing sinister – lung cancer, I think. Do you remember that she smoked to keep her weight down?'

I'd forgotten that she smoked. I don't think I've mentioned it in my description of her. Does that mean something?

'What about Gerry?'

'He held out until a couple of years ago. He became lonely and bored and drank too much. His children despised him and left home. He thought he could resurface in a small way and nothing would happen. Water under the bridge and all that. But the Russians did remember. By then they had a big presence in London and didn't want some relic of their ancient sins shooting his mouth off in half the clubs in town. So they killed him. There was a story in the papers about it, but I was the only person who knew what it all meant.'

That Thing slinks in. She glances indifferently at us all, then settles under a chair to chew on a mouse. I seem to take in the news of the deaths with the same indifference, but I think it's because I need time to process them. I shall probably find myself crying at an inappropriate time and place, the way crazy people do.

Then I realise that none of this has anything to do with Ludmila.

The Boys return unexpectedly early from Zurich. I'm at

273

home in bed when a taxi draws up outside our building. Someday my prince will come, and here he is with his two friends, cheering, yelling and waving a champagne bottle. They burst into the flat, where I'm putting on a dressing gown, and confront me, the three of them swaying like Mexican gunmen in a spaghetti western. Do they really see me in my nightwear with a face pack on? Full of their own glory, I'm not sure they do.

'Come on, old girl,' says the Boss. 'Get your glad rags on, it's time to celebrate.' Even as he's speaking, Call Me Gerry is on the phone to Hermione and Sergei is trying to reach Ludmila on his mobile. Somewhere in the noise I learn that we are off to the West End to celebrate in some casino and night club or other; Sergei's treat; money no object. I have no opinion on the subject. It doesn't occur to them that I might have.

'Hermione will be here in an hour,' Gerry announces. 'She was none too pleased to be woken out of her beauty sleep, but she'll be all right once she's scrubbed and polished.'

'Ludmila isn't answering,' says Sergei, puzzled.

'She may have taken a sleeping pill.'

He looks at me slantwise. 'She not taking sleeping pills.'

I say, 'Sometimes I think she does.'

'No, never.' He is firm on this and I don't contradict him.

The Boss proposes more drinks. 'There's shampoo in the fridge.'

I agree to a glass because I need to shift my sense of foreboding. Gerry and Sergei pour themselves a whisky; the Boss fixes himself a G&T. The mood of afflatus has faded to be replaced by anticipation, but I don't think any of us knows what we are anticipating. Sergei tries to phone Ludmila once more. He gets no answer and flings his phone at the wall, where it doesn't break, and so he picks it up again and slips it into his pocket.

Hermione arrives. She is glittering and ghostlike, nervously trying to pick up cues from the men. She says, 'We weren't expecting you. Were we?'

'We weren't expecting them,' I say.

'Ludmila is maybe not expecting me,' says Sergei.

Hermione looks at me, then at him. 'She's probably taken a sleeping pill.'

'She is not taking...' Sergei doesn't finish. He tries Ludmila's number again. 'We go round and wake her up, I think.'

'It's late. If she's tired...'

'Yes, we go round and wake her up.'

And so it's decided.

But first a moment of comedy. We discuss who is fit to drive. Sergei is angry and unsteady. Gerry struggles to stay awake. The Boss says he feels OK but declines to drive. Obviously, on an occasion like this, the two girls aren't going to drive, and in any case amid all the waiting I've put away two glasses of wine and Hermione has a large gin inside her. We call a taxi and sit around gloomily until it arrives.

So into the taxi. Fortunately it's a black cab since there are five of us. A sign says there's a cleaning charge if we vomit in the interior. I half expect the driver to make small talk about the famous people he's had in his cab, because that's what they're supposed to do, but he's a foreigner and spends his time speaking Foreign on the radio. The streets are wet and dreary and the bobbies are out in force. Someone remarks that it's not a night for driving while pissed and we all agree. Finally we arrive at Rotherhithe and Gerry settles the fare but tells the driver to wait because he suspects what will happen next.

As for now, Sergei tries the phone again, but we know that Ludmila isn't going to answer and she doesn't.

'I hope you're not planning on breaking in, Sergei, old man?' says Call me Gerry. 'Neighbours, police and all that.'

'I have key,' says Sergei so dully that it almost seems he's tired of the idea and we should go home and think about things in the morning. But we don't, of course. We go up to the flat and he opens the door and, oh gosh, no one is there. He goes to the bedroom and starts rummaging in drawers and wardrobes, but Ludmila has enough clothes that, if some are gone, he can't tell. Hermione and I check the bathroom and the dressing table, which are a surer guide. Her favourite perfume is missing.

'We go to Oliver,' Sergei says at last. 'I know where he lives.'

'And what then?' asks the Boss, who has largely stayed quiet through these events.

Sergei stares at him. 'We have a very serious conversation.'

'Do you remember that night when Ludmila went missing?' I ask the Boss.

He doesn't understand the question behind the question. 'I was drunk. I remember it, obviously, but not the details.'

The important moments in my life are not his. In any case I have to attend to the matter in hand.

'I saw Stephen Gregg at the house you visit. I remembered that he called here a couple of times before I got to know him. I didn't make the connection.'

'He thought you hadn't recognised him from the visits here, but when you turned up yesterday he realised you had.'

'So you've been deciding what story to tell me? What lies?'

He doesn't immediately answer, from which it's clear that he has at least considered the possibility of lying, though I don't know why. There's still some secret I haven't fathomed: something he's ashamed of: a truth he knows I won't accept.

'Why is Stephen Gregg in Dartcross? He says it isn't

276

because of the murder; and in any case he arrived here before it happened. What sort of policeman is he?'

'He's with the Met – the Fraud Squad.'

I should have expected this because I recall that Inspector Gregg joked that he was nothing more than an accountant. It was the night of the ceilidh, or possibly when we went to the theatre; not that it matters.

'I see.' I do vaguely see. A memory comes back of the Boss studying for his own accountancy exams in the early days of our marriage before we became whatever we became: the thing that, like so many other things, I no longer have words for.

I'm distracted. Ludmila preys on my mind. I say tearfully, 'Oliver wasn't at his place in Islington.'

'What? No, he wasn't. That has nothing to do with Stephen Gregg. Are you all right, darling?'

'I don't know.'

I'm trying to hold on to the narrative of my life, but I seem to have two stories that I think are the same story and I can't choose between them.

I ask, 'What does Oliver – I mean Stephen Gregg – what does he want?'

'Help with a case. It's a big case involving oil and diamonds, the Russian mafia and…'

I interrupt angrily. 'How did he find you? We vanished! We are no longer *us!*'

The Boss shrugs. 'Apparently we didn't vanish from everybody's radar. MI5 have always known where we are; that's what Stephen told me. A surprise. I wouldn't have thought we were of any interest to them, but apparently we were. They were curious about what Sergei was up to – he was KGB, of course – I mean in the early days. They struggled to get their heads around the idea that he was simply a crook who was robbing people. In that respect Gerry and I were quicker on the uptake.'

'And you're helping them: MI5 – Stephen Gregg – whoever.'

'Not a lot of choice really.' He looks at me boyishly – the little lad who was caught out. 'Back in the day, Gerry and I were rather naughty, as you must have guessed, and MI5 know some of it. And frankly, they're not very nice people.'

'You wouldn't be put on trial, surely? Not after so many years.'

'Oh, no. Nothing like that. But the point is that they know who I am and where I live, and there are other people who are even less nice who don't.'

'They'd tell the Russians?'

'They don't say so. Then again, they don't have to.' He looks away from me. 'My tea is going cold. I've told you all you need to know. I go to the house most days – a bit like going to the office – and Stephen and I work our way through P&L accounts and balance sheets, money transfers and share registers going back twenty years in some cases. Where necessary I do translation.'

'Translation?' This doesn't sound right, and I can tell he's said something he didn't mean to say.

'Correspondence, for example. Some of it is in Russian. Stephen doesn't speak Russian.'

The Boss, of course, does speak Russian, as well as being an accountant and an expert in investments and banking. I have forgotten, in my triviality, that he is a considerable person and that his role in the world after Communism has probably been more significant – if clandestine – than I've ever given him credit for. And now it's caught up with him.

Still, behind that word 'translation', he's hiding something. I suspect now that he does love me after all and that whatever it is that he doesn't want to tell me, it's because it's something appalling and he thinks it will destroy me.

I say, 'Someone is living at the house.'

'Stephen.'

'Don't lie to me! The curtains are drawn during the

day. Someone is living there who mustn't be seen. Someone who now and again needs a translator.'

I know who it is, of course. It isn't Stanislaw Walacaszewski. It isn't the mysterious Sarah. Instead it's the person who took away my happiness and now leaves me old and frightened of going mad.

I say, 'Sergei Nikitich is living there, isn't he?' And I wait because even now I can see he's wondering whether he can chance just one more lie, because I'm a person who can be lied to.

'Yes,' says the Boss, and adds, 'I'm sorry.'

31

'I've got the answers to that list of questions we wrote,' said Belle over breakfast. 'Not that it matters – not if you've solved the mystery. Which I think you have, by the way.'

'I'd still like to know,' said Janet. 'Maybe you've discovered something that would make me change my mind.'

'Chance would be a fine thing,' said Belle, but she was pleased that Janet valued her efforts. She took the handwritten list from her copious bag and unfolded it.

'OK. Question 1: "What was Sandra doing before she came to Dartcross?" Well, according to her, after Mr 'Wide as They Come' Wallace buggered off, she scratched a living for about five years: supermarket checkout assistant and that sort of thing. Then she ran into Joanie who got her interested in the psychic game. Joanie corroborates the story, so there's no reason to think it isn't true.

'Question 2: "Why did Sandra and her hubby split up?" She always said it was because he used to knock her about, which is plausible. I can't *prove* she's telling the truth, but at least she's consistent, because everyone's been told the same story. The only discrepancy – which doesn't seem to mean much – is that, as Sandra tells it, she threw hubby out; but, according to Joanie, Sandra was one of those poor cows who put up with it and it was Ray Wallace who ran off with some bimbo in the end. Joanie's version doesn't sound like Sandra, but there's no accounting for people.'

Janet nodded, but, unlike Belle, she believed the story that Sandra had stuck it out through a violent marriage, though she had no particular reason to think so beyond an indefinable sorrow in the other woman's voice whenever she mentioned the subject of her husband. Janet asked, 'What about Christine and Keith?'

'I'm getting there. Question 3 was about Keith's connection with Bulgaria and did it mean he had summat to do with Poland. Well, it seems he used to work in manufacturing: pumps and compressors – whatever they are. This is back in the days when we had a manufacturing industry and I was slim and beautiful. Keith was a salesman and his job took him all over Eastern Europe. Bulgaria, Poland, Russia: he's visited the lot. He lost his job at the back end of the eighties and turned his hand to marketing Christine's business selling New Age bits and pieces. He's good at it and they're doing very nicely, thank you. That said, it's an odd business for him to involve himself in, because by all accounts he's some sort of lay preacher.'

'Diana and Pierce?'

'I do wish you wouldn't rush me. Where was I? Oh, yes, Diana and the handsome Rev Pierce. Diana has always been a housewife – I use the term loosely, because I think she was the kind that rich husbands show off to their friends and wouldn't know an iron from a doorstop. Comes from a "county" family, as she tells it; and certainly she looks and sounds like it. But come down in the world. Pierce was "something in the City", as they say, but I can't find out what. Then he got religion about twenty years ago and chucked it all in in favour of Doing Good. They live in a nice house but she makes a point of telling other people that they're poor. Compared with how they used to be, they probably are. And – before you ask – I've got the lowdown on Jean and Stuart.'

'Go on.'

'They had a win on the Lottery. Not wealth beyond the dreams of avarice, but a tidy sum compared with living on benefit in Glasgow after Stuart lost his job in ship building. They came to Devon for no other reason than Jean had once had a holiday in Paignton when she was a kiddie. Stuart fell into the taxi driving after a conversation with a man in a pub, who wanted a partner so the business could cover the hours. It all sounds very casual, but that's the way some folk carry on.'

Yes, thought Janet, it was the way people carried on. 'Personal Development' gurus might talk about 'Life Plans', but in her experience chance played a larger part in life as it was actually lived. Indeed – now she thought of it – the encounter of the disciples with Jesus wasn't so far removed from bumping into a man in a pub. Probably something like that accounted for Pierce's conversion from City slicker to Anglican vicar or Keith's becoming a lay preacher. It was unlikely to have been on their Life Plans.

'And finally,' said Belle, 'there's Frieda and Harry. You had your doubts that a legacy from the sort of relatives they were likely to have would pay for that white elephant of a house. And, as usual, Smartypants was right. What swung it is that Harry also collected on some sort of personal accident claim – a car crash, I think. He's got more silver pins in him than a jewellers' shop and he's a bit subject to mood swings and confusion which he manages by walking the dog. Nowadays Frieda says they should have given more thought to that side of things before they bought a fixer-upper, but they had their eyes set on the fantasy not the reality.'

And that was that. Belle put her list back in her bag and looked at Janet expectantly.

'Well? Has anything changed?'

Janet shook her head. These stories of other people's lives were much as she'd expected from her own observations and she thought they were essentially true. Only one of them accounted for the death of Stanislaw Walacaszewski, but she knew which it was, and it made perfect sense.

'So?' Belle asked. 'Are you going to see her in her den?'

'Yes.'

'I don't suppose she'll try to kill you. That only happens in films.'

'It's more likely she'll offer me coffee and a biscuit,' said Janet.

'Probably,' Belle agreed and gave Janet an impromptu kiss. She added wistfully, 'After all that work, it'll be a bit of an anti-climax, won't it?'

In mild spring sunshine Station Road was still an undistinguished by-pass taking traffic away from Foregate and the High Street. Surveying the neat pebble-dashed semis either side, Janet wondered how she would have written the scene if it had ever come to that. The habit of authors – the 'pathetic fallacy' – was to provide weather to suit the occasion. A handy storm could complement indifferent writing when it came to describing a tense situation. But what was the present situation? The subject might be murder, but the substance of the scene would be two women 'of a certain age' (as the French say) having a chat, neither of whom was likely to break down in a show of emotion. From an artistic point of view it was highly unsatisfactory, but the contrast of subject and setting amused Janet. The oddness of Life. She never got over it.

She knocked on the front door and Sandra answered. Janet noted the attractive dress, shoes not slippers, some light make-up, and none of the usual Celtic rings. Evidently Sandra had been expecting her, and, of course, she would be.

'I thought you'd drop in today. Belle not with you?' Sandra closed the front door behind her visitor.

'I thought it would be better if just you and I had a chat. Less…'

'Intimidating? That's considerate.' Sandra opened the door to the sitting room, the same room where, less than three weeks before, Janet had noticed a copy of the local newspaper lying on a Parker Knoll table. She took a seat.

Sandra said, 'Tea? Coffee? I went out early and bought

some fruit scones; I had a recollection that you liked them.'

'Coffee please. Milk but no sugar. Yes, I should like a scone.'

'With jam and butter? The jam's in one those small pots, so you can decide for yourself. No clotted cream, I'm afraid.'

'I've never been one for clotted cream with scones.'

Sandra went to make the coffee. In the small house it was possible to hold a conversation from the kitchen, and she continued speaking, asking Janet in a general way how she had enjoyed Elspeth van Doorman's display of psychic powers.

'It was a first for me,' Janet said, 'but much as I expected.'

'You don't approve? No, I don't suppose you do. She's quite a performer, but I think an English audience prefers someone a bit less assertive and a bit more mumsy. Still, you have to admire her class. She didn't bat an eyelid when no one rose to the bait after the "Sarah" revelation; just finessed it and moved on to her prepared finale: that business with … "Eddie" was it? A real tear jerker; not a dry eye in the house. She had a stooge in the hall to pick up on that one; so it was a sure fire hit.'

Sandra came into the sitting room bearing the tray of refreshments and placed it on the Parker Knoll table. The two women went through the ritual of pouring coffee and buttering scones with a sacramental delicacy. There were no rules for this encounter, but it seemed that, where other people might be angry or frightened, they had decided without prior discussion to be tactful and polite. Janet did wonder at that, and supposed that each of them had given off subtle cues that led to this tacit agreement. She was glad.

Sandra said, 'Last night, I did ask myself why you started that conversation with me just when everyone was trying to get into the hall and find a seat. I realised you were manoeuvring me into sitting with you and Belle, but I had no idea what you were trying to pull off. I mean – who would have expected?'

'I'm sorry.' Janet wondered why she was apologising. Habit, she supposed.

'You took me completely by surprise with that "Sarah" business. Is there a real "Sarah" by the way?'

'No.'

'Oh, good. I thought I might be going mad.'

'I didn't want to humiliate you in public. It would have been cruel since we'd never spoken and I hadn't got your side of the story.'

Sandra dabbed her eyes with a napkin, but she spoke quite calmly. 'That really is kind. You're a nice person. I thought you might be, and it's good to be proved right. I suppose it was enough for you that we were close together and you could judge my reaction?'

Janet nodded.

Sandra said, 'It was the shock – exactly as you planned. It never occurred to me that that you understood how Elspeth van Doorman works her act and that you'd use it against me. How?'

'I read up on the subject. She planted one of her staff in the cloakroom to go through pockets and handbags, and she had others in the crowd listening to people talking and feeding back scraps: all she needs are a few hooks and the audience react as you did and provide the rest. I imagine she wears an earpiece under the big hair-do. All Belle and I had to do was get alongside the right person and talk.'

Sandra looked at her watch. 'Eleven o'clock. There's a bottle of wine on the rack in the kitchen. I'm going to have a glass. Don't get the idea I normally drink this early.' She didn't bother asking if Janet wanted any. From the kitchen she called out, 'What was it that gave me away?'

Janet explained about the copy of the *Advertiser* with the story of the body with a ring drawn around it.

'Any one of us could have done that,' Sandra said,

returning with a large glass of Rioja.

'Yes, they could. But in my experience women like us are careful with other people's property. It was always far more likely that the person who lived in this house had done it.'

'You mean you always thought I was the killer?' Sandra was incredulous. 'You certainly took your time in saying so.'

'I couldn't understand the motive. I was thrown by the dead man's name and the fact that he seemed to have come from Poland only a day or two before he was killed.' Janet explained about the discrepancy of an hour in the time shown on the mobile phone. 'It was Belle who put me on the right track. She pointed out that everyone has to come from somewhere, and that "somewhere" doesn't necessarily have to be relevant. It didn't matter that Stanislaw Walacaszewski was Polish. In fact he *wasn't* Polish in the strict sense.'

'He was born in Birmingham,' said Sandra.

'Well, there you are.'

'So what was my motive?'

'The one that explains most killings by women. He was your husband: Raymond Stanley Wallace.'

Sandra stared at her half-empty glass. 'I shan't have another.' She looked at Janet but without focussing. 'He called himself "Ray" after some kid who had a rock band when he was a teenager – not even someone famous. Quite a lot of Polish people changed their name if it was one that no one could pronounce. Ray was sick of people trying to say Walacaszewski and making a mess of it. It was the last straw when the other lads kept calling him Willy Wonka in front of the girls. He chose Stanley Wallace because it was near enough to his proper name, and Ray because he liked it. He didn't do it formally. His passport has his Polish name and my marriage certificate calls me Mrs Walacaszewska, though for obvious reasons it's not the name I use. I imagine the police don't know him as Ray

Wallace.'

'No,' Janet agreed. 'I don't think they do. But it's probably just a matter of time. By now they'll have discovered whatever name he used to book into the hotel in London and recovered his suitcase. His credit cards are probably in the name Wallace and so he'll have signed the register in that name, too. He flew here from Spain, didn't he?'

'Yes.'

Janet grinned at a recollection. 'Poland is two hours ahead of England. You can't imagine the hoops Belle and I jumped through trying to explain why the phone was only one hour ahead. If it hadn't been for that Polish name, the answer would have stared us in the face.'

Sandra briefly changed the subject – trying to establish a shared bond. 'Your husband's dead, isn't he?'

'Yes.'

'Were you happy? Yes, of course you were. I can see it. That self-confidence.' In a sudden flash of anger she said, 'Ray fucked off with that slag, Chelsea, just after he made his big score and I thought we were set up for life.'

'The UXE Bank Vault Raid?'

Sandra was surprised. 'How did you know about that.'

'Stephen Gregg told me that Ray was a suspect – though he knows him only as Walacaszewski.'

'Yeah. Well, he wasn't in on the actual robbery, but he financed it and fenced all the stuff they stole. Then he left me and went to Spain with a woman fifteen years younger and set himself up in property, bars and so on. But the trouble with Ray was he thought he was smarter than he actually was. He expanded his empire with loans from some very nasty people, and when the Crash came it all started to unravel. He lost the lot, and Chelsea with it.'

'So he came back to you.'

'Yes.'

For a moment neither said anything. Ray Wallace had turned to the woman he'd beaten and abandoned and expected her to take him in. What was anyone to make of that? Janet remembered that, according to Joanie, despite the beatings Sandra had never actually thrown her husband out. It was entirely possible that Ray thought the assaults were just part of the give and take of an everyday marriage and didn't bring them into his calculations. He would no doubt have rationalised them: Sandra had in some fashion been 'out of order' as the expression had it. It was beyond sad.

'You didn't find my number on Ray's phone?' Sandra asked.

'No.'

'He was paranoid; he probably had half a dozen of them. The fact is that, apart from knocking women about, Ray was a coward. He was scared shitless that his pals in Spain were going to find and kill him, and maybe they were. He called me and asked me to put him up while he made plans. He was full of plans about how he was going to claw his way back to the top again. Open another chain of lap dancing clubs. Rob another bank. Ray and Sandra together like in the good old days and no more mistakes such as Chelsea – as if that was possible: the wrinkly old sod.'

Sandra checked her watch again. 'Do you want to stay for lunch? I've got a nice quinoa and lentil salad.'

'I've promised to eat with Belle. Tell me about that Sunday night.'

Sandra seemed disappointed.

We're supposed to be friends, thought Janet. And friends have lunch together.

Sandra said, 'There's not a lot to tell. I put my foot down and told him there was no way he was staying at my house. I said I had visitors and he didn't want to be recognised – and the vain bugger believed me, as if Joe Public goes around with pictures of bank robbers in his wallet. We agreed to meet by the river, exactly where he was found. Knowing what he was like I intended to take a hammer with me for protection, but Joanie had left her stick behind, the last time I saw her.'

'I remembered you giving it back to her.' Janet didn't say she tested it for blood.

'You *are* sharp. I'm beginning to think I never had a chance, though I don't mind. In fact it's something of a relief. Anyway, I took it, the stick. And then...'

So far Sandra had been calm except for that one small show of tears. Now she seemed distressed. She said, 'Do I have to spell out the details?'

Janet shook her head.

'Then that's it, isn't it? Are you going to go to the police?'

'No. It isn't my business.' Janet meant that judging the other woman wasn't her business. How did one weigh the years of beatings and abuse against whatever happened on the river path on a night of fear and heightened emotion? She said, 'Sooner or later the police will work out Ray's connection to you and why he came to Dartcross. I suggest you go to them first and tell your story.'

'But I'll go to prison!'

Janet shook her head. 'You'll tell them you killed Ray in self defence. He has a history of violence against you as well as being a suspect in a robbery, and you're the only witness to what happened by the river. Whatever the police believe, there's no one to contradict your story. The Crown Prosecution Service will probably not even take the case to court, and, if they do, you'll certainly be acquitted, especially if you hand yourself in while the police are still in the dark.'

Janet wasn't lying. The police had no love for Stanislaw Walacaszewski, alias Raymond Stanley Wallace, and his death had spared them a lot of effort and the ratepayers the expense of locking him up.

In the broader picture, the question of whether Sandra had set out that night with the intention of murdering her husband was a secondary consideration and unfathomable.

32

Sergei is living in the house off Park Crescent.

'Only until Stephen Gregg and I are finished,' says the Boss, 'and then he'll be taken … I don't know where he'll be taken.'

There's a saying that it's the last straw that breaks the camel's back, but I wonder if sometimes we are so compromised that there is no last straw: only an illusion, a hope, that, if not this time, then the next will be it: the end of our self-betrayal; the reclaiming of the authentic person. In my heart I fear there's no getting rid of Sergei Nikitich Blok. He is our Mephistopheles and we cannot redeem our souls this side of death. Call Me Gerry and Hermione are dead. Oliver and Ludmila are…. No, I don't want to think about them. Maybe later.

I must go shopping.

– Grout cleaner for the shower

– Washing up gloves – medium

– Coffee – Fairtrade

– Frozen prawns

– Ibuprofen tablets

I need the ibuprofen for my headaches. I had another one this morning. I've tried *cimicifuga* and *cocculus indicus* but neither of them has worked. I know I should go to the doctor, but that would be an admission of defeat. "Healer, heal thyself." But, in truth, do we ever?

The Boss has gone for his meeting with Inspector Gregg. I detected a spring in his step. He has unburdened his secret and now he feels OK. How I might feel hasn't crossed his mind. Confession may be good for his soul but it's done nothing for mine. As often as not it's like Pass the Parcel. His guilt has become my guilt.

This morning he kissed me. I was betrayed by a sexual tingle. Even at my age it can still happen. I think he does love me, but so often love is asymmetrical, and I can't judge his feelings for me by my feelings for him. His kiss may have been caused by relief rather than affection. Mine by force of habit or inattention. Judas probably thought nothing of kissing Jesus. That gang probably gave each other man-hugs all the time like football players.

I wonder how many people ask themselves if their lives have been authentic? In my case was an authentic life ever possible?

Ludmila and Oliver don't reappear.

'I can believe it of Ludmila,' says Hermione. 'She always had something of that Slavic romantic gloom about her. Everything for love, darling! A bit like Greta Garbo, if Greta Garbo had been Russian, which she wasn't. I never thought anything of it. I put it down as a pose. If ever a woman was playing to the gallery, it was her.'

At the time I was shocked by this remark, but now I'm not. I think there *was* something of a pose in Ludmila's behaviour, but sometimes we are imprisoned by our poses if we are not to admit our insignificance. It didn't make her suffering less.

'It's Oliver I can't fathom,' says Hermione. 'It never occurred to me for a moment that there was a real person inside that suit. I thought he was playing with Ludmila's feelings and he'd back off once he realised it had gone too far. Not that he cares a bean for Sergei, but he must know what the bastard is like.'

I know what she means. In this thing of mine I've tried to draw a picture of the Oliver who would risk everything to run away with the woman he loved, but I never get beyond his grooming and impeccable manners. As Hermione knew, even now I can't find anyone inside the suit. Maybe there was never anybody there. But that would be unbearable. It would mean that everything that happened was just the unintended consequence of a trivial affair. Yet perhaps that's how it was. There are more miscalculations than tragedies.

In the meantime, for a few months, we carry on as before, but now with an added seriousness. Ludmila took with her all that lighter side of our life and left us with nothing but the naked making of money under the watchful eyes of Boris and Vanya. It was clear that Sergei hated them and – as I now understand – was looking for some way of breaking free. I suppose this was when he formulated his plan to rob his paymasters with the help of the Boys.

Boris and Vanya know of Ludmila's disappearance. When they speak English in my presence they are always polite and show a modicum of respect to Sergei, but the Boss says that, in Russian, they call him Little Dick and say he doesn't know how to keep his woman. Russian gangsters aren't high among Nature's sensitive souls.

To my surprise the Boss came back for lunch. I made him a sandwich. He says his business with Stephen Gregg is winding down, and he's exacted a promise that, once it's all over, we'll be left alone.

'But Sergei knows where we live – or, at least, he knows we live in Dartcross, which is all anyone needs in order to find us. What if someone finds Sergei?'

He has no answer to that one. I'm left to imagine moving again: to imagine leaving this house and the friends I've cautiously assembled over the years. If we move, my life will be a prison bounded by a man who is a stranger to me, a drooling dog, and a cat I hate. Senility may be a blessing.

'What will happen to him – Sergei?' I asked.

'They haven't told me. In the short run I fancy they'll take him to London to continue his debriefing. And then?

Some sort of witness protection programme, I suppose.'

'If he's really told everything, is there going to be a trial?'

'I very much doubt it. The Russian oligarchs have dug themselves into London only too well. There'd be a march of estate agents on Parliament if we threw them out. At a guess, I think the authorities will simply drop a few hints that they have the goods on that crew and use their knowledge to keep them quietly in order. No killing people on our patch – that kind of thing.'

That I do believe. Certainly I don't expect anything resembling justice.

The Boss finished his lunch, checked his watch and said he'd arranged an afternoon meeting with Rev Bev. She plans to launch her new evangelical crusade to time with Whit. According to the Boss, the Holy Spirit is particularly frisky around that time of year and might lend her a helping hand. But failing the Holy Spirit, she wants the Boss to chip in with a sermon plus a few baptisms if the crowd of converts gets too much for her. She's probably planning an overflow font to handle the rush.

As far as I'm concerned, Bev is welcome to him. I can put up with loneliness and silence, or with a painful exchange that thrashes out all the issues between us. What I can't stand is being in the same house with him while he pretends that we've cleared the air and said everything that needs to be said. Yesterday, just for a moment after he'd read these things that I've written, I thought we were going to have that conversation. But I know now that it isn't going to happen. Men don't think that way. Unless they're losing their tempers, they imagine that a few words and a grunt amount to a baring of the soul. He genuinely believes that everything is settled. His only comment on what I've written was to say, 'Sometimes you refer to yourself in the third person. Couldn't you make your mind up?'

He doesn't wait for an answer.

Once he'd left for his meeting, I remembered the ibuprofen and went to the chemists to buy some. My shopping list slipped my mind, so I didn't pick up the other items. I also forgot that I had a patient – a two o'clock appointment – and, even when I got a call from Jean, for the life of me it didn't ring any bells. I'm sure I checked my calendar this morning – but was it yesterday? Is this ordinary forgetfulness or something more sinister?

Fortunately Jean was calling to postpone. I'm treating her for a recurrent rash – not exactly critical. She told me that Stuart is poorly again and so, while he's manning the phone at the office, she's out and about in the cab; and someone with a disability needs ferrying to the hospital in Southquay. All being well, I'll see her tomorrow.

At least my memory has proved robust enough that I've noted the new time in the calendar, but when I look for the old one, it isn't there. Either Jean was mistaken when she thought we'd made an appointment, or she wasn't and I did indeed forget to write it down. One of us is losing it. Possibly both of us.

Now I'm sitting at my laptop trying simultaneously to manage trivia and stop my life and sanity from falling apart. Somehow these are the same thing and I shall succeed or fail at them together.

In his own way even a monstrous nonentity like Sergei Nikitich Blok carries his burden of suffering and humiliation. He knows that Boris and Vanya call him Little Dick. One night we have a grotesque conversation, the two of us, because he has arrived at the flat for a meeting with the Boss but the latter is delayed. Sergei settles in to wait and whiles away the time eating peanuts and putting away shots of chilled Stoli. He starts to speak and it comes out that he wants a tear-filled heart-to-heart about the agonies of his love life.

'You understand,' he sobs. 'Lovely English people! Beautiful poetry! Shakespeare and the other guy – you get what I am saying?'

It all comes out as he sees it. When he first discovers her, Ludmila is some sort of charity case, abandoned with a child by a shit-for-brains university academic, living in a hovel and turning tricks to make ends meet. 'But me,' says Sergei, 'I am all big heart. You have cigarettes? I am all big heart!'

In this version, Sergei takes Ludmila in and showers her with clothes and jewels and, because he's all 'big heart', sees to it that the child is taken care of. And in return all he asks is loyalty. 'Is so much to ask?'

No, it isn't so much to ask. It's the standard price for clothes and jewels and I've paid it myself.

I join Sergei in a drink and cosy alongside him on the settee. He keeps turning over the same story, repeating the same phrases about his 'big heart' and 'loyalty – is so much to ask?' He has to repeat himself because he understands so little. Why Ludmila might leave him is completely beyond him. 'That bastard queer is hypnotising her?' he suggests. 'There are drugs – you know, *drugs* – make people behave funny strange.'

My head swims with vodka but I have a sense that I'm listening to a sort of fairytale in which the roles have become unstable. Cinderella elides into the wicked stepmother, and Prince Charming needs to be rescued from the evil witch.

Then the Boss comes home. Gives me a filthy look. Packs me off to the bedroom to sleep off the Stoli while he and Sergei talk. Later I find him going through the Yellow Pages and making calls.

'What are you doing?' I ask.

'I'm looking for a reliable private detective,' he says.

Rev Bev isn't married. Lesbian? I have my doubts about C of E vicars, but in her case I haven't noticed the signs. She's in her late thirties; so could give the Boss a few miles. More than the existing model. Pretty features, plumped out just enough to keep the wrinkles at bay. Hair on the ginger side of blonde. A 'full figure', as the saying goes, but not fat. And cheery. Always cheery.

What does the Boss think when he comes back from one of his chats with her to the cold comfort of his half-mad wife, banging on with the latest horror story about the bloody cat? I can see her vividly – the mad wife – but I can't do anything about her.

He comes home to find me dozing to stave off a headache and because being awake leaves me tired and confused. He looks very cheerful for a man who's spent a couple of hours chatting about bringing 'the Good News of God's Love' to Dartcross, as if the last two thousand years of Christianity have been merely a warm-up for Bev's little act. I call his cheerfulness the Bev Effect. I've noticed it before, and thought that he'd be better off with her than with me. I am a relic of his Unfortunate Past: something that he carried away in a rush on that dreadful night when we did a midnight runner from the Hampstead flat so that Boris and Vanya wouldn't torture and kill us.

I have a suspicion that he has had the conversation with her that he won't have with me. He probably thinks that she understands him as he is now, and I don't. The truth is that she understands him and is interested, and I understand him but am appalled. I think my understanding is closer to the truth. If by any chance their relationship goes any further, she'll get to the same place in the end.

I don't know why I'm writing this. I have a vague idea that, if I were dead, he'd marry her, but I don't know where it comes from. He's given no sign of deserting me. Haven't I just written that I think he loves me in his way?

What troubles me is that I know what he's capable of. I saw him searching for a detective in the Yellow Pages so that Sergei could get on the trail of Ludmila and Oliver. What did he think that was about? What did he think would happen? Even when Sergei and I were getting plastered and sentimental, I didn't think a tearful reconciliation was what our Russian pal had in mind.

After our drunken conversation I never saw Sergei again. I couldn't. The Boys however continued, because, after all, business is business. And then, of course it came to an end when we threw away everything and ran.

But, before that, the final betrayal.

We are at home one evening, the Boss and I. Not something that happens often but the Boss is unexpectedly here and distinctly edgy. I stretch my culinary talents and produce an omelette and a salad and we watch a game show on television.

The telephone rings. The Boss takes the call, grunts his way through it and writes a few notes. He looks solemn but when I ask him what's wrong all he says is, 'We may have to go out after all.'

It seems we're waiting for Gerry. He arrives half an hour later with Hermione who is staring at me and mouthing questions. This isn't jovial, noisy Call Me Gerry, but a thoroughly miserable specimen I've never seen before, and it's clear that Hermione has no more idea what's going on than I have.

Gerry asks, 'Your car or mine? Mine, I suppose since I'm blocking you in.'

'Yes, yours,' says the Boss and we talk about coats and jackets. It's a summer evening but the sky is clear and these evenings can be deceptively cold.

We go down to the car. Oddly, neither Hermione nor I press the Boys to tell us where we're heading or why. We know that we can't because we sense that they are angry: not with us but with something else: something about our lives that has driven us to this. If we do ask, then all that anger will turn onto us, and we are too smart and too frightened.

So we drive through west London on a balmy evening, watching lads in shorts and girls in summer dresses as we used to be. We look at road signs and wonder: where would our lovebirds fly to, because that is surely where we are aiming? But we know. Where else but the Province of Cotswold where Ludmila has dreamt of being a doctor's wife taking tea in a garden filled with lupins and hollyhocks?

Night falls and we are somewhere between Whitney and Burford, motoring along country lanes overhung with beech and chestnut, the leaves splashed yellow-green by our headlights, and stripes of cinnamon and turquoise painting the horizon. Here, on our left, is a drive that snakes away from the road to a cottage of honey-coloured stone with wisteria growing against it and baskets of marigolds and alyssum hanging by the door. There are lights, but no one hears our car, or pays attention if they do hear, and so we park and for a moment sit there with the engine running like people who have come to a party, who suddenly realise that it's the wrong day and they should go home; but, perhaps, first they should let their friends know that they are here and they can all laugh at the mistake.

'Well, let's go in then,' says Gerry. 'Get it over with. You stay here,' he tells Hermione.

The Boss says nothing, but naturally I stay in the car too. The men get out and go to the front door and knock. No one comes, but the door is open and so they go in.

Now, at last, Hermione and I can talk. But we don't. We know what has happened but we don't want to say so because perhaps, at this last moment, we are mistaken and the rest of our lives will be different from what it will be if we go into that cottage. So we wait. Two little girls promising to be good.

Gerry comes to the door. He beckons us and, when we don't immediately respond, he comes to the car and says curtly, 'Get out. You have to see. For all our sakes there *have* to be witnesses.'

We get out and walk along the path and through the door into the house where the lovers have lived. And I recognise nothing except the lovely water colour by the

Swedish painter. Yet it tells me Ludmila's heart was here among the twee furnishings and wallpaper printed with small flowers.

'I never cared for these country places,' says Hermione to lighten things up. 'Dust, spiders' webs and nowhere decent to go in the evening.'

'Shut up!' snaps Gerry.

The shock causes her to make silent fish mouths.

We go into each of the ground floor rooms but see nothing except that Ludmila has become a good housekeeper.

'No touching,' says Gerry – as if we would.

'Here!' shouts the Boss from upstairs, startling us. There's nothing to do but follow the sound of his voice. We climb the irregular staircase, Gerry at the rear as if to stop us bolting. At the top are two bedrooms and a bathroom, each with rustic plank doors held with strap hinges, and the Boss is in the bathroom.

As, of course, is Ludmila.

She is in the half-filled bath, hair floating on the water, her pale skin mottled from being there too long. Eyes closed. Mouth closed in a neutral smile. Blue lips. Blue veins threading her white thighs. Strangled and drowned. Ophelia without the flowers.

Hermione throws up in the toilet basin, and Gerry tells her to get a grip on herself.

'There's no sign of Oliver,' says the Boss.

'What?' I don't understand what he means.

'He hasn't hung around after killing her.'

'Oliver killed her?'

'There's no sign that anyone else was here except us.' He means that it's self-evident.

I say again, 'Oliver killed her?'

'We'll call the police. They'll find him if he's around to be found.' The Boss is looking at me and he can tell I'm thinking about the telephone call that brought us all out here. He says, 'We're here because Ludmila invited us for drinks, and this is what we found.'

'That's right – drinks,' affirms Gerry.

Already the Boss is on the phone, as cool as they come, a man who knows how to act under stress. A man who – I now realise – can dissemble to become anyone the situation requires: public schoolboy, banker, go-between, fixer for the Russian mafia – even husband and god-fearing Anglican clergyman. The man who can read these things that I've written and tell me that he loves me.

We sit demurely on the three piece suite waiting for the police to arrive. Upstairs Ludmila still lies in the bath with her half smile on her pale face for ever hiding her mysteries.

I think of her and after all the years still miss her. The only woman I ever loved. Sergei killed her. Pierce helped him. And I stayed silent.

I created a fiction called Diana to hide my shame. She it is who waits for the monster who has just this moment come home. What thoughts are on his mind concerning his mad, guilty, inconvenient wife?

I no longer care. I have nothing else to say.

33

Today was Thursday and Janet hadn't seen or spoken to Stephen Gregg since the previous Saturday when they went dancing. She wasn't sure how she felt about that. She had no rules for this particular relationship and couldn't judge. She was puzzled, perhaps. Certainly not distressed. Yet it would have been nice if he'd called.

And now he did, in the middle of the morning, while she was writing and Belle was cleaning the bedrooms.

He was always good at anticipating her. 'I'm sorry I haven't called before. It isn't much of an excuse, but I'm working to a deadline. We're wrapping up our investigations here.'

'So, you'll be going back to London?'

'Yes.'

Well, that was inevitable and had been from the beginning.

'Come and have coffee with me at that place in the High Street,' he said. 'Only if you want to and have nothing better to do, of course.'

'I'd like that.'

'Excellent. Shall we say three o'clock?'

'Alright, three o'clock.'

And what do I wear to say farewell on a Thursday afternoon?

She told Belle.

'You're not asking your Auntie's advice, are you? I'm hopeless at that sort of thing. I suppose you could tie your stuff in a bundle and follow him to London like Dick Whittington. On the other hand you could just be grateful for whatever it is and be glad you have a nice man for a friend. At our age ... well, you know what I mean. You take what you're given.'

'I think they call it "living in the moment",' Janet suggested, still wondering what had happened.

'Silly beggars probably do,' said Belle. 'But not in Clitheroe."

It was a morning for calls. Janet was still writing but Belle was taking time out from chores and picked up the phone. She became quite solemn, punctuating the conversation with small gasps and questions Janet couldn't hear. When the call was finished she said she would put the kettle on.

'Well, that was a turn up,' she said at last. 'It was Jean on the phone. She was supposed to see Diana this morning. She has a rash where you definitely don't want one – Jean not Diana – I'll tell you about it sometime. Any road, she was supposed to see Diana because Diana dishes out those homeo-whatsit cures, if you believe it. Jean swears by them. So this morning, as arranged, she goes to Diana's house, but it's Pierce who answers the door. He stands there – she says – in a right state, tears running down his cheeks and all that. And he only tells her, Jean, that Diana is dead.'

'Dead?' Janet had a quick vision of the other woman: her reserve and natural elegance. How old? A good looking sixty? 'She wasn't ill, was she?'

'No, nothing like that. It was an accident, apparently. Pierce says that she's been suffering from confused spells – TIAs I think they call them – and he's surmising she got up in the night to go to the you-know-where and lost her bearings.'

'What happened?'

'He's guessing she tripped over the cat and fell head over heels downstairs. Broke her neck.'

They were silent for a moment, taking the story in as they poured cups of tea. Janet was conscious that we react to the death of comparative strangers differently from those we love. Unless the details are particularly shocking, we draw our responses from the stock of those we learn as appropriate; but sometimes they aren't. She was sad for the other woman's death, but couldn't wholly ignore the comedy of tripping over a cat and breaking one's neck – in other circumstances an amusing pratfall. Reality had a knack of demeaning our private tragedies.

Belle said, 'Jean probably knew Diana best. She says she wasn't as posh as she made out to be. They got on well.'

'I didn't really know her,' Janet said. 'I always had a feeling she was hiding something but I've no idea what. Probably I'm mistaken and it was just her manner.'

Belle didn't respond to this, instead saying, 'It only happened last night, so it's too early to talk about a funeral, though the service will be at St. Ivo's obviously; what with Pierce being a vicar.'

Janet nodded. 'There may be a delay before that happens.'

'Oh? Why?'

'Because, I imagine, there'll have to be an inquest. Diana wasn't ill and it isn't a natural death, so the police will have to be satisfied and the coroner will become involved.'

'Well, that all seems a bit OTT to me,' said Belle, 'when what we're talking about is a silly accident. What else could it be? Suicide?'

'Or murder.'

Belle stared at her friend. 'Don't be daft. You have murder on the brain.'

Do I? Janet wondered. She was a little offended at Belle's reaction. But, on reflection, it had been a rather cold remark to make, even if accurate.

She said, 'I'm only talking about the steps the police have to go through in this sort of case. I'm not suggesting Diana was actually murdered.'

'I should think not. I mean: why would Pierce murder her?'

Janet tried to think of Pierce and Diana as a couple: he

305

rather handsome and sociable; she simply pleasant and impeccably polite. Behind that surface she knew nothing at all.

'No, I don't suppose she was murdered,' Janet admitted, 'unless the cat did it.'

The unseasonably warm and sunny weather continued. Janet put on one of the dresses she favoured: it was printed with poppies and with a full skirt. She wondered if it was too girlish but liked it all the same and was in a good mood.

Stephen Gregg was waiting for her at a window table in the Anne Boleyn café. It was the quiet spell after the lunchtime trade. Only one other table was occupied by a bedraggled elderly man with a weary smile that displayed a gold tooth and, next to him, two young, beefy types who ignored him and talked to each other about football.

Stephen kissed her cheek. He looked preoccupied, even a little nervous. His job presumably, which meant that in the circumstances it was good of him to want to see her.

'Thanks for coming,' he said.

'So you're leaving today?'

'Yes. Not my decision. The higher-ups concluded last night that we were finished here. I'd hoped to give you more notice.'

Janet nodded. She accepted that he was too considerate to simply vanish. But now they were left to close something that neither of them had understood. So what were the right words?

For the present he gave them space by changing the subject. 'I have some news that may cheer you up.'

'Oh? What?'

'Yesterday your friend Sandra Wallace wandered into the station and confessed to killing her husband, our Mr Stanislaw Walacaszewski.'

'Ah.'

'You're smiling.'

'Am I?'

He grinned. 'You do realise that we'd have got there in the end – the police.'

'How do you know they would have?'

'I pick things up. At the hotel in Paddington they'd kept his suitcase after he didn't return from Dartcross. It contained a couple of passports and a second throwaway phone. The name "Wallace" was on our radar and I imagine that sooner or later we'd have got round to people in Dartcross going by that name. Still, it's obliging of Sandra to spare us the effort.'

'Where is she now?'

'On police bail.'

'Really? Despite being suspected of murder?'

'She claims self-defence, and I don't know that anyone is in a position to say otherwise – or inclined to. Stanislaw Walacaszewski wasn't Mister Popularity: in fact he was a cowardly, nasty piece of work. Sandra stood herself in good stead by coming forward and no one expects her to run away or bump anyone else off, so it would be a waste of tax payers' money to lock her up at this stage.'

'What will happen next?'

'The papers will go to the CPS and it's anyone's guess what they'll decide, though, frankly, I shouldn't think there's much chance that a jury will convict if she's well represented.'

'I hope so,' said Janet. 'I happen to like her.'

'She likes you too. She mentioned a conversation you both had a couple of days ago. You worked all of it out, didn't you? The killing?'

'I had some ideas,' Janet admitted. She glanced away. Across the road she saw Christine taking in the sunshine outside the Heart of Osiris bookshop, where she had first seen Sandra only a few weeks ago. Stephen Gregg followed her gaze.

He said, 'Seriously, what do you think really happened? Did she murder her husband?'

Janet was surprised he cared for her opinion, given that she no more knew than he did. Or perhaps she did know? When it came down to it, Sandra had gone to the meeting by the river armed with a weapon – Joanie's stick – and, despite his violent reputation, Walacaszewski hadn't attacked her before she killed him: at all events Janet had seen no defensive injuries on Sandra, neither had Sandra ever mentioned any. It was certainly possible that Sandra had simply decided she'd had enough of her husband.

'I shouldn't think she murdered him,' Janet said. Whatever her opinion, the truth was unknowable. Indeed she doubted even Sandra knew any more. We construct narratives after the event and, if they ease our mind, they become the version we live by.

Stephen checked his watch. He cast an eye at the other table, at the man with the gold tooth and the two younger types.

Janet asked, 'How long to your train?'

'An hour.'

'Are you going to tell me what brought you to Dartcross?'

He thought that over.

'If you like – but no names. A few months ago a Russian – a defector as we would have called him in the old days – presented himself at Scotland Yard, and said he had information he wanted to give us in exchange for protection from some of his fellow Russians. He was someone well known to us, even though we'd never been able to lay a hand on him. He was a bagman and money launderer for the KGB and then later for the oligarchs and the Russian mafia, and he had with him, on data sticks, the records of the operations he'd been involved in: the names, the places, the deals – the lot. He also had the name of someone – an Englishman – he'd worked with back in the day, whom he trusted and who could help interpret all the material he'd brought over. My job has been to make this happen.' He looked at Janet and sighed. 'I never know where I am with you. Did you suspect any of this?'

Janet shook her head. 'No, none of it.' She smiled to encourage him. 'I'm not really a detective. And I shan't ask you who the Englishman was who worked with your Russian.'

'I couldn't tell you anyway.'

Janet wondered if she could find out on her own account. But what would be the point other than her curiosity? She looked again at the man with the gold tooth and supposed he was the Russian in question, and the other two were presumably his police escort. It occurred to her that she'd solved one mystery only to discover that others were going on around her: this one and also the death of Diana, though the latter was probably an accident not a mystery.

'Do you ever get up to London?' Stephen asked.

'I have friends there,' Janet said, and wondered if she had occasion to visit them. When had she last done so? Friends so often drifted away and one didn't notice.

'I'll give you my telephone number. If you come to London we could perhaps go for a meal or to the theatre – even the ballet?'

'That would be nice,' Janet said; then thought: No, I should stop this here. Otherwise where does it go? Where does it end? She had an insight – possibly no more than a wild guess. She said, 'This is about grief, isn't it? Anne? David? Trying to hold on to feelings we remember? We've lost our partners and we're frightened we've lost what it was in us that made us love them.' She could think of no other explanation that accounted for his interest in a woman almost twenty years older than him: an *old* woman, some would say.

He ducked the question. He was a man after all. He said, 'I invited you on a date if you're ever in London because I like you. It isn't necessary to read anything more into it.' He looked at his watch again. 'I'm sorry. I have things to do – people to call – before we leave' He raised a hand for the bill and signalled to his companions who began to shuffle in their chairs and make signs of going.

Janet had nothing else to say. As endings go, this one seemed abrupt and only half-resolved. Perhaps anything more required greater courage or understanding than either of them had. She found herself picking up her bag and offering a contribution to the bill, which he refused of course. And then there was nothing to do except exchange another kiss on the cheek before she found herself leaving. Unaccountably it felt as though they had quarrelled when no such thing had happened.

'So how did your meeting with Sexy Stevie go?' asked Belle.

Janet felt tired and cross but hid the fact. She didn't want to take out her confused feelings on her friend.

'It was – "nice" is the word, I suppose. He's going back to London today; in fact his train leaves in the next few minutes.'

'You're not seeing him off, then? No *Brief Encounter* moment?'

'It isn't like that.'

'If you say so.'

'It *isn't*.'

Belle looked glum. 'You're probably right. OK, so tell me what happened.'

Janet gave her the story of Sandra's visit to the police station.

Belle said, 'You got it right as per usual when you thought she'd see sense and get her version of events in first. Mind you, if you ask my opinion, she did do it deliberately: murder her hubby. Behind all that New Age flummery she's quite a calculating woman and at no time during these last three weeks has she ever looked cut up about killing someone. Not that I can get excited either way as far as Ray Wallace is concerned, who deserved it if anyone did. What about Steve himself? Did he tell you what brought him to our neck of the woods?'

Janet reflected that he hadn't sworn her to confidence, so she told Belle as much as she knew herself about the defecting Russian gangster. Belle was enthralled.

'It's like James Bond, isn't it!'

'With the addition of accountants,' Janet suggested, but Belle pooh-poohed her.

'I love your description of the bodyguards, eating scones with cream and jam while keeping an eye out for assassins.'

'I never mentioned scones with cream and jam.'

Belle didn't care. 'Dramatic licence. It's a café; so they have to be eating summat. Scones or Bakewell tart, I don't see it makes much difference. And don't spoil the effect by telling me the bodyguards looked like those fat blokes who keep an eye on you in Marks & Spencers. Let me keep my dreams.''

Later, while cooking dinner, Belle asked who it was that Stephen Gregg had been working with: the English criminal who had aided and abetted the financial manipulations of the Russian mafia.

'He didn't say.'

'Make a guess.'

'I can't. It's probably someone we don't know.' When all was said and done, Janet thought, they knew only a handful of people in Dartcross.

'Well,' said Belle, 'we can let that one go. The fact still remains that we solved a murder mystery even if we can't be a hundred percent sure it was a murder. How many people can say that? Let's hear it: a victory for The Demented Lady Detectives' Club! Hurrah!'

Janet smiled. It was a while since that name had been spoken; and that was all it had ever really been – a name – hadn't it? Only she and Belle had taken the investigation seriously, and Belle had done it more out of her good nature than because she believed Janet was right. She was wonderful that way.

Over the meal Belle said, 'I'm thinking: maybe it's time to pack my traps and go back to Clitheroe. I've been here a good three weeks.'

Janet said, 'Do you have to? I mean: do you still have business there?'

'Well, I'm still trying to sort out Charlie's affairs – God bless him – but I'm not rooted to the place. First Puybrun and now Dartcross: I've seen the world.'

Janet wondered if she would be comfortable sharing her cottage or whether it was just a passing sentiment.

Belle read her thoughts. 'If I stay any longer, there'll be another murder in Dartcross and one less detective.'

'I don't think so. But it's a matter for you.'

'Why don't I go back to Clitheroe and you can see if you miss me?'

'Yes, we could try that,' Janet agreed.

It was a plan of sorts, like going to the theatre with Stephen Gregg if she happened to find herself in London. It was something to do and yet resolved nothing. Yet perhaps it was unreasonable to look for resolution, given the fluidity of human affairs. She should learn to 'go with the flow'. Wasn't that a Taoist notion? Or Mick Jagger? Either way there was something to be said for it. Even at her age.

She thought again about Stephen Gregg, whom she'd grown to like enormously. She found the idea of spending time in his company, of going to the theatre and ballet with him, very appealing. She suspected that the difficulty in defining their relationship arose only because there was nothing fixed that was capable of definition. Instead there was a process of *becoming*, which was far more exciting the more she thought about it. She didn't suppose for a moment that they would ever be more than friends, nor that she wanted anything else. Still the uncertainty reminded her that she was alive. Still capable of feeling.

Still capable of loving in one way or another.

On this evening, Janet did not feel old. She felt affirmed.

READERS' NOTES

On our 40th wedding anniversary, as a gift to my wife, I wrote *The English Lady Murderers' Society*. Now, on the occasion of our 45th anniversary I've followed with this sequel, which features three of the characters from the earlier novel. There are worse presents to give a much-loved wife.

Appropriately, both of these novels are told from the point of view of women. This is a deliberate choice, made for two reasons. One is a matter of personal exploration: an attempt to discover whether the experience of marriage has taught me anything. The second is as a technical exercise to stretch me as a writer. It's often said – probably with good reason – that male authors struggle to create realistic female characters. Those that they do create tend to be instruments to drive forward a male-oriented plot and there is little sense that the author inhabits the mind set or experience of his creations. I don't know that I've done any better, but the criteria by which I invite you to judge "my" women are authenticity, empathy and compassion. If I haven't displayed these qualities, then I've failed.

Given that I aim for authenticity, the humorous tone of much of the book may seem a contradiction, though it's balanced here and there by notes of seriousness – even tragedy. This was a conscious choice that reflects the way I experience life and a preference for "light and shade" in writing, which to my mind makes it more varied and interesting. I take joy in my women friends and wanted to reflect this.

Through the voice of Janet I've commented on the

experience of being an author and some of the technical issues that affect the writing of murder mysteries. It's common enough for novels to feature writers as their principal character, following the precept that one should write what one knows about. However the normal practice is to make the author successful and well-known – which, frankly, isn't the experience of most of us who bob along ignored except by a few fans who keep asking why the film of our latest has never been made. I've preferred to make Janet a mid-list author whom most people have never heard of. It's more truthful and it's a chance to poke fun at myself and my pretensions.

One of the attractions of the Golden Age of crime writing, which expired with the death of Agatha Christie, is that the plots ultimately comfort the reader by disrupting the natural order of things only to restore it in the finale when the Truth is revealed and Justice triumphs. Even now, in an age of world-weary detectives with addiction problems and failed lives, this essential model still survives beneath a superficial cynicism. The solution to the mystery is *the* solution to the exclusion of any other, and the unmasking of the killer is an exercise of justice, even if sometimes incomplete.

If you read closely, you will see that I haven't followed this model. In form *The Demented Lady Detectives' Club* has something of the appearance of a traditional "cosy" whodunit, but in fact the ending subverts the conventions. The proffered solution isn't the only solution, and justice may not have been done at all. Janet's method of investigation – as she acknowledges – is to follow only the most *probable* of the explanations that account for the evidence. In the case of Sandra's role in her husband's death, Janet opts for manslaughter, but she openly acknowledges that a good case can be made for murder – *there is simply no way of knowing*. It follows that we can't be sure that justice has been done. In the case of the death of Diana the uncertainties are even more pronounced. Murder, accident and suicide are all plausible explanations, and I've made no attempt to choose between them though I've tried to tantalise the reader by dropping enough hints for you to make your own case. As for Ludmila, her murder goes unpunished.

In the end, the "solution" to the mystery in both this and several of my earlier books is only provisional. It isn't so much the Truth as the version of events that attracts the most consent. You must make what you will of this.

"Dartcross" is a fictitious town even though it closely resembles Totnes in terms of detail. This has no great significance. Shirley and I happen to like Totnes and using it as a reference-point made research and consistency easier. The inhabitants are entirely my invention and are not intended as coded references to real people or events.

I owe thanks to Mark Turner for inspiring me to write again; to Adrienne Turner for reading and commenting on the text; to Toots Eveleigh for pouring justified scorn on me to my great amusement; and to Sue Webb for a detailed and useful set of notes and comments.

As for my wife Shirley – 45 years are not enough.

Jim Williams
October 2015

If you enjoyed reading *The Demented Lady Detectives' Club* then please share your reflections with others by posting a review online.

Connect with Jim Williams and Marble City Publishing

http://www.jimwilliamsbooks.com/

http://www.marblecitypublishing.com

Join Marble City's list for updates on new releases by Jim Williams at http://eepurl.com/vek5L or scan the QR code below:

Follow on Twitter:

http://twitter.com/MarbleCityPub

Other Marble City releases by Jim Williams

A disillusioned soldier looks for love. An exiled Emperor fears assassination. Agatha Christie takes a holiday. And George Bernard Shaw learns to tango.

In the aftermath of World War I, Michael Pinfold a disillusioned ex-soldier tries to rescue his failing family wine business on the island of Madeira. In a villa in the hills the exiled Austrian Emperor lives in fear of assassination by Hungarian killers, while in Reid's Hotel, a well-known lady crime novelist is stranded on her way to South Africa and George Bernard Shaw whiles away his days corresponding with his friends, writing a one act play and learning to tango with the hotel manager's spouse.

A stranger, Robinson, is found murdered and Michael finds himself manipulated into investigating the crime by his sinister best friend, Johnny Cardozo, the local police chief, with whose wife he is pursuing an arid love affair; manipulated, too, by Father Flaherty, a priest with dubious political interests, and by his own eccentric parent, who claims to have been part of a comedy duo that once entertained the Kaiser with Jewish jokes. Will Michael find love? Will the Emperor escape his would-be killers? Will any of the characters learn the true meaning of the tango?

The poet Shelley wasn't murdered. This book tells you whodunit.

A group of glamorous English socialites spend the summer of 1930 holidaying on the Italian Riviera where the poet Shelley died in a sailing accident in 1822. To pass the time, they tell amusing stories, much as Shelley, Byron and their friends had done a century earlier. For their theme they choose the death of Shelley and the stories progress towards a solution to the "murder mystery". Yet is that truly what the stories are about? Or, despite their witty surface, are they a code for dark and dangerous secrets hidden behind an urbane façade?

Guy Parrot, a naive young doctor, finds himself falling in love with the beautiful and enigmatic Julia, the truth of whose past flickers between the lines of the stories, tantalising both Guy and the Reader. Guy discovers that truth, and its terrible reality leads to two murders and the destruction of his happiness and sanity.

In 1945, in the aftermath of war, Guy returns to Italy with the army and is given an opportunity to re-examine the events of fifteen years before. This time will he understand what happened and finally redeem himself?

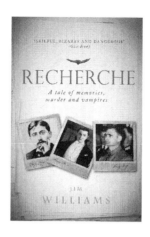

"A skilful exercise, bizarre and dangerous in a lineage that includes Fowles' *The Magus*."

Guardian

You get to be a lot of people when you are a vampire.

Meet old Harry Haze: war criminal, Jewish stand-up comedian, friend of Marcel Proust and J. Edgar Hoover. John Harper encounters him while spending the summer in the South of France with his mistress Lucy, and is entranced by Harry's stories of his fabulous past. Then Lucy disappears without explanation and both John and Harry fall under suspicion.

Yet how are we to know the truth when it is hidden in the labyrinth of Harry's bizarre memories and John's guilt at abandoning his wife? Nothing in this story is certain. Is Lucy dead? Is Harry a harmless old druggie or really a vampire? Deep inside his humorous tales is the suppressed memory of a night of sheer horror. And it is possible that one of the two men is an insane killer.

Summer 1941. France is occupied by the Germans but the United States is not at war. Four glamorous young Americans find themselves whiling away the hot days in the boredom of a small Riviera town, while in a half-abandoned mansion nearby, Teresa and Katerina Malipiero, a mother and daughter, wait for Señor Malipiero to complete his business in the Reich and take them home to Argentina.

The plight of the women attracts the sympathy of 'Lucky' Tom Rensselaer and he is seduced by the beauty of Katerina. Tom has perfect faith in their innocence, yet they cannot explain why a sinister Spaniard has been murdered in their home and why Tom must help them dispose of the body without informing the police.

Watching over events is Pat Byrne, a young Irish writer. Twenty years later, when Tom has been reduced from the most handsome, admired and talented man of his generation to a derelict alcoholic, Pat sets out to discover the facts of that fateful summer: the secrets that were hidden and the lies that were told. It is a shocking truth: a tale of murder unpunished and a good man destroyed by those who loved him most.

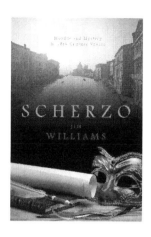

MEET two unusual detectives. Ludovico – a young man who has had his testicles cut off for the sake of opera. And Monsieur Arouet – a fraudster, or just possibly the philosopher Voltaire.

VISIT the setting. Carnival time in mid-18th century Venice, a city of winter mists, and the season of masquerade and decadence.

ENCOUNTER a Venetian underworld of pimps, harlots, gamblers, forgers and charlatans.

BEWARE of a mysterious coterie of aristocrats, Jesuits, Freemasons and magicians.

DISCOVER a murder: that of the nobleman, Sgr Alessandro Molin, found swinging from a bridge with his innards hanging out and a message in code from his killer.

Scherzo is a murder mystery of sparkling vivacity and an historical novel of stunning originality told with a wit and style highly praised by critics and nominated for the Booker Prize.

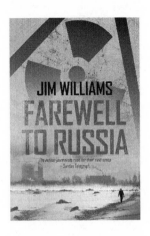

The unthinkable has happened at the Soviet nuclear plant at Sokolskoye. An accident of such terrifying proportions, of such catastrophic ecological and political consequence that a curtain of silence is drawn ominously over the incident. Major Pyotr Kirov of the KGB is appointed to extract the truth from the treacherous minefield of misinformation and intrigue and to obtain from the West the technology essential to prevent further damage. But the vital equipment is under strict trade embargo....

And in London, George Twist, head of a company which manufactures the technology, is on the verge of bankruptcy and desperate to win the illegal contract. Can he deliver on time? Will he survive a frantic smuggling operation across the frozen wastes of Finland? Can he wrong-foot the authorities ... and his own conscience? Is it possible to say farewell to Russia?

Farewell to Russia is the first of Jim Williams's astonishingly prophetic novels about the decline and fall of the Soviet Union.

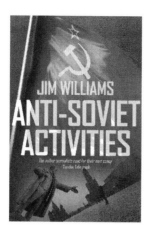

For Colonel Pyotr Andreevitch Kirov there is only one inescapable truth in modern Russia – if the old order does not change, it is impossible to bury the past.

When Kirov's routine investigation into black market antibiotics is linked to the former head of the KGB – and Kirov himself is put under investigation by his own men – the course for collision is set.

As the old and new factions in the Soviet machine grapple for power, the stock in trade is the hardest currency known to the Socialist Republic … murder. Will Mikhail Gorbachev share the same fate?

Anti-Soviet Activities is the second of Jim Williams's astonishingly prophetic novels about the decline and fall of the Soviet Union.

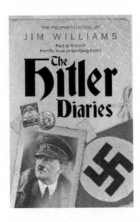

A stunning literary prophecy! The international bestseller that caused a sensation when it was published 9 months before the famous Hitler Diaries forgery scandal.

A French aristocrat and his mistress are murdered. A mysterious businessman offers the Fuehrer's diaries to a new York publishing house. Are they a hoax or a record of terrifying truth? A controversial historian and his beautiful assistant are commissioned to find out the answer following a trail that draws them into a terrifying web of conspiracy and slaughter as competing forces fight to publish or suppress Hitler's account of the War and of secret negotiations with his enemies.

But are the Diaries genuine or just a plot to destabilise contemporary politics? A shattering revision of history whose revelation must be prevented at all costs: or a fake, just a sinister manoeuvre in the Cold War?

If the Hitler Diaries are authentic, then who left the bunker alive?

Lord T'ien Huang controls the universe through poetry, telepathy and the violence of his insane Angels. His subjects consider him to be God. Emperor of a universe ruled by the Ch'ang, immortal but not invulnerable, his interest is aroused by Sebastian, a novice monk on the remote and wasted planet of Lu, who can see and speak to God. Should he destroy the boy or toy with him?

Sebastian is rescued from the Lord T'ien Huang's avenging Angels by Mapmaker, an ancient Old Before the Fall with a forgotten history of betrayal, and they journey to the snowbound north. They are accompanied by Velikka Magdasdottir, a girl belonging to the Hengstmijster tribe of warrior herdswomen who maintain a veiled harem of husbands.

In the frozen wastes they encounter the remains of the Ingitkuk who rebelled against the Ch'ang in antiquity and lost their witch princess, She Whom the Reindeer Love. Mapmaker knew her when she died half a millennium ago as Her Breath Is Of Jasmine.

Will Mapmaker lead Sebastian, the Hengstmijster and the Ingitkuk to their doom against the Ch'ang? Can Sebastian master his own powers? How will they survive against the Angel Michael, thawed and frozen more times than he can recall, with his power to destroy humanity by the billion?

Made in the USA
Charleston, SC
11 January 2016